Jill Mansell live⟨ ⟩h her family in Bristol. She used to work in the field ⟨ ⟩inical Neurophysiology but now writes full time. She ⟨wa⟩ ⟨ ⟩es ⟨ ⟩ too much TV and would love to be one of those super-sporty types but basically can't be bothered. Nor can she cook – having once attempted to bake a cake for the hospital's Christmas Fair, she was forced to watch while her co-workers played frisbee with it. But she's good at Twitter!

Just *Heavenly*. Just *Jill*.

'Bursting with humour, brimming with intrigue and full of characters you'll adore – we can't think of a better literary remedy' ***** *Heat*

'To read it is to devour it' *Company*

'A warm, witty and romantic read that you won't be able to put down' *Daily Mail*

'Slick, sexy, funny' *Daily Telegraph*

'Mansell's fiction is a happy leap away from the troubles of today' *Sunday Express*

'Jill Mansell is in a different league' *Sun*

Jill Mansell

FALLING FOR YOU

headline
review

First published in 2003
by HEADLINE PUBLISHING GROUP

First published in paperback in 2004
by HEADLINE PUBLISHING GROUP

This edition published in paperback in 2014
by HEADLINE REVIEW
An imprint of HEADLINE PUBLISHING GROUP

14

Cataloguing in Publication Data is available from the British Library

ISBN 978 0 7553 3262 5

Typeset in Times New Roman by Palimpsest Book Production Limited,
Falkirk, Stirlingshire

Printed and bound in Great Britain by CPI Group (UK) Ltd, Croydon CR0 4YY

Headline's policy is to use papers that are natural, renewable and recyclable
products and made from wood grown in sustainable forests. The logging and
manufacturing processes are expected to conform to the environmental regulations
of the country of origin.

HEADLINE PUBLISHING GROUP
An Hachette UK Company
338 Euston Road
London NW1 3BH

www.headline.co.uk
www.hachette.co.uk

For my mum

Chapter 1

If she jumped high enough into the air, Maddy Harvey could see the party carrying on without her, blissfully unaware of her absence. Well, she could see in a blurry, abstract kind of way – the lights in the house, the trees surrounding it and the outlines of other party-goers either drifting from room to room or dancing manically along to Kylie Minogue (truly a girl for all age groups).

I bet this never happens to Kylie.

It was an inescapable law of nature that sometimes you went along to a party, everything went right and you had the best time ever. The flip side of the coin, needless to say, was that sometimes you didn't. Everything that could possibly go wrong did go wrong.

Like tonight.

Maddy heaved a sigh and considered her current predicament. She blamed Bean for launching herself joyfully at the backs of her legs just as she'd been poised to put her left contact lens in. The little dog had caught her by surprise, the lens had flown off her fingertip and, in good old contact lens fashion, had promptly disappeared. It could have fallen into the sink and slipped down the plughole. It could have landed literally anywhere in the bathroom. Bean could have stepped on it, eaten it. Not for the first time, a tiny transparent sliver of plastic had simply vanished into thin air.

1

Since wearing only one lens was no use at all, she had been forced to wear her glasses instead. But only in order to be able to drive herself the few miles from Ashcombe into Bath. Not to wear to the party itself. Oh no, good grief, she was far too vain to actually wear her glasses at a party, which was why they were currently stowed away in the glove compartment of her car.

So that had been mistake number one. Mistake number two had come about when, desperate for a wee and discovering that there was a major queue for the bathroom, she had slipped outside in search of somewhere discreet and al fresco. And since there wasn't anywhere discreet in the back garden, she had climbed over a five-foot wall into next door's, where a weeping cherry tree promised absolute privacy.

If she hadn't been too vain to wear her glasses, she'd have spotted the nail sticking out of the wall, encouraging a clematis to entwine itself around it, and her trousers wouldn't have got disastrously ripped.

Mistake number three had been climbing over a five-foot wall with the help of a sawn-off tree trunk without pausing to wonder if the drop might be greater on the other side, and whether there would be another handily positioned tree trunk to enable her to get back.

And I'm not even drunk, Maddy thought, exasperated. At this rate she could be stuck out here for the rest of the night.

Never had the sound of a door clicking open been more welcome. Realising that this could be her big – OK, *only* – chance, Maddy started bobbing up and down again like Zebedee, waving her arms in the air to attract attention. Spotting the outline of a figure and feeling completely idiotic, she called out, 'Um, hello? Excuse me?'

Still, he looked tall. And tall was good, tall was definitely what she needed right now. Failing that, a circus dwarf with a stepladder.

Within seconds he'd crossed the lawn and was peering over the wall at her.

'Are you a burglar?'

In the pitch blackness, Maddy couldn't see what he looked like, but he had a nice voice. And she was hardly in a position to be choosy.

'If I was a burglar I'd have a swag bag,' she told him. 'And a stripy jumper and a mask.'

'Sorry. Of course you would.' He sounded amused. 'So . . . are you lost?'

'I'm stuck. I jumped over the wall,' Maddy explained, 'and now I can't get back. There's no other way out of this garden except through the house, and all the lights are off, which means the people who live here are either out or asleep. If they're asleep, I don't want to wake them up.'

'Probably don't want to have to explain what you're doing in their garden either,' observed the man she was rather relying on to rescue her. 'Out of interest, what were you doing in their garden?'

Oh dear.

'A gentleman wouldn't ask.'

'Get him to help you over the wall then,' he said lightly, beginning to walk away.

Letting out a muted shriek of frustration, Maddy hissed, 'Oh please, don't leave me, *come back.*'

This time, she heard him laughing. Returning, he gestured for her to move away from the wall, and the next moment had vaulted effortlessly over it.

Now he was close enough, despite the darkness and her own myopia, for Maddy to be able to tell that this was no troll. Dark hair, dark eyes, good cheekbones and a flash of white teeth as he smiled. She was about to be

3

rescued – hopefully – by a rather nice-looking man. Blurry, but nice.

'OK. Come and stand in front of me.' He beckoned to her. 'No, face the wall, then I'll lift you up.'

'Er . . . I ripped my trousers jumping down. They caught on a nail.' Maddy's hand moved protectively to the gaping hole at the back of her trousers; if he lifted her, he was going to see it – and her fluorescent orange knickers – at close range.

Smiling, he said, 'Don't worry, I'll close my eyes.'

He was impressive, she'd say that for him. One moment she was on the ground, the next his hands were round her waist and she found herself being whooshed up into the air. It was all very Torvill and Dean. Her own arms outstretched, Maddy made a grab for the top of the wall, raised one knee and landed on top of it. Not very elegantly, she dragged her other leg over, wriggled to the edge and dropped down on the other side.

Oh, the relief.

Impressively, her rescuer hauled himself over too, his feet landing with a soft thud on the grass.

'I've just been saved by Superman,' said Maddy. 'Thanks.'

'No problem.' He sounded entertained. 'Nice pants, by the way.'

'It hasn't been my night.' Twisting round, Maddy ruefully examined the rip in her white trousers. 'I'll have to go home now. God, they're completely wrecked.'

'You can't rush off. I've only just rescued you. Come on, there's a bench over there. We can stay out here for a bit.'

They sat down on the bench. He was wearing a pale grey shirt with the cuffs folded back, and black trousers that melted into the darkness. Breathing in, she smelled soap and the faint tang of aftershave, possibly Hugo Boss. Maybe the evening wasn't going to be such a disaster after all. Cheering up, Maddy said, 'So, Superman, what brought you out into the garden?'

'Keeping out of the way of a jealous husband.'

'Really? If he's that jealous, why did you marry him?'

He smiled. 'His wife wouldn't leave me alone. I wasn't encouraging her, but she's a bit drunk. Her husband was getting irritated so I escaped to the kitchen. Then, as I was looking out of the window, I saw a blonde head bobbing up and down like a ping-pong ball over the wall at the end of this garden. Thought I'd come out and see what was going on.'

'I'm glad you did.' Maddy shivered as the cool night air sank through her thin purple top. 'I wouldn't have slept well over there.' It struck her that as far as she could tell, she hadn't spotted her rescuer at the party. 'Have you been here long?'

'Here at the party? Twenty minutes. Or did you mean here in Bath?' His eyes sparkled. 'In which case, I grew up around here, then moved away years ago. I've been back a few months now, running a PR company. Callaghan and Fox.'

'Really? I know it!' Brightening, Maddy said, 'You're on the top floor of Claremont House. I deliver sandwiches to the accountants on the first floor.'

He tilted his head to one side. 'Sandwiches. Good ones?'

'Excuse me! Completely brilliant ones. We do baps, bagels, baguettes, cartons of rice and pasta and salady things, home-made cakes, everything you could want.' Spotting an oppor-tunity, Maddy said innocently, 'And very cheerful service. Everyone says we're the best.'

'Do they now? And you're reliable?'

'If we weren't reliable, everyone wouldn't say we were the best. Who does yours?' asked Maddy, although she already knew.

'Blunkett's, the place on Armitage Street.' Her rescuer pulled a face. 'They're OK, but sometimes they get to us late and all the best stuff has gone.'

'That must be so annoying. We make-to-order. One of our clients is pregnant and we take her chicken and banana baguettes with spring onions and Marmite. I just feel sorry for the baby.' Maddy shivered as another gust of wind sliced through her; it might be June, but this was England and everyone with an ounce of sense was inside.

'You're cold,' he observed. 'I'd lend you my jacket if I was wearing one. Look, take this.' Digging his wallet from his back pocket, he pulled out a business card.

'It's not going to keep me very warm.'

'Come and see us on Monday morning. Maybe it's time for a change.'

Yay, result. Maddy tucked the card in her pocket, delighted by the happy turn this evening had taken. Not only a nice-sounding man but a potential addition to her client list.

'Excellent.' Rising to her feet, she felt a draught as the L-shaped tear at the back of her trousers flapped open. 'Around eleven o'clock, is that OK? You'll be there then?'

'I'll be there. Just go to the reception desk and ask for—'

'I know.' Maddy patted the pocket containing his business card and broke into a grin. 'Ask for Superman.'

Kate was going home. Back to England, back to Ashcombe. Not because she wanted to, but because she didn't have a lot of choice. New York was no longer her kind of town. Swish Park Avenue hotels weren't interested in employing a receptionist with a scarred face; her appearance didn't fit with the ambience. Basically, she was a bit of a turn-off.

Kicking up an almighty fuss and threatening to sue them might have been an option, but she hadn't been able to bring herself to do it. She was sick of being treated like a freak anyway. Every time she ventured out onto the streets there were another million or so New Yorkers ready to point and stare at her. After a while it really got you down.

Turning away from the window of her loft apartment in East Village, Kate caught sight of her reflection in the oval mirror on the wall opposite. Even now, almost a year later, an unexpected glimpse of herself – that can't be me! Oh God, it *is* me – still had the power to give her a jolt.

There was no getting away from it, she was now officially ugly. Oh, how everyone in Ashcombe would laugh when they saw her. Not to her face, maybe, but certainly behind her back. She was under no illusions about that. It wasn't a comfortable thing to have to admit, but if anyone truly deserved their comeuppance, it was her.

'How's it going with the packing?' Mimi, her barely-there flatmate, poked her head round the bedroom door. Honestly, Mimi spent so little time at their apartment it was a wonder sometimes that Kate recognised her.

'Slowly.' Kate picked up a pair of Calvin Klein pink denims and half-heartedly folded them into one of the cases lying open on the bed.

'We're off to the movies, you're welcome to come along if you want.' Mimi flashed the kind of overbright smile that signalled: Look, I'm saying it but I don't actually mean it.

'No thanks. I'd better get on with this.' Kate wondered what would happen to Mimi's smile if she'd said, 'Oh yes please, I'd love to!'

'OK. Have a nice da-ay,' Mimi sang out, and swiftly disappeared before Kate could change her mind.

The apartment door slammed shut and Kate slumped down on the edge of the queen-sized bed, angrily brushing away a tear. She was glad to be leaving New York, so why should she care?

Except she already knew the answer to that one: going back to Ashcombe would undoubtedly be worse.

Chapter 2

Anyone living in a city might visit Ashcombe and call it a village, but officially it was a small town, ravishingly pretty and prone to tourists, nestling in a valley of the Cotswolds in true *Cider with Rosie* fashion. Everyone knew everyone and in-comers, traditionally, were regarded with suspicion. The unwritten rule was that until you'd lived there for over fifty years, you were a begrudgingly tolerated outsider. After that, if you were very, very lucky, you might be accepted as a local.

Somehow, when Juliet Price had moved down from London five years ago and opened the Peach Tree Delicatessen, the rules had been magically broken.

'I don't know how you do it,' said Maddy, when ancient Cyrus Sharp had shuffled out of the shop in his wellies, the carrier containing his morning *pain au chocolat* and a loaf of walnut bread tucked under one arm. 'You should have heard Cyrus in the pub five years ago when he found out the old ironmongers was being turned into a deli. Bloody yuppies and their fancy foreign food . . . stinking the town out with herbs and garlic . . . what's wrong with Fray Bentos pies and a can of peas . . . And just look at him now, practically your best customer! And he fancies you.' Maddy smirked. 'I'm telling you, you've definitely pulled.'

'He's a sweetheart.' Smiling, Juliet reached for the broom

and quickly swept up the dried mud – at least she hoped it was only dried mud – that had crumbled off Cyrus's wellies. 'If he was fifty years younger I'd take him up on it. Well, I might if he didn't smell so much of farmyards.'

It never failed to impress Maddy, the way Juliet had mysteriously, *effortlessly*, managed to become a bona fide local within the space of, at most, a couple of months. Maybe it had something to do with her lustrous dark eyes, glossy black hair and gloriously old-fashioned hourglass figure. Maybe it was her warm velvety voice and innate compassion, but whatever it was, it worked. Juliet was kind, wonderfully discreet and adored by everyone. A single parent, she had arrived in Ashcombe with two-year-old Tiff, who had inherited his mother's winning smile and – presumably – his absent father's blond hair. Now an entrancing, boisterous seven-year-old, Tiff – short for Christopher – was best friends with Maddy's niece Sophie. The two of them, almost exactly the same age, were inseparable.

'Anyway, look at you,' said Juliet as Maddy emerged from the kitchen lugging four cool-boxes. 'All done up on a Monday morning. Eyeshadow and mascara, I'm impressed.'

'Oh God, *too* done up?' Maddy pulled a face; normally she didn't make too much of an effort for her delivery round. 'I don't look like a dog's dinner, do I?'

'Don't be daft. The regulars are going to wonder what they've done to deserve it, that's all.' Juliet raised a playful eyebrow. 'And I'm pretty curious myself.'

'I'm touting for business.' Maddy rested the cool-boxes on the floor.

'Sweetheart, you'll get it.'

'Sandwich business, Miss Clever-drawers. I met someone at a party on Saturday night. Play my cards right and we'll have ourselves a new customer. He's with Callaghan and

Fox; they've been using Blunkett's until now.' Maddy couldn't help sounding a bit smug; winning clients from your rivals was always a thrill. Especially when that rival company was Blunkett's.

'And would this happen to be a rather attractive new customer?'

'Well, I didn't have my lenses in, but I *think* so.' Maddy grinned and reached for the cool-boxes once more as a couple of tourists wandered into the shop. 'I'll know for sure when I see him again.'

Juliet, her eyes sparkling, said, 'Just don't forget to come back.'

One of the best things about seven-year-olds, Maddy had discovered, was that when something was irretrievably lost, you could offer them fifty pence each to spend on sweets if they found it and they wouldn't give up until they did. On Sunday morning Tiff and Sophie had gone through the bathroom with all the attention to detail of a pair of forensic pathologists, finally locating the missing gas-permeable lens stuck to the side of a pack of make-up remover pads.

Solemnly presenting it to Maddy, Sophie had said, 'I think probably that might be worth a pound each.'

Delving back into her purse, Maddy shook her head sorrowfully. 'You are your father's daughter.'

Sophie looked at her as if she was mad. 'Of course I'm my father's daughter. Otherwise he wouldn't be my dad.'

Anyway, two pounds had been a complete bargain, her lenses were back where they belonged, in her eyes, and the dreaded glasses had been relegated once more to her bedside drawer. Poor old glasses, they weren't really that bad, they certainly didn't deserve to be regarded with such loathing and contempt. For a moment, as she headed into Bath, Maddy almost felt sorry for them. But she couldn't quite bring herself to do it. She had a deep psychological aversion to her glasses, hated them with a passion. When you'd spent your entire time at school being taunted and called Speccy Four-eyes – unoriginal but cruelly effective – it was hard not to. Just the thought of that first pair of hideous pink plastic NHS specs was enough to bring all those old feelings of inadequacy flooding back. She was nine again, not only short-sighted but distressingly plain, the archetypal ugly duckling with her badly cut hair, wonky teeth, pale eyelashes and matchstick legs. Basically, not a pretty sight. No wonder everyone had spent the best part of twelve years making fun of her.

Oh well, at least it had been character-forming. And, thank goodness, she had blossomed since then.

The traffic in Bath had slowed to its habitual morning standstill. While the engine was idling, Maddy checked her face in the rear-view mirror, making sure she didn't have cornflake bits stuck to her teeth (teeth that were no longer crooked, thanks to three years of intensive brace-wearing – oh yes, her other nickname had been Metal Mickey. She'd been an absolute stunner at school).

Ruffling her hair – it was blonde, layered and responded well to a quick ruffle – Maddy smiled experimentally at her reflection, as she would soon be smiling at . . . um, thingy. Superman. Like an idiot she'd chucked her ruined white trousers in the bin on Sunday morning, forgetting that the business card he'd given her was still in the back pocket. Oh well, didn't matter. She'd find out soon enough.

Another quick practice smile reassured Maddy that she was looking OK (God bless eyelash dye), her lipgloss was still intact and her nose hadn't gone shiny in the heat. She was wearing a turquoise top, above-the-knee pink skirt and green and pink striped sandals – smarter than her usual T-shirt and jeans, but the staff at Callaghan and Fox wouldn't know she was only doing it to impress their handsome boss – well, hopefully handsome – ooh, traffic's moving again. Nearly there now.

The offices were on the top floor of Claremont House. Having parked in the visitor's car park, Maddy delivered the regular order to the accountants on the first floor before venturing on up the stairs. Through a glass door she saw a plump girl typing away behind a sleek yellow and white reception desk. As Maddy's cool-box clunked against the door frame, the girl looked up. Maddy manoeuvred herself through the door and said, 'Hi, I'm from the Peach Tree Deli, I was asked to—'

'Oh brilliant, you're here!' The girl stopped typing and jumped to her feet. 'We were told to expect you – I can't tell you how excited we all are. Everyone's so fed up with being messed around by Blunkett's, but you just kind of get used to rubbish sandwiches after a while, don't you? If they bring something you actually like, it's a bonus . . . oh, wow,' she went on happily as Maddy began lifting out the contents of the cool-box, lining up the blue and white plates and deftly removing their cellophane wrappings. Within seconds they'd been joined by half a dozen other members of staff, all exclaiming greedily over the prospect of free food. But there was no sign of Superman.

'Is . . . um, your boss here?'

'In his office, on the phone to a client. He'll be out in a minute – ooh, is that smoked salmon?' The receptionist looked as if she might start drooling. 'And what's in that one – some kind of chickeny stuff?'

'Chicken in tarragon mayonnaise. Here's a list of some of the other things we do, and these are our prices.' Maddy felt her heart break into a gallop as somewhere, out of view, an office door opened and shut. All of a sudden realising how much she was looking forward to seeing her rescuer again, she prayed she wouldn't blush.

'About time too,' exclaimed the plump receptionist as foot-steps grew louder down the corridor. Glancing over her shoulder she sang out chirpily, 'Food's here! Any longer and we'd have started without you.'

Maddy looked up and saw him smiling at her. Her mouth went dry and her ears began to buzz. No, it couldn't be, it just couldn't.

'Hello there,' said Kerr McKinnon, coming over to join them. He clearly hadn't a clue who she was, other than the girl he had lifted over a high wall on Saturday night. Well, that was hardly surprising when you considered the evidence. His hair may have been a lot longer then, and he'd filled out generally, but otherwise he was more or less the same. She'd changed, far more than he had.

Oh God, this was horrible, *horrible* . . .

'Kerr, you'll have to break it to Blunkett's.' One of the other girls was greedily cramming a chilli tuna sandwich into her mouth. 'We don't want them any more, they're sacked. Josh, you big pig, don't eat both the prawn ones!'

'Looks like you've got yourself some new clients,' Kerr McKinnon told Maddy with a wink. Turning to the recep-tionist he said, 'See? Don't say I never do anything for you.'

Kerr McKinnon.

'Excuse me.' Maddy took an abrupt step backwards, her mind in such a whirl she almost couldn't speak. Clumsily, she turned away from the receptionist's desk.

'Are you OK?' Looking concerned, Kerr McKinnon reached out to put a hand on her arm. Maddy pulled away, nodding and wondering if she might actually faint, which would be *ridiculous* . . .

Needing to get out, she left the offices and stumbled down the stairs. The sun had turned the inside of the car into a furnace. Maddy sat sideways in the driver's seat with her feet outside the car and her head in her hands. The greatest shock wasn't seeing Kerr McKinnon again; if she had passed him in a crowded street in Bath, say, her knee-jerk reaction would have been far more straightforward: initial recognition swiftly followed by a rush of disdain. Or hatred. Maybe anger, followed by contempt. And then within a few seconds it would have been over. She wouldn't, for instance, have raced over and started attacking him. If he'd caught her eye she would simply have shot him a look of loathing, before walking on.

But this was completely different, and the greatest shock of all was realising how much, after meeting and talking to Kerr McKinnon on Saturday night, she had been looking forward to seeing him again.

Maddy let out a groan of despair. She'd really liked him, and he had seemed to like her. There had been a spark there, the chemistry of mutual attraction. She had spent all of Sunday thinking about him, hoping he was as nice as she thought he was and, ironically, wondering what his name was. If Marcella hadn't emptied the contents of the Hoover bag into the dustbin, all over her chucked-away white trousers, she would have hauled them out and retrieved his business card from the back pocket. Then she would have known.

Ah, but would she have come here today, to Kerr McKinnon's offices, bringing carefully prepared food to impress him with?

Of course she wouldn't. Absolutely not.

And now she'd left the cool-box upstairs.

'Hey, are you all right?'

Maddy jumped; with her face buried in her hands she hadn't seen him emerge from the building. Crouching down in front of her, Kerr McKinnon held out a bottle of iced water and said, 'You poor thing, you look terrible. When I saw you turn white back there I thought you were going to pass out.

Here, have a drink.' He unscrewed the top of the bottle for her. 'Are you still feeling faint?'

Maddy flinched as he pressed the flat of his hand against her forehead, just like Marcella used to do whenever she complained that she was too ill to go to school.

'Hot,' he observed. 'Being in this car isn't helping. Look, put your head between your knees. As soon as you feel strong enough, we'll go back up to my office. Or I could carry you, if you like.' He smiled briefly. 'I had no idea I had this much of an effect on women.'

He was being kind, reassuring her that it didn't matter. Maddy couldn't smile back. She took a couple of deep breaths and said, 'I'm not going to faint.'

'Well, that's good.' He waited, then said, 'It's really nice to see you again. I was starting to wonder what I'd do if you didn't turn up.'

He was even better looking than she'd imagined on Saturday night; he had the best eyelashes Maddy had ever seen. And as for those eyes . . . God, even George Clooney would be jealous. Worst of all, he was being so lovely, so concerned about her being ill and possibly about to throw up all over his shoes.

'By the way, they love the food,' Kerr went on. 'So it looks like we're going to be seeing a lot more of each other.' He paused. 'You could look a bit happier if you like.'

This was truly awful. It was no good, she had to tell him.

'Look, I'm sorry, but I don't think it's going to happen.' Maddy really was starting to feel sick now; why did he have to be so nice?

'I'm not with you.' Even as he spoke, he was encouraging her to drink more of the ice-cold water.

'You don't even know my name,' Maddy said helplessly.

'And that's a major problem? How about if I – this is just off the top of my head – how about if I just ask you?'

He thought it was funny, that she was making a ridiculous fuss about nothing.

'It's Maddy. Maddy Harvey.'

She saw it register, saw it click into place. Finally Kerr McKinnon's expression changed.

'Shit. Are you serious?' For a split second, doubt flickered in his eyes.

Maddy couldn't blame him. She nodded, shivering violently despite the heat.

'Maddy Harvey? But . . . but you've . . .'

For a traitorous second Maddy wished she hadn't said it. Everything was spoiled now.

'I know.' Almost unbelievably she found herself feeling sorry for him. 'I don't look like I used to. I've changed.'

JFK airport. Millions of people, and no one there to see her off. Kate was wearing her beige floppy-brimmed hat in the forlorn hope that it would divert attention from her face. When she'd stopped for a cappuccino at Heathrow three years ago, she'd been chatted up by a six-foot Australian archaeologist. He'd even bought her another cup of coffee.

This time nobody chatted her up, not even the ancient lavatory attendant. Kate wasn't surprised. She paid for her own coffee and thought of her mother, who was driving up to meet her off the plane at Heathrow.

At least someone would be pleased to see her again.

All my own fault, thought Kate, flicking distractedly through the *New York Times*. Nobody to blame but myself. She paused at a photo of Brad Pitt, arriving at the premiere of his latest film. Once upon a time she had fantasised about meeting a famous movie star, someone the whole world drooled over. They would bump into each other quite by chance, in a supermarket checkout queue or something, and fall effortlessly into conversation. Naturally, besotted by her

17

ravishing looks and winning personality, the famous movie star would fall in love with her – oh yes, it would have been *Notting Hill* all over again, complete with dazzling Richard Curtis script.

Crossing her legs, Kate flipped over the page with the Brad Pitt photo on it. She didn't bother having that fantasy any more.

Chapter 3

Jake Harvey had an audience, but he didn't let on that he was aware of it. This was the way potential customers liked it to be. He carried on working, they stood and watched, and after a few minutes he would turn and smile at them, maybe exchange a friendly greeting, then return his attention to the task in hand. It was a low-key, low-pressure sales technique and it worked for Jake. He enjoyed his job and it showed. Sooner or later, curiosity always got the better of his visitors. He allowed them to open the conversation. His easy manner, indicating that he really couldn't care less whether they stayed or not, more often than not did the trick. And when it didn't, well, he genuinely wasn't that bothered anyway. These were tourists, impulse buyers, quite as likely to leave Ashcombe with a couple of postcards or a pot of homemade jam from the Peach Tree. You couldn't win them all.

Then again, in his line of work, you never knew when they – or their relatives – might, at some time in the future, be back in touch.

Putting down his glue gun, Jake straightened up and stretched his arms. Stripped to the waist, wearing only a pair of drastically faded jeans, he knew he looked good. Working outside had tanned him to the colour of strong tea, and when he stretched, the muscles in his back rippled beneath his skin.

Turning finally, he saw that the girl waiting was the type least likely to buy anything: the Scandinavian backpacker. He knew she was Scandinavian because she was blonde, and wearing khaki shorts, sturdy hiking boots and white socks.

Actually, she wasn't even that pretty, but Jake flashed her a smile anyway. He didn't mind.

'Hi.'

'Hi. This is fascinating. I have never seen this kind of thing done before.' The girl's English was excellent. 'Is the coffin for someone in particular?'

Nodding, Jake ran his hand lightly over the lid of the casket, lacquered in lapis-lazuli blue and studded with the glass jewels he had been applying with the aid of the hot-glue gun. The coloured jewels glittered like fairy lights in the sun. 'Oh yes, this one's going to a seventy-six-year-old Englishwoman living in Cyprus.'

The girl pulled an appropriately sympathetic face. 'And she is dead?'

'Not at all. Fighting fit.' Jake grinned and took a swig of Coke from the can at his side. 'She's planning on using it as a coffee table in the meantime. She told me that when she goes, her body might be all wrinkled and ancient but at least her coffin will be gorgeous.'

'That is such a beautiful idea.' Entranced, the girl peered past him into the shadowy workshop. 'I think it's wonderful. But if your clients die first, how do you—'

'Just work faster,' said Jake good-naturedly. 'It's fifty-fifty. Some like to choose their own coffins and design them themselves. Other times, the relatives contact me after the death and we choose something together. As long as they don't want anything too complicated, I can finish it in a day and send it to them by ParcelForce. The caskets are made of cardboard, so they aren't that heavy. And they're cheaper too. Commissioning a hand-decorated coffin ends up costing about the same as a plain old wooden one. Feel free to look around,' he went on, waving towards the workshop where photographs were pinned up along the back wall. 'Those are some of my past works. And I have a portfolio of standard designs on the table in the corner.'

Having stopped for a break, Jake followed the girl into the workshop and switched on the kettle to make tea. She was studying the photos of a particularly extravagant coffin covered in vibrant purple velvet, trimmed with gold and painted with white regale lilies.

'Lili DeLisle, the rock singer. That was hers,' said Jake. 'Her husband asked me to do it after she died in that plane crash. You can't see from the photo, but the lyrics of her song "Take Me" are etched all the way round the gold border. Gave my business no end of a boost,' he said cheerfully. 'Everyone who saw it wanted to know where it came from. The stamens on those lilies were real diamonds.'

'And letters from satisfied customers,' exclaimed the girl, moving on.

'Well, maybe not the customers themselves. But after the funeral the relatives quite often write to tell me what a difference it made.'

'I like this one.' The girl touched the edge of a photo displaying a casket simply decorated with white clouds in a cerulean blue sky, with a silver bird soaring above them.

'One of my bestsellers. Fancy a cup of tea?'

'I'd love one. But I'm not about to die, so I won't be needing a coffin, if that's what you're hoping.'

'Don't speak too soon,' said Jake. 'You don't know what I could be putting into your cup.'

They sat outside together, companionably drinking their tea and chatting about the famous bits of Bath which Trude had spent the morning exploring.

'Very nice,' she said, nodding seriously, 'but so terribly

crowded. It would be far better if there weren't so many tourists.'

Jake managed to keep a straight face. 'Sometimes it can get a bit much.'

'You know, my grandmother is very old. I'm thinking she might enjoy one of your coffins. Do you have a leaflet, perhaps, so I could show her your work?'

'I do. Better still,' said Jake, loping into the workshop and returning with a brochure and a packet of biscuits, 'it has my website address on it. That's how I get most of my business.'

Trude tucked the brochure carefully away in one of the pockets on her backpack.

'I like your business, very much. But how did you start? What gave you the idea to do this thing? Oh, thanks.' Blushing slightly, she took a digestive from the packet, showering crumbs down the front of her khaki shorts.

'Well, my sister died when I was fourteen,' said Jake, and Trude shot him a look of anguish, unable to speak through her mouthful of biscuit.

'It's OK,' said Jake, 'I get asked this question all the time. Anyway, April was sixteen, and my dad thought she wouldn't want to be buried in a plain coffin. He made one himself, a proper wooden one, and painted it pale pink, because that was April's favourite colour. Then the rest of us put our hand-prints on it, and Dad painted wildflowers and butterflies over the rest. April would have loved it.' He smiled briefly. 'So there you go, that's how it all started. I knew at once it was what I wanted to do. I left school at sixteen and set up the business. And here I am, almost ten years later, still here.'

'In a tiny place like this,' Trude marvelled.

'Ah, but it's my tiny place.' Spotting Marcella and Sophie heading towards them along Gypsy Lane, Jake waved and broke into a grin. 'I've lived in Ashcombe all my life.'

Moments later Sophie hurtled the rest of the way down

22

Gypsy Lane and flung herself into his arms. It was like catching an exuberant wriggling puppy. Swinging her round, Jake kissed the top of her neatly braided head and said, 'I'm getting too old for this. What have you two been up to then?'

'Making daisy chains.' Proudly, Sophie showed him the bedraggled chain in her left hand, before placing it round his neck. 'This one's for you, Daddy.'

'Now everyone will think I'm a girl,' said Jake.

'They won't, because you've got stubble on your chin.' Lovingly, she ran a grubby finger over his jawline. 'Anyway, there's a surprise for later. At six o'clock in the back garden, and you have to put a shirt on.'

'What kind of a surprise?'

'Me and Tiff are getting married.'

'Really?' Jake raised his eyebrows at Marcella, who was leaning against the wall lighting a cigarette. 'Mum, did you know about this?'

Marcella gave a what-can-you-do shrug. 'Darling, I tried to talk them out of it, tried to persuade them to wait a couple of years, but would they listen? You know how it is with young people today.'

'Fine.' Jake lowered his daughter to the ground. 'Just so long as you aren't expecting a wedding present, because I haven't had time to get to the shops.'

Beaming, Sophie said, 'That's OK. You can give me a cheque.'

Behind Sophie, Trude was looking puzzled, clearly struggling to work out the dynamics of the family before her. Jake smiled to himself, because confusion was a fairly common occurrence and always a source of entertainment. He knew exactly what was going through Trude's mind.

'Come along, pet, we'd better start getting you ready.' Marcella held out a hand. 'Every bride has to have a bath before her wedding.'

'Oh Gran, *why*?' Sophie pulled a disgusted face. 'I just had a bath on Saturday.'

'No one wants to marry a girl with muddy knees.'

'Tiff wouldn't mind. He hates baths too.' Rolling her dark eyes, Sophie gave up and made her way over to Marcella. 'OK. And Daddy, don't forget. Six o'clock.'

Jake shook his head in mock despair as Marcella and Sophie headed back up the road to Snow Cottage.

'How old is she?' said Trude.

'Seven.'

'You were very young when you became a father.'

'Seventeen.'

'She's beautiful. You must be very proud.' Trude hesitated, as he had known she would. 'And the lady with her? You called her Mum. But she is your mother-in-law, right?'

'No, she's my mum,' Jake said easily.

Trude, confused all over again, said, 'Please, forgive me if this is impertinent, but your daughter is . . . um, black.'

'Well spotted,' said Jake with a grin.

'And your mother, she is the same.'

Jake said helpfully, 'Black.'

Poor Trude was now frowning like Inspector Morse, doubtfully eyeing Jake's streaky blond hair, green eyes and golden-stubbled chin.

'So, I'm sorry, but you're not . . . um . . .'

'It's OK.' Jake nodded encouragingly. 'You can say it. I'm not black.'

'Exactly,' Trude exclaimed with relief. 'But I don't understand. How is it that you are white?'

Chapter 4

When Robert Harvey had lost his young wife Annabel to acute lymphoblastic leukaemia, he was devastated. Left alone to grieve and bring up their three small children, he couldn't imagine ever finding love again. Two years later, meeting Marcella Darby in a cafe in Keynsham where she was working as a waitress, he wondered what he'd done to deserve a second chance of happiness. Marcella, then twenty-two, was funny and irreverent, feisty and passionate. Robert, convinced there had to be a catch somewhere, tried – with spectacular lack of success – to conceal his true feelings. But it soon became apparent that there was no catch. Within weeks he knew he'd found his soulmate.

Unable to believe his luck, he brought Marcella back to Ashcombe and introduced her to his children. April was by this time six years old, Maddy five and Jake four. It was risky, but it had to be done. Marcella hadn't been scared off when he'd told her of their existence; indeed, she had declared that she loved kids, but saying it and actually meaning it were two different things. There was no guarantee that it wouldn't all go horribly wrong.

It hadn't. The bond between Marcella and Robert's children had been instantaneous, irrevocable and touching to behold. Marcella had adored all three and made her feelings so plain that they in turn had adored her. A fortnight after that first meeting, Maddy and Jake had asked their father why Marcella couldn't live with them. The following weekend she moved in, and by the end of the month all three children were calling her Mummy. Three months after that, they were married.

Marcella's arrival in Ashcombe caused a bit of a stir. Some of the older residents got quite het up about it, never having seen a black person in the flesh before. But most of the villagers, sympathetic to the family's tragic past and delighted to see Robert smiling again, welcomed Marcella with genuine warmth. Marcella herself, with her natural enthusiasm, exuberance and dazzling smile, soon won over the rest, the ancient old farmers who seemed to expect her to start smoking spliffs in the pub and turn Ashcombe into a den of vice, and those doubters who whispered that she had only married Robert Harvey for his money.

Not that he had any, but that was the first rule of small-town tittle-tattle: when stuck for a spurious excuse, make one up.

But who could doubt Marcella's genuine love for her new family when, at that year's summer fête, April was crowned carnival queen. Nobody could have been prouder than Marcella, who had spent weeks sewing sequins onto the Barbie-pink dress she had painstakingly made by hand. The little girl, who suffered from cerebral palsy and had never won anything before in her life, had insisted on making her own faltering speech at the crowning ceremony, and Marcella had applauded with tears of joy in her eyes.

Eight years later, the unthinkable happened. Tragedy struck again one sunny Saturday afternoon in May. April left the cottage and made her way up Gypsy Lane to visit a friend. A car, losing control as it rounded a bend at speed, mounted the pavement and catapulted April fifty feet into the air. According to the coroner at the inquest, she was probably dead before she hit the ground.

Robert and Marcella were inconsolable. Their grief was compounded at the trial when it was suggested that April's handicap had contributed to the accident, that she had been wandering in the road when the car had rounded the bend.

'April *never* wandered in the road,' Marcella stormed. 'She always kept to the pavement. How dare they say that, just to try and get that snivelling little fucker off the hook?'

In the end it didn't, and the seventeen-year-old snivelling little fucker – Kerr McKinnon's younger brother – was found guilty of dangerous driving. Den McKinnon was sentenced to two years' imprisonment, which didn't pacify Robert and Marcella one bit.

'Two years,' Marcella wept on the steps of the court, so incandescent with rage she could barely get the words out. 'Two years ... how can that make up for killing our beautiful girl? If I ever see that murdering bastard again, I'll kill him with my bare hands, I swear I will.'

Marcella had done a lot of swearing during those dark days, not least when a rumour spread through Ashcombe that the mother of the teenage driver had been heard outside the courtroom pointing out that it wasn't as if the Harveys had lost a normal child, everyone knew the girl wasn't all there. When Marcella heard this, she had to be physically restrained. 'Jesus Christ, are these people *human*? What are they saying, that April had cerebral palsy so they've actually done us some kind of *favour*? That killing her was on a par with running over an animal? Is that it? Am I hearing this right?' Wild-eyed with grief, she was almost literally tearing her hair out. 'So what do they think we should do to cheer ourselves up, *buy a cute little rabbit*?'

But as the months passed, the family gained strength from each other. Love pulled them through. Somehow they survived and learned how to be happy again. Marcella and Robert devoted themselves to making the remainder of

Maddy and Jake's childhood idyllic and when Maddy wrote in a school essay that she had the very best mum and dad in the world, she knew that – unlike all the other kids in her class, who only thought they had – she was writing the absolute truth.

Estelle had reached Heathrow in plenty of time to meet her daughter off the flight from New York. Now, waiting at the arrivals gate for Kate to appear, she found herself being jostled by an excited family unfurling a huge homemade Welcome Home banner. Touched by the sight of them, Estelle wondered how Kate would react if she emerged through the doors to find her mother waving a Welcome Home banner. Well, maybe not. It wasn't the kind of gesture Kate would appreciate. Somehow, they just weren't that kind of family.

The toddler in the pushchair next to her spat his dummy out on Estelle's shoe. Retrieving it and handing it back to him, she was rewarded with a face like thunder, as if it was all her fault. Strongly reminded of Kate at that age – the haughty attitude, the indifference – Estelle straightened up and quelled the butterflies in her stomach. She loved her daughter, of *course* she did, but she was also slightly afraid of her.

Oh Lord, that was an awful thing to even think. Not afraid, intimidated. Kate had inherited her father's somewhat aloof manner, and the emotional distance had been furthered by the school she had attended. Estelle hadn't been convinced that sending her to super-expensive Ridgelow Hall was necessary, but Oliver had insisted. 'Can you imagine how she might turn out if we dumped her in the nearest comprehensive?' he'd demanded. 'Good heavens, woman, are you out of your mind?' So Estelle had capitulated, thinking that maybe she was wrong after all, but the long-suppressed doubts had come back to haunt her. And as for the local comprehensive, well, it hadn't seemed to do Maddy and Jake Harvey any harm. They may not have PhDs and stratospheric careers, but they were thoroughly nice people and had grown into the kind of young adults of which any parent would be proud. Plus, of course, they adored their mother. Despite all the truly terrible things that had happened to Marcella over the years, Estelle secretly envied her.

'There he is! Dad, Dad, over here!' The family at her side began screaming and Estelle was forced to dodge out of the way to avoid getting entangled with their frantically flapping banner. Dad, letting out a roar of delight, raced over and hauled several small children into his arms. As they showered him with kisses and he told them how much he'd missed them, Estelle saw him catch his wife's eye and mouth: *Love you.* The wife, who was forty if she was a day, beamed like a teenage bride and blew him a kiss, happy to wait her turn.

Estelle's eyes suddenly filled with tears. Now she was reduced to envying total strangers – total strangers waving the kind of banner her own daughter would sneer at and pronounce naff.

She wouldn't mind betting this couple would be having fabulous sex tonight.

Then she straightened, because Kate was coming through, pushing a trolley piled high with cases and looking like a celebrity travelling incognito in a sleek charcoal trouser suit, dark glasses and trilby-style hat.

'Darling! Yoo-hoo,' Estelle called out (slightly naffly), waving an arm to attract her attention. Catching sight of her, Kate altered course and came over, proferring the undamaged side of her face for a kiss. Hugging her rather too enthusiastically in a feeble attempt to keep up with the neighbours, Estelle dislodged the trilby, which managed to land in the lap of the toddler in the pushchair.

The small boy stared at it as if it were a bomb. Kate

snatched it up and thrust it back onto her head. Estelle flinched as one of the small children said, 'Mum, what's happened to that lady's face?'

'Sshh,' his mother chided. 'It's not nice to say things like that. Poor girl . . .' She pulled a sympathetic face at Kate. 'I'm so sorry. You know what children are like.'

Shooting the woman a look that could have pickled walnuts, Kate said brusquely, 'Mum, can we get out of here? *Now?*'

Kate waited until they were racing down the M4 in the Lancia before speaking again. 'Will Dad be there when we get home?'

Estelle shot her an apologetic look. 'Sorry, darling. He had to work.'

'Par for the course.' Kate watched her mother light a cigarette. Estelle, a furtive smoker when her husband was around, had needed the boost of a Marlboro in order to brave the terrors of the motorway.

'But he'll be home soon,' Estelle went on brightly, as she had done for the last twenty-odd years, 'and he can't *wait* to see you.' She paused. 'I thought we'd have dinner tonight at the Angel, just you and me.'

Kate shuddered. The Fallen Angel was the only pub in Ashcombe. Just you and me could be roughly translated as: the two of us sitting at a table while everyone else in the pub ogles us from the bar and sniggers at the posh bird's comeuppance.

She hadn't asked to be the posh bird, they'd just saddled her with that label God knows how many years ago, and ever since then she'd been stuck with it.

'Darling. I know. But you have to face them at some stage.' Estelle was only too aware of what gossipy small-town life was like.

Kate sighed and gazed out of the window as Berkshire

sped past them in a blur of motorway-constructed emerald-green turf and geometrically planted trees. She knew her mother was right.

Aloud she said, 'We'll see.'

'You'll have to tell Mum,' said Jake.

'I can't tell Mum.' Maddy covered her face with her hands. 'She'll go ballistic.'

'You still should. She at least has a right to know he's back.' Jake kept his voice low. They were outside in the back garden of Snow Cottage, Maddy sitting cross-legged on the grass and Jake lounging in the hammock, his eyes shielded by dark glasses, a can of lager in his hands. Upstairs, Sophie was having her hair rebraided by Marcella, in preparation for the ceremony.

'He's been back for months and she hasn't known about it. He's living in Bath,' said Maddy. 'What are the chances of her bumping into him?'

'About the same as the chance of *you* bumping into him,' Jake pointed out. 'And you managed it. Jesus, I can't believe he didn't recognise you. You must have been even uglier than I remember.'

'I was.' Memories had nothing to do with it; Maddy had the unfortunate photos to prove it, but she reached over and gave the hammock a shove anyway, causing Jake to spill ice-cold Fosters over his bare chest.

He flicked lager back at her with his fingers. 'Thanks. So what happens now? I take it you won't be delivering to his company.'

Maddy paused. She'd already told Juliet, who could be trusted to be discreet, and Juliet had reacted with typical pragmatism: 'Look, I'm not just saying this because it means more business for us, but we are only talking sandwiches here. And you did say his staff were keen on our stuff. I mean, why should they miss out?' She'd shrugged, then gone on in her gentle way, 'Of course, it's entirely your decision. Whether *you* want to or not. You said he was a nice man; what did he have to say about it?'

'That it was up to me.'

'Well, just think it over.'

This was what Maddy had been doing ever since.

'Daddy!' A cross voice bellowed out and Sophie's head appeared at her bedroom window. 'Put some *clothes* on. I can't get married if you're not wearing a shirt.'

Rolling sideways out of the hammock and landing with practised ease on his feet, Jake handed Maddy his half-empty can of lager.

'I still think you should tell Mum.'

Maddy pictured Marcella's reaction. As far as family feuds went, the Harveys and the McKinnons knocked the Montagues and the Capulets into a cocked hat. She thought of Kerr and her stomach contracted.

'Maybe. But not yet.'

Chapter 5

Marcella worked as a cleaner at the Taylor-Trents' house, which was how Maddy knew that Kate Taylor-Trent would have arrived home by now. It seemed almost incredible to imagine that they had once been best friends, playing happily together and sharing everything, right up until the age of eleven.

Then Kate had been sent away to boarding school – Maddy vividly remembered their tearful parting – and that had been the beginning of the end. When Kate returned from Ridgelow Hall after her first term there, she had invited along her new best friend, a confident twelve-year-old called Alicia whose father was a newspaper magnate. Alicia had resisted Maddy's efforts to join in with them, and Kate, anxious to impress Alicia, had begun to slavishly follow her lead. Finally, Maddy had overheard Alicia drawling, 'She wears those awful glasses, her father drives a taxi for a living and her step-mother's *black*. Daddy would have a fit if he knew I was associating with someone like that.' Bursting into the Taylor-Trents' vast kitchen, Maddy had given Alicia a resounding slap before racing out of the house. For the rest of the afternoon she'd expected Kate to come over to the cottage and apologise. She didn't, and Maddy hadn't set eyes on her for the rest of the school holidays.

After that, Kate only had time for her bitchy rich school-friends. When they did encounter Maddy in the town, they smirked and sniggered behind her back, but always loudly enough for her to hear. Glossy-haired and immaculately turned out themselves – teenage It-girls in the making – they made fun of Maddy's clothes, the clanking great braces on her teeth, her general gawkiness and, of course, her National Health specs. The rest of the time they talked loudly about their parents' wealth, the exotic holidays they were taking this year, and how ghastly it must be to be poor *and* knobbly-kneed.

Oh, how they'd laughed at her knees.

Maddy hadn't let the experience mentally scar her for life. Kate and her snobbish new friends may have found it amusing to sneer at her and her friends, but it had been just as enjoyable making fun of them in return, ruthlessly mimicking their la-di-da voices and loudly discussing whose daddy had the biggest helicopter or the plushest yacht.

This had carried on until Kate had left Ridgelow Hall. From then on, throughout her time at finishing school in Switzerland, followed by university, then the move to New York, their paths hadn't crossed. Very occasionally Kate paid fleeting visits home, but never ventured into the town. More often, Estelle and Oliver flew out to visit her, or to meet up with her for long holidays in glamorous locations across the globe.

Then had come news of Kate's accident, and Maddy hadn't known what to think. Vacationing out in the Hamptons with a group of friends, Kate had crashed the car she was driving and had sustained horrific injuries to her face and neck. Estelle, naturally enough, had been distraught. Oliver had organised the best possible medical care and lined the pockets of the world's most skilled surgeons. Maddy had been horrified and ashamed to discover that although it was a terrible, *terrible* thing to have happened to anyone, a small subversive part of her couldn't help picturing Kate's beautiful smirking face and thinking *serves her right*.

Now, almost a year on and despite the best efforts of the surgeons, Kate Taylor-Trent was arriving back in Ashcombe with a face that bore the still very visible scars of the accident. If she saw her – and sooner or later they were bound to bump into each other – Maddy wondered if she would have to be nice to Kate, the one-time friend and latter-day enemy she hadn't set eyes on in over eight years. Despite the countless hurtful names Kate had once called her, Maddy didn't suppose she'd be allowed to retaliate now. When you were twenty-six, it was probably one of those things that was frowned upon. Even if you did sometimes still feel fourteen years old inside.

The wedding was a huge success, despite Tiff and Sophie's refusal to kiss each other when Marcella declared, 'You may now kiss the bride,' on the grounds that kissing was, *yeeugh*, gross. .

Now, having spent the evening watching a celebratory Rugrats video, the bride and groom were upstairs in their bunkbeds, fast asleep. Sleeping over at each other's houses two or three times a week suited their single parents perfectly, and when both Juliet and Jake wanted to go out on the same night, like tonight, Marcella was always happy to babysit. (Not that anyone was allowed to call it that. As Sophie had loftily pointed out, 'We aren't babies. You just look after us.')

Looking in on them, Maddy tucked her niece's spindly brown leg back under the duvet and carefully removed a cross-dressed Action man (wearing one of Barbie's tutus) from under Tiff's neck. She headed downstairs and found Marcella stretched across the sofa eating jalapeno-chilli crisps and watching a documentary on BBC 2. Since meeting

Vincenzo d'Agostini three years earlier and moving into his house up on Holly Hill, Marcella had found new – and much deserved – happiness. Everyone adored Vince and declared that they were perfect together. With a pang, Maddy saw that the documentary was about foster carers. Marcella's inability to have children of her own had been a source of sorrow to all of them; even now, at the age of forty-three, she still harboured powerful maternal urges.

'I could do that.' Marcella pointed at the TV screen with a crisp. 'D'you think they'd let me, or am I too old and decrepit?'

Maddy leaned over the back of the sofa and gave her mother a big hug. 'You'd be brilliant, but don't just rush off and come back with one as a surprise. It's the kind of thing you need to talk about first.'

'That was different, Bean was only a puppy.' Marcella recognised the dig. 'There wasn't time to discuss it. The man said if I didn't take her, it'd be curtains for Bean. So what else could I do?'

'Ooh, I don't know, how about wave a placard saying, "Go on, tell me a heartrending story, I'm a total pushover"?'

'But look at her!' Marcella reached for Bean, who was curled up beside her, and swung the little dog into the air. 'Even if the man was lying to me, how could I have said no? If you'd been there, you wouldn't have been able to either.'

'I wouldn't have paid him fifty pounds,' said Maddy, because Marcella truly was the queen of gullibility. The traveller who had sold Bean to her on a busy street corner in the centre of Bath surely hadn't been able to believe his luck.

'Are you saying Bean wasn't worth it? Oh, sweetheart, don't listen, cover your ears! Anyway,' Marcella went on, folding the puppy's long floppy ears lovingly under its jaw, 'isn't it time you were gone? If this programme's going to make me cry I'd rather do it in peace.'

Maddy imagined telling her mother that the man she'd met on Saturday night and liked so much was in fact Kerr McKinnon. Marcella might not burst into tears, but the torrent of abuse that would pour forth would be spectacular.

Surely it was kinder not to let her know.

The Fallen Angel was busier than usual that Monday evening. Joining Jake and Juliet at the bar, Maddy was struck once again by the beauty of the pair of them, Jake so lean and blond and tanned, like a surfer, next to Juliet with her bewitching dark hair and eyes, lily-white skin and voluptuous figure. They made the perfect couple visually, got on like a house on fire and adored each other's children, yet there wasn't so much as a flicker of chemistry between the two of them. It was such a waste, but there was nothing anyone could do about it; they simply didn't fancy each other – ooh, drink.

'Thanks.' Maddy sat down next to Juliet, who had thrust the glass of Fitou into her hand. 'No sign of the other team yet?'

Monday night was darts night and this evening they were up against the Red Fox from the neighbouring village of Claverham.

'They're always late. So did you tell Marcella yet?' Jake waved his empty lager bottle at Nuala, behind the bar. 'Another one of these, darling, thanks. Well?' He returned his attention to Maddy, one eyebrow raised.

'No, I just couldn't. That smells fantastic.' Keen to change the subject, Maddy lifted her head as one of the waitresses emerged from the kitchen with an array of plates balanced on each arm. To the right of the bar was the restaurant area, where several tables were already occupied.

'Coward,' retorted Jake.

Juliet gave him a prod. 'Leave her alone. I don't see why Maddy has to tell her at all. Even if Marcella does find out that this chap's moved back to Bath, she could always pretend she didn't know he had.'

Maddy nodded. That made sense, actually. OK, so maybe it was a little underhand, but if she was only doing it in Marcella's best interests . . .

Anyway, why had it suddenly gone so quiet in here? As the conversation died, Maddy swivelled round on her stool, realising that someone had just walked into the pub behind her.

Oh shit, please don't let it be Kerr McKinnon.

It wasn't, although the new arrival had caused just as much of a stir. Although stirs were supposed to be noisy, weren't they? And this was the opposite of noisy, more of an anti-stir.

Along with everyone else, Maddy couldn't help gazing at Kate Taylor-Trent. She would have done it anyway, even if Kate's accident hadn't happened; it had been eight years since she'd last seen her, after all. But the livid scars were there for all to see, despite the baseball cap pulled down over her forehead. As Kate followed her mother through the pub to the restaurant area, she gazed determinedly ahead, refusing to catch anyone's eye.

Under his breath, Jake murmured, 'It's like that bit in *High Noon*.'

Apart from a few of the locals acknowledging Estelle with a nod and a mumbled, 'Evening, Mrs Taylor-Trent,' nobody else was speaking. Desperate to break the embarrassing silence, Maddy burst out laughing as if she'd just heard a brilliant joke, then realised too late that she sounded as if she was laughing at Kate. Hurrying to cover the faux pas, she said brightly, 'Juliet, you should have seen them, they were so *funny,*' and promptly realised that this only made her sound more guilty.

For good measure, Kate chose this moment to look back over her shoulder and stare directly at her. Feeling dreadful and prickling all over with embarrassment, Maddy pretended she hadn't noticed and took a huge glug of Fitou.

'Who were so funny?' said Juliet, puzzled.

Highly entertained, Jake ruffled Maddy's hair and said, 'Nobody. Well, apart from my sister.'

'Tiff and Sophie, I was talking about.' Maddy decided to go for the bluff and pretend she hadn't just been blurting out any old rubbish. 'They looked so sweet tonight in their bunkbeds, that's all I meant. Sophie insisted on sleeping in her wedding dress.'

'And you're still blushing,' Jake couldn't resist pointing out.

'Oh, shut up.' Seeing Kate had caused her to regress; she was feeling stupid and inadequate all over again and now to cap it all she was redder than her glass of red wine. Right, stop it, *enough*.

Nuala Stratton leaned across the bar, agog. 'Is that her? Is that the one who was always so horrid to you?'

As if Estelle Taylor-Trent were likely to bring any number of half-stunning, half-scarred 26-year-olds into the restaurant for dinner.

'Come on,' said Jake cheerfully, 'time we hit the dart-board before the opposition gets here. We could all do with the practice.'

Kate was hating every moment. Everyone was pretending not to look at her. They had ordered from the menu and now she longed for a cigarette, but the dining section was non-smoking and she definitely wasn't going to venture through to the bar to be ogled at close quarters.

'Hungry, darling?' Valiantly attempting to pretend there

was nothing wrong, that this was just a normal, happy mother-daughter outing, Estelle was struggling to keep the conversation going. 'The new chef's much better than the old one. Daddy and I had a fantastic bouillabaisse last time we were in.'

Kate pointedly examined the salt cellar. In desperation, her mother gazed around the other tables.

'Ooh, those mussels look nice.'

How could mussels *look* nice? Mussels were mussels, for crying out loud, nothing more than a heap of black shiny shells.

'Sweetheart, trust me, everything's going to be fine,' Estelle whispered. 'Just give them a few days to get used to you and—'

'Oh please, Mum, don't treat me like a kid,' Kate hissed back. 'Everything *isn't* going to be fine. How can it, with me looking like this? I've had almost a year to get used to it,' she went on bitterly, 'and it hasn't happened yet.'

'But darling, it's only a few little scars! How you look on the outside isn't important, you're still you . . . oh Kate, where are you going? Sweetheart, *come back.*'

Chapter 6

It was no good, she couldn't do this. Feeling horribly trapped, Kate stood up so fast she almost tipped her chair over. If she was going to cry, she had to get out of here before it happened. But pushing back through the crowded bar – past the darts teams limbering up for their match – would be too much of an ordeal.

Glimpsing the corridor to the right, Kate abruptly veered towards it. The ladies' loo was through a door on the left. Locking herself into the cubicle with trembling hands, she collapsed onto the lowered lavatory seat and took several deep breaths, tilting her head back and willing the tears to go back down.

Thankfully it worked. When it was safe to return her head to the upright position, Kate snapped open her Prada bag, took out her cigarettes and lit one. This was what she was reduced to now; hiding in the toilet, smoking a Marlboro Light, hideously aware that out in the bar people were laughing and talking about her, and there wasn't a damn thing she could do to stop it.

All her life she'd adored being the centre of attention. But not like this.

Exhaling furiously, Kate pictured Maddy Harvey, whom until tonight she hadn't seen for eight years. The change in her was amazing; Maddy had been the original ugly duckling.

If Estelle hadn't kept her up to date with developments, she might not have recognised her. But having been told what to expect, she had known at once that the sparky blonde at the bar was Maddy. She'd heard the burst of laughter, too, after she and Estelle had made their way through the bar. And when they'd been seated at their table she'd found herself covertly glancing over at her. Being prepared for an improvement was one thing, but this much of a transformation had come as a major shock. Maddy may only have been wearing a little black vest and black trousers, but the colour enhanced her bouncing, layered, white-blonde hair and golden tan. As she drank and joked with the visiting darts team, she exuded down-to-earth glamour and the kind of easy confidence that—

Oh hell.

Kate shrank back instinctively as the door handle to the loo began to jiggle. She stared at it, willing the intruder to give up and leave her in peace.

The jiggling stopped, then started up again, accompanied by the creak of wood as someone leaned against the door. *Go away*, thought Kate, wondering if it was her mother come to see how she was. *Just go away.*

'Hello?' called a voice that clearly didn't belong to Estelle. 'Is anyone in there?'

Drawing hard on her Marlboro, Kate rose to her feet, lifted the wooden lavatory seat and dropped the rest of the cigarette down the loo. Then she flushed it away.

'Oh, sorry!' the voice sang out. 'Sometimes you think there's someone in there and it's just that the door's got stuck.'

A shiver went down the back of Kate's neck. Was that Maddy's voice? Swivelling round, she peered up in desperation at the tiny window, but it was no bigger than a cat flap. You might just be able to squeeze a loaf of bread through there, but a grown woman? Forget it.

So she was trapped. The only way out was through the

door. Meanwhile, the more she thought about it, the more convinced she became that the voice on the other side belonged to Maddy Harvey.

Bracing herself, Kate unlocked the door.

And there she was, leaning against the sink, looking even more spectacular close up, those emerald-green eyes no longer hidden behind geeky spectacles.

'Oh. Hi.' Maddy hesitated. 'Sorry about the door. It gets stuck sometimes.'

Kate reached the second door, the one that would lead her back out into the corridor.

'And I'm sorry about your . . . um, accident,' Maddy went on awkwardly.

Bitch. I'll bet you are.

'Yes.' Kate fixed her with a look of utter derision. 'I heard you laughing.'

Maddy flinched as if she'd been slapped. 'Oh, but I wasn't laughing at—'

'You,' Maddy insisted to Jake and Juliet when she rejoined them. 'I was about to say, "I wasn't laughing at you," but she just slammed the door shut in my face! God, it was awful, I was only trying to be polite. And then when I came out of the loo they were sitting there eating their meals and I wondered if I should go over and explain, but what if she'd started causing a massive scene in front of everyone, chucked a bowl of mussels over me or something?' Maddy shuddered. 'I just couldn't bring myself to do it, and now everything's more awkward than ever.'

'So?' Jake was typically unconcerned. 'Don't let it bother you. Scars or no scars, she's always been a bitch. Anyway, we've got a match to play.'

'And someone here has his eye on you.' Juliet gave Maddy a nudge. 'You could be about to pull.'

The last time they'd played the team from the Red Fox, Maddy had been charmed by their captain, a burly rugby-player type called Ed. Throughout the evening they had flirted happily with each other, until last orders were called and Ed had regretfully confided that he'd love to take her out some time, but he had a girlfriend. Which was sweet, of course, and showed he was the faithful, trustworthy type, but at the same time not what she'd wanted to hear.

Maddy glanced across at Ed now, throwing darts and pretending he didn't know he was being watched.

'He's already seeing someone.'

'Wrong. He sidled over when you were in the loo and asked if you were available.' Juliet looked smug. 'Then he casually mentioned that he'd finished with his girlfriend. I think you've definitely made a conquest.'

Maddy wished she could feel more enthusiastic. Before, she had been quite taken with Ed, but somehow this news no longer filled her with delight. It was like seeing a great pair of Timberlands and not being able to afford them, then walking into the shop two months later with your birthday money in your purse, realising that the yearning to own them had evaporated and that, actually, you'd much prefer a pair of fantastically sleek stiletto-heeled boots.

Oh God, was she seriously comparing Kerr McKinnon with a pair of boots?

'Come on, you're miles away.' Jake pushed her forward. 'You're next.'

Needless to say, they lost the match. Not because Maddy's mind wasn't on the job but because they invariably lost. They were the worst team in the league, the upside being that their opponents were always delighted to play them.

'Bad luck,' said Ed, joining Maddy at the bar where she was sitting with Juliet.

Spotting the glint of intent in his eye, Juliet slid off her stool and murmured, 'Back in a minute.'

For a single woman with no love life of her own, Juliet was an incorrigible matchmaker. Whenever Maddy tried to interest her in a man she simply pulled a face and said easily, 'He's nice, but not my type.'

'Hi.' Now that his way was clear, Ed said casually, 'Did you hear I'd broken up with my girlfriend?'

'Well, yes. You told Juliet. She told me. I'm so sorry,' said Maddy. 'You must be devastated.'

He looked offended. 'No, no! I finished with *her*. Anyway, the thing is, I wondered what you were doing this weekend, Friday or Saturday night. Maybe we could go out somewhere.'

'Oh, what a shame,' Maddy said sorrowfully, 'I can't. I have to babysit my niece.'

'Both nights?'

'Both nights. Sorry.' Aware that Jake was listening behind her, she prayed he wouldn't give her a dig in the ribs and say embarrassingly, 'That's not true.'

But Jake waited until Juliet was back from the loo and Ed had slunk off in defeat before saying, 'Hey, Juliet, fancy a wild weekend in Paris?'

'Why?'

'Maddy's babysitting Sophie on Friday and Saturday, so she may as well have Tiff too. That leaves you and me free to do whatever we want – brilliant restaurants, loads to drink, *fabulous* sex . . .'

'Thanks,' Juliet gave his arm a consoling squeeze, 'but you're not my type.'

Behind the bar, vigorously polishing glasses, Nuala said with frustration, 'You always say that. But what kind of man do you go for? I mean, what was Tiff's dad like?'

Since Juliet had spent the last five years not elaborating on the subject of Tiff's father, Maddy didn't get her hopes up.

True to form, Juliet simply smiled her dazzling, enigmatic smile.

'Oh, he was definitely my type. But he was married.'

'Enemy on the move, enemy on the move,' Jake murmured in Maddy's ear. 'Approaching at three o'clock . . . draw your weapons . . .'

Flushing, Maddy saw that Kate and Estelle had finished their meal and were heading back through the bar.

'She isn't my enemy.'

'She may not be *your* enemy,' Jake whispered wickedly, 'but I think you could be hers.'

As first Estelle then Kate made their way past them, Kate shot Maddy a look of disdain.

Oh great. Maddy turned away.

'Blimey,' Nuala exclaimed as they swept out, 'did you see her *face*?'

The door hadn't completely closed. It swung back open, Kate glared ferociously at Nuala, spat, 'At least I'm not *fat*,' and slammed out again.

Visibly shaken, Nuala clutched the Guinness pump for support.

'That's not fair! She took it *completely* the wrong way. I didn't mean did you see the ugly scars on her face, I meant did you see the *look* on her face! And now she's called me fat,' wailed Nuala, who was ultra-sensitive about her weight.

Feeling both guilty and relieved that it had happened to Nuala too, Maddy said, 'Welcome to the club.'

Chapter 7

'I didn't know whether we'd see you again,' said Kerr. 'Come on through to my office.'

'But—'

'Seriously.' He took the cool-boxes from her and put them on the floor next to the reception desk. 'We need to talk.'

Heart in her mouth, Maddy followed him down the corridor and into his office. The desk, she noticed, was strewn with papers and three empty coffee cups. Not naturally tidy herself, Maddy was heartened by the sight of another person's chaos. Over-organised people automatically made her feel nervous and defensive.

'Coffee?'

'Um, no thanks.'

'OK.' He paused, sat down opposite her in his swivel chair, picked up a Biro and began to tap it against the edge of the desk, probably because there wasn't any space to tap it on the surface. Maddy was further reassured by the pen, so few people seemed to own them these days. Computer-only offices gave her the heebie-jeebies.

Kerr was looking on edge, hardly surprisingly under the circumstances. To get the conversational ball rolling, she said, 'I wasn't going to come back. I talked to my boss about it – her name's Juliet – and she said it was up to me, but she didn't see why your staff should be deprived of brilliant sandwiches because of something that has nothing to do with them.'

Kerr considered this, then nodded. 'We should have brought the cool-boxes in with us. They'll be out there helping themselves to all the best ones.'

'That's OK, you'll love the maggot and cress baguette.' Maddy stopped and laced her fingers together; she was joking and she shouldn't be. It was inappropriate. Nerves were getting the better of her. Anyway, who was she trying to kid? If she didn't find him so attractive she wouldn't have dreamed of coming back. Putting the blame on Juliet was nothing more than a bare-faced lie and she should be ashamed of herself.

The thing was, did Kerr know that?

He looked at her. 'Why don't you sit down?'

Relieved, Maddy sat.

'I'm so sorry about your sister.' Kerr came straight to the point. 'There isn't a day goes by when I don't think about what happened. I don't blame your parents for reacting the way they did. How is your mother, by the way?'

'She's fine. Very well.' They were finally talking about it; Maddy resolved not to cry. 'She wouldn't be fine if she knew I was here, talking to you.'

'Even though it happened eleven years ago? And it wasn't actually anything to do with me?'

'Sixty years wouldn't be long enough for Marcella. You're a McKinnon and that's all that matters. As far as she's concerned, you're all beneath contempt.'

Kerr paused, digesting this statement. 'But I wasn't even in the country when it happened. I was in the French Alps—'

'Nobody ever apologised,' Maddy blurted out, 'that's what she could never get over. Your family lived three miles away. OK, we may not have moved in the same social circles, but we knew who you were, and you knew us by

48

sight. Then the accident happened and your family didn't even have the decency to say sorry. No message, no letter, nothing. As if we weren't even worth apologising to. That's what Mum's never been able to get over. Well,' she amended, 'that and . . . something else that was said.'

Sitting very still, Kerr McKinnon said, 'Which was?'

'Apparently your mother was heard outside the court saying it wasn't as if April had been normal.'

The room was silent.

Finally Kerr spoke.

'I did apologise.'

Maddy shook her head. 'Nobody did. That's what made Marcella so mad.'

'OK, listen. Before the trial, my brother's lawyers stressed that none of us should make any attempt to contact your family. That was their number one rule. But after the trial, when Den had been sentenced, I *did* apologise, to your father.' Kerr waited. 'At least, I tried to. He didn't want to hear it. I came over to your house one morning when I knew you and your brother would be at school. I wanted to see Marcella as well, but she wasn't there. I did my best to tell your father how sorry we all were, but he wouldn't let me get more than a few words out. Basically he told me to clear off out of his sight and never come near him or his family again. I thought he was going to punch me. I'd gone there to try and make things better and all I was doing was making things worse. So I did what he wanted me to do and left.' Shaking his head, Kerr said, 'And he never even told anyone I'd been there.'

'Never. Not a word.' Maddy wondered if she was being gullible here. Could Kerr McKinnon be spinning her a sob story?

Catching the look in her eyes he said flatly, 'You don't believe me? It's the truth. Ask your father.'

Maddy stared at him. 'I can't.'

'Look, it was eleven years ago. I'm not expecting him to forgive me for being a McKinnon, but he could at least admit that I went to your house that day and did my best to apologise for what happened.'

'He couldn't,' said Maddy. 'He's dead.'

Now it was Kerr's turn to look at her in dismay.

'God. I'm sorry. I didn't know.'

'Clearly.'

'When did that happen?'

'Six years ago. He had a heart attack.' Maddy blinked hard. 'He was only forty-four. I don't know, life doesn't seem fair sometimes, does it? We didn't have any warning. Poor Marcella, as if she hadn't already had enough to cope with.'

'Not only Marcella,' Kerr said gently.

'She's amazing. I don't know how she does it. We're so lucky to have her.'

'She's lucky to have you.'

Maddy swallowed the lump in her throat; sympathy was the last thing she needed. 'Anyway, Mum's fine now. Three years ago she started seeing this new chap who'd just moved into the village. His name's Vincenzo d'Agostini, he's a master carpenter and we all really like him. They live together now in his house on Holly Hill, and he's only thirty-eight so we call him the toyboy. We keep dropping hints about wedding bells but Mum says it's more fun living in sin.'

For the first time that morning, Kerr smiled.

'Well, good for them. I'm glad she's happy. And how about your brother, where's he living now?'

Maddy began to relax. 'Oh, still in Ashcombe. Jake has a seven-year-old daughter—'

'Jesus. *Seven?*'

'Yes, well, it wasn't exactly planned. He and Nadine were both seventeen. She didn't want the baby, but Marcella persuaded her to go through with the pregnancy. Actually, she paid her not to have an abortion. After Sophie was born, Nadine handed her over to Jake and took off. Jake was granted sole custody. Mum helps out, of course, but he's brilliant with her. To be honest, I never thought he'd manage it, I expected him to get bored after a couple of months, like he did with his Lego space station when he was eight. But it's been seven years now and he hasn't got bored yet.'

'And you're in Ashcombe as well. Whereabouts?'

'With Jake and Sophie. We're still in our old house. Marcella's the only one who's moved out.'

'Snow Cottage,' said Kerr, remembering the name.

'The three of us,' said Maddy with a wry smile. 'Not the most conventional of set-ups, but then our family never did specialise in being run-of-the-mill. Anyhow, it works for us. We're happy.'

'Good,' said Kerr, and he sounded as if he meant it.

'How about you? Your family, I mean.' She felt obliged to ask, but was curious too. Following the trial, Den had gone to prison. Kerr had returned to complete his university degree, then taken a job in London. Meanwhile their mother Pauline had retreated, alone, to the secluded family home midway between Ashcombe and Bath. Pauline McKinnon was rumoured to have become an eccentric recluse – though Maddy had always wondered how, if she was such a recluse, anyone could possibly know she was eccentric.

'My family?' Kerr sighed. 'Haven't done as well as yours, I'm afraid. When Den was released, he moved to Australia. He wasn't happy, couldn't settle, drifted from job to job and from woman to woman . . . we lost touch over five years ago. I have no idea where he is or what he's doing now. And as for my mother, well, she's a chronic alcoholic, incapable of looking after herself. I've hired maybe a dozen housekeeper-companions over the years but they never stay more than a few months. Last Christmas I had to arrange for her to go into a home. That's why I moved back to Bath. I'm going to need to sell the house to pay the nursing home fees. According to the doctors, she shouldn't even still be alive, but apparently she has the constitution of an ox.' He paused. 'Needless to say, she's not happy either. Maybe your mother will be pleased to hear it.'

Maddy automatically opened her mouth to defend Marcella, then shut it again. He was probably right. OK, be honest, he was right. How many times had Marcella vehemently declared that she hoped the McKinnons would burn in hell?

Whereas it was, in truth, just terribly, *terribly* sad. Pauline McKinnon had been through the mill and had declined into alcoholism as a result. She too had been widowed when her children were only young, losing her Scottish architect husband to a brain haemorrhage. And now her house was having to be sold to pay her nursing home fees. She wasn't to blame for what had happened. The accident had been a tragedy affecting more than just one family. And Kerr – Maddy truly believed him now – *had* attempted to apologise to her father . . .

'I'd better be getting on.' She rose to her feet, realising how long they'd been closeted in his office exchanging family histories. 'My other customers will be getting restless.'

'But you'll carry on coming here,' said Kerr. When she hesitated he added, 'I won't always be around. I'm away in London a lot of the time, dealing with clients.'

Was that meant to be an incentive? Maddy nodded, already feeling oddly bereft at the thought of not seeing him while he was in London. 'I'll carry on.'

Another flicker of a smile. 'Maybe when I get back we could go out to dinner one evening. If you wanted to.'

He was looking at her, gauging her reaction. Maddy

wondered if he had the remotest idea how she was feeling right now.

If you wanted to.

Oh, she wanted to, all right. But wanting something and actually doing it were two entirely different things. She pictured Marcella's reaction upon discovering that she'd had a civilised conversation with a McKinnon, let alone a dinner date.

Put it this way, there'd be no roof left on Snow Cottage.

'Thanks.' Maddy hesitated. 'But that might be a bit . . .'

Kerr raised his hands in acknowledgement. 'OK. I know. Sorry, I shouldn't have said that. Oh, before you go, there's one other thing that's been puzzling me.'

Lovely. Something embarrassing, I hope. 'What's that?'

'On Saturday night you didn't recognise me. On Monday morning you did. I mean, I know it was dark in the garden, but it wasn't that dark.'

Phew. Only semi-embarrassing, what a relief.

'Vanity,' said Maddy. 'I'd lost one of my contacts and couldn't bear to wear my glasses.'

'So that's what you're wearing now? Contact lenses? I can't see them at all,' Kerr marvelled, moving closer.

'Actually, that's the general idea.' Maddy obligingly tilted her head, allowing him to peer into her eyes. There was that aftershave again, and the giveaway fluttering action in the pit of her stomach. OK, surely ten seconds was enough . . .

Shifting her gaze, she saw that Kerr hadn't been studying her lenses at all. He was looking at *her*. As their eyes met, the wing-flapping of the hummingbirds in her stomach intensified. Was he going to kiss her? He wanted to, that much was for sure. And she wanted him to, and he knew she wanted him to . . .

It was easy, Maddy discovered, to break the spell. All you had to do was imagine Marcella bursting into the office.

Maddy took a step back and gave Kerr McKinnon a look of reproach.

'Sorry.' His smile rueful, he pushed his hair back with his fingers and shook his head. 'Cheap trick.'

'Very cheap trick.'

'I couldn't help myself.'

'Just picture my mother with a gun in her hands.'

'Right. That's very helpful. Thanks.'

'Any time,' said Maddy, realising as she let herself out of the room that they were doing it again. Making jokes about something that really wasn't a joking matter.

Chapter 8

It was midday on Thursday and Kate was still in bed, buried under the duvet because in all honesty what was the point of getting up?

But she wasn't asleep, which was hardly surprising considering the racket going on downstairs. Her mother had visitors, judging by the snatches of laughter, the doors slamming and the click-clacking of high heels across the parquet flooring in the hall.

Finally she heard Estelle climb the staircase and call out something muffled.

Kate groaned and rolled over onto her back, wincing as the sunlight streamed in through the bedroom window and into her eyes. But trying to ignore her mother was pointless; when she wanted a reaction she was as persistent as Jeremy Paxman.

As the bedroom door swung open, Kate said wearily, 'You've got a what?'

'A surprise! Darling, come on, just slip some clothes on and come down to the kitchen. You'll love it, I promise.'

Kate doubted it.

'Who's downstairs?' She had successfully avoided Marcella Harvey so far, by the simple expedient of staying in bed until mid-afternoon.

'No one.'

'I heard noise. And voices.'

Looking suspiciously smug, Estelle said, 'Oh, that was Barbara Kendall. She's gone now. Come along, sweetheart, I can't wait to show you!'

Grumpily, Kate crawled out of bed and pulled on a grey T-shirt and baggy jogging pants. At least if the house was empty she needn't bother with make-up.

Triumphantly, her mother flung open the door to the kitchen. Presented with not one but two unwelcome sights, Kate took a step back and said, 'Oh, good grief, what's *that*?'

The thing straining towards her was dark brown, snuffly and grossly overweight. Its claws scrabbled against the quarry-tiled floor while its stubby tail – like half an old discarded sausage – juddered with excitement. Sitting on one of the kitchen chairs, hanging on to its lead, was Maddy Harvey's mother.

'Isn't he wonderful?' cried Estelle. 'His name's Norris!'

Norris the bulldog. 'He's gross,' Kate declared. 'And I thought you said there was no one here.' She avoided looking at Marcella as she said it, but was acutely aware of the bright glare of sunlight on her own unmade-up face.

'Darling, I just meant that Barbara had gone. Marcella isn't a visitor, she's part of the family.'

Family, indeed. Kate bit her tongue; now she knew her mother was officially losing it.

'Hello, Kate, it's been a long time,' Marcella said easily. Raising herself from her chair she said, 'Now why don't I take a good look at you, then that'll be the awkwardness put behind us.'

'Good idea,' said Estelle. 'I'll take Norris, shall I?'

Take Norris and drown him in a bucket preferably, thought Kate, scarcely able to believe that she was standing there like a statue in a bloody art gallery, allowing Marcella Harvey to walk round her studying her face from all angles. How

Estelle could possibly think this was a good idea was beyond her. The woman was hired to clean their house, for crying out loud.

'Well,' Marcella said finally, 'I haven't run screaming from the room. It's only a bit of scarring, when all's said and done.'

Only a bit of scarring. Kate could have slapped her.

'You were lucky not to lose that eye,' Marcella observed. Catching the mutinous look on Kate's face, she smiled and said, 'OK, I know, there's nothing more annoying than being told to count your blessings. But all I'm saying is, it doesn't change who you are.'

Of course it does, you stupid old witch, it changes *everything*.

'Not unless you let it change you,' Marcella went on, 'and it'd be a real shame if you did that. You're still a pretty girl, you know.' Kate flinched as Marcella reached out and gently stroked her face, first one side then the other. 'Anyone who can't see that isn't worth bothering with.'

Appalled, Kate realised that quite suddenly she was on the verge of tears; Marcella's gentle fingers and matter-of-fact tone had got to her. She was talking absolute rubbish, of course, but at least it made a change from the endless sympathy.

She wondered if Maddy had told Marcella about the incident in the pub, and guessed that she hadn't. Marcella's loyalty to her own family was legendary. Giving herself a mental shake, Kate said, 'So what's the dog doing here anyway?'

'He's Barbara's dog,' Estelle proudly explained. 'She rang me yesterday in a terrible state. They're all off to Australia in a few days and they'd arranged for Norris to be looked after by a neighbour, but the neighbour's broken her hip and all the boarding kennels are booked up, so I said why didn't we have him here with us?'

Kate could think of lots of reasons, not least that Norris was diabolically ugly, as fat as a pig and – on the current evidence – a champion drooler. If there was a national saliva shortage, they could donate Norris to the cause.

'It's only for six weeks,' Estelle chattered on, 'and he's such a poppet, he has a lovely nature. You'll be able to take him for lots of long walks, darling . . . it'll do both of you the world of good. To be honest, Barbara spoils him rotten and he doesn't get nearly enough exercise. I thought we could put him on a bit of a diet while he's with us, work out a fitness regime—'

'I don't need to lose weight.' Kate was stung by her mother's comment that it would do her the world of good.

'Darling, I know you don't. But you can't spend all your time in bed, you should be out in the fresh air, and taking Norris for a walk would be such a nice way of meeting people.'

'I don't want to meet people.'

'But you must! Sweetheart, you're twenty-six,' Estelle pleaded, 'you can't hide away like a hermit. Anyway, it was Marcella's idea, and I think she's absolutely right. Since they got Bean, they can't imagine life without her. And Norris is here now; we can't kick him out into the street, can we?' Bending down and cupping Norris's lugubrious face in her hands she cooed, 'Eh? Of course we wouldn't do that, because you're beautiful, aren't you?'

The world had gone mad. Her mother had never shown the remotest interest in dogs before and now look at her, crawling around on the floor making goo-goo noises like some besotted new mother.

Was this what happened when you hit the menopause?

'Well, I'd better make a start on those windows,' said Marcella.

About bloody time too. But Kate couldn't help covertly

watching as Marcella crossed to the utility room, took a yellow
bucket out from under the sink and began to fill it with water
and a dash of Fairy. She was wearing lime-green cotton Capri
pants, a raspberry-pink shirt knotted at the waist, and orange
flip-flops. Her skin was the colour of Maltesers, her black
hair tied back with a glittery pink scrunchie. Marcella had to
be in her early forties, but she possessed an enviable figure.
As she vigorously swirled the Fairy Liquid around in the
water, her high bottom jiggled like a 25-year-old's. And her
waist was tiny, Kate noted. Unlike Estelle, who had been
letting herself go lately and could do with shifting a couple
of stone.

'Don't drink it, you daft animal,' Marcella gently chided
as Norris investigated the contents of the bucket with snuffly,
snorty interest. That was something else about Marcella: she
had a beguiling voice, warm and husky with that hint of a
Newcastle accent betraying her upbringing on Tyneside.

'He's thirsty. I'll get him a bowl of water,' said Estelle.
'And we're going to need some cans of food for him.
Sweetheart, why don't you have a shower and get dressed,
then you could pop down to the shop and pick some up.'

Kate sighed; this whole charade was nothing more than
a conspiracy to get her out of the house.

'Can't you do it?'

'I have to hold the ladder while Marcella's doing the high-
up bits. Otherwise she might fall off.' Estelle grinned. 'And
then who'd clean the windows?'

Shooting a look of hatred at Norris, Kate moved towards
the door.

'Actually, could you do me a favour?' said Marcella. 'When
you see Jake, tell him to take the lamb chops out of the freezer.
If he spreads them out on a plate they'll defrost in a couple
of hours. And remind him that Sophie has to be at the village
hall by five o'clock for Charlotte's birthday party.'

Could the day get any worse? Kate gritted her teeth; the very last thing she needed was to be forced to speak to Maddy Harvey's brother. With barely concealed irritation she said, 'Why don't you just ring him?'

'Because to get to the store you have to go right past Jake's workshop. It's sunny, so he'll be sitting outside. Anyway,' Marcella concluded with a dazzling smile, 'why add to your parents' phone bill when it's not necessary?'

Oh, for crying out loud, thought Kate, increasingly tempted to literally cry out loud. My father's a multimillionaire, a phone call costs less than ten *pence*, what are you *talking* about, woman?

But Marcella, armed with her brimming bucket and a whole host of window-cleaning paraphernalia, had already left the room.

Of course, Marcella had more than likely done it on purpose.

This thought struck Kate as she made her way down Gypsy Lane with Norris ambling along at her heels. It was by this time one o'clock; showering, washing her hair, dressing then carefully applying enough make-up to minimise the horror of the scarred side of her face had taken fifty minutes. The irony of this ritual didn't escape her; once upon a time she had been a strikingly attractive girl and make-up had made her breathtakingly gorgeous. These days it was a tool necessary to prevent small children screaming with fright at the sight of her.

So long as it didn't melt in this heat.

Thinking dark thoughts about Marcella, Kate rounded a bend and was brought up by the sight of the flowers on the verge opposite, a sudden profusion of poppies, ox-eye daisies and dog roses marking the spot where April Harvey had been killed. Marcella had planted them herself, shortly after the accident. Each time she walked up the lane to Dauncey

House, she passed them and was reminded afresh of April's death.

Although flowers or no flowers, she was hardly likely to forget it.

Kate paused to gaze at the flowers, remembering April with her funny, wobbly gait, slurred speech and lopsided smile. To her shame, she also remembered the way she and her friends from Ridgelow Hall had made fun of April whenever they saw her, mimicking her mannerisms and comical way of speaking. At least, they had when the rest of April's family weren't around. Anyone caught making fun of her would have been swiftly and efficiently dealt with by either Maddy or Jake.

It was deeply embarrassing to recall now, but she had been only young at the time. Making fun of people because they weren't perfect was what children did. It had never occurred to her that one day she might not be perfect herself.

Bored with waiting, Norris strained at his lead. Slowly Kate made her way on down the dappled, tree-lined lane. As they rounded the final bend, where Gypsy Lane joined the town's broader Main Street, she saw Snow Cottage ahead of her on the right and beyond it the row of craft shops and galleries set back from the road, where metal-workers and artists and ceramicists produced and displayed their wares for visiting tourists.

And there was Jake Harvey, as Marcella had predicted, sitting outside his own workshop, chatting animatedly to an old woman while she examined one of his bespoke caskets.

Stripped to the waist in a pair of white jeans, Jake looked like something out of a Coke ad. Deeply tanned, shinily muscled, with overlong hair streaked by the sun into fifty shades of blond, he was the archetypal bad boy at school, the one your mother always warned you not to get involved with. Not that Kate had ever been tempted herself; during her teenage years she and her friends had spent their time lusting after public-school educated boys with names like Henry and Tristram.

Reluctantly she approached the workshop, aware that her stomach was jumping with trepidation. God, all this hassle for the sake of 10p.

Chapter 9

'It's perfect,' the elderly woman was saying as she ran a gnarled hand over the glossy deep crimson surface of the casket. Alerted by the sound of footsteps – and possibly Norris's laboured sumo-like breathing – she turned and greeted Kate with a cheerful smile. 'Hello, dear, come and take a look, hasn't this young man done a marvellous job?'

At least concentrating on the casket meant not having to meet Jake Harvey's eye. Kate studied the picture of a leggy brunette in mid high-kick, presumably dancing the can-can. Frowning, she struggled to work out the significance.

'It's me,' the woman explained with pride. 'I was a dancer at the Moulin Rouge. I was nineteen when this photograph was taken. It's where I met my husband. Such happy days.'

Intrigued, Kate peered more closely at the lid of the casket, wondering how the effect had been achieved.

'You make an enlarged colour photocopy of the original print,' said Jake, reading her mind, 'and cut around the figure you want to use. Then you soak it in image transfer cream, place the copy face down on the lid and rub over it with a cloth. When you peel the paper away, the photo's transferred to the lid. Couple of coats of varnish and you're done.'

'It's beautiful,' Kate told the woman, careful to keep the left side of her face out of view.

'I know, I can hardly wait to get in it!' Her eyes bright

63

with laughter, the woman said, 'And it's going to drive my children demented.'

'Why?'

'Ha! If you met them you wouldn't need to ask. I have three,' said the woman, counting them off on fingers weighed down with glittering rings. 'A bank manager, a Tory MP and a perfect-wife-and-mother who lives in Surrey. I don't know where I went wrong. They're dreadfully ashamed of me. I'm the bane of their lives, poor darlings. Oh well, can't win 'em all I suppose. Jake, would you be an angel and pop it into the truck? I want to show it off to my friends.'

Jake effortlessly loaded the casket into the back of the woman's muddy Land Rover. Reaching up, she kissed him on both cheeks, leaving scarlet lipstick marks, then hopped into the driver's seat and with a toot and a wave roared off.

Norris was by this time flat out on the dusty ground, snoring peacefully in the sun like a drunk.

'Business or pleasure?' said Jake.

'Sorry?'

'Are you here to buy a coffin?'

Kate suppressed a shudder. 'No.'

He smiled briefly. 'So, pleasure then.'

Hardly. 'Not that either. Your mother asked me to tell you to take the lamb chops out of the freezer.'

Jake laughed. 'Sounds like one of those coded messages. You say, "Take the lamb chops out of the freezer," then I nod and say, "Lamb chops are excellent with mint sauce." Are you sure you aren't a secret agent?'

She hadn't expected him to sound so normal, friendly even. Stiffly, Kate said, 'And she also said not to forget about Sophie's party.'

'Ah yes, the party.' Still nodding in a spy-like manner, Jake said, 'Five o'clock, in ze village hall. Zat is when ze party begins. I haff ze situation under control – oh bugger,

64

actually I don't.' He looked at Kate then, quizzically, at Norris. 'Where did the dog come from?'

'We're looking after him for a friend of my mother's. Just for a few weeks. Actually, it was *your* mother's idea,' said Kate.

'Tell me about it.' Jake's greenish-yellow eyes narrowed with amusement. 'Ideas are my mother's speciality.'

'She thought a dog would get me out of the house.'

'And here you are, so she was right. Would you be on your way to the shop, by any chance?'

'Yes.' Kate eyed him warily. 'Why?'

'Ze party at five o'clock. I haff ze present, but no paper in vich to wrap it.'

'OK,' sighed Kate; was this where her future lay, as some kind of lowly gofer? She jiggled Norris's lead and he opened a baleful eye. 'Norris, come on, get *up*.'

'Leave him with me,' Jake said easily. 'You'd only have to tie him up outside the shop.' Taking the end of the lead, he looped it over the gatepost, then dug a pound coin out of his jeans pocket. 'There you go. Actually, I'm holding him hostage to stop you running off with my money. Bring me the wrapping paper and you'll get the dog back.'

'You're assuming I want him back,' said Kate.

'And von more zing,' Jake called after her as she headed along Main Street.

She turned. 'What?'

'Ze wrapping paper. No Barbies. No pink.'

The general store, a kind of mini supermarket-cum-tardis, was owned by a garrulous old spinster called Theresa who had run the place for the last forty years and knew everything that went on in Ashcombe. Kate couldn't get out of there fast enough.

'Hello, dear, heard you were back, look at your poor old face, eh? What a shame, what a thing to happen, that's

65

America for you though, isn't it, everyone drives like maniacs over there, rushing around, I've seen 'em doin' it on the telly, what I always say is take your time and get somewhere safely, better than goin' too fast and not getting there at all . . . What're you doin' buying dog food then?' Beadily she eyed Kate's basket, as if suspicious that the cans of Pedigree Chum might be lunch. 'You 'aven't got a dog.'

'Just ring them up on the till and stop yabbering, you nosy cow.'

Kate smiled blandly and wondered how Theresa would react if she'd actually said the words aloud instead of just thinking them.

'We're looking after one for a friend. And I'll have a sheet of that wrapping paper. The dark blue one.'

'Blue? Not your dad's birthday, is it? Although if it is, we've got some nice boxed hankies, or maybe he'd prefer—'

'It's not his birthday,' interrupted Kate.

'Thought it wasn't.' Theresa looked relieved to have been proved right. 'He's January, isn't he? Your poor mum and dad, must've been a terrible shock for them, seein' you with your face like that and—'

'How much do I owe you?' said Kate.

'In and out of Theresa's in under twenty minutes.' Jake shook his head in admiration. 'Better contact the *Guinness Book of Records*.'

'What an old witch. She was bursting to know who the wrapping paper was for.' Kate felt her mood lighten, like the sun coming out. The last time she'd properly known Jake, he'd been Maddy Harvey's irritating little brother, a skinny ten-year-old covered in grazes, with a much prized dried worm collection. Now, all grown up, he was . . . well, all grown up. For some local girl there was no denying he'd be quite a catch.

'Are you looking at my chest?' said Jake.

'No!'

'Oh. Just wondered. Actually, you could give me a hand with the wrapping if you like.'

Kate followed him into the cool gloom of the workshop. Bemused, she said, 'A *gun*?'

'Don't sound so shocked, it's not a real one.' Spreading out the sheet of cobalt blue paper on the workbench, Jake picked up the imitation pistol. 'Fires potato pellets. Here, you make a start with the Sellotape.'

'I thought it was a birthday party for a girl.'

'It is, but Sophie chose this. She's already got one, so now she and Charlotte can have shootouts. Or murder other girls' Barbies. Sophie thinks dolls are feeble,' said Jake. 'She wants to be a police officer when she grows up. Last week I caught her and Tiff aiming a hairdryer at passing motorists. When I asked what she was doing she said, "Being a speed-trap."'

Together they managed to wrap up the potato gun, although the end result was secure rather than stylish.

'I'd better get back,' said Kate.

'Before they send out the search parties.' Jake picked up the unused rectangle of paper. 'Do you think I should wrap up a potato too?'

He was teasing her. Realising she had to say something, Kate began awkwardly, 'Look, thanks for . . . you know, talking to me. Being . . . um, normal.'

'That's OK.' Jake clearly found this amusing. 'I am actually quite a normal person. Plus, I always do as I'm told.'

'Told?'

'By Marcella, anyway. Life wouldn't be worth living otherwise.'

Suspicion crawled over Kate's skin like ants. 'You mean . . . ?'

Smiling, Jake said, 'She told me to be nice to you.'

'When?' She could barely get the word out.

'Two minutes before you got here, I imagine.' He patted the phone lying on the bench. 'Hey, it's OK.'

'It's *not* OK. It's humiliating. I don't *need* to be patronised—'

'Don't get your knickers in a twist.' Jake's green eyes were by this time bright with laughter. 'I was going to be nice to you anyway.'

But then he would say that, wouldn't he? For just a few brief minutes, Kate realised, her mood had magically lifted and she'd almost forgotten about her scarred face.

Now everything was spoiled.

Nuala Stratton, having slipped away from her barmaiding duties for five minutes, was observing the exchange between Jake and Kate with a mixture of intrigue and indignation. From her bedroom window above the pub she had a clear view into his workshop. She knew, of course, that Jake was an habitual charmer who flirted effortlessly and always made you feel extra-special, even when all he was doing was ordering a pint of Guinness and a packet of crisps, but why on earth was he doing it now with Kate Taylor-Trent?

Maddy would go mental when she found out.

Sucking in her stomach – something she found herself doing almost instinctively whenever she looked at Jake – Nuala watched him saunter over to the bulldog, unhook its lead from the fencepost and cajole the overweight animal to its feet. Then he said something else to Kate, handed the dog over to her and gave her forearm a reassuring squeeze.

What a traitor. So much for family loyalty. Didn't Jake realise that some people didn't deserve to be smiled at like that?

'Nuala?' Dexter's voice bellowed up the stairs. 'Get a

bloody move on, will you? If you've fallen asleep up there, you're sacked.'

Not that she was jealous of the attention Jake was paying Kate. Not properly jealous anyway. She had Dexter – she and Dexter *lived* together – and he was all she wanted. It was just that you could be perfectly happy with one man and still harbour a teeny crush on another. If they were honest, probably every woman who met Jake had a teeny crush on him. It must be quite strange to be Maddy, having Jake as a brother and not secretly fancying him.

'*Nuala!* Get your backside down here this *minute*.'

Hastily, Nuala kicked her discarded four-inch turquoise stilettos under the bed and slipped her feet into less exotic but far comfier two-inch heels. She had Dexter and she was happy with Dexter, but he did like to see her dressed like a glamour girl and, being a man, he simply had no idea how excruciating four-inch stilettos could be. God knows, she'd never make it as a Playboy Bunny. Two hours of crippling pain was as much as she could bear in one shift. Tonight she would put the turquoise ones on again, but for now the low-heeled suede mules would just have to do. Quickly checking in the wardrobe mirror that her reddish-brown hair wasn't too messy, that her cream top was still free of drink stains and that her new caramel skirt didn't make her bum look vast, Nuala exhaled with disappointment. Failed on all three counts, and the wet patch of lager was situated directly over her left breast. Hastily she brushed her hair, slicked on another layer of glossy toffee lipstick and jacked the belt round her waist in by another notch.

Dexter wasn't what you'd call an easygoing character. She loved him to bits but there was no denying that sometimes he could be tricky to live with. Volatile and impatient, he could teach Basil Fawlty a thing or two about being temperamental. Living and working with Dexter was like standing too close to a pyromaniac with a box of fireworks – at any moment the whole lot could go off.

'We need another crate of Cokes from the cellar,' said Dexter when Nuala arrived downstairs. His gaze dropped to her feet. 'Got your granny shoes on, I see.'

He wanted her to be Liz Hurley, Rita Hayworth and Jessica Rabbit all rolled into one. Nuala's only comfort was in knowing that, with his receding hairline, expanding paunch and waspish put-downs, Liz Hurley wouldn't look twice at Dexter.

Besides, it wasn't as if she was the only one he insulted – anyone was fair game. And he was actually a lot nicer in private, when it was just the two of them together. Rolling his eyes in despair and mocking her shortcomings was his way of entertaining the customers; she knew he didn't mean it, deep down.

'My feet were hurting. It's either these or my furry slippers,' said Nuala.

'God save us,' Dexter roared, to his audience. 'She's turning into Nora Batty.' Shaking his head in disgust at Nuala he said, 'You are such a frump.'

Nuala smiled; she knew she wasn't a frump.

'I've just seen Jake chatting to Kate Taylor-Trent.' Then, because he was looking blank, 'The one who called me fat the other night.'

'So? You are fat.'

He didn't mean it. All for show.

Chapter 10

The lamb chops were sizzling under the grill when Maddy arrived home from work. Foil-wrapped potatoes were baking in the oven and a bowl of salad sat on top of the fridge. With Sophie out at her party, the house was silent apart from the hiss of the shower running upstairs.

By the time Jake appeared, wearing a red and white striped towel around his waist, Maddy had boiled the kettle and made two mugs of tea.

'Thanks.' Taking a mouthful, Jake froze then spat it back into the mug. 'Jesus, what did you put in that?'

'Tabasco. And salt. And mustard,' Maddy added serenely, because Jake particularly loathed mustard.

'Why? Oh fuck, that is *disgusting*, my tongue's going to drop off.' Racing to the sink as the slow-burn of Tabasco kicked in, he put his mouth under the mixer tap and tried to rinse away the taste.

'Good. Maybe if you didn't have a tongue you wouldn't be able to chat up girls like – ooh, let me see, girls like Kate Taylor-Trent.'

'I wasn't chatting her up. Mum just said be nice to her. Polite, that's all.' Still vigorously rinsing and spitting, Jake reached blindly for the kitchen roll.

'From what I hear, you were being more than polite. She's

a stroppy cow and you have no business chatting her up when she's been so vile to me.'

Jake straightened up, drying his mouth with kitchen paper.

'Look, you're both adults now. She's back, and in a place this size you can't just ignore her. It's stupid. Put it behind you.'

He really had no idea. He'd heard all her grievances before, but he hadn't been the one on the receiving end of Kate's snide remarks.

'She and her schoolfriends used to make fun of me because Marcella was black, Kate said *hateful* things about her—'

'And she probably regrets it now. We all do stupid things when we're young.' Swallowing and pulling a face, Jake added pointedly, 'Look at you, you're twenty-six and still doing stupid things.'

'You're supposed to be on my side.' Maddy watched him refill the kettle and drop a teabag into a fresh mug. 'If she regretted it that much, she would have apologised.'

'OK, I'll tell her that, shall I?' Jake raised his eyebrows. 'I'll be the go-between, let her know that if she says sorry *really* nicely, you'll be friends with her again.'

Maddy gave him a pitying look. 'It wasn't just me, you know. She said horrible things about you as well.'

'Not any more she doesn't.' Amused, Jake said, 'She fancies me rotten now. Anyway, who told you about me talking to Kate?'

Maddy counted on her fingers. 'Nuala was watching you from the pub. Juliet saw you. *And* Theresa from the supermarket.'

'Ah, the usual suspects.' Pouring boiling water into the mug, Jake added modestly, 'They all fancy me too.'

When Kerr McKinnon had moved back to Bath five months ago, he had rented a flat in the heart of the city, just a few hundred yards from the offices of Callaghan and Fox. He drove out to his mother's old house every week or so just to keep an eye on the place, check that it hadn't burned to the ground or been taken over by an army of squatters, but he hadn't ever driven the extra couple of miles and revisited Ashcombe.

This time, purely out of curiosity, he did.

OK, it possibly had something to do with Maddy Harvey, but he thought it would be nice to see how the place looked, find out if it had changed much in the last ten years.

With the evening sun now low in the sky, Kerr put on his dark glasses and switched off the stereo as he approached the outskirts of the tiny town. There was the primary school – his old school – on the right. Slowing, he passed over the hump-backed bridge that crossed the River Ash. Ahead of him, he saw the war memorial. To the left lay Main Street; to the right, Gypsy Lane. Turning left, he drove even more slowly past the Fallen Angel and an assortment of shops – some he recognised, others he didn't. There was the Peach Tree Delicatessen where Maddy worked, then a couple of antiques shops, the small supermarket . . . Carrying on up Holly Hill, Kerr reached the outskirts of the town where a new housing development had been built. He turned and headed back down the hill, this time concentrating on the row of craft and workshops on the left hand side of Main Street. There was the sign for Harvey's Caskets, Jake's business. And now he was passing Snow Cottage where Maddy lived with Jake and his daughter; ridiculously, he found it hard to tear his eyes away from the low, honey-coloured Cotswold stone building. It was like being a teenager again, wondering if Maddy was in there, but he couldn't stop, mustn't draw attention to himself. Instead he carried on, turning into Gypsy Lane, mentally bracing himself for the moment when he would follow the winding road round to the left and reach the spot where the accident had happened.

There it was. And he hadn't even realised he'd been holding his breath. Exhaling slowly, Kerr saw that the wild flowers planted by Marcella Harvey were still there, marking the place where her beloved stepdaughter had died. Strangers arriving in Ashcombe might wonder about the story behind this sudden burst of colour along an otherwise undistinguished stretch of roadside. He knew that April was buried in the churchyard, and that her grave would bear a profusion of flowers too.

Continuing up the narrow lane, he saw the figure of a woman ahead, walking a dog. With her back to him, wearing a baggy grey jogging suit and a baseball cap on her head, it was impossible to gauge the identity of the dog-walker.

Of course if this was a Hollywood movie, the dog would lurch suddenly off the pavement and into the road, dragging its owner after him. Kerr, paying attention, would brake in plenty of time but the juggernaut screaming down the hill at sixty miles an hour wouldn't be able to stop or swerve to avoid them. If he hadn't leaped out of his own car at superhuman speed and snatched the woman – and her dog – to safety, they would have been killed outright. And – this still being a film – it wouldn't be until the woman turned to face him, gibbering with tearful gratitude and thanking him for saving her life, that he'd realise it was Marcella Harvey . . .

Well, it was a nice fantasy. Kerr smiled wryly to himself as he passed the woman with the waddling, overweight bulldog huffing to keep up. Beneath the peak of her cap he couldn't see much of her face, just enough to let him know that she was white, and younger than Marcella.

At the top of Gypsy Lane he swung the car round yet again. Heading back into the town, as he approached the entrance to Dauncey House, he saw the girl and her dog turning into the driveway. This time she briefly turned to look at him and he felt a flicker of recognition. A momentary glimpse of profile wasn't much to go on but he was almost sure it was Kate Taylor-Trent.

Putting his foot down, Kerr sped past. He had an early start tomorrow, and wall to wall meetings in London. Time to head back to Bath.

When he was out of sight, Kate turned and stared down the empty, tree-lined lane. Had that been Kerr McKinnon? God, had it really? But what was he doing here in Ashcombe? As far as she was aware, he'd moved to London years ago and stayed there.

Then again, if his mother was still living in the same house, he must have to visit her sometimes. Although no one seemed to know for sure if Pauline McKinnon was still alive; according to Estelle, nobody had clapped eyes on her for years.

Kerr McKinnon, driving a dark blue Mercedes and wearing dark glasses. It had been quite a while – OK, a decade – since they'd last seen each other, but Kate knew instinctively that it was him. Her heart was still beating like a tom-tom inside her ribs. She felt overheated and frozen at the same time. And Norris was at her feet, giving her the kind of world-weary look that signified he knew exactly what was going through her head.

She was fairly sure Kerr hadn't seen the scars. She certainly *hoped* he hadn't seen them – although this was a pointless exercise if ever there was one. If she was never going to see Kerr McKinnon again, what did it matter? And if they did meet up, well, sooner or later there was a chance he was going to notice her spooky new resemblance to Quasimodo.

Oh, forget it. If it wasn't for her accident, she'd have been overjoyed to see Kerr again, may even have waved and gestured for him to stop the car. She had been smitten with him once and, modesty aside, he'd been pretty interested in return. Who knew, if he hadn't left to go back to university at the end of that summer . . .

Anyway, too late now. The accident had happened, and unexpectedly bumping into old boyfriends was no longer a joyful experience.

'Who's uglier, Norris? You or me?'

Snuffling, Norris gazed up at her.

'Except it's easier for you.' Kate gave his lead a let's-get-going tug. 'You've always looked like that.'

Estelle greeted them at the door with a beaming smile on her face.

'Darling, fantastic news! Guess who just rang?'

Kate couldn't help it; for a split second her thoughts flew back to Kerr McKinnon. He'd recognised her . . . been too shy to stop . . . reached for his mobile and dialled directory enquiries, then rung their number . . . If she hadn't spent the last ten minutes gazing after him in the lane before dawdling back up the drive, she'd have been here to pick up the phone herself . . .

'Daddy!'

'Oh.' Bending, Kate unclipped Norris's lead and watched him waddle like John Wayne through to the kitchen in search of food. Oh well, served her right for getting carried away. And in all honesty, since when had Kerr McKinnon been shy?

'He's coming home tomorrow,' Estelle gabbled on, over-doing it as usual, 'for a whole week! Isn't that brilliant?'

'Brilliant.' Dutifully, Kate forced herself to smile. Not that she didn't want to see her father, but it was hardly the most earth-shattering news in the world. Like most business tycoons, he was a workaholic, spending most of his time in London and jetting off at a moment's notice around the world.

When he was at home, he was constantly on the phone. It wasn't as if she was suddenly going to have a dad to play endless cosy games of Monopoly with. Oliver Taylor-Trent preferred to play Monopoly with real money and proper hotels.

'He'll be here around midday, and he's sorry he couldn't get down before now, but he'll make it up to you tomorrow.' Her eyes sparkling, Estelle confided, 'I think he's bought you a present.'

It was like being seven again. Her father never changed.

'You mean he's told his secretary to pop into Harvey Nichols and buy me a present.' But Kate couldn't be cross, she was too used to it. Besides, it might be shoes. God knows, anything that drew attention away from her face had to be worth a try.

Chapter 11

The next morning was even hotter. With Oliver due home at lunchtime, Estelle had rushed into Bath to do a big super-market shop. It wasn't Marcella's day to work. Finding herself alone in the house – well, apart from Norris, who didn't count – Kate had changed into a pink bikini and wandered out to the pool. Now, after a few desultory lengths, she was stretched out on one of the recliners soaking up the sun. Swimming alone was no fun.

Closing her eyes, Kate remembered a magical summer long ago, when she and Maddy Harvey had played endlessly together in this very pool. They had been like sisters then. The following year she had been sent to Ridgelow Hall and had made new friends. She recalled the scorching, dusty after-noon when she and a couple of her new best friends had bumped into Maddy outside the sweet shop. How old had they all been? Eleven, maybe twelve? Nudging her compan-ions, she had said gaily, 'Hey, fancy a swim?'

Maddy, her thin little face lighting up, had said, 'Oh, that'd be great.'

And she had smirked – God, actually *smirked* – and said, 'Better go and jump in the river then. Bye!'

It had seemed funny at the time. She and her friends had screeched with laughter at the look of disappointment on Maddy's face. Now, Kate inwardly cringed at the memory.

There was no getting away from it, she had been a snobby little cow, seduced by the my-dad's-richer-than-your-dad mentality of her fellow pupils. Once, visiting the spectacular home of one of the girls and discovering that the pool there was twice the size of her own, she had promptly broken off the friendship in order not to have to invite her back to Dauncey House. For weeks after that, she had even badgered her father to buy a helicopter purely to compensate for the embarrassment of not owning an Olympic-sized pool.

A cloud had drifted over the sun. Brushing a fly from her shoulder, Kate opened her eyes a fraction then let out a yelp of surprise, because it hadn't been a cloud after all; the shadow on her face had been caused by a complete stranger who—

'Sorry, sorry, didn't mean to scare you! Crikey, what must you think of me? I honestly thought you were asleep. Sorry, all my fault, I did ring the doorbell but there was no reply.'

Kate stared at him. If this was a burglar, he was the friendliest burglar she'd ever encountered.

'And you are . . . ?'

'Will.' He smiled, extended his hand and shook hers vigorously. When Kate continued to look blank, he said, 'Will Gifford? And you must be Kate. Good to meet you, *really* good to meet you. Oh dear.' He paused and shook his head in sorrowful fashion. 'He didn't tell you, did he?'

'Who didn't tell me what?'

'Your father. God, I'm so sorry, I just assumed he'd have mentioned me.'

He was also the most apologetic burglar she'd ever met. Except it was fairly obvious now that he wasn't a burglar.

'Hang on. You rang the doorbell,' said Kate, 'and no one came to the door. So you assumed everyone was out and just decided to explore the back garden anyway?'

'Oh Lord, it sounds terrible when you put it like that. I

mean, I didn't break down the front door, just wandered round the side of the house. I didn't know how long I'd have to wait, you see. And Oliver did invite me. I've got my case in the car.'

His case? 'You mean you're *staying* here? Look, I'm sorry,' oops, now she was doing it too, 'but who *exactly* are you?'

Kate was mystified; whoever this Will Gifford might be, he didn't look like a business colleague of her father's. In his mid-thirties, he was tall and indescribably scruffy, wearing crumpled black trousers and a baggy un-ironed checked shirt. His dark brown hair was all over the shop, sticking out in tufts, and his spectacles were Harry Potterish. The overall impression was of a gangly overgrown schoolboy, quite shy and clever but incapable of wielding a hairbrush.

As Will Gifford opened his mouth to reply, Estelle came into view, hurrying across the lawn calling, 'Hello, I'm ba-ack.'

Will Gifford turned and said charmingly, 'Mrs Taylor-Trent.'

Puffing, catching her breath, Estelle said, 'Oof, it's hot. You must be Will, how lovely to meet you. And please, do call me Estelle. You're early!'

'I'm a bit of a one for getting lost,' Will confided, 'so I set off from London at nine o'clock, to give myself that extra hour to get lost in. But it was like a miracle, I got the entire journey right first time.' He shook his head, clearly delighted with this achievement. 'Never happened to me before. Remarkable.'

Kate's suspicions were growing. Her father had invited this man here to stay with them. Her mother had been expecting him, but hadn't mentioned it to her. Was Will Gifford some kind of self-help guru, hired by her parents in order to teach her that looks weren't everything?

They certainly weren't as far as he was concerned. The man looked like a cross between a mad scientist and a scarecrow.

Oh God, was he supposed to be her *present*?

Gaily, Estelle said, 'Right then, why don't I make us all a nice pot of tea?'

Kate waited until her mother was back inside the house before saying, 'I still don't know what you're doing here.'

'Relax, you're looking at me like I'm a dentist.' Will grinned and flopped down on the grass a few feet away from her.

'Is it something to do with me?'

'Nothing at all to do with you, crosspatch. I'm making a documentary about your father and he was kind enough to ask me to stay for a few days. Although since the idea of the programme is to see Oliver Taylor-Trent both at work and away from it, of course I'd like you to feature in the film.'

A documentary. Well, she hadn't seen that one coming.

'Can I say no?'

'Of course you can say no.'

'Good. In that case, no.'

Mildly, Will Gifford said, 'That's a shame. Why not?'

'Oh please, don't tell me you hadn't noticed.' Kate gazed steadily at him, hoping he'd be embarrassed.

'Your face, you mean? Oliver told me about your accident. But I'm sorry, I don't see how it's relevant.'

'OK, let me put it this way. Why on earth would I *want* to appear on TV, so that even more people can see my scars? Don't you think it's hard enough for me, just walking down the street?'

It was meant to be the ultimate riposte. Will Gifford spoiled it completely by tilting his head to one side and saying easily, 'With dress sense like mine, you get used to it.'

If she hadn't been lying flat on her back, Kate would have stamped her foot.

'It's hardly the same thing, is it? Please don't try and compare your hideous shirts with my *face*—'

'Yoo-hoo, here we are! Dad's home,' sang Estelle, heading up the path with a tray of tea in her hands and Oliver Taylor-Trent following in her wake.

Despite everything, Kate felt a lump form in her throat. Being back in Ashcombe was having a weird effect on her hormones; for a split second she'd longed to scramble to her feet and hurl herself into her father's arms. But since they weren't a huggy family and Oliver certainly wouldn't appreciate getting suncream all over his Hugo Boss suit, she stood up and gave him a decorous kiss on the cheek instead. The next moment he was briskly greeting Will Gifford, while Estelle fussed around with the tea tray and attempted to tear open a packet of shortbread with her teeth.

'Will, welcome to Dauncey House. I don't think we want tea, do we? Got a bottle of something decent in the fridge, darling? We should raise a toast to an interesting and mutually profitable project . . . and Kate, maybe you'd be more comfortable slipping some clothes on?'

As ever, Oliver had taken charge of the situation, reorganising the family to his satisfaction. As Estelle rushed back inside with the no-longer-required tea and biscuits, he put his hand on Will's frayed shirt cuff and said, 'While we're waiting, why don't I show you the grounds? Afterwards you can see the rest of the house, then later on I'll take you on a guided tour of our little town.'

Our town, thought Kate. Like he owned it.

'Fantastic.' Winking at Kate, Will rubbed his hands together with boyish enthusiasm. 'Can't wait.'

Kate pointedly ignored the wink. What an utter prat.

Deliveries completed, Maddy was back in Ashcombe by one o'clock. Racing over to the Angel, she said, 'Dexter, I know that deep down, beneath that horrid grumpy exterior, you're actually a sweet and lovely man.'

'No I'm not.' Dexter carried on hanging up beer mugs by their handles.

'You see? Modest too.' Plunging on, Maddy said, 'And now I need a favour. Can I borrow Nuala, just for ten minutes?' It was Friday lunchtime and the pub was quiet; Dexter could easily handle the few existing customers himself. For good measure she added, 'Please?'

'It'll have to come out of her wages.'

Naturally. Maddy flashed him a brilliant smile. 'I'll pay you the thirty pence myself.'

'Blimey, you must be desperate.' Aware of Maddy and Nuala's intensive gossip sessions, Dexter raised an eyebrow. 'Not pregnant, are you?'

'I just need to talk to Nuala.' She heaved an inward sigh. 'And you're her boss, which is why I'm being so nice to you.'

'OK. What d'you want to drink?'

Hooray. 'Two Cokes please.'

'Go ahead then, take her outside.' Dexter waved a dismissive arm in the direction of Nuala, emerging from the storeroom with a box of salt 'n' vinegar crisps. 'Just for ten minutes. And she'll have Diet Coke,' he added. 'There's hardly room for both of us in one bed as it is.'

'Back garden,' Maddy told Nuala when she'd dumped the box of crisps and Dexter had served their drinks. As he dropped the change into Maddy's hand he said, 'Time starts . . . *now*.'

'Actually,' Nuala said brightly when they were seated outside, 'I prefer Diet Coke. Once you get used to the taste, it's—'

'No you don't,' Maddy interrupted, 'you've just brainwashed yourself into thinking you prefer it because Dexter

83

won't let you drink the normal kind.' A lot of their conversations ran along these lines, with Nuala defending Dexter
and Maddy vainly attempting to make her see sense.

'But—'

'Anyway, enough about you, we're here to talk about me.
If I don't tell you my stuff, I may have to explode.'

'And Dexter would make me clear up all the mess.'
Instantly diverted, Nuala leaned her elbows on the table and
said eagerly, 'Go on then, tell me. Is this to do with the bloke
you met last week at the party?'

'Yes.'

'I *knew* it! Is he completely gorgeous?'

'Yes, but—'

'And you really really fancy him?'

'*Yes*—'

'And he really really fancies you? Oh wow, that's so brilliant, when did all this happen and why didn't you tell me
bef— *Ow!*'

'Sorry,' sighed Maddy, because the only way to stop Nuala
when she got this carried away was to pinch her wrist hard.
She hadn't meant to grind the bones like that, though.

'That hurt!'

'I know, sorry sorry, but we don't have time to play twenty
questions, and the thing is, it *isn't* brilliant because—'

'God, he's *married*, what a bas— oh no you don't.' Nuala
snatched her wrist away just in time. 'OK, sorry, I'll shut
up.' Pause. 'But I'm right, aren't I? He's *married*.'

'He isn't.' Shaking her head, Maddy explained the whole
sorry McKinnon saga in four minutes flat. This time Nuala
listened intently and didn't interrupt once.

'Shit,' she said flatly when Maddy had finished.

'I know.'

'This isn't good.'

'Tell me about it,' agreed Maddy, draining her Coke and

feeling pretty drained herself. At least, her brain felt drained, but underneath the wooden trellis table her hopelessly overexcited knees were jiggling away like mini Michael Flatleys. Taking an envelope from her jeans pocket and placing it in front of Nuala, she added, 'And now this.'

Nuala whisked the enclosed sheet of paper from the battered envelope and read the brief handwritten note.

'He wants to meet you tomorrow! God, this is so romantic! I mean, I've had phone calls and text messages in my time, but nobody's *ever* written me a letter.'

'It's not romantic when he's only doing it because a phone call would be too risky.' Fraught, Maddy raked her fingers through her already drastically-raked hair. 'He's in London today. He left the envelope with his receptionist to hand over to me.'

'But don't you see? That's even more romantic! "I need to see you, properly."' Nuala swooned as she read aloud. '"Saturday night, seven o'clock, my flat. Let me know if you can't make it. Hope you can. Kerr." Ooh, *nice* flat,' she added with approval, noting the address. 'And lovely masterful handwriting. If you aren't up for it, can I go instead?'

'I want to go, more than anything.' Maddy watched a ladybird inch its way along the edge of the table, then spread its wings and take off like a Harrier jump jet. 'But how can I?'

'What d'you mean, how can you? Are you mad?' squeaked Nuala. 'You *have* to go!'

'Marcella would kill me.'

'What Marcella doesn't know won't hurt her,' Nuala blithely retorted. 'How's she ever going to find out? My mum's next-door neighbours got divorced last summer, it turned out that the husband had been having an affair for the last fifteen years and his wife hadn't had any idea!'

As if that made it all right, thought Maddy. 'But—'

'Anyway, you already know you'll go.'

'What?' Maddy stared at her. 'How can you say that?'

'Oh, come on. Why else would you show me the letter? That's why you're here, isn't it?' Looking pleased with herself, Nuala said, 'Because you knew I'd say you had to meet him. Face it, you know me. I'm hardly likely to tell you never to see him again, am I? You want me to persuade you to go to his flat tomorrow night, so it's my decision and not yours.' Squishing an ant with her thumb, she beamed across at Maddy. 'Plus, of course, it'll be my fault if anything goes wrong.'

Maddy couldn't speak.

'See?' Nuala said happily. 'I'm not as daft as I look, am I?'

'God, I didn't even *realise* what I was doing.' Maddy let out a wail, snatching the letter and shoving it back into her pocket. 'I hate it when you're right!'

'So there you go, you have my permission to see him. And wear something sexy.'

'We're only going to *talk*.'

'Good grief, are you mad? If he's as gorgeous as you say he is, and meeting him is this risky, what on earth's the point of just talking?' Nuala raised her eyebrows in disbelief. 'I mean, if Marcella's going to go ballistic anyway – not that she will find out, of course, but *if* she did – you may as well be hung for a sheep as for a lamb.' Pausing, she frowned. 'You know, I don't actually understand what that means. I mean, why would anyone want to hang a sheep *or* a—'

'*Time's up*,' bellowed Dexter like a sergeant major from the back door of the pub.

'Honestly, he's such a bossy-boots,' Nuala grumbled, but she was already on her feet, gathering up their empty glasses.

Maddy, wondering why on earth she was asking advice from someone whose idea of a perfect partner was Dexter

Nevin, said, 'Will you two end up getting married, d'you think?'

'Good grief, no.' Vigorously, Nuala shook her head. 'Not a chance.'

Oh well, that was something to be grateful for.

'I've already asked him,' Nuala went on, blowing her fringe out of her eyes. 'He turned me down flat.'

'What are you, a three-toed sloth?' bawled Dexter. 'Get a bloody move on, woman, there's customers dying of thirst in here!'

Wishing she'd thought to bring Sophie's potato gun along with her, Maddy shook her head and said, 'Wouldn't it be nicer to have a boyfriend who isn't horrible to you the whole time?'

'Dexter isn't horrible,' Nuala said fondly. 'That's just his way. It's only a bit of fun.'

Chapter 12

'Lunch? We stop serving lunch at two.' Dexter jerked a finger in the direction of the clock on the wall. 'It's five past.'

Bolshy pub landlords didn't faze Oliver Taylor-Trent.

'Tell me about it,' he said jovially. 'My wife burned ours to a cinder. We're starving. My invited guest here is starving. I've told him all about your miraculous bouillabaisse – he's a documentary maker, by the way. Will, meet Dexter Nevin. Dexter, this is Will Gifford.'

'Blimey, you must be really hungry.' Dexter's dark eyes glinted with sardonic humour.

'More than you can imagine. Cooking's never been my wife's strong point. We'll have a bottle of Laurent Perrier, by the way. Oh, and would you have any objections to Will doing a spot of filming here in the pub?'

'For TV? What, *now*?' Dexter looked taken aback.

'Not now.' Will spread his arms reassuringly. 'See? No camera. But within the next few days. The thing is, I'm making a film about Oliver,' he explained. 'And Ashcombe's such a great place. I wouldn't want to leave the pub out of it. Could be good publicity for you,' he added with a winning smile, 'but don't worry, feel free to say no if you'd rather not.'

'Two bouillabaisses?' said Dexter, who wasn't stupid.

'I think we'll take a look at the menu,' Oliver replied with satisfaction. 'And there are three of us. My daughter's waiting outside.'

See and be seen was Oliver's motto. Despite the fact that the Fallen Angel had a perfectly good restaurant area and a ravishingly pretty rear garden, he had insisted they eat at one of the tables at the front of the pub. Kate, waiting self-consciously for her father and Will Gifford to re-emerge, watched as one of the locals ambled past and turned to stare at her. Oliver had persuaded her, against her far better judgement, to join them for lunch while Estelle set about the task of fumigating the kitchen and scraping cremated salmon fillets off the baking tin she had put into the oven and promptly forgotten all about until the smoke alarm had gone off. Oh well, she couldn't hide away for ever. Safety in numbers and all that.

'Quite a character, that landlord,' announced Will, sitting down next to her and handing her a menu.

Glancing at it, Kate prayed no one passing by would assume they were a couple. More specifically, she hoped Jake Harvey in his workshop across the road wouldn't think it.

'I'll have the steak in port. And a glass of red.'

'Your dad's on his way out with another bottle of champagne. What it must be like to be wealthy,' Will marvelled. 'You wouldn't believe the lengths I normally have to go to to get a glass of champagne – blagging my way into celebrity parties, getting turfed out on my ear when they realise I haven't been invited, the humiliation of realising I'm actually a pint of bitter man through and through – excuse me, but is that dog all right?'

Norris was snorting and grunting at her feet. Kate shrugged. 'I don't know. He always breathes like that.'

'He might be thirsty. I'll ask for a bowl of water while we're ordering the food.' Unfolding his long legs, Will said, 'Back in a sec. By the way, you don't happen to know the name of the pretty barmaid, do you? Curvy redhead, cute dimples?'

Honestly, what *was* it with men? One-track minds or what?

'I only moved back here this week. I don't have a clue.' This was perfectly true; she and the barmaid hadn't got as far as exchanging names, only insults.

'Fine, fine.' Will raised his hands in mock terror, as if dodging a poison dart. 'No problem anyway, I've just had a brilliant idea.'

Kate wondered if he was capable of a brilliant idea. Bored, she said, 'What?'

'I'm going to call on my expertise in the field of investigative journalism.' Will's brown eyes sparkled. 'And ask her.'

The champagne helped, which was something to be grateful for. Before long, Kate's knees were feeling nicely relaxed. When Will realised that the bowl of water hadn't arrived for Norris, her father said brusquely, 'Kate, go and sort it out,' and she found herself rising automatically to her feet.

The abrupt transition from bright sunlight to dim smoky gloom was disorientating, not helped by the fact that she was still wearing her dark glasses. Removing them and blinking, waiting for her eyes to adjust, Kate saw the door from the kitchen swing open and heard a voice saying, 'Back in a moment, there's something I forgot to – *ooh*.'

The curvy redhead with the dimples, carrying something in both hands, had caught sight of Kate in the pub and frozen for a millisecond. Sadly, a millisecond was all it took for the swing doors to swing shut again, before she had a chance to escape them. Realising too late what was about to happen, the girl lunged forward, getting caught anyway. She let out a squeak of alarm as the bowl ricocheted out of her hands, sending up a beautifully choreographed fountain of water before hitting the flagstones with a loud *craaacckk*. Kate gasped. The girl gazed in dismay at the shattered remains of the bowl, now strewn across the floor, and at the sopping wet front of her white shirt and navy skirt.

A roar of fury made them both jump. Erupting out of the kitchen like a maddened bear, the landlord bawled, 'You bloody idiot, can't you do *anything* right? Is a bowl of water too difficult for you?'

'I'm sorry, the doors swung shut on me.' Flushing, the girl knelt and began frantically scooping up the scattered shards, wincing as a splinter of china dug into her knee.

'Possibly because they're *swing doors*,' jeered the landlord. 'But then you've only been here for two years, haven't you, so how could you possibly be expected to have known that? Oh, for crying out loud, stop faffing about and clear it up. Get a dustpan and brush, if you know what they are, and try not to get blood all over the flagstones . . . Yes, can I help you?' As the girl scurried off, the landlord turned his attention to Kate for the first time. 'My apologies for the scene of carnage – you can't get the staff these days.'

'It was an accident,' said Kate.

He gave a snort of derision. '*She's* the accident.'

'No wonder you can't get the staff,' Kate bristled, 'if this is the way you treat them. Why do you have to be so rude?'

The landlord smiled, but not in a friendly way.

'Because it's fun. I enjoy it. Why, what's your excuse?'

Eyeing him with contempt, Kate retorted, 'At least I'm not a bully.'

'No? Hardly Julie Andrews though, are you?' He was openly smirking at her now. 'I mean, forgive me if I'm wrong, but aren't you the one who was in here the other night hurling insults at Nuala? Calling her a fat cow and reducing her to tears?'

'I didn't call her a fat cow.' Kate was seriously regretting coming here now, but she was damned if she'd back down.

'No?'

'No. Just . . . fat.' Thank goodness the barmaid – Nuala – was still off somewhere hunting down the dustpan and brush.

'You made her cry.'

Oh God, she hadn't, had she?

At that moment the kitchen doors swung back open. Surveying the scene – Kate and the landlord facing each other across the wooden bar – Nuala said, 'That's not true.' Turning to Kate she added, 'Don't take any notice of him, he'll say anything to win an argument.'

'Been listening at the door, have we? Very classy,' drawled the landlord as Nuala bent down and began sweeping up the bits of broken bowl.

Not to mention embarrassing, thought Kate. Addressing Nuala, she said in disbelief, 'Why do you let him speak to you like this? I mean, what are you doing here, working for someone who treats you like dirt?'

Nuala, hurriedly brushing the last splinters of china into the dustpan, mumbled something unintelligible.

'Ah, but she doesn't just work for me,' the landlord declared with satisfaction. 'She's my girlfriend. We live together. Didn't you know?' He raised his dark eyebrows in mock surprise. 'We're love's young dream.'

'You've been ages. We were about to send in a search party.' Will Gifford patted the space on the bench beside him. 'What was all the crashing and shouting about in there? Is that your way of getting reacquainted with the locals?'

Kate wondered if his scruffy, bumbling Hugh Grant act was meant to be endearing. 'I'm fine. The landlord's a dickhead, that's all.'

With a shout of laughter, Will said, 'Oh good grief, you mean it *was* you?'

Emptying the lukewarm dregs of her champagne into an

oak barrel overflowing with geraniums, Kate held out her glass for a refill from the bottle in the ice bucket.

'Your daughter doesn't suffer fools gladly,' Will told Oliver, and Kate shot him a meaningful, take-note look.

'That's Kate for you.' Oliver nodded with pride. 'She's always known her own mind.'

Nuala appeared, carrying a fresh bowl of water for Norris. As she placed it on the ground next to their table she glanced awkwardly across at Kate.

'Look, thanks for sticking up for me in there. I heard what you said to Dexter.' Despite feeling she needed to express gratitude, she clearly wasn't comfortable saying it.

Kate shrugged. 'I meant what I said. He's a bully.'

'He isn't really. A lot of it's just for show,' Nuala insisted. Duh?

'Fine.' Kate picked up her drink. 'If that's what you think, good luck to you. You'll need it.'

'Honestly,' complained Will, 'this is so unfair, I miss all the fun.' His eyes bright, he looked at Nuala. 'So what happens now? Is she banned from the pub?'

'*Banned?*' It was Dexter, emerging with their lunches. 'You must be bloody joking. Had the guts to stand up to me, didn't she? I've always respected a girl with a bit of spirit.' Deftly, he laid down the plates, straightened the cutlery and refilled their glasses with the remainder of the Laurent Perrier. 'Besides,' he went on, acknowledging Oliver with a nod, 'what landlord in his right mind would ban the daughter of a man who spends two hundred quid on a pub lunch?'

'Anyway,' Nuala murmured when Dexter had whisked open their napkins with a flourish and disappeared back inside the pub, 'I just wanted to . . . um, apologise for the other night, although I didn't say what you thought I said.'

'Fine,' Kate replied stiffly, aware of Will bristling with curiosity beside her. 'Let's just forget it, shall we? In future, you don't make fun of my face and I won't make fun of your fat.'

'There you go.' Will Gifford gave her a comforting nudge when Nuala had left them. 'Sounds to me like you're settling back in a treat.'

Chapter 13

'Right,' Oliver announced with a flourish of platinum Amex, 'how about that guided tour now?'

Norris, nudged awake by Kate's foot, spotted a small, sandy-haired terrier some distance away and lumbered to his feet, snuffling with interest.

'No,' Kate warned, but Norris ignored her. Like a new graduate from an assertiveness training course, he raced across the dusty road dragging her along in his wake. The terrier, eyeing him in return, let out a volley of high-pitched barks and rushed up to greet him like a besotted groupie.

This had to be the famous Bean, Kate realised as Jake Harvey emerged from his workshop and whistled to attract the little dog's attention. Bean glanced back, then promptly ignored him, far more interested in discovering what a hulking great bulldog looked like close up.

And smelled like close up, Kate discovered, as the two animals investigated each other thoroughly, indulging in that dreadful bottom-sniffing thing dogs loved to do in order to embarrass their owners. Mortified, she tugged at Norris's lead and prayed they wouldn't attempt anything more gymnastic.

Laughing, Jake sauntered over. 'Bean, you're under age. Plus, he'd squash you flat. How was lunch?' He grinned broadly at Kate.

'Pretty good.' Actually, it had been excellent. 'But I don't think much of the landlord.'

'Dexter? Oh, he's in a league of his own. Actually, we're fairly sure he's the secret love child of Simon Cowell and Rosa Klebb. Saw you talking to Nuala,' he went on innocently.

'That girl shouldn't let him speak to her like that. What is she, some kind of doormat?'

'Nuala? Her motto is better the devil you know than no devil at all. Anyway, how about you?' He nodded over at Will Gifford, currently shrugging his way back into his shabby jacket. 'Who's the mystery man? Boyfriend of yours?'

Oh God, was this the conclusion everyone was going to jump to? Now that she was ugly, would they automatically assume that someone like Will was the best she could hope for?

'Please,' Kate shuddered, 'I'm not that desperate.' In fact, if anyone physically resembled a battered old doormat, it was scruffy, tufty-haired Will; should you need to wipe your feet on something, he'd be perfect.

'You're looking a bit happier today,' said Jake.

Was she? Really? Well, maybe she wasn't feeling quite so suicidal. Then again, this could be due to picturing herself trampling all over Will Gifford in spike-heeled boots.

'Either your heart's beating very fast indeed,' Kate observed, 'or someone wants to speak to you.'

The pocket of Jake's white cotton shirt was vibrating like a humming-bird.

'I was enjoying the buzz.' With a wink, he took out his mobile and answered it. Much to Kate's relief, Norris and Bean had stopped investigating each other's bottoms, evidently having decided to keep their relationship platonic. Norris was now lying on his side on the dusty ground while Bean, rather sweetly, attempted to clamber all over him.

'Hello, you,' Jake murmured smiling into the phone and

raking tanned fingers through his blond hair. 'I know, me too.' He paused to listen, then laughed. 'Now there's an offer I can't refuse. No, definitely free tonight.' Another pause, then he broke into a grin. 'You're a bad, bad girl. OK, eight o'clock, I'd better go now. See you there.'

Kate had never been more glad of her dark glasses. Was every conversation with Jake Harvey destined to lift her spirits, then bring her crashing back to earth with a bump?

'Sorry about that. Sophie's headmistress,' said Jake.

'*Really?* Oh.' Too late, she realised he was joking.

Entertained, he said, 'You haven't seen Sophie's head-mistress. Anne Robinson on a broomstick.'

'Well, I'd better be going too.' Kate gave Norris's lead another tug, before Jake could start telling her all about the stunning girl he'd arranged to meet tonight. Across the road she saw that Oliver had finished settling up; if he and Will made their way over now, Will would be bound to say something excruciating.

'So who is he?' Clearly curious, Jake nodded over at Will.

'He makes documentaries. He's doing one on my dad. He'll be filming around here too,' said Kate.

'Filming?' Jake let out a low whistle. 'Anyone with something to hide had better watch out then.'

'Does that include you?' Kate couldn't resist the dig.

'Not me.' He flashed her a wicked grin. 'Luckily, I'm not the secretive type.'

'Who's he?' said Will.

Honestly, and women were supposed to be the nosy ones.

'Local coffin-maker. Thinks he's it. I'm taking Norris home,' said Kate, because Norris was casting lovelorn looks over his burly shoulder at Bean and she didn't trust him not to drag her back across the road.

'We won't be long,' said Oliver. 'Just a quick tour of the town then we'll be back.'

Sophie and Tiff were playing with a cardboard box on the pavement outside the Peach Tree.

'Takes me back a bit,' Oliver said jovially as he and Will approached the delicatessen. 'Playing with cardboard boxes because we couldn't afford proper toys.' He liked to exaggerate the circumstances of his childhood, play up the poverty aspect. 'Hello there, you two, having fun? This is Sophie, by the way, our housekeeper's granddaughter. And Tiff is the son of Juliet, who owns the deli.'

'Hi,' said Will, eyeing the box with its letterbox-sized slit in the top. 'Playing postmen?'

Sophie shot him a pitying look. 'It's a toll booth.'

'It costs fifty pence to get into the shop,' said Tiff.

'No *it doesn't*,' an exasperated female voice called out from inside the delicatessen. 'Tiff, let them in.'

Tiff and Sophie gazed up at Oliver.

'Outrageous opportunism,' Oliver tut-tutted, pulling a handful of coins from his trouser pocket and slipping them into the box. Sophie and Tiff exchanged smug glances – Oliver Taylor-Trent was always a soft touch. Then their eyes swivelled in unison to fix upon his younger, scruffier companion.

'Don't look at me,' Will protested. 'I'm like the Queen, I never carry cash.'

'Appalling children,' sighed Juliet, appearing in the doorway and ushering in her potential customers. 'You shouldn't give them any money.'

'Nonsense,' Oliver said briskly. 'Couple of young entrepreneurs in the making. Reminds me of myself when I was young.'

'More like a couple of highway robbers.' Juliet smiled apologetically at Will. 'What must you think of us?'

It didn't take a mind-reader to guess what Will was thinking. Juliet was wearing a white, peasant-style Indian cotton blouse and a swirling calf-length skirt strewn with poppies. Her dark hair was tied back in a loose glossy plait. Her eyes, darker still, were alight with gentle humour. Oliver, watching Will's reaction to Juliet, wondered whether it was those eyes or her glorious hourglass figure that appealed to him most.

'How's business?' Oliver said easily.

'Oh, pretty good. We get by.' Dimples appeared in Juliet's cheeks. 'I'm sure trade will pick up now that you're back.'

'Funny you should mention it. Estelle forgot to buy Parma ham this morning.'

'Customers with expensive tastes and more money than sense,' Juliet told Will cheerfully as she crossed to the chill cabinet, 'are my favourite kind. Three packets or four?'

Oliver thought about it. 'Better make it six.'

'Gravlax?'

'Go on then.'

'How about those olives you like?'

'You've twisted my arm.'

'And we've got the most amazing Sevruga caviar.'

'Now you're pushing your luck,' said Oliver.

'Oh well, worth a try.' Juliet laughed as she rang up his purchases on the till and expertly packed them into a Peach Tree brown paper carrier with string handles. 'Thanks very much, I'll put it on your account. And we look forward to seeing you again soon.'

'Bye, Mr Taylor-Trent,' chorused Tiff and Sophie as they left the shop.

'Bye,' said Oliver. 'Don't spend it all at once.'

'It wasn't *that* much money,' Sophie told him. 'Only three pounds twenty pee.'

'Wow,' breathed Will, when they were out of eavesdropping range of the children. 'I mean . . . *wow*.'

'She has that effect on men,' Oliver agreed. 'I tell you, if I were twenty years younger, I'd be tempted myself.'

'It's not just her. This whole . . . place.' As Will Gifford spread his arms to encompass Ashcombe, a button went *ping* and parted with his shirt. 'I mean, are any of the people who live here *normal*?'

'Funny you should say that.' Oliver steered him up the road towards the mini supermarket. 'Brace yourself, you're about to meet Theresa Birch.'

You knew your subconscious was up to something when you went into Bath to buy a new pair of trainers and a bottle of contact lens cleaning solution, and scuttled home three hours later with a lime-green silk and velvet bra and knicker set instead.

What a trollop.

Worse still was hearing the front door open and guiltily stuffing the carrier bag containing your new bra and knickers under the sofa.

'Hi, darling.' Marcella came bursting into the living room. 'Buy something nice?'

Maddy pulled a face. 'Couldn't find any trainers I liked.'

'Oh, what a shame. So you didn't get anything at all?'

'No, just looked around the shops.' Not just a trollop, but a wicked *lying* trollop. Wondering if this was how people felt when they smuggled hard drugs through customs, Maddy hurried through to the kitchen and put the kettle on. She imagined the hidden underwear pulsating and glowing like kryptonite, signalling its presence to Marcella. 'Chocolate biscuits?'

'No thanks, but I'd love a raw carrot.' Marcella grinned. 'What a ridiculous question. Of course I want chocolate biscuits – ooh, here come the rabble.' She jumped to one side as the door crashed open again. Jake, Sophie and Bean came clattering down the hallway and erupted into the kitchen. Sophie, covered in grass stains and dust, was clutching a football and looking triumphant.

'She's lethal,' complained Jake. 'Almost broke my leg. She's Vinnie Jones in a skirt.'

'He lost,' Sophie said matter-of-factly. 'And I don't wear skirts. Anyway I've never heard of Vinnie Jones. Who's she?'

'That reminds me,' said Marcella. 'Vince and I are having a barbecue tonight, if you fancy coming along.'

'Great,' said Jake.

'I can't.' Maddy used the excuse she'd had the foresight to prepare earlier. 'I'm meeting up with Jen and Susie in Bath.' She looked suitably regretful. 'We're having a girly night out.'

'Oh well, never mind. Give them my love,' said Marcella warmly, which only made Maddy feel worse. 'And if you're home before midnight, come on over, we'll still be going strong – oh, darling, what have you got there? Is that a present for me?' Bending down, she reached for the glossy black carrier Bean was dragging into the kitchen, and Maddy felt herself break into a light sweat. For a panicky moment she wondered if she could get away with pretending it was a present for Marcella, but it wasn't her birthday and the bra was the wrong size and her mother wasn't stupid. So basically she wasn't going to be able to get away with it at all.

'I say, these are a bit special.' Lifting out the tiny velvet-trimmed bra and knickers, Marcella's dark eyes danced with mischief. 'Been out buying for a lady friend, darling?'

'Nothing to do with me.' Jake raised his hands, absolving himself.

'Maddy? I thought you said you didn't find anything you liked.'

'I . . . I changed my mind.' Maddy stammered, uncomfortably aware of Jake's gaze upon her. 'I mean, I *did* like them, so I bought them, but I'm going to take them back to the shop. Too . . . um, expensive,' she added hurriedly as Marcella glanced at the price tag and let out a low whistle. 'It was a moment of madness, I don't know why I did it. I mean, you know me, it's usually Marks and Spencer's multipacks.'

Maddy knew she was gabbling, but this part of the lie was actually true. She could get worryingly excited about tearing open a pristine M & S multipack.

'You don't know why you did it? Spent sixty pounds on *these*? Well, I think I can probably hazard a guess. *So*,' Marcella gave her a less than subtle, tell-us-everything nudge, 'who is he?'

Now Maddy really couldn't meet Jake's eye. She didn't know where to look.

'No one. Really. I just saw them and liked the colour.'

'See that?' Marcella pointed out of the kitchen window. 'Flying pig. Sweetheart, you must have your eye on someone – hey, I know, why don't you invite him to the barbecue? Bring Jen and Susie along too, then it won't be so obvious, just tell him it's a casual get-together for a few friends. Wouldn't that be a fabulous idea? Then we can all meet him and see what we think!'

What Marcella would think truly didn't bear thinking about. Shovelling the bra and briefs back into their black carrier, Maddy said, 'Mum, I promise you, there isn't anyone. This stuff's going back to the shop, I'm meeting Jen and Susie in Brown's at seven and if it's OK with everyone, I'd quite like a bath before I go.'

'She thinks I was born yesterday,' Marcella said cheerfully as Maddy squeezed out of the crowded kitchen, 'but she's forgotten two important things.'

Ever inquisitive, Sophie said beadily, 'What important things?'

'I'm her mother,' Marcella told Sophie, raising her voice so that Maddy could still hear as she escaped up the stairs. 'And I'm *always right*.'

Chapter 14

The glorious bra and knicker set, now destined never to be worn, was back at the cottage. Wearing a bronze lace top and tight black trousers – because she was, after all, supposed to be out clubbing with Susie and Jen – Maddy parked in Armitage Close, an anonymous cul-de-sac around the corner from Kerr's house. Feeling like a fugitive, she checked all around before sliding out of the car, then made her way hurriedly to his address.

He answered the door so quickly that Maddy knew he'd been looking out for her. Now that she was actually here, she could barely make out what he was saying, so loud was the adrenalin-fuelled pumping of blood in her ears.

She took a deep breath. This was it; she was *here*.

'I'm sorry, I'll calm down in a minute. I just feel so bad about deceiving Mum . . . Marcella . . .' Managing a shaky smile, Maddy said, 'And then I thought about not coming here tonight and that made me feel worse.'

Kerr led her through the panelled hallway, into a high-ceilinged sitting room. Primrose-yellow walls and a cream carpet didn't go at all with the heavy, reddish-brown mahogany furniture or the dark blue rugs sprawled across the floor.

'I know.' Kerr intercepted her gaze. 'It's horrible, a complete nightmare. I rented it furnished. The kitchen has to be seen to be believed. Anyway, that's not important.' He shook his head. 'Being appalled by my kitchen tiles isn't why you're here. Bloody hell, life would be a damn sight easier if it was.'

Maddy nodded, acknowledging this with feeling. If only she were Laurence Llewellyn-Bowen, life would be a doddle. Apart from having to wear the clothes, obviously.

'I still can't believe this is happening,' Kerr went on. 'It's only been a week, for heaven's sake. This time last Saturday I hadn't even met you.' He paused. 'And then at the party, *bam*. Since that night I haven't been able to stop thinking about you. Nothing like this has ever happened to me before.'

He was wearing a dark blue cotton shirt and faded jeans, the body beneath them – frankly – to die for. Her stomach knotted with lust, Maddy whispered, 'I know. Me too.' There was no point in trying to deny it; the attraction was fairly obviously mutual. She cleared her throat. 'But what if we're feeling like this because we know it can't happen? Like being on a diet and knowing you can't have chocolate mousse?'

'OK, I thought about that too. That's why I invited you here tonight.' Moving towards her, Kerr smiled slightly and reached for her hands. 'Come here, mousse.'

Pulling her towards him, he kissed her on the corner of her mouth, then on the other corner, then properly, and Maddy thought, *At last*. It was like going to heaven, feeling Kerr's warm body pressed against her own and his fingers (thank goodness she hadn't used hair gel) sliding unimpeded through her hair. All too soon he pulled away, surveying her with an expression in his dark eyes that almost made her want to cry.

'OK, you have to bear with me now because I'm not used to saying this kind of stuff. I'm not sure, but I think I love you.'

'Oh God, don't say that . . .' Maddy covered her mouth, not meaning it for a moment; this was what she wanted to hear him say more than anything. But it was just so scary, so impossible. How could anything but misery result from a situation so dire?

'It's the only way. We both know how we feel, it's too late to back down and pretend it hasn't happened. Not seeing you again would only make me want you more.' Kerr waited. 'Right, so this is the plan. We *are* going to see each other. We'll be incredibly discreet, no one else will know, and with a bit of luck we'll discover we don't like each other as much as we think we do.'

Maddy stared at him in disbelief. 'With a bit of luck?'

'I know, I know.' He shrugged helplessly. 'But what other choice do we have? And it could happen, you know. In fact, the odds are that it will. How many boyfriends have you had?'

Taken aback by the bluntness of the question, Maddy said cautiously, 'Well . . . quite a few, I suppose. All in all.'

'OK, same here. Maybe a bit more than quite a few.' A flicker of a smile crossed his face. 'I'm sorry. If only I'd known, I'd have saved myself. But the point is, we went out with other people because we liked them. And each time, sooner or later, and for whatever reason, we stopped going out with them. Fingers crossed, that's exactly what'll happen to us.'

It didn't help that while he was saying this, he was running his fingers magically down the side of her face, touching her neck, looking very much as though he wanted to kiss her again.

'But you said . . .' Maddy's throat constricted with emotion '. . . you said that you thought you might, um . . .'

'Love you. I know. But it could still happen, couldn't it? Give it a couple of weeks and I might realise I can't stand the sight of you. Or you may decide you never want to see me again.'

Right now, that seemed about as likely as deciding that your favourite sandwich was cat food and mustard.

'And if we don't?'

'If we don't, it's officially a disaster. We'll just have to run away together.' Kerr drew her towards him once more, his dark eyes fixed on hers. 'We'll have to find somewhere where Marcella can't track us down. Join up with the VSO or something, and devote the rest of our lives to helping homeless smelly old tramps in Siberia. It'll be vile, but at least we'll be together. God,' he pulled a face, 'I really hope it doesn't come to that. Talk about an incentive to get you out of my system.'

'Maybe we should write down a list of our bad points, to get the ball rolling,' Maddy said helpfully. 'You know, I could go off you really quickly if you told me lots of completely hideous things about you.'

'You think? Like what?'

'Oh, like if you watch Sky Sports all the time. And get really worked up about football. And you hate dogs. And you're really irritatingly tidy. Or if you only change your socks once a fortnight. And you tell bad jokes all the time and expect me to laugh at them over and over again.' Actually, this was easy, all she had to do was remember all the things that had annoyed her about previous boyfriends. 'Or you're proud of the fact that you've never done the washing-up in your life, or you play with model trains, or you think it's funny to mock people with speech impediments, or like to pretend you've got a huge spider in your hand when you know perfectly well someone's terrified of spiders—'

'Stop, *stop*.' Kerr held up his hands in protest. 'Jesus, what kind of men have you been associating with? That's the most appalling list I've ever heard. Do you seriously think I'd do any of those things?'

'Well, no.' Maddy was embarrassed.

'Apart from the spider trick, of course.' He nodded matter-of-factly. 'I've done that.'

'Really?'

'When I was about sixteen. But if you think it would help, I could do it again.'

'No thanks. How about you?'

'What puts me off girls, you mean? God, loads of things.' Sliding his arms around her, Kerr said, 'Girls on diets, girls asking if their dress makes them look fat, girls reading out your horoscope even though they know you aren't interested, girls who think spending a fortune on clothes and manicures makes up for not having a person-ality, girls who eat crisps with their mouths open, girls who pee in other people's gardens then expect to be rescued when they can't climb back over the wall – OK, not true,' he said as Maddy shot him a warning look, 'I love it when girls do that.'

'Where can we go?' said Maddy.

'I told you, anywhere in the world. Actually, Siberia's bloody freezing. How would you feel about Barbados?'

'I mean here, while we're secretly seeing each other and doing our best to hate each other. Every time we go out I'll be terrified Marcella might see us, or friends of Marcella might see us and tell her.' She gestured in desperation. 'Or friends of friends, and God knows there must be thousands of *them* around. Don't you see, we can never go *anywhere*.'

'Fine.' Kerr shrugged, unperturbed. 'We'll just have to stay here and make our own entertainment.'

'But it'll be like being stuck in a prison cell,' wailed Maddy. 'It'll be boring!'

'I've been called a lot of things in my time. But never

boring. Anyway, why does it have to be? We can play card games. Watch documentaries on the TV. Make Airfix kits, do giant jigsaw puzzles . . .'

He was teasing her. Maddy squirmed with pleasure as his hands settled around her waist, his thumbs idly stroking her back. She was getting the distinct impression that the jigsaw puzzles he had in mind comprised two pieces.

'This isn't going to work.' She held her breath as his warm mouth brushed her collarbone.

'OK, you're right, let's forget it.' Abruptly spinning her round, Kerr marched her back to the hall, yanked open the front door and—

'Noooo!' shrieked Maddy.

He closed the front door.

'Think it might work after all?'

She exhaled slowly. Kerr, having successfully called her bluff, regarded her with amusement.

'Maybe.' Trembling again, Maddy leaned back against the wall.

'Sorry. Not good enough.'

'OK. We'll do it.' What choice did they have, after all? The alternative – not seeing him again – was unthinkable.

'Wise decision.' Smiling, he kissed her again. Feeling as though her whole body was on fire, Maddy wrapped her arms round his neck and kissed him back. *Twannggg,* went her bra strap and for a split second she thought Kerr had unfastened it.

'That definitely wasn't me.' Raising his hands, he protested his innocence. 'I didn't do that.'

Bugger, he was right. With impeccable timing, Maddy realised, her left shoulder strap had chosen this moment to snap.

'Sorry, it's an old bra.' Wryly, she added, 'The excitement must have been too much for it.'

'You see? That's one of the things I like about you. What colour is it?'

'Um . . . sort of coffee coloured.' Mocha, actually, but Kerr was only a man. He wouldn't understand.

'And what colour are your knickers?'

Oh, the shame. But since modesty clearly wasn't an option, Maddy said, 'Black.'

Anyway, with a bit of luck he'd find this out for himself before too long.

'Do you know how much I love it that you're wearing a brown bra and black knickers?' Kerr said happily.

Brown? The horror. Unable to help herself, Maddy blurted out, 'Mocha.'

There was a difference.

'Whatever. I just . . . all my life, whenever I've been out with girls and undressed them for the first time, they've always been wearing brand new super-lacy matching bra and knickers. It's so contrived, it makes me feel as if I've been set up. The situation just doesn't feel spontaneous any more.'

'If you feel that strongly about it, you could always try not undressing them,' Maddy pointed out.

'It doesn't put me off that much. Anyway, I'm just saying it makes a refreshing change, and I really like it that you aren't the kind of girl who meets a new man and rushes out to buy a sexy new bra and knicker set.'

'This isn't going to work,' said Maddy. 'I'm supposed to be putting you off me.'

'Sorry, but you haven't.' Kerr's eyes glittered. 'In fact you've failed, with flying colours.'

'But I *did* buy a sexy bra and knicker set! This morning! It's at home, I was going to wear them tonight, but Bean found them under the sofa,' Maddy babbled, 'and then

Marcella saw them and started teasing me about having a new man, so—'

'Nice try.' Kerr tilted her face up to meet his and slid the broken bra strap down over her shoulder. 'In fact, excellent try. But you can't fool me.'

Chapter 15

'OK, I need you to know something. I'm not normally the type of girl who jumps into bed with someone on the first date,' said Maddy an hour later.

'No?' Grinning down at her, Kerr said, 'You did it very well.'

'I just don't want you to think I'm a complete slapper, because I'm not.' She ran her hands through her drastically rumpled hair. 'But this is different, because putting it off would only have made us want each other more. So by sleeping together as soon as possible we've got all that breathless anticipation stuff out of the way, which made it the right thing to do, don't you agree?'

'God, yes, absolutely. I'm starting to get bored with you already. Any minute now I'll roll over, fall asleep and start snoring like an elephant seal,' said Kerr. 'That'll be your cue to prod me awake and say in a whiny voice, "Why can't you give me a cuddle? Why can't we just lie here and talk about *us*?" Then I'll chuck you my phone and tell you to call yourself a taxi. Ten minutes later you'll wake me up slamming the front door as you let yourself out of the flat, and when I get up the next morning there'll be rude words scribbled in lipstick on my bathroom mirror.'

'Wow, you really are a pig,' Maddy marvelled, deeply impressed. 'Who pays for my taxi?'

'What am I, a walking cash machine?'

The trouble was, nothing he said was managing to put her off. In desperation she asked, 'Do you snore?'

'Like a tractor. Stick around and you'll find out.'

'I'm not staying. I can't.' Maddy knew she couldn't bring herself to go to Marcella's barbecue, to just turn up as if nothing had happened, but she couldn't stay here tonight either. Jake, who didn't miss a trick, was suspicious already. When he'd seen the new bra and knickers earlier, the look he'd given her had made her flush with guilt.

It was so unfair. When it came to the opposite sex, Jake was no saint; if she had a pair of shoes for every girl he'd slept with, she'd be Imelda Marcos and Tara Palmer-Tomkinson rolled into one. But now, just when it was her turn to have some fun, he was threatening to come over all disapproving simply because of who Kerr was related to.

'Sure I can't change your mind?' Kerr's hand disappeared beneath the rumpled duvet, sliding down her hip.

Maddy shook her head. Why did everything have to be so difficult?

'I have to get back.'

'But not just yet.'

Oh God, this wasn't just difficult, it was completely impossible. But he was right; it was still only nine thirty. Giving herself up to a fresh surge of lust, Maddy smiled and insinuated one leg between his own.

Not just yet.

Marcella and Vince's garden bore all the morning-after signs of a truly successful party. Discarded cans and bottles were strewn across the lawn and in the flowerbeds, plastic glasses glinted in the sunlight, leftover burger remnants were being helpfully wolfed up by Bean and the tables on the patio were piled high with overflowing ashtrays, discarded CDs and empty bowls that had once contained mayonnaise, pickles and Cajun dips.

Vince, busy cleaning the well-used barbecue, waved when he saw Maddy and called out, 'You're too late, you've missed it!'

'Morning, darling!' Marcella, wearing a scarlet satin dressing gown and dark glasses, was busy filling a black bin liner with empty lager cans. The party might have gone on until 5 a.m. but Marcella and Vince would still be up at eight to make a start on the clearing up. Pointing to the honey-suckle-covered gazebo she said, 'I need to get up there. You couldn't be an angel, could you, and fetch the stepladder from the garage?'

Maddy carted out the stepladder, then watched as Marcella climbed to the top step, reached into the depths of the honey-suckle and shook out three mismatched shoes, a string of uncooked sausages and a pink sequinned T-shirt.

'Don't ask,' said Marcella.

'So it was a good party.' Maddy held the ladder steady as her mother jumped down.

'The very best. You don't know what you missed.' Turning, Marcella enveloped her in a hug. 'And how did your night go? Did you have a lovely time?'

A lovely time? It had possibly been the best night of Maddy's life. Adding to her litany of shameless lies, she said, 'Great. Jen's got her eye on one of the new barmen at Brown's. Susie's convinced he's gay. We ended up at the Crash Club.' Even as the words were tumbling out, she realised she was going to have to warn Jen and Susie, explain to them that they were her alibis and that if Marcella should bump into them, they had to back her up. Preferably without knowing the real reason why she needed alibis, since it went without saying that the fewer people who knew about this, the better.

God, getting complicated already.

'Oof, my poor head.' Marcella groaned as she bent down to pick up an empty Côtes du Rhône bottle.

'Hangover?'

Looking rueful, Marcella said, 'Ozzy Osbourne impression. We had a bit of a karaoke thing going. Should have stuck with Diana Ross – far less headbanging involved.'

'Here, let me do it.' Taking the black binbag away from her, Maddy said, 'I'll clear this lot up. You go and put the kettle on.'

'You should have come along,' said Marcella. 'We missed you. Nuala and Dexter came up after the pub shut – you haven't lived until you've seen Dexter doing his Rod Stewart impression.'

You haven't lived until you've been to bed with Kerr McKinnon, thought Maddy, not daring to look at Marcella and busying herself with the black bag.

'So do you think he's gay?'

Good grief, no! Startled, Maddy said, 'What? *Who?*'

'The new barman at Brown's.' Marcella laughed. 'Dear me, you're away with the fairies this morning.'

'Sorry. Too busy picturing Dexter singing, "Do ya think I'm sexy."' Bending down, Maddy picked up a charred baked potato. 'And yes, I think the barman was gay – it's always a bit of a giveaway when they wear a Barbra Streisand T-shirt. But that's the kind of luck Jen has with men.'

'She'll find the right one sooner or later. There's plenty of lovely men out there if you know where to look. Jen'll end up with her Mr Perfect one day.' Marcella glanced fondly across at Vince as she spoke. 'And so will you.'

Guilt swept through Maddy like a bushfire.

Raising a teasing eyebrow, Marcella went on, 'That is, unless you've already found him.'

'Honestly, I do the decent thing, turn up early to help you with the clearing up, and you start having a go at me.'

'I'm not having a go. I'm on your side,' Marcella protested. 'Look at how happy your dad and I were. And now I've got Vince and he's every bit as wonderful. Sweetheart, I just want you to be happy too.'

Last night's bedroom antics had left Maddy with aching trembly limbs. Dumping the black bag on the grass she said, 'And when I do find him, I'll tell you. Come on, we'll finish the rest of this later. Let's have a cup of tea.'

No one ever escaped with just a cup of tea at Marcella's house; she was physically incapable of not cooking for anyone who happened to drop in. Vince carried on clearing up outside. Maddy, who adored the cosy, comfortably cluttered kitchen, sat in one of the sunny window seats with Bean on her lap while Marcella got busy with the frying pan. Within minutes, two vast plates of crispy smoked bacon, eggs, potato and mushroom hash, grilled tomatoes and doorsteps of buttered toast were on the table. Fifteen thousand calories each, no problem, Maddy decided. Then again, she'd probably used up that many during last night's shenanigans, five thousand calories per—

Oh God, stop it, don't even *think* about that now.

'I invited the Taylor-Trents last night,' said Marcella.

'What, all of them?' Maddy paused between mouthfuls of perfect bacon. 'Not Kate, surely.'

'Come on, give the girl a break. I popped up to borrow Estelle's lovely big serving dishes for the potato salad. How could I not invite Kate?'

'She'd kill any party stone dead.' Maddy envisaged Kate Taylor-Trent throwing herself into a bout of no-holds-barred karaoke. Surely not.

'Well, they couldn't make it anyway.' Marcella shrugged

comfortably. 'They already had dinner booked at the Hinton Grange. And they have a guest staying with them for a few days.'

'Lucky guest.' Maddy pulled a face.

'I met him, he seems charming. His name's Will and he's going to be making a TV documentary about Oliver. And for your information, they were all in the pub on Friday afternoon and Kate gave Dexter Nevin a bit of a tongue-lashing. He'd been yelling at Nuala so Kate laid into him big-time. She and Nuala have buried their differences, by the sound of it.' Meaningfully, Marcella went on, 'You could do worse than follow their example.'

Bloody Nuala, what a traitor.

'She called Nuala fat. *Once.*' Maddy gestured irritably with her fork. 'It's hardly the same as spending years making someone's life a complete misery.'

'Just a thought, darling.'

'And you've got streamers in your hair.' Reaching across the table, Maddy gently removed a tangle of rainbow coloured paper ribbons.

'We couldn't get hold of any fireworks, so it was party poppers at midnight. Oh, we had such a good time.' Marcella beamed. 'You really should have come along.'

'I was shattered.' At least this wasn't a lie. 'Drove home, fell into bed at one o'clock, didn't even hear Jake and Sophie come in.' Also true, but at least when they had arrived home, Jake would have seen her car outside and known she was back. In her current guilt-ridden state, this had seemed particularly important.

'I know it's never going to happen, but I do wish Jake and Juliet could get together.' Regretfully Marcella shook her head. 'They'd make such a great couple. They did Sonny and Cher last night.'

'Sonny and Cher got divorced,' Maddy pointed out. Then

she said, 'What?' because Marcella's expression had abruptly changed.

'Kerr McKinnon. Heard anything about him lately?'

Maddy almost fell off her chair. The air was knocked from her lungs as if she'd just been punched by a giant fist.

Was this some kind of test? No, it couldn't be; Marcella wasn't the game-playing type. If you'd done something wrong she confronted you outright, more often than not with a frying pan in her hand. She didn't pretend everything was fine, then suddenly launch into an attack.

'Who? Kerr McKinnon? Why would I have heard anything?' Her skin prickled all over with the effort of sounding normal.

'Oh, I know, daft question. It was just something Kate Taylor-Trent said last night. We were in the kitchen when she asked if he was back living around here. Gave me a jolt, I can tell you.'

She wasn't the only one. Staring at Marcella, who was looking decidedly fierce, Maddy said, 'What made her say that? I thought he'd moved to London for good.'

'Let's hope so. It was just that Kate thought she saw him the other day, driving down Gypsy Lane.' Marcella's mouth narrowed as she jabbed a fork into her tomato, splattering juice.

'She probably made a mistake. Nobody's seen him for years, they wouldn't even know what he looked like these days. People change,' said Maddy, her legs wound rigidly around each other like barbed wire under the kitchen table.

'Ha!' Marcella's eyes were colder than ice. 'Not that family. I'd recognise any of them, and that's a promise.'

Oh Lord. 'I'm sure it wasn't him.'

'Better not have been. Driving through Ashcombe as if nothing had ever happened.' Bitterly Marcella went on, 'Although as far as they're concerned, I'm sure nothing ever did. Arrogant bastards, the lot of them. I daresay they've forgotten all about it by now. Oh, don't let me get started on that family . . .'

That was the trouble with Marcella, Maddy decided helplessly; she didn't differentiate between the various McKinnons, just lumped them together as a single entity. It was no good trying to explain to her that Den McKinnon had been the one driving the car and that Kerr had been out of the country at the time. They were brothers and as far as Marcella was concerned that was all that mattered. Anyone who was a McKinnon could rot in hell.

'*Now* look what they've made me do.' Crossly Marcella rubbed at the mark on the front of her scarlet silk kimono, as if Kerr McKinnon had personally erupted into the kitchen and fired tomato juice down her front. Glad of a diversion, Maddy jumped up and fetched a J-cloth from the drainer. Her mobile, lying on the kitchen table next to her plate, promptly began to chirp.

'Nuala.' Having glanced at the caller display, Marcella handed over the phone in exchange for the damp J-cloth. Taking it with trepidation, Maddy thought that on balance she'd have preferred to keep the cloth.

Chapter 16

True to form, Nuala wasted no time in coming straight to the point.

'"Sex bomb, sex bomb,"' she sang down the phone, evidently still in raucous karaoke mode. 'So don't hold back, tell me everything, how did it *go*?' Then she laughed dirtily, like Benny Hill. 'Or should that be, how's it *going*? Are you still at his place? Been getting jiggy-jiggy, have we? Come on, come on, I need to *know*!'

Maddy had the phone pressed so tightly against her ear it was a wonder it hadn't burst through the other side. Nuala could be nerve-wrackingly loud when she wanted.

'Yes, I've been hearing all about it,' she replied brightly. 'I'm here at Mum's house now. Marcella was just telling me about Dexter doing his Rod Stewart thing—'

'OK, OK, I get the message,' Nuala interrupted. 'Just give me a few clues to be going on with. I know, we'll play the yes/no game. First, did you—?'

'Actually,' Maddy broke in hurriedly, 'we're just having breakfast and my sausages are getting cold. Why don't I ring you back later?'

'Boring! No, you aren't wriggling out of it that easily.' Bossily Nuala said, 'I'm the one who persuaded you to go over there, remember? And there's nothing wrong with a cold sausage, so I want to hear all about it *now*.'

120

Confiding in Nuala had been a huge mistake, Maddy now realised. How could she have been so stupid?

'OK, thanks, I'll call you back in an hour.' Cutting off Nuala's outraged protests with a flick of a switch, Maddy slid the phone into her shirt pocket and said to Marcella, 'You know what Nuala's like, she'll be wittering on for hours. Is there any more coffee in that pot?'

'I'm not deaf, you know.' Marcella shook her head, surveying Maddy with resignation. 'I know what's going on.'

Oh crikey.

'What? Mum, I keep telling you, nothing's going on.'

'And you've always been a hopeless liar.' Refilling their cups, Marcella said, 'You're seeing someone and you don't want me to know about it.'

Prevaricating, feeling sick, Maddy stammered, 'Why would I do that?'

'Oh, come on, it's pretty obvious, isn't it? He's married.'

Married. Going red had its uses, Maddy discovered. Marcella, automatically mistaking fervent relief for miserable guilt, said, 'There you see, I *knew* it. Oh darling, what have you got yourself mixed up in? How did this happen? How long has it been going on?'

Lost for words, Maddy shook her head helplessly.

'A married *man*,' Marcella continued. 'Someone with a *wife*.' She heaved a sorrowful sigh. 'Sweetheart, this is bad news, you have to think about how you'd feel if you were married to someone who was cheating on you.'

Maddy shifted uncomfortably in her seat; what had seemed like a brilliant idea twenty seconds ago was turning out to be less brilliant than she'd thought. Marcella's disappointment was almost as hard to bear as her incandescent fury would have been.

Almost, but not quite.

'He's separated from his wife,' Maddy mumbled defensively. 'Well, pretty much. As good as. They're getting a divorce.'

'Are they? Truly? Or is that just what he tells you?' Pushing her plate to one side, Marcella lit a cigarette and exhaled, the ruler-straight stream of smoke signalling her disapproval. For all her unorthodox lifestyle, she was a woman of high moral standards, with a strong sense of right and wrong.

'They're getting a divorce,' Maddy promised.

'Children?'

'Oh, no.'

Marcella raised an eyebrow. 'And is that true? Or could he be fibbing about that too?'

Outraged at the implied slur on her imaginary boyfriend's character, Maddy wailed, 'Why are you so suspicious? Of course he doesn't have any children.'

'Have you met his wife?'

'No!'

'Does she know you're seeing her husband?'

Actually, make it too much of an amicable separation and Marcella might want to meet him too. Hesitating, Maddy said, 'Well, no.'

'And you wonder why I'm so suspicious,' sighed Marcella. 'Sweetheart, he lied to her. What makes you think he wouldn't lie to you?'

'He just wouldn't. Anyway, don't lecture me. I don't want to talk about this any more.'

'It'll end in tears. You have to finish it now,' Marcella said gently. 'Sweetheart, you know you must.'

'Like I keep telling you, with your cigarettes.' Maddy glanced pointedly at the Silk Cut smouldering in her mother's hand. 'And look how much notice you take of me.'

'Fine.' Marcella ground the half-smoked cigarette into the ashtray and fixed her with a challenging stare. 'Let's both give up what's no good for us, shall we?'

'It's not the same thing!'

'You just said it was.'

Maddy jutted out her chin like a teenager. This was ridiculous; they were about to have an argument about a boyfriend who didn't even exist.

Except . . . he did. He just wasn't married.

He was Kerr McKinnon, which was worse.

'OK, I won't see him again. But you mustn't nag me about it. *And*,' she said truculently, 'you have to give up smoking.'

Marcella looked as if she'd like to say a whole lot more, but was holding it inside her with enormous difficulty. Finally she said, 'I'm only worried because I love you. Getting involved with someone like that won't make you happy, sweetheart. You aren't the marriage-wrecking type.'

'I didn't wreck his marriage, it was over months ago. But we aren't talking about this any more, remember? Now, do you want some help with the clearing up or shall I go and see Nuala?'

'I'd rather you went and saw lover boy, told him it was over.'

Thinking fast, Maddy said, 'I can't. Sundays aren't . . . good.'

'You mean he spends them with his wife.' Marcella's tone was sorrowful, but tinged with triumph. 'Sweetheart, what does that tell you? He's never going to leave her!'

'He will. Just you wait.'

'Oh please, have some dignity. You deserve so much better than this.'

'I told you, I'll stop seeing him,' Maddy insisted. 'It's just that Sundays are difficult. I *will* do it, I promise. Just not today.'

'We're shut,' said Dexter. 'Can't you tell the time?'

Actually, he was looking rather attractive this morning in

123

a dishevelled celebrity chef kind of way. Dexter might be the world's stroppiest character, but he definitely had sexy eyes. If you didn't mind a few bags and wrinkles.

Or insults.

'I need a quick word with Nuala.' Maddy flashed him a bright smile, because Dexter didn't scare her.

'God, another one? Hurry up then, don't take all day about it.' Begrudgingly, Dexter allowed her inside the pub. Raising his voice he roared, 'Nuala? Get down here, you lazy lump. Someone here to see you.'

'It's OK, I'll go on up.' Darting past him, Maddy headed for the staircase.

'That's it, and make sure you close the door behind you so I can't overhear. She'll be dying to catch you up on all the latest news,' said Dexter with a smirk.

Maddy's mouth went dry. 'What kind of news?'

'Made a fool of herself last night at the barbecue, didn't she. Thinks she stands a chance with that brother of yours – ha, as if he'd look twice at a pudding like her.'

Oh Lord, this didn't sound promising. What had Jake been up to now?

Upstairs, Nuala was practising staying upright on a pair of brand new, ludicrously high-heeled shoes. As she teetered across the living room and collapsed onto the overstuffed yellow sofa, Maddy said, 'Never do that again.'

'I know, Dexter says I look like Lily Savage out on a bender, I think it's because the ankle straps are too loose.'

'Don't give me that rubbish. Marcella was listening to that phone call. You *know* she mustn't find out who I was with last night.'

'Oh, come on, lighten up, it was just a bit of fun.' Waggling her outstretched feet, Nuala admired her impractical lilac shoes.

'Take it from me, it *wasn't* fun. I almost wet myself.'

'Don't try and blame your weak bladder on me. Anyway, how could I give anything away? I didn't even mention his name.' Nuala looked impossibly smug. 'The dreaded K-word never once passed my lips, I was the *soul* of discretion – ooh, the *sole* of discretion, get it?' Kicking up her legs, she pointed to the bottom of her shoes. Delighted by her own wit she cried, 'And you know I'd never give away your naughty secret. If I did that, I'd be an utter heel!'

'So what's this I hear about you and Jake?' said Maddy, and Nuala's face abruptly lit up.

'Oh, my God, who told you about that? Was it Jake?'

'No.' When she'd left the house this morning, Jake had still been asleep. 'Your live-in lover happened to mention it.'

Nuala wriggled with delight. 'In a jealous way?'

'Actually, in more of a what's-the-silly-cow-playing-at-now sort of way.'

'That means I've got him worried. Anyhow, I didn't start it. Jake was the one doing all the flirting. You know, I think he secretly really fancies me. Has he ever mentioned anything to you?'

Oh please.

'Jake's Jake. You know what he's like. Female plus pulse equals potential shag.' Maddy was deliberately blunt; sometimes you had to be cruel to be kind.

'Oh well, not that I ever would, of course.' Nuala tried to hide her disappointment. 'It's just nice, sometimes, to be flirted with.'

'Instead of publicly humiliated.'

'Exactly. I mean, I know Dexter doesn't mean it, it's just his way, but if he sees other men chatting me up it might make him appreciate me a bit more.'

'Hmm, maybe.' Trussing Dexter up with barbed wire and lowering him head first over a tank of alligators wasn't likely to make him appreciate Nuala a bit more, but Maddy didn't say so. For the first time, Nuala was actually acknowledging that the endless insults were starting to get her down. Since any attempt to persuade her to dump Dexter would only cause her to leap to his defence, Maddy left it at that.

'Anyway.' Brushing aside the subject of Dexter and Jake, Nuala leaned forward eagerly. 'Your turn now. Tell me about last night. Was he spectacular in bed?'

Never backwards in coming forwards, that was Nuala.

Maddy's childhood drama classes came flooding back.

'I didn't sleep with him,' she protested, as convincingly as she knew how.

'Liar liar pants on fire,' crowed Nuala. 'Look at your face.'

Oh well, it had been worth a try.

'OK, but you mustn't tell anyone. Really, I mean *really*, really.'

Nuala nodded vigorously. 'Cross my heart and hope to die.'

'Good,' said Maddy, 'because if you breathe one word about this, you *will* die. And that's a promise.'

Chapter 17

Hillview was the name of the house. Maddy tensed as she reached the entrance to the property and saw, half-hidden by an overhang of ivy, the battered wooden sign.

Checking for the hundredth time that the road was empty both ahead and behind her as far as the eye could see, she turned the Saab into the bumpy driveway. Then her heart began to race as she realised the danger of being spotted was behind her now. When she'd rung Kerr on his mobile she'd assumed he was at home; it had come as something of a shock when he'd told her he was here instead. It had come as even more of a shock when he'd invited her over to join him.

'Come and take a look at the place. I could do with a second opinion.'

Maddy shivered with a mixture of lust and trepidation. 'But what if someone sees me?'

'They won't, how can they? The house is completely hidden from the road. And, trust me, nobody ever comes here. Not even Jehovah's Witnesses.' Kerr's voice was persuasive, as irresistible as melted chocolate. 'You'll be quite safe, I promise.'

'OK.' Maddy had swallowed hard. As if she could say no.

Hillview. Well, it was situated on a hill and many years

ago there undoubtedly *had* been a view, but that was before Pauline McKinnon had instructed her gardener to get planting those leylandii. Now the fiendishly fast-growing trees surrounded the house like a fortress. Intimidating but, under the circumstances, useful.

Kerr's dark blue Mercedes was parked at the head of the drive. Pulling up behind it, Maddy exhaled slowly and gazed up at the house itself. Hillview was a rambling Victorian property built from honey-coloured Bath stone, with diamond-leaded windows and steeply sloping gables. The garden was hopelessly overgrown, the window frames could do with a paint job and the shadows cast by the towering leylandii created an air of gloom, but these were all problems that could be solved. She could just see it, advertised in *Country Life*. This house was eminently marketable and would fetch a good price.

The front door opened and Kerr appeared on the top step, wearing jeans and a bleached blue rugby shirt. Feeling the tug of an invisible elastic band, Maddy jumped out of the car and raced into his outstretched arms. It might not be the cool thing to do, but she didn't care. Nobody had ever made her feel like this before and if she didn't kiss him this minute she might self-detonate.

It was no good, Kerr McKinnon was everything she'd ever wanted. Clinging to him as his tongue slid into her mouth, Maddy realised that this was what she'd been missing out on all these years. He was the elusive piece of the jigsaw making her feel, for the first time in her life, complete.

Oh God, he was electrifying, how could she ever bear to give him up?

'This is hopeless,' Kerr murmured, holding her close. 'You're meant to be putting me off you. I don't think you're even trying.'

'OK. Sorry.' Quick, think, what was the most off-putting

thing a besotted girl could say? 'I love you, I want to marry you, can we get engaged?' whined Maddy. 'Then we can live happily ever after and have lots of babies. In fact, I think I may already be pregnant . . .'

'Sorry, nice try, it just doesn't seem to be doing the trick. Maybe I should show you over the house.' Taking her by the hand, Kerr led the way across the shadowy hall and up the winding staircase. 'I'd especially like you to see my old bedroom.'

Guessing from the look in his eyes that his intentions were – thank *goodness* – completely dishonourable, Maddy said innocently, 'Got any etchings up there?'

'No,' Kerr gave her waist a squeeze, exploring the sensitive gap between her top and her jeans, 'but I've got a double bed.'

Oh God in Heaven, how could she ever, in a million years, get bored of an experience as indescribably stupendous as that?

'I can't believe I'm here. In your mother's house,' whispered Maddy when she was finally able to speak normally again. Breathe normally, too, rather than pant like a dog.

'It's where I grew up. It was my house too,' Kerr reminded her.

'I know. It feels a bit funny, though. You'd feel a bit funny if we'd just done this in my family home.'

'I'd be bloody terrified. Imagine being caught by Marcella.'

Heavenly though it would have been, they couldn't spend the entire afternoon in bed. After a quick shower, Maddy headed downstairs where Kerr was in the kitchen making a pot of coffee.

'OK? I'd have opened a bottle of wine but you said you'd told Marcella you were going shopping.' He kissed Maddy on the mouth. 'If you're hungry I've got some stuff in the fridge.'

'I'm not hungry.' That was the great thing about new-man syndrome, it shrank your appetite to thimble-sized proportions. 'Marcella knows I'm seeing someone, by the way. She was dying to meet you, so I had to tell her you were married.'

'I wouldn't have thought you were the type. A married man?' Kerr raised an eyebrow. 'That's terrible.'

'Your wife doesn't understand you.' Maddy's tone was reassuring. 'It's a hopeless situation, you've both been miserable for years and you're on the verge of splitting up. Plus, of course, she's a complete bitch.'

'Oh well, goes without saying. That's all right then.'

'Marcella doesn't think so. She isn't thrilled. We nearly had a big fight about it.'

'But not so big a fight as if you'd told her who you were really seeing,' said Kerr. 'Do I have a name, by the way?'

'No. Easier not to give you one. You're just . . . married.'

'Any kids?'

'No way. I'm not that much of a cow. Although,' Maddy was struck by a thought, 'maybe you could have had just one, then found out it wasn't yours after all . . . Oh well, never mind, too late now. Anyway, let's not talk about Marcella. When are you going to put this place on the market?'

'Well, that's one of the reasons I asked you to come over and see it. *One* of the reasons,' Kerr said with a smile. 'You see, I had a word with my bank manager yesterday. Business is good at the agency and I may not need to sell the house after all. I can take out a second mortgage, which would cover the nursing home fees. That way, my mother's taken care of and I could move out of that flat. Live here instead.'

Here. Crikey. Good grief.

'Well?' prompted Kerr. 'What d'you think?'

Maddy shook her head; she didn't know what to think. It

all depended on how their relationship panned out, didn't it? Because secretly seeing each other and hoping to God that the novelty would wear off and that sooner or later they'd call it a day was all very well, but the chances of it happening by mutual agreement were, frankly, slim. It was far more likely that one of them would get bored first and finish with the other, and although it didn't seem terribly likely at present, Maddy was rather hoping to be the finisher rather than the finishee. If she could just manage to persuade herself to go off Kerr McKinnon, how much easier it would be, knowing that he was living here, just a couple of miles from Ashcombe. If, on the other hand, he broke her heart and left her bereft, it wouldn't be easy at all.

Maddy gave herself a mental slap. This was ridiculous; whether Kerr lived two miles away here or five miles away in Bath, what difference did it make? She had to get a grip, act like a mature and sensible adult. Whatever happened between them, Kerr was entitled to live wherever he liked. And this was a beautiful house.

Now, why was he looking at her like that? Oh yes, waiting for her to say something.

Brightly, Maddy said, 'Great.'

'Come on, finish your coffee. I'll show you around.'

'You said that before, and we didn't get too far.'

'I know, sorry about that. My motives were pure, I promise you.' Kerr's eyes glittered with wickedness. 'I was pretending to be a sex-crazed seducer, to put you off me. I just hope it worked.'

Maddy thought about it. 'Good tactics. But this time I'm actually going to see the rest of the house?'

'Not making any promises,' Kerr murmured into her still-damp hair. 'I may have to seduce you in a few more rooms en route. But we'll give it a go.'

* * *

131

'Marcella told me. She's not thrilled.'

'Didn't expect her to be,' Maddy retaliated with a care-less shrug. Fresh from the bath, she was in the kitchen making herself cheese on toast. She had no intention of being intimidated and lectured to by, of all people, Jake.

Watching her, Jake said evenly, 'So, who is he?'

Had he suspected, earlier, that it could be Kerr?

'No one you know, no one you've heard of, and I'm not telling you his name because there's no point. Now, do you want some cheese on toast or not?'

Jake leaned against the door, his hands folded.

'Marcella wants you to finish with him.'

'Oh, for heaven's sake, of course she wants me to finish with him!' Shaking her head in defiance, Maddy prodded the bubbling slices of cheese on toast under the grill with her knife. 'But it's not as easy as that. Which is why you've been dragged in to put the pressure on, presumably.' She raised her eyebrows at Jake. 'Although why I should take a blind bit of notice of anything you say, I've no idea. You sleep with married women, why can't I do it too?'

'There's a difference,' said Jake. 'OK, I may have slept with a few married women in my time, but it was never serious. Just a bit of fun, to cheer them up and tide them over while their husbands weren't doing their share. I don't get emotion-ally involved and I certainly don't put their marriages at risk.'

'What a hero,' Maddy said crossly. 'Your trouble is, you never get emotionally involved with *anyone*, married or not. But Sophie's seven now, doesn't it ever occur to you that maybe you should give it a go? I mean, you can't spend the rest of your life just shagging your way round Bath for the hell of it. Don't you think it's about time you found your-self someone nice and settled down? You never know, if you carried on seeing a girl for longer than three days, you might find out you actually liked her.'

'Here comes Sophie,' said Jake as the back door banged and Sophie and Bean raced in. 'Tell you what, you don't lecture me and I won't lecture you.' Strolling over and turning off the smoking grill he added, 'Even though I know exactly what I'm doing and you haven't a clue. These are wrecked, by the way. I'll have the one on the left.'

'Bugger off.' Maddy pushed him out of the way. 'You can have the one on the right. Unless Sophie wants some.' Turning, she said, 'Soph? Fancy some cheese on toast?'

Sophie, who adored rude words and was swinging from the door jamb, said happily, 'Bugger off, I want one that isn't burned.'

Chapter 18

It was probably PMT, but that didn't make all the little irritations of the day any less irritating. Estelle, having stacked the dishwasher and discovered that the only things she actively disliked washing wouldn't fit into it anyway, was at the kitchen sink scrubbing futilely at a roasting pan that was determined not to relinquish its welded-on bits of caramelised parsnip.

This wasn't turning out to be one of her better days. Kate had been so snappish all morning that when she had taken Norris out for a walk after lunch, it had been a relief. Oliver had, in the space of the last couple of hours, managed to criticise Estelle's roast potatoes, her dress sense *and* her less than intellectual taste in novels, leaving her with an ego like a deflated condom and the urge to punch him on the nose. Now Oliver had left as well, departed for London for the day, and as far as she was concerned London was jolly well welcome to him.

'Oh *fuck it*.' Estelle leapt back from the sink as her vigorous scrubbing caused a wave of washing-up water to sloosh down the front of her turquoise linen shirt. Not lovely clean, bubbly washing-up water, of course, but brackish greasy water complete with floaty burned bits. Just what you needed to accessorise a linen shirt.

'Shit, *shit*,' whispered Estelle, snatching up the tea towel and pressing it to her front – for all the good it would do.

134

'Are you OK? Did you cut yourself?' Will's voice behind her made her jump; she hadn't heard him come into the kitchen.

Turning round, shaking her head helplessly, Estelle showed him her sopping wet front. 'Just making a mess of this, like I've made a mess of everything else today.'

'Well, I'm glad it's only water. Can't stand the sight of blood.' Will's eyes crinkled reassuringly at her behind his glasses, and he was holding something wrapped in a plastic carrier bag that looked as if it might be a large bone for Norris. 'Go and change into something dry,' he went on gently. 'And don't be silly, you haven't messed up anything else. That was a fantastic lunch.'

Upstairs, Estelle stripped off her shirt and as an act of rebellion changed into a pale pink sweatshirt – the one that, according to Oliver, made her look like a giant marsh-mallow. And not in a good way. Sod Oliver, Estelle told herself resentfully, thinking she really should run a comb through her hair and deciding she couldn't be bothered. He wasn't even here, and she liked this sweatshirt. At least Will, with his non-existent clothes sense, wasn't likely to criticise it.

He was leaving too, heading back up to London this after-noon with the first few hours of recorded videotape under his belt. As she made her way downstairs, Estelle realised how sorry she'd be to see Will go; he was such a genuinely nice, easygoing character, which certainly made a change from Oliver's air of preoccupation and picky, often pedantic, manner.

'Oh!' Estelle stopped short in the kitchen, overwhelmed by the sight of the roasting tin, now scrubbed sparkling clean, propped up on the drainer. 'Oh Will, you didn't have to do that!'

'Hey, it's only a roasting tin. It's not as if I built a

conservatory.' Waving aside her protestations, he reached for the carrier bag on top of the fridge. 'Anyway, this is for you. A little thank you present for making me so welcome. It's not much, but . . .' As he handed it over, Estelle saw that his flapping shirtcuffs were now damp where he'd neglected to roll up his sleeves before setting to with the Brillo pad. Taking the carrier bag and opening it, she saw that it didn't contain a ham bone for Norris but an assortment of bath products. Tears sprang into her eyes as she saw that Will had bought her a bottle of lavender oil, several cellophane-wrapped bars of fruit-scented soaps, a tube of geranium foaming shower gel and a loofah.

He either thought she stank to high heaven and was keen to remedy the situation fast, or he was the sweetest, most thoughtful man she'd ever met.

'Oh Will, this is just . . .'

'Are they OK? I'm rubbish at buying presents, but the girl in the shop said they'd be fine.' Eagerly he went on, 'And I'm sorry I didn't wrap them properly but I'm hopeless at wrapping stuff up too – oh God, don't cry, *please* don't cry.' Will moved towards her, attempting to grab the bag back. 'What's the matter? Did I buy the wrong things? I know you're probably used to more expensive brands, but the people in the shop were just so friendly . . . I can't believe I've upset you like this . . .'

'You haven't, I promise.' Shaking her head vigorously, Estelle managed a watery smile. 'Will, I love my presents. It's not them and it's not you. I just . . . well, I'm not having a very good d-day, that's all, and people being unexpectedly nice to me always makes me cry. And yes, OK, maybe I *am* used to expensive brands' – the gloriously gift-wrapped baskets that Oliver ordered over the internet every Christmas from Jo Malone sprang to mind – 'but these mean so much more. You chose everything yourself and that's wonderful.'

Wiping her eyes, she hiccupped, 'Especially the loofah. Nobody's ever given me a loofah before.'

Will looked relieved. 'Really? You're not just being polite? To be honest, I'm not absolutely sure what a loofah does, but . . . hey, you're still crying. It's not just the present, is it? Come on, tell me what's wrong.'

Feeling utterly drained, Estelle allowed him to steer her onto a kitchen chair. Will took a glass down from the wall cabinet and filled it to the brim from the half-empty bottle of Beaujolais left from lunch.

'It's nothing. I'm just being silly.' Nevertheless her hand sneaked out and clutched the glass.

'You aren't being silly.' He paused. 'And I'm not stupid. I do have eyes in my head, you know.'

The room-temperature wine slipped comfortably down Estelle's throat, warming her stomach and soothing her frazzled nerve endings, but she didn't dare speak. To cover the awkward silence she took another hefty gulp instead.

'It's OK,' Will said eventually, 'I can guess what's bothering you. You're loyal to Oliver and I'm a TV journalist. But I promise you, I'm not the blabbing kind. I don't do hatchet jobs, that isn't my style. If I did,' he went on with a brief smile, 'I'd soon run out of subjects. Nobody would let me film them. So you see, it's not even in my interests to dig the dirt. You can talk to me as a friend and I swear I'd never use anything you told me. But I do think you shouldn't bottle things up. And, as I said, I do already have a pretty good idea.'

Estelle found a hanky in her pocket and blew her nose. Of course he had a pretty good idea, he was a documentary maker, for heaven's sake. Trained to observe everything and never miss a trick. Then again, he was right about it not being in his interests to dig the dirt. Having now had a chance to see videos of his previous programmes she knew that Will's style was affectionate and quirky, never under-hand or sly.

'The thing is, I know how lucky I am.' Hearing her voice wobble, Estelle took another gulp of wine to steady it. 'Living here in this beautiful house with a swimming pool, a nice car, no money worries – crikey, that's what everyone dreams of, isn't it? It's why people buy lottery tickets. And I'm healthy, I'm not dying from some horrible incurable disease. What reason do I have to moan and feel sorry for myself? But sometimes I just . . . Oh God, I don't know, most women would give their right arms to have my advantages . . .'

'But you're not happy,' Will said gently. 'And you feel guilty because you think you should be. Estelle, millions of people buy lottery tickets thinking that hitting the jackpot will solve all their problems, but only the ones who've actu-ally done it discover the truth. If you aren't happy in your-self, no amount of money will change that. It isn't going to solve fundamental problems in, say, a marriage.'

Estelle swallowed hard. It was so obvious he already knew, what was the point of even trying to deny it?

'Oliver's not a bad man.' Her voice was low. 'He doesn't drink, or beat me up, or flaunt mistresses under my nose. But sometimes he's . . . hard to handle. He has his career, he gets picky sometimes, and he can be a bit abrupt.'

'Autocratic, even,' Will suggested mildly.

'OK, yes, autocratic. But we've been together for twenty-seven years. Since I was eighteen. For heaven's sake, you'd think I'd be used to it by now.'

'He's always been the same?'

'Well, no. I mean, Oliver was always the one in charge, but that was just his character. Over the last year or so, though, it's got worse. I've started to feel completely unimportant, I don't know why I'm *here* any more, I just feel . . . pointless.' Feeling her eyes fill with tears again, Estelle took a shuddery breath. 'Fat and pointless, that's me. And I've been trying so hard to pretend nothing's wrong, but having Kate back here doesn't help. I know she doesn't mean to, but she's treating me just like Oliver does. I feel like one of those plate-spinners, rushing from plate to plate desperately trying to keep everything up in the air . . . All I want is for us to be a normal happy family, but it's just not w-working and I don't know what else I can possibly d-do . . .' Her voice breaking, Estelle covered her face with her hands and wailed, 'Because no matter how hard I try, nothing I *do* do ever seems to be good enough!'

'Hey, hey, don't blame yourself.' Will's voice was wonderfully soothing. Whereas Oliver, if he were here now, would have barked, 'Oh for God's sake, don't *cry*,' Will simply passed her a handful of kitchen roll and allowed her to get on with it. 'You mustn't blame yourself, you know. I'm sure Oliver doesn't mean to upset you. And Kate's . . . well, she's having a hard time adjusting, that's all. She's going through a prickly stage.'

Bloody prickly, thought Estelle. And in all honesty, when something had lasted for fifteen years, did it still count as a stage? She could barely remember a time when she hadn't felt intimidated by her daughter.

'But what am I supposed to do?' Blowing her nose on the kitchen roll, she watched resignedly as Will refilled her glass.

'Ah, well now, that *is* up to you. Do you want to stay with Oliver, or leave him?'

Estelle's bottom lip trembled. 'Stay, of course. I still love him, I *want* us to be happy again, I just don't know how to make it happen. I'm not even sure there's anything I *can* do. Sometimes, as far as Oliver's concerned, I just feel invisible.'

'I can't advise you,' said Will, which was a massive letdown; she'd secretly been hoping he might have the most brilliant plan. 'But if it's any consolation,' he leaned back on his chair and fixed Estelle with a smile that told her he was on her side, 'you don't deserve to be treated like that. If I were lucky enough to be married to someone like you, I'd be over the moon. Then again,' he looked almost comically disconsolate, 'who'd ever want to be saddled with a case as hopeless as me? My last girlfriend was always complaining that I looked as if I'd got dressed in the dark. She once found a mouldy sausage roll in my bathroom cabinet. And when we went to her Uncle Bill's wedding I called the bride Megan, which was the name of Uncle Bill's first wife.'

Despite everything, Estelle found herself snorting with laughter.

'That's terrible. And Megan, the first wife, was . . . ?'

'Dead.' Will heaved a sigh of resignation and nodded. 'I'm just a walking disaster. No wonder my girlfriend dumped me.'

'Just because of that?' Estelle felt absurdly indignant on his behalf. 'But anyone can make a mistake!'

'You're forgetting the sausage roll. Actually, she compiled this whole list of reasons why she deserved better than me. Read them out to me like a school register.' Will pulled a face. 'It took ages. So you see, it's no wonder I'm still single. But that's enough about me. Are you feeling any better yet?'

He'd made her laugh, with his self-deprecating humour and gentle encouragement. God knows, he was the polar opposite of Oliver, who was hardly what you'd call encouraging and who'd never been self-deprecating in his life. Smiling back at Will, Estelle nodded and discovered there was a lot to be said for getting things off your chest. She'd never confided her feelings of inadequacy before, not to a living soul. Pretending that everything was fine had always been her way of muddling through.

'Much better. You won't say anything about this to Oliver, will you?'

'I told you, you can trust me. I won't breathe a word,' Will said comfortably. As he fiddled with the damp cuff of his shirt, the button pinged off and he watched it roll across the floor. When it disappeared under the freezer he shrugged, unconcerned. 'You could always give it a go yourself, though. Sit him down and tell him how you feel.'

This really did make Estelle smile. 'We'll see.' There was more chance of her swimming the Channel with bricks strapped to her feet. 'Thanks anyway. I can't believe I've told you all this.'

'Ah well, that's me, I have a listening face.' Will tilted his head at the sound of the front door being pushed open. 'And here's Kate back now. I suppose I should be making a move.'

Estelle wished he didn't have to go. As Norris noisily emptied his water bowl, Will lugged his battered weekend bag out to the car and said his goodbyes. Feeling as if she'd lost her only ally, Estelle waved as the dusty Volkswagen bumped off down the drive. Back in the kitchen beadily eyeing first her mother then the almost empty bottle of wine, Kate said, 'What's been going on?'

'Nothing. Will helped me with the washing-up. He's a nice man, don't you think?' Quite daringly for her, Estelle said, 'So thoughtful.'

Kate's gaze narrowed as she surveyed her mother's pink-rimmed eyes.

'Have you been crying?'

For a moment Estelle hesitated, wondering how Kate would react if she blurted out the truth, just as she'd done with Will. But no, she couldn't bring herself to do it.

'Of course not.' She smiled brightly at her daughter. 'I just rubbed my eyes earlier when there was washing-up liquid on my hands. Silly me.'

'Then again, who could blame you?' Picking up the fruit-scented soaps, sniffing them and pulling a face, Kate said, 'If someone gave me this lot as a thank you present, I'd cry too.'

Chapter 19

In the Peach Tree, Juliet was writing out price labels and Maddy was on the floor unpacking a fresh consignment of plum chutney when the door clanged open and Jake erupted into the shop.

'Sorry,' said Maddy, 'no winos, no undesirables, we're a classy establishment, we are—'

'Do me a favour, just go and sit in my workshop. When a blonde in a red MG asks where I am, tell her I'm out delivering a casket. *Move*,' said Jake, grabbing hold of Maddy like a rag doll and hauling her to her feet.

Ooch, pins and needles . . .

'Say please.'

'*Please.*'

'And you'll do dinner tonight,' prompted Maddy, whose turn it was to cook.

'OK, fine, just go.'

Laughing, Maddy sauntered out and across the hot dusty road. As Jake hovered at the back of the shop, Juliet peered through the window.

'Who is it this time?'

'Her name's Emma. Luckily I was inside the workshop when she drove past, so she didn't spot me. God knows what she's doing here now. I thought she was in court today.'

Juliet's dark eyes widened. 'What did she do?'

'She's a stalker.' Grinning, Jake said, 'Actually, a solicitor.'

'She's pulling up now,' Juliet reported as the scarlet MG, having completed its U-turn, slowed to a halt outside Jake's workshop. 'Honestly, Jake, you are hopeless. If you don't want to see her, why don't you just tell the poor girl? Put her out of her misery.'

'I have told her! She won't take no for an answer! We only went out a couple of times. I didn't even sleep with her,' Jake protested.

'Really?'

'I didn't! And I told her it was over last week, *really nicely.*'

'Let me guess,' said Juliet. 'You're a great girl, Emma, it's not you, it's me. All the usual tosh.'

'Well, yes.' Jake looked hurt. 'What's wrong with that? I can hardly say it's not me, it's you, can I? Anyway, I gave it my best shot, thought I'd done a good job. But she won't accept it, she keeps phoning me, it's really awkward, *and* she drove past the cottage last night.'

'Maddy's talking to her now,' Juliet announced. 'She's pointing over here . . . Crikey, Emma's heading this way, she's taking a knife out of her handbag.'

'You're not serious.'

'Of course I'm not serious. Ha, had you going though, serves you right for being so irresistible.' Clearly amused, Juliet moved away from the window. 'It's OK, Emma's climbing back into her car. She's driving off now. You're safe. And who said you could have that?' She eyed the apricot Danish Jake had filched from the glass cabinet.

'Stress makes me hungry. God, why does life have to be so complicated?' grumbled Jake.

'That's what happens when you're a professional love rat. Go around breaking girls' hearts and you'll get grief,' Juliet said cheerfully. 'That's just the way it goes. Maybe it's time you thought about meeting someone nice and settling down.'

Had she and Maddy been discussing him behind his back?

'Pot, kettle.' Swallowing a mouthful of Danish, Jake gave her a pointed look. 'Anyway, speaking of girls getting their hearts broken, what's Maddy playing at? Has she told you who she's seeing?' He made it sound as if *he* knew but was wondering if Juliet had been let in on the secret.

'No,' Juliet lied, perfectly well aware that Jake didn't know and would certainly hit the roof if he did. 'Just that he's married. Here she comes now,' she added. 'And don't nag her about it, OK? Because nagging won't help.'

Jake had already guessed that Juliet would be on Maddy's side. Tiff's father had been a married man. Beyond that, no details were known; he and Juliet may have been friends for years, but Juliet had remained resolutely silent on the subject. Privately, Jake wondered how anyone, married or otherwise, could have dumped Juliet.

'All sorted.' Maddy, looking pleased with herself, re-entered the shop and sat back down cross-legged on the floor in front of her jars of plum chutney.

'Well? What happened?' said Jake.

'I told her you'd been battling with your sexuality.'

Jake choked on his Danish pastry. 'Excuse me?'

'But that you'd reached a decision at last, and from now on you were only going to go out with people with hairy chests.'

'You're joking.' Juliet's eyes sparkled. 'And she actually believed you?'

'I'm not joking at all,' said Maddy, 'and no, of course she didn't believe me, but it did the trick. She said, "Jake doesn't want to see me any more, does he?" and I said, "Sorry, no he doesn't." So she did that wobbly-lip thing and said, "I thought we had something special together," and I said, "Trust me, he's not worth it, he's not special at all."'

'Thanks,' said Jake.

'You're welcome. So after that Emma said, "Tell him I won't phone him again, I promise, but he's got my number if he changes his mind." Then she climbed back into her car and drove off, still trying not to cry. So there you go,' Maddy concluded cheerfully, 'I've done your dirty work for you. I think we'll have lasagne tonight.'

Jake, who knew when he was beaten, turned to Juliet. 'Fancy bringing Tiff over? If I'm making lasagne, may as well make a big one.'

'Great,' said Juliet, because lasagne was Jake's signature dish. 'I'll bring a bottle. What time, sevenish?'

'Actually, can we eat earlier than that?' Maddy did her best to sound casual. 'I'm going out at seven.'

Opening his mouth to say something caustic, Jake caught Juliet's look of warning and closed it again.

'Fine. We'll lock the kids in the attic and have a romantic candlelit evening together, just the two of us.' Winking at Maddy, he said, 'She won't be able to resist me.'

'Or,' Juliet said prosaically, 'we could play Scrabble.'

'*Oof*,' Kate gasped as the small boy, barrelling round the corner of the pub, ran full tilt into her stomach.

Tiff, staggering backwards in the wake of the impact, gazed up in horror at Kate and wailed, 'Oh no, my ice cream!'

The chocolate ice cream he'd been clutching had ricocheted out of his hand and landed with a soft *phut* on the pavement, the cornet sticking out like Pinocchio's nose.

It served him right, of course, but that was boys for you. Kate found herself feeling quite sorry for him.

'You shouldn't have been running so fast,' she said kindly, because tears were now welling up in the boy's blue eyes.

She didn't see why she should have to buy him another one, it wasn't her fault after all, but in all likelihood she probably would. 'It's OK, don't cry – oh, look at Norris, he's such a pig.' Smiling nicely to cheer the boy up, she nodded at Norris, who was enthusiastically slurping away at the ice cream and chomping up the cone.

'I-I'm sorry,' the boy whispered, backing away from Kate in dismay.

She knew who he was. He belonged to Juliet Price, who ran the delicatessen. His name was Tiff, that was it, and he spent most of his time with Jake's daughter Sophie. With his messy white-blond hair and startlingly bright eyes, he was actually rather sweet looking. Abruptly, it dawned on Kate that the cause of his terror could be the sight of her own scarred face. Hurriedly she dug into her back pocket for a couple of pound coins. Determined to show him she wasn't as scary as she looked, she said encouragingly, 'Here, don't worry, I'll get you an even better ice cream – aaarrghh!'

Belatedly glancing down, Kate discovered the real reason for the boy's agitation. The front of her trousers was sporting a brown stain the size of a baked potato, complete with splatter marks and drips all down one leg. She gazed at the mess in paralysed disbelief. This couldn't have happened while she was wearing her usual jeans, could it? Oh no, of course not, because life didn't work that way, did it? Instead, it had to happen on the one day she was wearing her brand new cream linen John Galliano trousers.

Kate's head felt as if it might explode with the effort it took not to scream and hurl abuse.

'Had a bit of an accident, have we?' Dexter Nevin, emerging from the pub, eyed Kate's trousers with ill-concealed amusement.

'They're Galliano.' Kate spat the words through gritted teeth. 'I bought them in Bloomingdale's.'

'Ah well.' Dexter shrugged easily. 'I'm more of a Next man myself.'

'They cost a *fortune*.'

'I said s-sorry.' Tiff turned fearfully to Dexter. 'It was an accident, I promise.'

'Oh, for crying out loud.' Before he had a chance to burst into fully-fledged sobs, Kate shoved the pound coins into the boy's hand. 'Just be more careful next time, OK?'

'I thought you were going to kick him,' said Dexter when Tiff had disappeared in a cloud of dust.

'Don't think I wasn't tempted.' Kate grimaced. 'But you'd only have called the NSPCC.'

'If you come inside, I'll lend you a cloth.'

'Oh yes, that'll do the trick.' Kate sighed. 'A nice greasy dishcloth, that'll really work. OK, stop it, it's all gone now,' she told Norris, who was greedily Hoovering up the last remnants of ice cream with a slurp and a flourish.

'You never know, we might be able to rustle up a clean dishcloth,' Dexter said mildly. 'You can bring him in with you, you know. We're a dog-friendly pub.'

'You don't say. I didn't think you were anything-friendly.'

He laughed at the truculent look on Kate's face. 'Animals are fine. It's humans I have a problem with. So are you coming in or aren't you?'

Kate hesitated for a moment, then shook her head.

'I'll get home. These'll have to go to the dry cleaners in Bath.'

'Don't mention it,' Dexter called after her as she headed towards Gypsy Lane.

Turning, Kate shielded her eyes from the sun and scowled. '*What?*'

'Sorry.' Dexter was standing there with his hands on his narrow hips, smirking at her. 'I thought I heard you say thanks.'

Chapter 20

At Dauncey House, Kate found her parents out in the garden around the pool. Estelle, wearing a black tankini that cruelly emphasised her bulging midriff, was valiantly attempting to read last year's Booker prizewinner. Since Danielle Steel was more her line of country, this was an exercise doomed to failure, on a par with expecting a stroppy teenager to enjoy sheep's eyeballs in aspic.

Looking up, only too glad to be distracted from her book, Estelle cried, 'Oh, darling, whatever happened?'

'They're bloody ruined, that's what happened.' As Kate showed her mother the damage to her trousers, Oliver swung round and she realised he was on the phone.

'Yes, yes, that's Kate you just heard.' He paused, then smiled at Kate and said, 'Will says hi.'

In no mood to exchange pointless pleasantries, Kate said, 'It's chocolate ice cream, it's never going to come out and they're my best trousers.'

'Oh darling, you don't know that, maybe we can soak them in Ariel,' suggested Estelle. 'How did it get there?'

'That bloody kid from the deli ran straight into me. I could have strangled him.'

'Tiff Price?' said Estelle. 'Juliet's little lad? Oh, he's a poppet, I'm sure he didn't mean to do it.'

Oh well, that was all right then.

'My trousers are *ruined.*' Kate's voice rose in exasperation. 'They cost me six hundred dollars!'

'Kate,' Oliver chided, 'you're overreacting. He bumped into you, it was an *accident.* Dear me, anyone would think you'd been stabbed.'

Eyes narrowed, Kate watched her father return to his phone conversation, laughing off the incident as if it was nothing at all. She vividly recalled once, as a child, spilling Coca-Cola over some business documents and Oliver yelling furiously at her until she'd burst into tears. Yet here he was now, acting all ultra-reasonable and telling her not to make such a fuss, purely because Will was listening on the other end of the phone and Oliver was determined to create a good impression and demonstrate that he truly was an all-round great guy.

Nuala, snuggled up in bed, thought happily that, contrary to what other people might think, life with Dexter wasn't all bad.

It was four o'clock on Friday afternoon and they'd been making the most of their precious free time in the nicest possible way. The pub had closed at two thirty and would re-open at six. Having reacquainted themselves with each other's bodies, a little doze was now in order, then maybe—

'Nu, fancy a cup of tea?'

See? He was all right really. Smiling to herself, Nuala wriggled and said, 'Mmm, lovely.'

'Great. Make me one while you're at it.'

'Oh, not fair.' Nuala groaned, tugging the tartan cotton duvet more tightly around her and nudging Dexter's legs with her feet. 'I'm sleepy.'

Dexter nudged her in the ribs. 'Me too. Come on, it's your turn.'

This was true; he had brought her a cup of tea in bed this morning. OK, so it had been way too strong and he'd forgotten to put any sugar in, but it had, technically, been a cup of tea.

'OK, we'll just have a little sleep first,' Nuala bargained, 'then I'll make it.'

Whisking the duvet off her and rolling her efficiently out of bed, Dexter said, 'No, *now.*'

'You're so mean.' Grumbling, Nuala covered her nakedness with her oversized white towelling dressing gown.

'I'm not, I'm just helping you use up a few more calories.' Lying back against the pillows with his hands resting behind his head, he winked at her.

Nuala weakened; when Dexter was happy, she was happy. He might not be the most perfect specimen physically – his rumpled brown hair was starting to recede and he was developing a paunch – but there was still that indefinable something about him that got to her every time. And let's face it, if he were drop-dead gorgeous he would never have been interested in her in the first place.

As she reached the door, Nuala warned, 'Don't fall asleep before I get back.'

'Wouldn't dream of it.' Dexter turned onto his side. 'Zzzzz . . .'

The dressing gown, miles too big for her, had been appropriated from a hotel by Dexter during a precious weekend away together last year. When he'd presented it to her, she'd been guiltily delighted. A week later, the hotel had written to Dexter billing him for the stolen dressing gown. Laughing, he'd chucked the letter in the bin. Nuala, mortified, had fished it out and secretly settled the account herself. The really annoying thing was that if she'd known she'd be paying seventy quid for a dressing gown, she would have at least bought one that was the right size.

Anyway, tea, thought Nuala as she made her way downstairs, and maybe a spot of pâté on toast then, who knows, perhaps they might even go for a repeat—

Aaarrgh.

Oh *God* . . .

'*Ow!*' screamed Nuala, crashing down the stairs like a skittle. 'Ow, ow, *ouch*.'

Twenty seconds later Dexter appeared at the top of the staircase.

'What's all the racket? Bloody hell, Nu, what are you doing on the floor?'

'Fell down.' Nuala managed to get the words out through teeth gritted with pain. 'Tripped over the hem of my dressing gown. Oh fuck, it hurts. Dexter, it really *hurts*!'

Naked, he made his way down the stairs and helped Nuala into a sitting position. Supporting her with his strong arms, he studied her face.

'Bit of a shiner there. Teeth feel OK?'

Tentatively checking with her tongue, Nuala nodded.

'Well, that's good. You're going to look like a boxer with that eye. And you've got a bump on your forehead, but no blood. You'll live,' he reassured her.

'My shoulder . . .' Nuala gasped, feeling sick with the pain, and Dexter gently pulled back the lapel of the dressing gown.

'Looks like you've broken your collarbone. How's the rest of you? Back? Legs?'

Bracing herself, Nuala moved her legs, then her spine. 'They're OK.'

'Right, just stay here, don't try to move.'

For a terrifying moment Nuala thought he was heading back to bed. As he rose to his feet she whimpered, 'Where are you going?'

'To get some clothes on, you idiot. I'm taking you to casualty.'

By the time Nuala emerged from her hospital cubicle with her left shoulder securely strapped and her arm in a sling, it was seven in the evening.

Maddy, waiting in reception, rushed to meet her.

'You look terrible!'

'Thanks.' Nuala had already seen her face in the bathroom mirror; her eye had blackened dramatically over the course of the last three hours. 'Are you giving me a lift home?'

'No, I thought I'd make you hitch a lift. Of course I'm giving you a lift home.' Maddy's expression softened as she held the door open to let Nuala through. 'You poor thing, does it really hurt?'

'They gave me some pills. Thanks for coming to pick me up. God, I'm such a twit.' Nuala's smile was self-deprecating as they made their way towards the car park. 'And now look at me. Clumsy or what?'

'Hmm,' said Maddy.

What was 'hmm' supposed to mean? Trying to laugh, Nuala said, 'Did Dexter tell you how it happened?' Having spent the first hour with her in the waiting room, Dexter had been forced to leave her there and drive back to Ashcombe in order to open the pub at six. He'd promised to find someone to come and pick her up and Nuala had been glad he'd managed to get Maddy. Dexter was just as likely to have sent along one of his cider-guzzling regulars on a tractor.

'He said you'd tripped on your dressing gown and fallen down the stairs,' said Maddy. She stopped, regarding Nuala gravely. 'Is that true?'

'Why wouldn't it be true?' Mystified, Nuala said, 'My dressing gown's too big for me. I got the hem caught under my foot and went flying. Poor Dexter, gave him the shock of his life! Oh, but he was so sweet, looking after me and carrying me to the car. He even had to put my knickers on for me because I couldn't reach past my—'

'Nuala, listen. This is me. We're friends, aren't we? You can tell me.' Maddy gave her a meaningful look.

'Tell you *what*?'

'Look at yourself. Black eye, bruised forehead, cracked collarbone. Come on now,' said Maddy, her tone supportive.

Realisation finally dawned. Nuala's eyebrows shot up as if she'd been electrocuted.

'My God, I don't believe it, you think Dexter did this to me! You actually think *he* gave me a black eye and chucked me down the stairs!'

'Didn't he?' said Maddy.

'Of course he didn't!' Her voice rising in disbelief, Nuala tried to stamp her foot and flinched as the sudden movement jarred her shoulder. 'I can't believe it even crossed your mind. Dexter's never laid a finger on me, he'd *never* hurt me!' Shaking her head – ooch, more pain – she said, 'And you have to believe me, because I swear to God that's the truth. You can strap me to one of those lie detectors if you want—'

'OK, OK.' Maddy nodded, to show she believed her. 'I'm sorry. I just had to ask.'

They'd reached the car. Carefully, Nuala climbed into the passenger seat.

'But why? Why would you even think that?' Even as the words came out, deep down Nuala already knew the answer. Oh Lord, did this mean everyone in Ashcombe was going to think Dexter had beaten her up?

'Well, you and Dexter . . . the way he is . . . I mean, you just said he'd never hurt you.' Maddy could be horribly blunt when she wanted. 'But he does sometimes, doesn't he? Maybe not physically, but verbally. When he calls you a lazy lump or a fat-arsed camel. You can't tell me you enjoy it.'

Her cheeks flaming, Nuala said defensively, 'He does it to everyone, that's just Dexter's way. When we're on our own he's *lovely* to me—'

'Wrong. No.' Maddy was shaking her head. 'He doesn't do it to everyone. He's brusque, he's sarcastic, he can be downright cantankerous, but he doesn't verbally abuse the rest of us. Only you, because he knows he can get away with it. And a man who treats you like that in public – well, you can't blame us for wondering what else he might do when the two of you are on your own.'

Nuala gazed blindly out of the side window, hot with shame. Everyone *was* going to assume she was a battered girlfriend. With a shudder, she imagined the regulars in the pub eyeing each other meaningfully, muttering behind their hands, watching her and Dexter and drawing their own wrong conclusions every time he came out with one of his mock derogatory remarks.

'I'll talk to him about it,' she said. 'Tell him he has to stop, you know, saying those things.'

Maddy drove out of the car park. 'Right, you do that.'

She sounded horribly unconvinced.

'I *will*. Don't give me one of your looks,' Nuala protested. 'God, I'm not going to be able to work for weeks.' She plucked gingerly at her sling. 'How's Dexter going to manage without me in the pub?'

'Grumpily, I'd imagine.' Swinging round a corner, Maddy said, 'He's already asked me if I'll help out tonight.'

'Really? And are you?'

'No chance. I've already made plans.'

'Great.' Mischievously Nuala said, 'Can I come along with you?'

A faint smile tugged at the corners of Maddy's mouth.

'How can I put this? Not a chance in the world.'

Chapter 21

'Come on, you stupid animal.' Kate tugged at Norris's lead as he dawdled along like a recalcitrant toddler. It was Saturday afternoon, the temperature had shot up into the nineties and she was beginning to regret this attempt at a longer than usual walk.

Since embarking on a keep-fit plan for Norris, they had done their best to restrict his eating, but last night he had wolfed down an entire Dundee cake that had been carelessly left out in the kitchen by Estelle. Today, in an effort to work off a few of the ten thousand or so calories he had guzzled in ninety seconds flat, Kate had changed into jeans and trainers and resolved to bring him out on the equivalent of a doggie marathon. Leaving the village behind them, they had set out along Ashcombe Lane, the hilly, winding road that would eventually take them into Bath. Not that they'd get that far, but at least the scenery was spectacular and it made a change from endlessly circling Ashcombe itself.

Feeling like an American sergeant major harassing the latest unfit arrival at boot camp, Kate chivvied Norris past a promising clump of creamy white cow parsley – he could spend forever searching for the perfect place to pee – and dragged him on up the hill. Huffing and grunting in protest, Norris waddled more slowly than ever. Honestly, at this rate *ants* would be overtaking them.

'Not much further,' said Kate, pushing her hair back from her face as they reached the brow of the hill and the wall of trees ahead of them came into sight. 'Norris, you really are hopeless, it hasn't even been two miles yet.'

By the time they reached the entrance to Hillview, Norris had had more than enough. When Kate stopped walking he sank down onto the grass verge with a grunt of relief. The road was deserted in both directions. The sun blazed relentlessly down. Norris's tongue, attractively, was lolling sideways out of his mouth.

'Two miles,' Kate told him. 'Well done, you. One day you'll have more muscles than Schwarzenegger.'

Then, turning, she gazed once more at the battered sign, half hidden by ivy. She hadn't deliberately planned this, not *really* deliberately. If Norris had been skipping along like a spring chicken, more than happy to set off back home, then that's what they would have done. But seeing as he was on his last legs and clearly desperate for a drink, well, it would be cruel to deprive him. And where was the harm, anyway, in knocking on Pauline McKinnon's front door to ask for a bowl of water? The advantage of calling on someone who was a recluse was that they were bound to be home. She could talk to Mrs McKinnon, casually ask her how Kerr was doing these days, maybe hear some news about him.

And if the woman was so reclusive she refused to answer the door, Kate remembered there had been a decorative stone water trough and a small pond to the side of the house, years ago. Since they were unlikely to have been removed, Norris could still have a drink.

Norris groaned when she attempted to pull him to his feet. Bending over, Kate hauled him up into her arms – God, he weighed a ton, it was like carrying the world's fattest baby – and headed up the bumpy, weed-strewn driveway.

Her heart leaped into her mouth as she rounded the last

bend and saw the car parked on the gravel. A gleaming midnight-blue Mercedes – surely this was the one that had passed her that day on Gypsy Lane. Oh good grief, Kerr must actually *be* here now, in the house, visiting his mother . . .

With adrenalin swooshing through her body – whether it was due to terror or excitement she couldn't tell – Kate clumsily shifted her hold on Norris, freeing one of her hands just enough to be able to comb her fingers frantically through her hair and rub the beads of perspiration from her upper lip. She really hadn't been expecting this, but was it such a bad thing to have happened? Maybe it was fate bringing them together today, maybe they were *meant* to meet again and when Kerr saw her he wouldn't even notice her scars . . .

OK, so maybe that was a fantasy too far, not even Stevie Wonder could fail to notice these scars, but Kerr would see them and instantly, magically, dismiss them because *she* was all that mattered, her personality was what was important and he didn't give a toss about physical imperfections.

Shit, shit, shit. Kate ground to an abrupt halt. Having ventured another twenty yards up the drive she was now able to see a second car parked behind Kerr's Mercedes. A silver Saab.

A silver Saab, silver Saab – the wheels were clicking in Kate's brain. She'd seen it before, parked in the Main Street outside – God, outside Jake Harvey's workshop. But this made no sense. Why would it be parked here now? Either Pauline McKinnon had just died and Jake was measuring her up for one of his bespoke coffins or Jake and Kerr were gay, conducting a furtive homosexual affair.

Creeping up the driveway, taking care not to crunch the gravel, Kate lowered her face to Norris's fat neck and shushed him before he could even think of betraying her with a bark. Approaching the house, she veered away from the front door and headed over to the long sash windows of the sitting room. Her pulse was thundering now, crashing against her ribs. If the silver Saab belonged to Jake, what on earth could he be doing here?

Breathing shallowly, Kate reached the sitting-room window at last. Clutching Norris tightly in her arms, she half knelt, half crouched in the untended flowerbed and peered inside.

What she saw made her cry out in disbelief.

The sitting room was empty but the house was narrow, longer than it was broad, with a clear view, via the two sets of windows at the front and back of the house, through to the back garden.

And there was Kerr, not with Jake Harvey at all, but with Maddy.

With with Maddy, that much was self-evident. Feeling as though she'd been punched in the stomach, Kate realised that what she was seeing here was a couple who were, without question, a *couple*.

Maddy was wearing a pink bikini. She lay on her front on a green and blue striped rug, smiling at something Kerr said as he massaged suncream into her back. Suddenly twisting round and seizing the bottle of Evian at her side, she squirted water at Kerr. He in turn grabbed her, pinning her down and tickling her until she shrieked for mercy. Still rooted to the spot, Kate watched him kiss Maddy, and Maddy's arms winding round his neck. Kerr, wearing only dark glasses and a pair of white shorts, was as tanned and athletically constructed as she remembered. His hands were roaming over Maddy's back . . . God, it was almost impossible to take in, Kerr McKinnon and Maddy Harvey, cavorting together in the garden.

More to the point, where was Pauline McKinnon while all this was going on?

Stunned, but realising that she could hardly stroll round

to the back of the house and ask them, Kate slipped away from the window and headed back down the driveway. Norris weighed a ton but she didn't dare put him down. Spotting the lily-strewn pond, he began to whimper pathetically, but Kate ignored him. Maddy and Kerr. It was unbelievable; surely Marcella couldn't know about this.

Feeling hotter and wearier than ever, Kate reached the bottom of the drive and unceremoniously plonked Norris down on all fours. Norris promptly lay down in the road and closed his eyes, tongue lolling and baggy jowls drooping in defeat.

So much for being offered a lift home by Kerr McKinnon. With a sigh, Kate pulled out her mobile and called a taxi company to come and pick them up.

At nine thirty on Sunday morning, Dexter Nevin was outside the Fallen Angel watering his hanging baskets when he heard footsteps coming down the road. Swivelling round on his ladder, he saw the answer to his prayers heading along the Main Street towards him.

Well, let's face it, he was desperate.

'Morning.' Dexter's mouth twitched at the look of disdain Kate shot him. Her face might be less than perfect but she had an enviable figure, he'd say that much for her; in low-slung khaki cargo pants and a tiny white cropped top, she moved like a catwalk model. Lithe, that was the word he was after. Maybe even slinky. Shame about the stroppy manner, but beggars couldn't afford to be choosers.

'Morning.' Kate's reply was cool.

She was on her way to the shop, Dexter guessed, to pick up the Sunday papers.

'You know, I could do you a favour.'

That stopped her in her tracks.

'Sorry?' said Kate suspiciously.

'Well, we could do each other a favour.' Dexter climbed down from the stepladder and began gathering up the coils of garden hose. 'Nuala's off work for a while – the clumsy article fell downstairs and cracked her collarbone. So,' he paused and surveyed Kate speculatively, 'how about you taking her place?'

'As a barmaid, you mean?'

'Of course as a barmaid. I wasn't actually suggesting you hop into my bed.' Dexter did his best to keep a straight face. 'Then again, it's entirely up to you, if that's one of your conditions—'

'Let me get this straight,' Kate interrupted. 'You want me to come and work for you, behind your bar, because your regular barmaid has a fractured collarbone. So, I'm sorry, but how exactly would *you* be doing *me* a favour?'

'You're bored to tears,' Dexter said bluntly, 'rattling around in that big old house up the hill. You spend all your time walking that fat dog of yours because you don't have anything else to do. I'm telling you, it's no life for a girl your age. A bit of socialising, that's what you need. Trust me, it'd work wonders. Because moping around feeling sorry for yourself isn't doing you any good at all.'

'Blimey, you must be desperate,' said Kate.

'Of course I'm desperate.' Dexter broke into an unrepentant grin. 'I've asked practically everyone else in the village and they've all turned me down.'

Kate widened her eyes. 'No. How *could* they? You'd think they'd be clamouring to work for someone with such a sparkling personality.'

'Ever done bar work before?'

'No, and I have no plans to start now.' Bar work, ugh; Kate suppressed a shudder of revulsion.

'Don't you look down your nose at me,' Dexter retaliated. 'You're not tall enough, for a start.'

Indignantly Kate took a step back as he advanced towards her.

'Miss Hoity Toity,' Dexter murmured, softening the insult with a faint smile. 'You think it'd be so far beneath you, don't you? It hasn't even occurred to you that this could be the answer to all your prayers.'

Oh for heaven's sake, was the man on drugs? Frostily Kate said, 'I promise you, it wouldn't.'

'Trust me,' said Dexter. 'Just give it a try. Today, twelve 'til four. If you don't like it, you don't have to do it again. But I still think you might be pleasantly surprised.'

Kate hesitated. One half of her couldn't believe she was even considering his offer. Then again, what if Dexter was right? And she *was* bored to tears, with nothing to do all day long other than drag Norris out on walks he passionately didn't want to take.

'What about my face?' Blurting out the question, she forced herself to meet Dexter's gaze. 'Aren't you scared I'll frighten away the customers?'

By way of reply, he stuck his fingers in the corners of his mouth and gave an ear-splitting whistle. Moments later the bedroom window above him was thrown open and Nuala, clearly used to being summoned like a dog, popped her head out.

'Now you see why I asked you.' Dexter casually indicated Nuala's spectacular black eye and dramatically bruised forehead. 'See? Compared with that, you're Nicole Kidman.'

'Flattery will get you everywhere,' said Kate.

'Ooh, are you going to be our new barmaid?' Hanging precariously out of the window, surrounded by a picturesque tangle of wisteria, Nuala looked delighted.

'She hasn't said yes yet,' Dexter announced. 'I'm still working my mysterious magic on her.' And he surveyed Kate with an expression of such infuriating self-confidence that for a moment she was tempted to slap him, hard.

Instead, a vision of the rest of her day intervened, hours and hours of boredom stretching endlessly ahead, and Kate found herself saying, 'OK, just this once. I'll give it a go.'

'There you are.' Dexter nodded with satisfaction. 'Wasn't so hard, was it?'

Against her better judgement, Kate found herself smiling. Shaking her head in disbelief, she murmured, 'Mysterious magic indeed.'

'Didn't think I had any, did you? You see, that's what makes it so mysterious.' As he wound up the last of the garden hose, Dexter winked at her. 'Works every time.'

Chapter 22

Sunday lunchtimes were one of the busiest sessions of the week at the Angel. A child-friendly pub selling excellent food, it attracted customers from miles around. Following a crash course in pouring pints and fathoming out the till, Kate was so rushed off her feet she barely had time to be self-conscious about her face. Occasionally, glancing up, she caught customers she didn't know gazing at her with a mixture of pity and horror, but the regulars had grown used to her, had seen her walking Norris around Ashcombe often enough by now for the novelty of her scars to have worn off.

Much to her amazement, Kate was enjoying herself. The pointy lace-edged sleeves of her white shirt were wrecked from dangling in the drip trays, but she'd wear something more sensible next time. On the plus side, everyone was so cheerful – apart from Dexter of course – and friendly. But even working behind the narrow bar with someone as professionally grumpy as Dexter Nevin somehow managed to be fun. Every time he berated a hapless customer, Kate promptly berated him in return. She flatly refused to take any nonsense. In no time at all they were like a long-established double act, and the more they bickered the more the customers enjoyed it.

'You've got the knack,' said Nuala, lost in admiration.

Perched on a leather upholstered bar stool with one arm in a sling and the other clutching a half of lager, she was discreetly advising Kate whenever advice was required. 'Stop, not Pepsi Cola.' She lowered her voice as Kate reached for a bottle. 'When someone asks for whisky and pep, they mean peppermint. The cordial bottle next to the lime.'

'That's disgusting. Whisky and peppermint?' Kate made a face. 'That shouldn't be allowed.'

'Shift your fat bottom, let me squeeze past,' bellowed Dexter, carrying four brimming pints of Blackthorn.

Using the steel tongs, Kate picked a cluster of ice cubes out of the ice bucket and deftly dropped them down the front of Dexter's denim shirt. His whole body stiffened, his eyes widened, but like the pro he was, he didn't spill a drop of cider.

'I do not have a fat bottom,' Kate said clearly, 'and I don't appreciate being spoken to like that. So just *stop it*, OK?'

After a brief stunned silence, a cheer went up around the bar. Unable to resist it, Kate curtsied to the applauding regulars.

'Oh God,' Dexter gave a snort of disgust, 'don't encourage her. She'll be unbearable.'

'If you want to keep your staff,' said Kate, 'try treating them with a bit of respect.'

'If you want to keep your job,' Dexter rejoined, 'you'll get this ice out of my shirt.'

'I think you're forgetting who needs who here.' Blithely, Kate busied herself with the next order.

'Come here.' Standing up on her barstool and leaning across the bar, Nuala lovingly unfastened the bottom button on Dexter's shirt with her good hand and shook out the lumps of ice. 'See? There are still some things I can do.'

Having assumed that no one else in Ashcombe would be aware of Maddy's affair with Kerr McKinnon, Kate began to think she'd got it wrong. Maddy herself had only popped into the pub briefly at one o'clock to return a video she'd borrowed from Nuala. Feeling like a spy in possession of classified information, Kate had stayed in the background stacking the dishwasher while Maddy and Nuala chatted at the bar. Maddy, looking sunkissed and golden in a pale yellow halter-neck top and black Capri pants, had glanced at Kate then turned away again without saying anything. Before long, jangling silver bracelets and wafting perfume as she waved goodbye, she was off again, her departure provoking a round of good-natured joking amongst the locals. A couple of them pressed Nuala for details but she just shrugged, professing her total innocence. The locals then turned their attention to Jake, who had sauntered in from the pub garden to fetch a lemonade and a packet of crisps for Sophie.

'Come on, Jake, tell us what that sister of yours is up to,' complained Alfie Archer from Archer's farm. 'Pops in for two minutes, then we don't see her for dust. Can't tell us there isn't something suspicious going on. Who's the latest lucky chap?'

'Sorry, Alfie, my lips are sealed. Not allowed to talk about it.' Gravely Jake shook his head. 'Marcella's orders. Let's just say she's not thrilled about Maddy's choice in men.'

Hmm, thought Kate. Interesting.

When Dexter called time at four o'clock, Kate realised that despite the sopping wet lacy sleeves and aching feet, she had in fact thoroughly enjoyed herself. She almost laughed out loud when Dexter pressed a twenty-pound note into her hand – she bought lipsticks that cost more than that. Were there really people in this country who survived on wages of five pounds an hour?

'You're not bad,' said Dexter, which Kate realised was his way of telling her that, in barmaiding terms, she was phenomenal. 'How about tonight?'

As Kate piled up the washed and dried ashtrays, she caught sight of Jake and his daughter making their way back through the pub. 'Fine,' she said absently, her heart leaping with foolish anticipation. Along with most of the pub regulars, Jake and Sophie were heading over to the cricket pitch to watch the match being played out between Ashcombe's first (and only) eleven and the team from neighbouring Monkton Combe. Not wanting to go home, Kate was counting on Jake to invite her along, not because she fancied him or anything, purely because it was the kind of sociable, easygoing offer he would make. Plus, of course, it would be interesting to hear more about his views on Maddy's liaison with Kerr.

'Seven o'clock we open,' said Dexter.

'Soph,' Jake called over his shoulder, 'come along.'

'I'm off then. See you back here at seven.' Hastily squeezing past Dexter, Kate just managed to reach the front door at the same time as Jake, Sophie and Bean.

'Hi. Was that fun?' Jake greeted her with that devastating surfer's smile of his and Kate's stomach promptly disappeared.

'Not so bad. I'm working again tonight.' She prayed she didn't sound as hopelessly out of practice as she felt. 'Um . . . going up to the cricket?'

'That's the plan. Soph, stay on the pavement,' Jake instructed as Sophie and the little dog raced ahead, 'and don't let Bean off the lead. That animal's a nightmare with cricket balls,' he told Kate. 'It's her life's ambition to disembowel one.'

Rather awkwardly, they were by this time outside the pub and Jake still hadn't invited her to join them. Out of sheer desperation, Kate heard herself saying hurriedly, 'Plenty of interest in Maddy's new chap then, by the sound of things.'

Jake raised an eyebrow, then shrugged.

'You said your mum wasn't thrilled,' Kate persisted, pulling a face. 'I'd have called that the understatement of the year.'

'Marcella's been talking about it, has she? Well, I suppose she was bound to tell Estelle. Of course, she doesn't approve,' said Jake, 'that goes without saying. But Maddy's over eighteen. You can't stop her doing what she wants, even if you know she's making a big mistake.'

They were starting to move now, heading down Main Street towards the war memorial, from where she could either turn left up Gypsy Lane or carry on round to the right with Jake.

'I have to say, I'm impressed,' Kate went on, to keep the momentum going. 'Last week, all I did was mention his name and Marcella went completely ballistic. I thought her head was going to explode. Of course, maybe she's had time to get used to the idea now.'

Next to her Jake slowed, gave her an odd sideways look. Casually he said, 'What did you say to Marcella?'

'Just that I thought I'd seen him driving past our house. It was completely innocent,' Kate insisted. 'I had no idea that anything was going on between him and Maddy, I only wondered where he was living because I suppose I'd assumed he was still in London. Anyway, as soon as I mentioned Kerr's name, Marcella went bananas.'

'*Kerr?*' Jake stopped dead in his tracks. He swung round, his green eyes boring into hers. 'Kerr McKinnon?'

Confused, Kate stammered, 'W-well, yes, but you already knew that. Oh God.' She felt the blood drain from her face in horror. 'You *didn't* know? But all that stuff about Marcella not being thrilled—'

'All Marcella knows is that Maddy's seeing a married man,' Jake said soberly. 'That's what she isn't thrilled about. If she found out it was Kerr McKinnon – well, heads would definitely explode. How do you know about this anyway?' He gave her a sharp look. 'Who told you?'

Rather wishing she hadn't raised the subject now, but at the same time experiencing a tiny flicker of schadenfreude, Kate said, 'I saw them together.' Then, because nobody liked a peeping Tom, she added hastily, 'In his car.'

'But they were definitely together?'

'Oh yes. Absolutely.' The image of Maddy and Kerr cavorting semi-naked on the lawn was indelibly imprinted on her mind.

'Right.' Jake's expression was grim.

Clearly he was intending to confront Maddy, and not in a supportive brotherly way. Beginning to envisage the repercussions, Kate said, 'Look, don't involve me in this. I'm not exactly Maddy's favourite person as it is.'

'Right now, she isn't my favourite person either,' said Jake.

'I'm serious.' Kate clutched his arm. 'I've just started working at the pub, this is important to me. Don't tell Maddy it was me who told you,' she begged Jake. 'Promise.'

He looked at her, then nodded. 'OK, I promise. You did a good job in the pub today, by the way.'

'Thanks, I—'

'Sophie, get down from there,' Jake yelled, spotting his daughter making her wobbly way along the top of the bridge over the River Ash. 'If you fall in I'm not rescuing you. Look, I'll see you around,' he told Kate distractedly, setting off up Ashcombe Road and leaving her standing by the memorial.

'Yes, fine. Bye.' Attempting to sound casual but actually feeling bereft and abandoned, Kate watched him go. Oh well, cricket was boring anyway.

She just hoped Jake wouldn't forget his promise.

Chapter 23

As she pushed open the front door of Snow Cottage at ten o'clock that evening, Maddy realised that she'd at last discovered the true meaning of the expression dancing on air. She actually knew how it *felt*, and it was as addictive as any drug. Once you'd danced on air, how could you ever be satisfied with trudging on boring old ground again?

'Good time?' Jake glanced up from his computer screen.

'Not so bad.' Maddy beamed, flinging her car keys onto the dresser and suppressing the urge to do a little jig to show him just how deliriously happy she was. A little jig several inches above floor level, needless to say. David Blaine, watch out.

Stretching and leaning back on his chair, Jake raked his fingers through his dishevelled blond hair. 'His wife's been here.'

'What?' Halfway to the kitchen to put the kettle on, Maddy turned. 'Whose wife?'

'Your man's. Remember?' Jake prompted. 'The married one you've been seeing? Big mistake.' He shook his head sorrowfully. 'Really. It's always bad news when the wife finds out.'

Maddy was beginning to wonder if she'd stepped into a parallel universe. This was like falling asleep during one film on TV and waking up in the middle of another. Bemused, she said, 'What did she look like?'

'Funny, I'd have thought you'd've been a bit more shocked,' Jake said idly. 'Horrified, even. Almost as if you can't believe what you're hearing because you know for a fact that this chap of yours doesn't have a wife.'

'OK, I don't know what you're talking about, but I'm off to bed.' Something dodgy was going on here; loftily refusing to join in, Maddy did an about-turn and headed for the stairs.

'Oh no you don't.' Jake's hand shot out, his fingers curling round her wrist as she attempted to slip past him. 'And keep your voice down, because Sophie's asleep.'

'I'm not shouting.'

'We haven't started yet.'

Maddy went hot and cold all over. Surely he couldn't know. They'd been so careful. But what other explanation could there be for the look in Jake's eyes? And why was she even bothering to wonder, when she was clearly about to find out?

'Go on then, let's get it over with.' Defiantly she wrenched her wrist free and turned to face him.

'Kerr McKinnon,' said Jake coldly. 'Are you out of your mind?'

Oh God.

'Who told you?' Maddy demanded.

'Never mind that.'

'*Who?*'

'I'm not telling you.' Firmly, Jake shook his head. 'I gave my word I wouldn't and don't change the subject. Have you considered Marcella for one *moment*? Can you even comprehend what this would do to her?'

'She isn't going to find out,' said Maddy, feeling sick. 'Because you aren't going to tell her.'

'I found out, though, didn't I? I bloody wish I hadn't, but I did. Because secrets don't stay secrets around here.' Jake took a gulp of cold coffee and grimaced. 'You're going to have to finish with him. You know that, don't you?'

In the space of five minutes, Maddy discovered, one of the most idyllic days of her life was turning into one of the very worst. And she knew who she had to thank for it too. Nuala, unable to work, had spent the afternoon in the Angel knocking back drink after drink. From there she had headed on down to watch the cricket. Keen to get the lowdown on Maddy's married man, Jake had paid her a bit of flirtatious attention and in turn Nuala, her tongue by this time thoroughly loosened, would have tipsily confided in him. It was all so obvious, so predictable. Nuala had always been a blabbermouth.

'Where are you going?' demanded Jake.

In the split second before the front door slammed, Maddy shouted, 'To sort something out.'

Nuala was upstairs in the living room wrestling with her long-sleeved T-shirt when she heard footsteps on the landing. With her top pulled half inside out over her head and her bra on show, all she could do was call out in a high-pitched voice, 'Who's that?' and pray it wasn't an after-hours gas man come to read the meter.

'Me.'

Maddy. Well, that was good news. 'Perfect timing,' Nuala said happily. 'I'm completely stuck. Can you give me a hand getting this off? Oh, and I can't undo my bra either.'

'How could you?'

Blindly, Nuala turned in the direction of Maddy's voice. 'What are you on about? I can't, can I? That's why I'm asking you to do it for me.'

But the expected help didn't materialise. Instead she heard Maddy say coldly, 'You just couldn't keep quiet, could you? I asked you not to tell anyone but you couldn't resist it.'

Trapped within the confines of her T-shirt, Nuala's face burned with indignation. 'What are you talking about?'

'I really thought I could trust you,' Maddy retaliated furiously, 'which just goes to show how stupid I am. You told Jake about Kerr and now, thanks to you, *everything's ruined.*'

'I didn't! I didn't tell Jake! Oh, for *God's sake.*' With her good arm, Nuala managed at last to wrench the T-shirt back down over her head. 'Did he tell you I did?'

'You and Juliet are the only ones who know. Juliet would never breathe a word.'

This was true; Juliet made sphinxes look garrulous. Appalled, Nuala recalled lying on the grass all but ignoring the cricket, far more interested in chatting away to Jake. Let's face it, she'd had a fair few drinks this afternoon – oh God, had she somehow managed to give the game away without even realising it?

'I-I'm sure I didn't,' Nuala faltered, but it was too late; Maddy had seen the worried look in her eyes.

'You mean you didn't do it on purpose, it just slipped out,' she hissed. 'Well, thanks a lot, I won't forget this in a hurry. I won't be telling you anything in future that I don't want broadcast all over town. In fact, I probably won't be telling you anything at all.'

Kate was serving large gins to a tweedy weekend couple when Maddy stomped back out through the bar without so much as a glance in her direction. Ten minutes later, as she was fetching fresh supplies of peanuts from the storeroom, she heard a voice plaintively calling her name from halfway up the stairs.

'What is it?' Popping her head round the corner, Kate saw Nuala looking pale and subdued.

'Um, sorry, is Dexter busy?'

'He's shouting at the washer-upper. Want me to fetch him for you?'

'Oh crikey, no, it's not urgent. I just, well, I can't get out of my T-shirt.'

Plonking the cards of dry- and honey-roasted peanuts back down on the shelf, Kate checked over her shoulder that no one was waiting to be served.

'Here, I'll give you a hand.' As she reached the top of the stairs, she saw that Nuala had been crying. 'Hey, are you OK?'

'Fine.' Nuala nodded falteringly, then shook her head as she reached the sanctuary of the living room. 'Sorry, it just seems so pathetic, not being able to take off your own clothes. All I want to do is go to bed – oh bugger, and now I need another tissue . . .'

Grabbing the box of Kleenex on the coffee table, Kate freed one just in time for Nuala to catch the tears dripping from her reddened nose.

'Come on, what's really wrong?'

'Oh God, this is going to sound so stupid,' Nuala blurted out, 'and I know you and Maddy don't get on, but she's my best friend. The thing is, she told me something in confidence the other day and now she's mad with me because she thinks I told someone else.'

Kate felt sick. So that was why Maddy had come storming over here.

'And . . . did you?'

Standing patiently, like a child being undressed by its mother, Nuala waited for Kate to free first her good arm, then her head, before carefully unrolling the T-shirt down over her immobile shoulder. Finally she shook her head.

'I can't remember doing it. I wouldn't hurt Maddy for the world, but there's no other way it could have got out. It *must* have been me. I keep racking my brains,' Nuala went on in desperation, 'but I honestly can't *remember* it. God, it's like having that thingy disease, you know, that whatjacallit . . .'

'Alzheimer's.'

'You see? *You see?*' Nuala wailed. 'That could be what's wrong with me! Either that or I'm going completely mad.'

This was the moment to come out and say it, to set the record straight and put poor Nuala out of her abject misery.

This was the moment . . .

OK, one, two, three, here it comes, here it comes . . .

'I'm sure you didn't do it,' said Kate, realising that these weren't quite the words she'd had in mind. Deeply ashamed of her lack of moral fibre but not ashamed enough to blurt out the truth, she went on, 'It'll be OK. Now, d'you need a hand with this bra?'

Nodding, Nuala turned her back. Kate unclipped the bra and helped Nuala into her dressing gown. Still racked with guilt – why couldn't she say it, *why?* – she jumped as they both heard Dexter bellowing, 'Hey, new girl, where are you?'

The next moment he appeared in the doorway.

'What's going on up here then?' demanded Dexter. 'Hot lesbian sex?'

'Yes,' said Kate. 'Too bad it's all over now. You missed it.'

'Has it occurred to you that I'm trying to run a pub here? I've just called last orders and there are punters queuing three deep at the bar, so why don't you get your . . . self down there and start serving?'

He'd corrected himself, Kate realised; having been about to tell her to get her fat backside downstairs, he'd actually bothered to modify his language.

'Fine,' she told Dexter. 'Keep your hair on.' With a sweet smile she added, 'What's left of it.'

Chapter 24

'I'm sorry, I'm *so sorry*,' wailed Maddy the next morning. 'I just want to kill myself, I can't believe I said all those horrible things, of course you didn't tell Jake about me and Kerr.'

'I didn't? Really? Oh, thank God for that!' Clutching her chest with relief, Nuala sank sideways against the door frame. Last night she had slept terribly, racked by dreams of herself clambering onto the pub roof, calling the entire village to attention and announcing through a megaphone that Maddy was bonking Kerr McKinnon but that . . . *sshhh* . . . nobody must breathe a word because it was TOP SECRET.

After that, being woken by the doorbell at seven thirty had come as a welcome reprieve.

'What can I tell you?' Maddy's hair was looking distinctly bird's-nesty, as if she hadn't slept well either. 'I'm so ashamed.'

Since she hadn't been too ashamed last night, Nuala said, 'What changed your mind?'

'Jake, of course. He'd gone to bed by the time I got back. Deliberately, so I couldn't interrogate him. Then this morning I told him what I'd said to you and he went, "Oh, it wasn't Nuala." Just like that, the bastard, as if I'd been trying to guess the mystery ingredient in a casserole. So I said, "Oh *fuck*," and of course that was the moment Sophie came into the kitchen and said, "That's a very rude word, Mrs Masters says only stupid people say fuck." Which was, of course, the very reason I was saying it,' Maddy concluded, 'because I *had* been stupid.' Looking anguished, she added, 'I'm sorry. Really and truly. Will you still be my friend?'

'Go on then.' Nuala was just glad it was all over, dizzy with relief that she hadn't let slip the secret to Jake when, in all honesty, she could so easily have done. 'You'll have to help me get dressed though – *ow!*' she winced as Maddy threw her arms round her like an over-enthusiastic bridesmaid catching a bouquet.

'Sorry, sorry!'

'So who did tell Jake?' Nuala was bursting to hear.

'I don't know! He won't say! What am I going to *do*?'

'Finish with Kerr?' Nuala ventured.

Maddy's face crumpled. 'I don't think I can.'

'OK, so you have to tell Marcella.'

With a shudder Maddy said, 'I definitely can't do that.'

'Only one other thing for it, then. Find out who told Jake and hire a professional assassin.'

'Excellent. Much the best way. And afterwards,' Maddy said hopefully, 'they could assassinate Jake.'

Monday night was darts night at the Fallen Angel. It was also discovery night for Maddy. Every time she looked over at Kate working behind the bar, Kate hurriedly looked elsewhere. The real giveaway, however, was the expression on her face. With a jolt like accidentally sitting on an electric fence, Maddy knew that the person who had told Jake was Kate.

'You're wrong, it can't be.' Nuala, her eye by this time a dramatic explosion of magenta, inky-blue and yellow, was going for the sympathy vote tonight, perched on a high bar stool with her white denim skirt riding up to reveal tanned thighs. Revelling in the attention she'd been getting from the visiting team, her cheeks were pink and her eyes bright. Now, though, she shook her head. 'Kate was with me last night, she knew why I was so upset. She would have said something if it had been her.'

Maddy doubted it. She still hadn't the faintest idea how anyone, let alone Kate Taylor-Trent, could have found out about herself and Kerr, but somehow it had happened.

The bad news was that she had planned on speaking to the instigator privately to explain how vital it was that Marcella shouldn't find out and generally appeal to their better nature. Well, what a waste of time that would be, seeing as Kate Taylor-Trent didn't have one.

'Let me get you a drink,' one of the visiting team offered Nuala. 'Who blacked your eye then? Jealous boyfriend?'

Dimpling, Nuala said, 'I tripped and fell down the stairs. And thanks, I'd love a white wine spritzer.'

Dexter, serving behind the bar, glanced at Nuala's legs. 'Fasten the buttons on that skirt,' he said curtly. 'You look like an old tart.'

'That's a coincidence,' Kate chimed in, 'you sound like an old fart.'

Nuala spluttered with laughter. Even Dexter, initially taken aback, managed to crack a smile.

'See?' Nuala whispered to Maddy. 'She's all right really. Not as bad as you think.'

Seriously? Was Nuala right? Maddy looked across the bar at the girl who had belittled her for so many years. For a split second their eyes met and Maddy wondered if, just this once, Kate might acknowledge her with a brief smile.

Who was she kidding? It didn't happen. Whether out of guilt or indifference or plain dislike, Kate turned away and Maddy knew two things for sure.

Kate was the one who had told Jake about herself and Kerr.

And Nuala was wrong; Kate was every bit as bad as she thought.

Just the sound of Kerr's voice on the phone had the ability to melt Maddy's insides like chocolate. She loved ringing him so much she couldn't imagine how she'd ever managed to get through life without it.

'Change of plan,' she murmured from the back room of the delicatessen, having triple-checked that no customers had ventured into the shop. 'I can't make six o'clock. Marcella just rang Jake and left a message for the two of us to meet her at six.'

'When you say the two of us,' said Kerr, 'you don't mean—'

'No, not you and me and Marcella with a shotgun.' Maddy smiled because, miraculously, when she was talking to Kerr nothing else seemed to matter. 'She wants to see Jake and me. No idea why, but apparently she sounded fine, so it can't be anything too scary. Anyhow, I'm sure it won't take long, so I'll be over by seven.'

'Do you want the good news or the bad news?' said Kerr.

Maddy's stomach flip-flopped like a landed fish.

'The bad news.'

'I still haven't gone off you.'

Bastard! Overcome with relief, she said, 'And the good news?'

Kerr's voice softened. 'You haven't gone off me.'

Maddy made her way back through to the shop with a dopey smirk on her face. Juliet, carefully slicing up a kiwi-lime torte, said, 'You're going to hate me for saying this, but it's all going to end in tears.'

Stubbornly, Maddy said, 'Don't be such a pessimist.'

'Take it from me, a secret is only a secret if *nobody* else knows about it. Even a secret shared between two people

180

can be risky. It only works if they both have watertight reasons for wanting it kept.'

'I know, I know, but we're managing.' If there had been any sand around, Maddy would have stuck her head in it.

'I'm just warning you, that's all.' Juliet's dark eyes were luminous with compassion. 'You and Kerr know. I know. So does Nuala and Jake. And now there's someone else as well. You think it's Kate Taylor-Trent but you're not completely sure. At this rate there aren't going to be many people left in Ashcombe who aren't in on the secret.'

Not wanting to hear this, Maddy reached for the silver tongs and began placing rum truffles from the glass-fronted case into one of the glossy cream boxes. Rum truffles were Marcella's favourite. Having weighed the box, she said, 'Six pounds fifty,' so that Juliet could add the extra amount to her slate.

'That's what a guilty husband does when he's been spending too much time with his mistress,' said Juliet. 'Stops off at a garage and grabs a bunch of orange carnations for the wife.'

'Is that what Tiff's father used to do?' Maddy felt mean, but she couldn't resist the dig. Life was complicated enough right now, without being subjected to lectures from well-meaning friends who hadn't exactly led blameless lives themselves.

'I'm sure he did,' said Juliet with a faint smile. 'Although I'd like to think he did a bit better than a few grotty carnations smelling of petrol.'

Juliet had never deliberately set out to steal another woman's husband, Maddy knew that. She hadn't discovered until it was too late that he had a wife at home, and by then Tiff had been on the way.

'Do you miss him?' said Maddy.

'You mean do I wish we could still be together, like a

normal happy family?' Juliet slid the torte back into the chiller cabinet and moved towards the till as a retired couple came into the shop. Lowering her voice, she murmured, 'No, I don't. Tiff and I are fine together.'

'Just the two of you? Don't you ever want anyone else?'

'We can't always have what we want, can we?' said Juliet. 'Sometimes we just have to settle for what we can get.'

The bus trundled along Main Street, finally slowing up as it reached the war memorial. Marcella would normally have collected her bags together by now, made her way to the front of the vehicle and chatted to the driver while she waited for the bus to come to a halt.

This time she stayed in her seat, clutching her pink raffia bag to her chest, until the bus stopped running and the door opened.

'Thought you'd fallen asleep,' said the driver when she finally reached the steps.

'Not me.' Marcella smiled absently at him. 'Thanks, Mickey. See you.'

'What happened to all your bags?' He looked surprised; one of life's great shoppers, Marcella was invariably loaded down like a packhorse.

She shook her head as she climbed down and waggled her fingers at him. 'Didn't buy anything today, Mickey. Nothing caught my eye.'

It wasn't true of course, but she could hardly show him the one item she had bought; there were some things it just wasn't appropriate to share with your friendly neighbourhood bus driver.

Still in a bit of a daze, Marcella waited until Mickey had driven off along Ashcombe Road before turning to face Snow Cottage. It was hard to believe quite how drastically life was about to change.

'Mum!' Her gaze shifting to the upstairs window, Marcella saw Maddy waving at her. 'Come on, we've been waiting for you! You're late!'

Darling Maddy, she loved her with all her heart. And Jake. And Sophie too. Her wonderful family – oh Lord, here she was, off again, how completely ridiculous.

Upstairs in her bedroom, Maddy saw the tears tumbling down Marcella's smooth brown cheeks and felt her heart sink like a stone. Marcella didn't cry; she was the strongest, bravest person she knew.

This had to be bad.

Either bad, or something to do with Kerr McKinnon, in which case it was a catastrophe.

'Jake?' Suddenly terrified, Maddy backed away from the window and clattered downstairs. 'Open the front door quick, Mum's here,' she heard her voice falter, 'and she's crying.'

By the time Maddy reached the hall, Jake had opened the door and there was Marcella in her denim jacket and primrose-yellow pedal-pushers, with her hair wrapped up in a spectacular pink scarf and tears rolling down her face.

Hardly daring to breathe, Maddy said, 'What is it? What's happened?'

Fumbling for a tissue that was already shredded and damp, Marcella shook her head. 'I've got a bit of news. Brace yourselves now, you two.' She broke into a huge, unrepentant grin. 'I'm pregnant.'

Chapter 25

'Oh my God, oh my *God*!' Shocked and delighted, as well as vastly relieved that it wasn't anything to do with Kerr – at least, she certainly *hoped* it wasn't – Maddy threw her arms round Marcella. 'Really? That's fantastic . . . it's just the most amazing news ever!'

Simultaneously laughing and crying, Marcella said, 'I know. I think I'm still in shock. Poor Vince, he really should have been the first to know – oh, thanks, darling.' She beamed at Jake, who had thrust a box of Kleenex into her hands. 'But he's on one of his fishing trips and his phone's switched off and I just couldn't wait to tell you. I still can't believe it. I'm pregnant, I'm actually having a baby, it's my biggest ever dream come true . . .'

Tears of joy were streaming unstoppably down Marcella's cheeks now as Jake hugged her and they made their way through to the kitchen. Wiping her own eyes, Maddy said, 'I'm so happy for you,' and meant it. This had been Marcella's fantasy for so many years; she had been a perfect mother to them, yet the longing for a child of her own had never faded. And now she was going to have one. It was like a miracle.

'I had absolutely no idea! Guess how I found out?' Pulling out a chair at the scrubbed oak table, Marcella said eagerly, 'What do I smell of?'

'Um . . .' Mystified, Maddy sniffed. 'Well, nothing.'

'Exactly! And I've been into Bath!'

Maddy twigged at last; Marcella's regular shopping jaunts invariably included a trawl through the perfume hall of Jolly's department store, squishing herself with enough scent to fell an elephant.

'They banned you from Jolly's?'

'Ha, they wouldn't dare! No, I went in there as usual, all ready to start squishing, and it was so weird, I just kept picking up the bottles, sniffing them, then putting them down again. I didn't feel sick exactly, I just couldn't bring myself to actually squirt any perfume *on* me. Well, it was just the strangest thing; even the sales girls thought it was odd. In the end it was Daphne, from the EstÈe Lauder counter, who said, "You're not pregnant, are you?" and I just laughed, because she'd only said it as a joke. But then I went for a coffee at that nice place on Pulteney Bridge – you know, the one where you're actually allowed to have a fag – and when I pushed open the door it was so smoky in there I had to come out again.' Marcella waggled her hands in disbelief. 'Well, that's something that's *never* happened to me before, so I began to think hey-up, what's going on here? So I went to the chemist, bought one of those tests and popped back to Jolly's because their loos are so nice. And . . . then I did the test, and it was . . . it was . . . p-positive, and I realised I was . . . p-p-pregnant. God, look at me, off again, I'm like the Trevi fountain.' Dragging another handful of tissues from the box she rubbed away her tears. 'It's the hormones, Dr Carter told me. They've just swirled up and knocked me for six – oh, thanks love.' Smiling gratefully up at Jake, she took the mug of tea. 'We should be cracking open the champagne really, but Dr Carter says no alcohol, to be on the safe side.'

'Hang on, how can you have seen Dr Carter already?' Maddy frowned, because it was easier to get an audience with the Pope than it was to persuade Dr Carter's dragon of a receptionist to give you an appointment this side of Christmas.

'Oh, it was fab. I made the receptionist an offer she couldn't refuse.' Marcella looked pleased with herself. 'I turned up at the surgery and she tried to fob me off with an appointment in twelve days' time, so I told her that wasn't good enough, and that I was going to sit there in the waiting room until I was seen. Then the old trout tried telling me I wasn't urgent and I said I'd spent the last twenty years trying to get pregnant and now that it looked as if I might actually *be* pregnant I wanted it confirmed *this minute.*'

'You're brave.' Maddy was filled with admiration.

'Not really, just desperate. Then I started crying again, really loudly, and that was when Dr Carter came out and took me into his office. He'd been in there dictating his letters, listening to the whole shouting match and having a good laugh, the sod.' Marcella's smile was rueful. 'He said nobody's ever stood their ground quite like that before now. Usually his receptionist boots them out. But when he heard me say I was pregnant he had to come and get me for the sake of my blood pressure. Anyway, so he examined me and confirmed it, and we both got a bit emotional because he knew how much it meant to me. Then he gave me all these leaflets and a big lecture on how to look after myself, because things can still go wrong, especially with me being so ancient.'

'Ancient,' Maddy scoffed, because Marcella had always looked so young for her age; she had the face and figure of a thirty-year-old.

'I'm forty-three.' For a moment Marcella's smile slipped. 'I've never been pregnant before. Dr Carter warned me about the risk of miscarriage. No cigarettes, obviously. No alcohol. No unpasteurised cheese or raw eggs or climbing ladders. He made a point of telling me I should be taking things easy, avoiding any stress. No physical exertions and definitely no emotional turmoil.' With a beatific smile, Marcella sat back and gently patted her flat stomach. 'Just inner calm and relaxation classes and general blissfulness.'

Oh Lord. Maddy inadvertently caught Jake's eye and instantly wished she hadn't.

'Hear that? No stress.' Jake raised a meaningful eyebrow and Maddy glowered back at him.

'Yes, darling, I was going to talk to you about that anyway,' said Marcella. 'Call me shameless, but I'm taking advantage of my delicate condition. Promise me you'll stop seeing this married man of yours.' Leaning across, she gave Maddy's hand a squeeze. 'Sweetheart, I've never asked you for anything before, but I'm asking you now. Please give him up. For this baby, if not for yourself.'

It was ten past seven. Back in the cottage, Jake was busy cooking a mushroom risotto while Marcella, with enormous relish, read aloud scary passages from the copy of *You and Your Pregnancy* she hadn't been able to resist buying in WH Smith. Maddy, who had volunteered to pick Sophie up from her Thursday night dance class in Batheaston, rang Kerr as soon as she was safely inside the car.

He answered on the third ring, as she was heading out of the village.

'D'you want the good news or the bad news?'

'Well, you aren't here,' said Kerr, 'so I can guess the bad news.'

'I can't see you tonight. We've got Marcella with us. She's pregnant, can you believe it? You've never seen anyone so happy.'

'That's fantastic. I'm glad for her.' Kerr knew all about Marcella's years of longing for a baby. Ruefully he added, 'Even if she does wish I was dead.'

'Not dead. Just . . . preferably not on this continent.'

Maddy smiled as she said it, but her fingers tightened round the steering wheel.

'So was that the good news, or is there more?'

Good news? Apart from Marcella's pregnancy, when had there been *any* good news? Longingly Maddy pictured Kerr in his flat, stretched out across the sofa, drinking a lager and flicking through the TV channels, winding down after a hard day's work, waiting for *her* . . .

'Hey,' Kerr prompted, breaking into her muddled thoughts. 'When am I going to see you? And I'm not talking about delivering sandwiches to the office,' he added. 'I mean when am I going to really see you?'

Maddy's throat tightened. Now was the time to tell him if she had a shred of decency about her, an honest bone in her body, an ounce of loyalty towards Marcella.

'Tomorrow evening.' Her mouth was dry with shame; it took an effort to unstick her traitorous tongue from the roof of her mouth. 'Tomorrow, seven o'clock. I promise.'

At nine thirty, sunburned and windswept and smelling of the sea, Vince arrived at Snow Cottage to pick Marcella up. Having greeted Maddy and Jake, he bent over the back of the sofa and gave Marcella a kiss.

'How was it?' Marcella had made sure the incriminating book was out of sight, under a cushion.

'Fantastic. Perfect conditions.' Vince's dark hair flopped over his forehead as he tickled the soles of Sophie's bare feet. Proudly he said, 'Five sea bass, three plaice and a dozen mackerel.'

'Oh darling, that's brilliant. And guess what else? We're going to have a baby.'

Vince stopped tickling Sophie's feet.

'What?'

'I think you heard,' Marcella said happily.

'It's a surprise!' screamed Sophie, beside herself with excitement. 'I wanted to tell you, but Dad said I wouldn't get any pocket money for a year.'

Vince was gazing at Marcella. His dark eyes filled with tears of joy. Barely able to speak, he whispered, 'A baby? *Really?*'

Marcella smiled and nodded. Maddy, watching Vince, knew how desperately he had always longed for children of his own.

The tears were sliding unashamedly down his cheeks now. With his Italian blood coursing through his veins, Vince made no attempt to hide them.

'Oh, poor Vince.' Scrambling off the sofa, Sophie rushed to fling her arms around him. 'Don't cry, babies aren't that bad. We thought you'd be pleased.'

Chapter 26

Lurking in the bushes wasn't something Maddy had much experience of doing. She was discovering that it involved close acquaintance with a lot more insects than she'd imagined.

It was eleven twenty, kicking out time at the Fallen Angel. Since waiting outside the entrance to the pub would only arouse the curiosity of departing regulars, Maddy was forced to skulk in the shadows with leaves tickling the back of her neck, moths flitting past her face like mini kamikaze pilots and grasshoppers making their raucous, ratchety grasshopper noises at her feet.

Jerking back in horror, Maddy discovered a spider had been busily constructing a cobweb between her hair and a handily positioned section of hedge. With a shudder of revulsion she pummelled the cobweb away and leaped to one side, time-warp style, as a grasshopper rasped in the vicinity of her left foot. Honestly, nature, sometimes there was just that bit too much of it.

Moments later, thankfully, the pub door opened and into a pool of light stepped the object of Maddy's attention.

Maddy waited until the door had swung shut, extinguishing the pool of light, before emerging from the depths of the hedge.

Having finished her shift, Kate was on her way home. With her Prada bag slung over one shoulder, her skirt swirling and her high heels clacking along the pavement, from this angle she looked like a model on TV advertising the latest in confidence-boosting tampons.

It wasn't until she turned her head, as Maddy crossed the road towards her, that the scars on her face were visible.

'Can I have a word?' said Maddy, wishing with all her heart that she didn't have to do this, but knowing she must.

'Fire away.' Kate didn't stop walking, or even slow down. Maddy kept pace with her as she headed for the junction where Main Street met Gypsy Lane.

Here goes.

'Do you know?'

'Do I know what?'

It was too dark to see whether Kate's expression had changed, but she'd paused for a moment before asking the question.

'OK,' said Maddy, 'I think you *do* know. But just in case you don't, I'd rather not say.'

This time Kate didn't hesitate. 'I'm sorry, I haven't a clue what you're talking about.'

That sounded genuine enough. Phew, the relief. My mistake, thought Maddy; jumping to the wrong conclusion as usual.

'Unless you mean the thing about you and Kerr McKinnon,' said Kate.

Bugger.

'Well, yes, that's the thing I mean.' Humiliatingly, Maddy heard her voice wobble halfway through, making her sound like a petrified fourteen-year-old boy asking a girl out on a date.

'Thought it might be.' Kate sounded annoyingly confident; she had the upper hand and she knew it. 'Well, well, you and Kerr. I take it Marcella doesn't know yet.'

Maddy braced herself.

'No, and that's why I need to talk to you, because—'

'She'll go ballistic? Disown you? Disembowel you?'

'No,' said Maddy. 'That's not the reason.'

'It must give you a bit of a thrill,' said Kate. 'I bet you never thought you'd get a look-in with Kerr McKinnon.' She paused, allowing Maddy to recall the time, all those years back, when Kerr had caused every girl's heart to beat faster. At seventeen and physically irresistible, he'd been as out of reach to ordinary mortals as Robbie Williams or David Beckham today. As for those so-called ordinary mortals with tragic haircuts, beer-bottle spectacles and knock knees, well, who in their right mind would spare them so much as a second glance? Whereas Kate, already precociously advanced in the bosom department and supremely confident of her own looks at thirteen, had undoubtedly felt that before long she would have her chance with Kerr . . .

Anyway, now wasn't the time to dredge up silly child-hood rivalries. Especially ones she'd so spectacularly lost.

'Marcella's pregnant,' said Maddy. 'She's forty-three and she's just found out she's pregnant.'

This stopped Kate in her tracks.

'But I thought she couldn't—'

'That's what we all thought. But it's happened, which is why I need to talk to you. The doctor's warned Marcella that she has to take things easy, not exert herself, not get het up about anything.'

'Oh, I get it.' Kate's lip curled. 'Emotional blackmail.'

Maddy swallowed. 'This isn't blackmail.'

'Come on, of course it is. You're worried sick about your big secret getting out, and you're warning me to keep my mouth shut. Because if I don't, Marcella might lose the baby and then it would all be my fault.'

That wasn't fair. OK, so it might be kind of true, but it was still unfair.

'I'm just saying,' Maddy hesitated, 'it's pretty obviously Marcella's only chance. You wouldn't want it to go wrong, would you?'

They'd reached the entrance to Dauncey House. Facing her, Kate said, 'Don't you think you're going about this the wrong way? Hasn't it even occurred to you to stop seeing Kerr McKinnon?'

Maddy felt sick. Why did people have to keep on saying that, as if it was the simplest thing in the world?

'I'm going to. I will.' Seeing that Kate was turning away, about to disappear up the drive, she blurted out, 'How did you know?'

'You mean how did I find out about you and Kerr? You really want me to tell you?'

Gripped with desperation, Maddy said, 'Yes.'

'I don't think so.' Kate smiled. 'You see, that's the whole point. You think you're being *so* careful, but there's always that chance you'll be caught out. I'll just leave you to think it over, wonder where you slipped up.'

What a *cow*.

'You haven't told Estelle, have you?' Maddy blurted out, because Kate was heading up to the house.

'I think you'd have heard, don't you?'

'And you won't say anything to Marcella?'

'She's probably tougher than you think,' said Kate.

Yes, but what if she isn't?

'Please,' Maddy called out, but all she heard was Kate's laughter as she disappeared from view.

Not a lot of work was getting done when Maddy arrived at the offices of Callaghan and Fox the next day. The air was thick with hairspray, the female staff were all wearing far more make-up than usual and Sara, the receptionist, was busy brushing bronzing powder into her pillowy cleavage.

193

'Blimey,' Maddy plonked the cool-box onto the desk, 'are we auditioning for *Baywatch*?'

Sara beamed; having overdone the bronzer on her face, she'd gone an alarming shade of Dale Winton.

'God, could you see me in a bikini? But we are going to be on TV,' she went on brightly. 'Kerr had a call from someone at HTV this morning, asking if they could come and do a piece for a careers slot on the local news – you know, what it's like to work in PR kind of thing. Isn't that so cool? I've never been on the telly before, apart from the time I told all my friends I was off to Glastonbury Festival and they saw me on TV queuing up with my mum for *The Antiques Roadshow*. Which didn't do wonders for my street cred.' Sara pulled a face, then added chirpily, 'But this is completely different. I won't be wearing a sad old anorak this time, oh no! Everyone's going to see me looking dead cool, working in a trendy PR agency for my hunky boss. How about you, Maddy, you're single, aren't you? D'you think Kerr's hunky?'

Rather sweetly, Sara had begun dropping hints like this over the last week or so; absolutely unaware that anything was going on between Kerr and Maddy, she was making unsubtle attempts to pair them up.

Since she could hardly deny that Kerr was attractive – because that would be like saying, 'George Clooney? God, yuk, he's got a face like a warthog' – Maddy shrugged and smiled. 'Kerr? He's not bad. I've seen worse.' She tapped the cool-box. 'Now, d'you want me to leave this in the coffee room?'

'Don't worry, I'll take care of it. Ooh, I've just had a brainwave!' Excitedly Sara said, 'The TV crew are going to be here from eleven till two, so why don't you go off now and do the rest of your deliveries, then come back with our stuff while they're in the middle of filming. Wouldn't that be great? Then you can be on telly too!'

Maddy pictured the scene; Marcella watching TV at home, initially repulsed by the sight of Kerr McKinnon, then boggling in disbelief as her own daughter pranced into view behind him. Oh yes, that'd do Marcella's blood pressure the world of good. Plus, they'd have to buy a new TV set to replace the one she'd smashed.

'I can't.' Maddy looked regretful. 'I've got a million deliveries then Juliet needs me back at the shop. When's it going to be shown, anyway?'

'They can't say for sure. Maybe tonight, maybe next week. But they'll let us know,' Sara said confidently. 'I made Kerr ask, so my mum could phone everyone she's ever met in her life.'

'Well, I'll definitely watch it,' promised Maddy. 'Is Kerr in his office?'

'He is.' Beneath the trowelled-on make-up, Sara's eyes gleamed with matchmaking interest. 'Do you want to see him?'

'No need.' Maddy knew she'd be seeing Kerr at seven o'clock tonight. 'Just tell him that he wanted white bread with his BLT, but we ran out. So just for today he'll have to make do with wholemeal instead.'

Chapter 27

Nuala was lying on the sofa devouring the book that was about to change her life when the knock came on the living-room door. As guiltily as a teenager caught with a copy of *Playboy*, she shovelled the paperback behind a green velvet cushion and called out, 'Who's that?'

'Only me.' Pushing the door open, Kate Taylor-Trent said, 'Sorry, I didn't know if you were asleep. Dexter needs to send the VAT stuff off to the accountants. He says the folder should be in the filing cabinet in his office, and you'll know where to find it.'

'I'll get it.' Levering herself awkwardly up off the sofa with her good arm, Nuala watched as the book slithered out from under the cushion and landed with a plop on the floor. Just as well it wasn't *Playboy*.

By the time she returned from the office with the relevant folder, Kate had picked up the book and was leafing through the pages.

Flushing, Nuala said defensively, 'I know, I'm pathetic.'

'At least you're doing something about it. These things are huge business in the States. My flatmate had hundreds. I've never read one,' said Kate.

'It was you who made me buy it,' Nuala confessed, blushing more deeply than ever but feeling emboldened.

'Me?'

'That title: *Don't Be A Doormat*. I mean, look at the way Dexter treats me. I've got so used to it I just put up with it, but you don't let him get away with anything. And you're absolutely right, which is why I'm going to *change*.' Grabbing the book back from Kate, Nuala found the relevant chapter headings and jabbed at them eagerly with her index finger. 'See? Lay Down The Law! You're A Person Too! Startle Him To His Senses! It's all here in black and white – I can't *believe* I've been such a wimp. From now on, I'm going to give as good as I get and really stand up to Dexter.' Proudly, she straightened her spine and concluded, 'I'm going to be just like you!'

Kate looked impressed. At that moment Dexter shouted up the stairs, 'Hasn't the silly bat found it yet? What is she, *blind*?'

Hurriedly Nuala handed over the folder bulging with VAT receipts.

'Look, I'm only up to Chapter Seven. Anyway, I can't do it yet. Not in front of other people.'

Kate raised an eyebrow. 'When then?'

When indeed?

'Later,' said Nuala, feeling determined and panicky. 'I promise.'

Don't Be A Doormat was hidden inside a Marks and Spencer carrier and stuffed out of sight at the back of the wardrobe, but Nuala could still hear it whispering to her as she and Dexter lounged on the sofa together watching TV. She'd finished the rest of the book earlier this afternoon and every word of it had made absolute, earth-shattering sense. It was like picking up the Bible and suddenly becoming a born-again Christian, without having to wear unflattering Alice bands and flat sandals. And it wasn't as if she had anything to lose, Nuala reminded herself; they would be redefining their relationship, that was all. Nothing but good could come of it. How did that song go? Oh yes – 'Thinnnnngs Can Only Get Betterrrrr . . .'

Crikey. Put like that, what on earth was she waiting for?

'Do you mind?' complained Dexter, turning up the TV.

'Hmm?'

'That bloody awful noise. You're singing under your breath. Stop it.'

Thinnnngs can only get betterrrr . . .

'I like singing,' said Nuala.

'Well, that's fine, I'm glad. I just don't like having to listen to it,' Dexter snorted. 'You sound like a cat being neutered.'

Don't Let Him Diss You, Nuala recalled being instructed by one of the chapter headings in the book. You Deserve Respect. And I *do*, Nuala thought indignantly, because I'm A Human Being Too, and if I want to sing, I jolly well *can* . . .

Exasperated, Dexter said, 'You're doing it again.'

'So?'

'It's horrible.'

'You always have to criticise me, don't you?' Bravely, Nuala turned to face him. 'Every single thing about me is wrong, according to you.'

Dexter shrugged and yawned. 'I wouldn't say *every* single thing.'

'Yes you would! OK, how about those trousers?' Pointing accusingly at the TV screen, where Kylie Minogue was currently twirling and pouting along to her latest single, Nuala demanded, 'What would you say if I bought a pair like that?'

Kylie's trousers were primrose yellow, shimmery and skin-tight. Her perfect little bottom was now wiggling fetchingly this way and that in time with the music.

'Are you serious?' said Dexter in amazement. 'With your thighs? You'd look bloody awful.'

'You see? That's *exactly* what I mean.' Nuala's voice rose an octave. 'You have no respect for me. You criticise me all the time and I've had enough. I'm not going to put up with it any more.'

'OK,' said Dexter.

'And you can stop watching that!' Realising that his attention had been drawn back to Kylie's pert, gyrating bottom, Nuala snatched the remote control away from him and switched off the TV. 'This is important! We're having a discussion here and the least you can do is listen!'

Actually, the authors of the book advised that all discussions be carried out in a calm and civilised manner, but this was easier said than done.

'*We* aren't having a discussion,' Dexter pointed out. 'You're just having a rant. All *I'm* trying to do is watch the TV in peace.'

'You treat me like dirt,' Nuala exploded. 'Like a piece of old rubbish! And I'm not putting up with it any more.'

'You've said that already.'

Empowerment, thought Nuala. Self-respect. *Don't Be A Doormat.*

'I'm serious,' she insisted. 'I mean it. You have to stop belittling me, criticising me, making me feel small.'

'Or you'll do what?' Dexter was sounding supremely disinterested.

Right. Shock Him To His Senses.

'Or it's all over between us,' said Nuala, her heart beginning to clatter. 'Finished.'

With Kylie no longer doing her twirly thing on TV, silence filled the room. Finally, nodding slowly, Dexter said, 'OK. If that's what you want.'

What? What was *that* supposed to mean? Nuala's eyes widened in panic. Surely she'd misunderstood.

Tentatively she said, 'So . . . you'll stop doing it?'

Dexter gave her a measured look. 'Come on, it's not working, is it? You're absolutely right. Ending it now would be the best thing all round.'

'B-but . . . you can't mean that!' Feeling as though she was sinking into a hole of her own making, Nuala croaked desperately, 'I only said it to give you a scare.'

'No you didn't.'

'I did! I don't want us to split up,' Nuala wailed.

'You say that, but subconsciously you do,' said Dexter, 'and you're right. I mean, look at us, we're hardly love's young dream, are we? You couldn't call us *happy*. One of the old blokes in the bar the other night asked me if I'd blacked your eye, can you imagine that? He actually thought *I'd* thumped you and chucked you down the stairs.'

Numbly, Nuala said, 'So did Maddy.'

'Well then, there you go. If that's what people think I do to you, there has to be something seriously wrong.'

Oh God, panic attack, this wasn't supposed to be happening. Beginning to hyperventilate – and jettisoning the first and most important rule of *Don't Be A Doormat* – Nuala whimpered, 'But I love you!'

'No,' shaking his head, Dexter hauled himself to his feet, 'you don't. You're just scared of being on your own.'

'Don't do this to me,' begged Nuala, scarcely able to take in what she was hearing. 'I didn't mean to say it, I was only trying to be more like Kate.'

'Exactly. You can't try to be more like somebody else,' Dexter's tone was almost sympathetic now, 'because it never works. You're *you*, Nuala. You shouldn't have to change. We aren't right for each other, that's all. And deep down, you know it as well as I do.'

'Where are you going?' Nuala whispered as he headed for the door.

'It's ten past five. I've got a pub to open up.'

A sensation like cold cement trickling into her stomach caused Nuala to grip the side of the sofa. Fearfully she said, 'And where . . . where am I going?'

Pausing in the doorway, Dexter ran his fingers through his receding hair.

'That's up to you. I'm not a monster, Nuala, I'm not about to turf you out into the street. I'll sleep on the sofa until you find somewhere else to stay.'

Oh God, this was unbearable, already he was being far nicer to her than he'd been in months. Maybe if she hung on for a while, he might—

'I'm not going to change my mind,' said Dexter, who had always possessed the uncanny ability to know what was going on inside her head.

In desperation Nuala blurted, 'But you don't know that for sure! You might realise you've made a horrible mistake.'

'I won't, because I haven't.' Calmly, Dexter checked his watch. 'Nuala, I'm sorry, but I have to open the pub. Trust me, you'll be fine. In fact, give it a few weeks and you'll thank me for this.'

Which just goes to show how stupid *you* are, Nuala thought hysterically, tears filling her eyes as Dexter made his way downstairs. Because all I want to do is *die*.

Chapter 28

'OK, OK, this isn't going to help.' Jake was seriously beginning to regret opening the front door now. Girls with boyfriend trouble, hell bent on unburdening themselves, weren't his forte at the best of times, but when he had a night out planned in Bath they were a complete pain in the bum.

Jake was fond of Nuala, it went without saying, but she had only come over to the cottage to regale Maddy with her woes. When he'd told her Maddy wasn't here, he'd expected Nuala to leave, but she'd come in and started offloading her woes onto him instead.

'I don't care! I'm going to sue the bloody woman who wrote this sodding bloody book!' Ripping out yet another page and crushing it into a ball, Nuala wailed, 'Eight pounds ninety-nine, can you believe that? I actually paid her eight pounds ninety-nine to completely bugger up my life . . . *aaarrgh!*'

Jake, who'd been in the shower when the doorbell had gone and was only wearing a purple towel, ducked as the balled-up paper missile whistled past his head. The kitchen floor was awash with them and Nuala evidently planned to keep on going until she'd used up every page, fuelled by the bottle of Bombay Sapphire gin she'd brought along with her from the Angel.

'You shouldn't be drinking that stuff on its own,' said Jake. 'At least put some orange juice with it.'

'Don't bully me. This is my worst night ever. Do you think he'll change his mind?' Nuala pleaded, sloshing another inch of gin into her glass.

'Honestly? No.'

'*No?*' She looked distraught. 'You don't mean that!'

With a sigh and a surreptitious glance at his watch, Jake saw that it was eight o'clock already. Maddy, having left her mobile phone at home, was uncontactable. Sophie was staying over at Tiff's house tonight. And since he clearly wasn't going to be allowed to abandon Nuala in her current state of drunken grief, he may as well give up any thought now of going out.

'Look,' he said. 'These things happen. You and Dexter were never right for each other. You'll be over him in no time.'

'Never.' Misjudging the angle of her glass, Nuala dribbled gin down her chin.

'You deserve so much better,' Jake persisted, this being a useful line he often resorted to himself.

'Oh, do me a favour, I'm not that stupid. Anyway, you have no idea how I feel,' Nuala said miserably. 'How can you? You've never been rejected in your life.'

Jake smiled briefly to himself as he opened the fridge and pulled out a carton of orange juice. If only she knew.

Aloud he said, 'That's absolutely not true. I wrote a love letter to Madonna when I was twelve and did she write back? Never, not one word. I was distraught.'

As he edged towards the door, Nuala looked up fearfully, clearly terrified of being left on her own. 'Where are you going now?'

Jake indicated the bath towel slung round his hips.

'Call me old-fashioned, but I thought I might put some clothes on.'

Still wary, she said, 'And after that?'

'After that?' Realising that he really was stuck here for the evening, Jake decided he may as well make the best of it. Ruffling Nuala's already ruffled hair, he said affectionately, 'I'm going to help you finish that bottle of gin.'

'Thanks.' Nuala's mouth began to wobble with relief; she couldn't have handled being abandoned by two men in one night. 'Just to warn you though, I may get a bit weepy.'

'Hey, don't be daft.' Jake flashed her a grin; he'd had to cope with more than his fair share of weeping females in his time. 'Shoulder to cry on? I'm your man.'

By eleven o'clock the bottle of Bombay Sapphire was finished.

'Empty. Bugger.' Nuala looked bereft. 'What are we supposed to do now?'

'Stop drinking?' said Jake. 'It's a miracle you're still awake.'

'I'm too depressed to sleep.' She pulled a suicidal face. 'OK if I stay here?'

'Course you can. The bed's made up in the spare room.'

'Oh God, what am I going to *do*?' Nuala closed her eyes in despair; every so often she forgot what had happened, then the next moment it all came rushing back to her, making her head spin with misery. 'Everyone's going to be sniggering behind my back. I feel so humiliated. I'll be the laughing stock of Ashcombe.'

'That's rubbish. Why would anyone laugh?'

'Because Dexter doesn't want me any more and that makes me look *stupid*.' Nuala only realised her right elbow had been propping her up when she moved it. She promptly slid sideways on the sofa, ending up in Jake's lap.

'You don't have to look stupid.' He was attempting to haul her upright again but Nuala decided she was happier horizontal. 'Act like you're not bothered. Put on a brave face, do yourself up and flirt for England. Isn't that better than moping around like a wet weekend?'

'Mmm.' Nodding, Nuala thought how delicious Jake smelled, and how fantastic the soft cotton of his shirt felt against her cheek. He really was lovely, and – in theory – what he was saying made a lot of sense.

'Show Dexter what he's missing.' Above her, Jake was still carrying on with his pep talk. 'Make it clear you don't need him.'

'Because I can do so much better, you mean? Come on, look at me.' Nuala groaned. 'Black eye, bruises, cracked collarbone – oh yes, they'll really be queueing up for me; Ewan McGregor, George Clooney . . . How am I ever going to be able to choose?'

'Don't put yourself down.' Jake gave her hip an encouraging squeeze. 'By this time next week your bruises will be gone.'

'Big deal,' Nuala muttered into Jake's shirt.

'Stop it. You're not ugly. And you *do* deserve better than Dexter.'

Turning her head, Nuala blinked up at him. Jake Harvey was possibly the best-looking male she'd ever encountered in the flesh. You couldn't look at him and not be bowled over by those cheekbones, that chiselled mouth, those incredible eyelashes of his. And he was still stroking her hip . . .

'You're better than Dexter,' said Nuala, suddenly realising what would help her over this.

'Well, thanks.' Jake smiled down at her, taking it as a compliment.

Hurriedly, before she lost her nerve, Nuala said, 'You could cheer me up.'

'What, tell you a few jokes?'

'Sleep with me,' Nuala blurted out. 'That would make me feel better.'

Jake's hand stopped stroking her hip. 'What?'

'No strings,' Nuala went on hurriedly, in case he thought

she was expecting an engagement ring. 'Just sex. You sleep with loads of girls, so why not me? A one-night stand, that's all I'm saying. We could do that, couldn't we? It'd be fun. And it would piss Dexter right off.'

Crikey, what an offer. Jake tried his hardest not to smile.

'Nu, thanks for the offer, but I couldn't. Really. We're friends, and I don't want to spoil that.'

Eagerly Nuala said, 'But we wouldn't spoil anything!'

'You don't know. It wouldn't feel right.' Jake was doing his utmost to be tactful.

'I'm too ugly!'

'You're not too ugly. We've just both had a bit to drink. Trust me, when you wake up tomorrow morning you'll be glad we didn't do it.'

'But I want to!' cried Nuala, clearly taking the rejection personally. 'This isn't fair. How many girls have you slept with in the last five years? Why can't it be my turn now?'

'Because I'm doing the decent thing for once and behaving like a gentleman.'

'That's what men say when they don't fancy you,' Nuala grumbled.

'It's what men say when they don't want to lose a good friend.' To his immense relief, Jake heard the Saab pulling up outside the cottage. Thank God for that. 'Maddy's back,' he told Nuala, helping her to sit up and this time making sure she stayed up. 'You can tell her about you and Dexter.' Actually, it wasn't eleven thirty yet; now that Maddy was here he could shoot into Bath after all.

He just hoped for Maddy's sake that she'd finally come to her senses and finished with Kerr McKinnon.

'Blimey, what's been going on here?' Maddy gazed at them, taking in the empty gin bottle and Nuala's air of dishevelment.

'Dexter's dumped me. I've never been so miserable in my life. No boyfriend, no job, nowhere to live,' said Nuala. 'So anyway, I came over to talk to you about it, but you were out so I talked to Jake instead, and he said not to worry, I could move in with you.'

'I *didn't* say she could move in with us,' Jake hissed at Maddy in the kitchen. 'She said she was too depressed to sleep, then she said was it OK if she stayed here, and I said yes, because I thought she meant just for tonight, not *forever*. You'll have to tell her.'

'How can I? She's my friend.' Energetically frying bacon for sandwiches, Maddy leaped back as the fat spattered like fireworks in the pan. 'Anyway, it's too late now, you've already said she can live with us.'

'But I don't want her to!'

'That's just mean. She needs somewhere to stay.' Maddy frowned. 'What have you got against Nuala?'

Exasperated, Jake said, 'She fancies me. It's not exactly relaxing, sharing a house with a girl who just wants to jump on you and rip all your clothes off.'

'Oh, don't talk such rubbish. She's upset about Dexter,' Maddy scoffed. 'Just because you flirt with every girl you meet doesn't automatically mean they fancy you back.'

'But—'

'Hi, can you do my bacon really crispy?' Appearing in the kitchen doorway, oblivious to their furious whispers, Nuala held out her good arm and tottered unsteadily over to Jake. She hugged him hard, then said, 'I've been having a think. It's better if we don't have sex. OK?'

Maddy raised an eyebrow. Jake marvelled at Nuala's ability to make it sound as though he'd been the one begging her to sleep with him.

'OK,' he said.

'Great.' Happily disentangling herself, Nuala reeled across the kitchen and peered at the frying pan crowded with bacon. 'God, you have no idea how hungry I am. Any chance of a couple of fried eggs with that?'

Chapter 29

At lunchtime on Monday Marcella arrived at the Peach Tree. Maddy's car wasn't outside, which meant she was still out on her delivery round, but patience had never been one of Marcella's strong points.

Juliet was delighted to see her. Coming out from behind the counter she said, 'Maddy told me. Congratulations! How are you feeling?'

'Fine. Thanks. I need to ask you something,' said Marcella with characteristic bluntness.

'Fire away. What, about pregnancy? You think you'll never get over the morning sickness, but you do.'

'Not about pregnancy. About Kerr McKinnon.'

'Oh!' The colour abruptly rushed to Juliet's cheeks. 'Well . . . I couldn't . . . it's not for me to say.'

Taken aback by the vehemence of her response, Marcella said, 'Of course it is.'

Clearly appalled, Juliet shook her head. 'Really, I can't. You'll have to talk to Maddy.' Her voice wavering, she said faintly, 'How on earth did you find out?'

'Does it matter?' Still mystified by the extent of Juliet's reaction, Marcella experienced a pang of deep unease. 'Why don't you tell me when it started?'

'I can't, I can't, but I *know* Maddy never meant to hurt you,' babbled Juliet, who normally never babbled. 'It was just one of those things . . . they met each other and that was it. But she's going to finish with him, I promise.'

On her way back from Bath, Maddy drove over the brow of Ashcombe Hill and saw Marcella heading towards her. From the armful of flowers her mother was carrying, she knew that Marcella was on her way to visit April's grave, something she still liked to do on a weekly basis. Slowing to a halt as she reached her, Maddy swung open the passenger door and said, 'I thought you were supposed to be taking things easy. Jump in and I'll give you a lift.' Pausing, she added, 'Mum, are you OK?' because Marcella was looking strained and distant, decidedly unlike her usual easygoing self.

But all Marcella did was nod, clutching the huge bunch of freshly picked honeysuckle, roses and ox-eye daisies to her chest.

The churchyard was deserted, the air hot and dry. Birds sang in the trees, but otherwise the silence was absolute. Marcella, still without speaking, cleared away the old flowers from April's grave, rinsed out the steel water-holder and carefully arranged the fresh blooms in their place. Maddy had never seen her mother like this before; she was normally chatty and eternally cheerful. Was it something to do with the pregnancy, the risk of losing this longed-for baby as heartbreakingly as they had lost April eleven years ago?

Marcella was kneeling by the grave with her back to her. Maddy reached out and touched her on the shoulder.

'Mum? Tell me what's wrong.'

Slowly Marcella rose to her feet.

'That's April in there. Your sister.'

'I know,' said Maddy gently. Oh dear, she'd never heard Marcella sound so subdued; her hormones were clearly running riot.

The next moment Marcella did something far less subdued. Raising her hand, she slapped Maddy hard across the face.

'April, your sister, is *dead*,' Marcella shouted furiously. 'And you're carrying on with Kerr McKinnon as if she never even existed! You have no shame, do you hear me? I don't know how you can *live* with yourself. Of all the men in the world, you had to get involved with him!'

Oh Lord. Maddy felt sick. Marcella had never laid a finger on her in her life. She should have ended it with Kerr while she still had the chance. Wide-eyed with shock, she took a step back before Marcella could slap her again.

'I'm ashamed of you,' Marcella raged, shaking her head in disgust. 'This is your family, don't you think you owe your sister a bit more loyalty than that?'

'Kerr wasn't the one driving the car.' Maddy knew even as she said it that any form of argument was hopeless. 'He didn't kill anyone.'

'I DON'T CARE!' bellowed Marcella. 'The McKinnons treated us like *dirt*, I can't believe you even—'

'I won't see him again,' Maddy blurted out, because what other choice did she have? This time, for Marcella's sake, it had to happen. She couldn't put it off any longer. Trembling, meeting Marcella's icy gaze, she nodded and said, 'I mean it, I'll never see him again, just don't shout any more, you know what the doctor said about staying calm and not getting worked up.'

'Promise me.' Marcella reached urgently for Maddy's hands.

What else could she do?

'I promise,' whispered Maddy.

That was it; all over now.

Marcella hugged her, tears spilling from her luminous dark eyes.

'You don't need someone like that. Come on, let's go home.'

As she followed Marcella back through the sun-dappled graveyard, Maddy thought, Oh, but I *do*.

Checking her watch – twenty to two – Maddy dropped Marcella home and headed back into the centre of Ashcombe. Juliet wasn't expecting her back in the shop before two. Pulling up alongside Snow Cottage, she saw Jake sitting at one of the tables in front of the pub, drinking a pint of orange juice and chatting to Malcolm, who sold his surreal paintings from the workshop next to his. By sitting outside, they were able to take a lunch break and keep an eye out for passing potential customers.

Fury boiled up inside Maddy at the unfairness of it all. How *dare* bloody Jake sit there without a care in the world when her own life was collapsing around her ears?

Leaping out onto the pavement, slamming the driver's door so hard it almost parted company with the car, she marched across the road.

'Did you tell Marcella?'

Jake looked up, surprised.

'Tell Marcella about what?'

'So you didn't?' said Maddy, double-checking. She wasn't about to make *that* mistake again.

Comprehension dawned. Jake, his eyebrows shooting up, said, 'You mean she found out about Kerr McKinnon?'

Right, that was all the confirmation she needed. Marching past him into the pub, Maddy saw Kate behind the bar, wearing a lime-green sleeveless linen top and her customary superior smirk.

'Well done,' Maddy said loudly, not caring that there were customers in the pub. Since there was no longer any secret to keep, she could be as loud as she jolly well liked.

Turning, Kate said, 'Excuse me?' in that irritatingly disinterested way of hers.

'I asked you not to tell Marcella and you told her. I explained *why* I asked you not to tell her,' Maddy went on furiously, 'but you went ahead and did it anyway.'

'I—'

'What the bloody hell's going on?' Dexter, his eyes flashing, had loomed up behind Kate.

'Ask your new barmaid,' Maddy spat back, aware that everyone was staring at the red, hand-shaped slap mark Marcella had imprinted on her cheek. 'But let me just say, if my mother doesn't have a miscarriage it'll be no thanks to *her*.' Pointing a trembling finger at Kate, who was looking gobsmacked and clearly hadn't expected to be confronted like this in public, she went on, 'My God, I knew you didn't like me, but even I never thought you'd sink this low. I mean, it doesn't matter that you've ruined *my* life, but how you could do this to Marcella, I'll never know.'

It was just as well there weren't any customers in the deli. Maddy was sitting on a crate in the back room shaking uncontrollably, raging against the world and knocking back a miniature of Amaretto.

Jake, strolling into the shop, said, 'Well, I hope you're proud of yourself.'

'Oh, bugger off, don't you start.' Maddy glared at him. 'She deserved it.'

'Did she? I've just been to see Marcella.'

'Oh no.' Juliet, who had been attempting to console Maddy, said, 'You mean it wasn't Kate?'

The look of disdain on Jake's face began to make Maddy feel queasy. 'It has to have been her. It definitely couldn't be Nuala, not after last time.'

'At midday, Marcella was doing exactly what the doctor had told her to do,' said Jake. 'She was taking things easy, relaxing, just having a cup of tea and watching the local

213

lunchtime news. When up came a piece on careers for school leavers, and guess whose company they were featuring today?'

Maddy's mouth was dry. There had been no cameras around while she'd been in the offices of Callaghan and Fox last Friday.

'I know. It's where Kerr works,' she told Jake. 'So? It's not as if he keeps a photo of me on his desk.'

'Maybe not, but several of the staff had stuff from here on their desks,' said Jake. 'Marcella recognised the blue and white wrappers at once.'

He was being deliberately maddening, Maddy decided. '*And?* That doesn't prove anything.'

'Oh my God,' whispered Juliet, her hand sliding from Maddy's shoulder. 'Oh no, please don't say what I think you're going to say.'

Her dark eyes were fixed on Jake, willing him to come up with a happier alternative. Signalling regret, he shook his head.

'What?' Maddy demanded. '*What?*'

Faintly, Juliet said, 'It was me.'

'WHAT?'

'The wrappers didn't prove you were having an affair with Kerr McKinnon,' said Jake, 'but they were certainly enough to bring Marcella down here, demanding to know what this deli was doing supplying sandwiches to his company, when just the other day you swore you had no idea where he worked.'

'I'm sorry,' groaned Juliet. 'The way Marcella said it, I thought she already knew everything.'

'Oh hell.' Maddy buried her head in her hands. 'I don't believe this is happening.'

'I'm *really* sorry,' Juliet repeated helplessly.

'Not you. It was an accident. I suppose something like

this was bound to happen sooner or later.' Maddy reached across and clumsily hugged Juliet, who was looking utterly distraught. 'I just can't bear the thought of having to apologise to Miss Smirky-knickers.'

'You're going to have to,' said Jake, so reasonably that Maddy longed to punch him.

Abruptly, all the adrenalin seeped out of her body and delayed shock set in. Her eyes filling with tears of exhaustion, she said, 'I know I do. Oh *fuck*.'

Chapter 30

Kate was doing her best to carry on working, but it wasn't going well. Aware of Dexter's beady gaze upon her, she fumbled in the till drawer for change and handed it over to Abel Trippick, whose eyes promptly widened with delight. As he scuttled away from the bar clutching his pint of Blackthorn, Dexter said, 'You just gave him eight quid change from a fiver.'

'Sorry.' Swallowing hard, Kate began clearing away empties. 'I'll pay you back.'

'I thought you were more than a match for Maddy Harvey.'

'So did I. Oh God—' Kate made a grab for one of the half-pint mugs as it slipped out of her hand, but it was too late. The glass shattered on the flagstones and she braced herself for the inevitable explosion of fury from Dexter.

Instead, his tone conversational, Dexter said, 'If I shout at you, will you shout back?'

Blindly, Kate shook her head. 'No.' It came out as a croak, like a frog phoning in sick.

'Oh well, no point in bothering then. Shift your bottom,' Dexter said brusquely, and tears began to slide down Kate's cheeks as she realised he was kneeling down, wielding a dustpan and brush and clearing up the mess.

Then she jumped as a warm hand came to rest on her arm and a familiar voice said, 'Hey, it's all right.'

Could have fooled me, thought Kate as Jake peered over the bar and said to Dexter, 'It's almost closing time. OK if I take this one home with me?'

Dexter straightened up. Finally he shrugged. 'May as well. She's not much use here.'

'Who says I want to go home with you?' Kate looked truculent, but it was a token show of protest. Flashing a grin, Jake raised the wooden flap that formed part of the bar and drew her through to his side.

'OK, here's the thing. Maddy shouldn't have shouted at you, she knows she has to apologise, but she's in a bit of a state right now, what with everything hitting the fan the way it did. So if you wouldn't mind, she'd like to make her grovelling apologies later.' As he spoke, he was leading her towards the door.

Kate said suspiciously, 'So why are you taking me home?'

'Because damsels in distress are my speciality. Besides,' Jake gestured over the road to where Malcolm was now sitting with a sketchpad outside his workshop, 'any excuse for an afternoon off.'

Dauncey House was cool and empty, with Oliver up in London as usual and Estelle off on one of her periodic half-hearted health and fitness kicks. This involved paying a visit to the ruinously expensive gym to which she belonged, gingerly attempting a few exercises on the less terrifying machines, then greeting her female friends with delight and repairing to the terrace for a good gossip over salad and a Diet Coke. Since this left them feeling every bit as virtuous as two hours on the treadmill, and involved far less sweating, it was a popular pastime amongst the wealthy wives who went there during the afternoon. Estelle was unlikely to be back before five.

'Hey, damsel, you've got mascara on your cheeks.'

They were in the kitchen. Kate instinctively made a move towards the downstairs cloakroom to wash her face, but Jake stopped her. Running a piece of kitchen towel under the tap, he drew her towards him and gently rubbed at the black marks under her eyes. Realising that he was removing the carefully applied scar concealer at the same time, Kate tried to pull away but Jake shook his head and said, 'Don't be silly, it's fine. You're not as scary as you think.'

He was so close to her now. She couldn't bring herself to look at his face, but he smelled of shampoo and outdoors and, very faintly, acrylic varnish. Kate was under his spell; she normally removed her mascara with Clinique cleanser at twenty quid a tube and supersoft cotton wool pads. Yet here was Jake Harvey rubbing away at her delicate under-eye areas with a wodge of wet kitchen towel – and she didn't want him to stop.

'Not as tough as you like to make out either,' Jake observed and she felt her throat tighten. He was being so kind.

'It's not much fun being accused of something you didn't do.' Kate shook her head. 'I would never have told Marcella.'

'I know that.'

'But Maddy didn't. That's what really got to me, I think. She seriously thought I had. I mean, I know we don't get on,' Kate blurted out, 'but I wouldn't risk Marcella losing the baby, would I? I'd *never* do that!'

'Damsel, calm down. I told you, Maddy's going to apologise. She's not having the best time right now. Crikey, none of us are having the best time.' Jake rolled his eyes. 'Let me tell you, it's no picnic sharing a house with Nuala.

When she isn't bleating on about Dexter and how she's never going to get another boyfriend, she's asking me to help her on with her trainers. It's like living with a three-year-old all over again.'

Kate felt a pang of solidarity with Nuala; she often wondered if she'd ever find another boyfriend herself.

'Anyway, how about you?' said Jake, changing the subject as they made their way through to the conservatory. 'You've been back a few weeks now. Looks to me as though you've settled right in.'

'Kind of,' Kate conceded. Certainly, she'd never imagined herself working in the pub and, more astounding still, actually enjoying it.

'You're a natural behind that bar.' Collapsing onto one of the squashy lime-green sofas, Jake patted the space next to him. 'I bet you never thought it would be that easy to get back to normal.'

'Normal?' Kate's laughter was hollow. How could he possibly think her life was back to normal?

'Isn't it? Oh, come on,' Jake protested, 'you're doing brilliantly. Nobody in the pub even notices your scars any more.'

'My accident happened fourteen months ago. I haven't been kissed by a man since then, let alone had sex with one. How normal do you suppose that feels?' The moment she'd finished blurting the words out, Kate wished she hadn't. What's more, how on earth could Jake be expected to have an inkling how it felt? He'd probably never gone without sex for as long as fourteen days.

He was definitely looking flummoxed.

'Sorry.' Kate gazed at the floor. 'Shouldn't have said that.'

'Are you serious? Nothing at all? Not even in New York?'

Ha, especially in New York.

'I think I'd have noticed.'

'But why not?' Jake was genuinely concerned.

'Why d'you think? Who'd look at my face and be overcome with lust?' Irritated, Kate said, 'People see my scars and they run a mile.'

'Wrong.' Jake was shaking his head.

'Don't patronise me. I know what I look like.'

'People see you with your defences up, snapping and snarling and not giving an inch, and that's why they run a mile. Trust me, it's not your face that scares them off,' Jake said bluntly. 'It's you.'

'Well, thanks.' Kate's jaw tightened.

'Just being honest, damsel.' Unperturbed by her frosty manner, Jake said mischievously, 'So, feel like giving it a go?'

Kate stopped breathing; she actually felt her lungs freeze in mid-flow.

'What?'

His eyes danced. 'You heard.'

'I don't know what you mean.'

'Of course you do.'

Kate was tingling all over with furious indignation. How *dare* Jake suggest such a thing? This was outrageous . . . and what exactly did he mean, anyway? Was he talking about a kiss or . . . well, *other* stuff?

Oh good grief, what would *that* be like? Lust shot through her like a bolt of lightning. And all the time Jake was sitting there watching her, utterly relaxed and laid-back, smiling his irresistible boyish smile. In all seriousness, what did he *expect* her to say?

'Fine. I'll take that as a no then.' Jake shrugged good-naturedly and Kate heard a squeak of protest escape – completely involuntarily – from her throat.

'Or maybe . . . a maybe?' said Jake.

Kate's cheeks began to burn. In fact her whole body felt as if it was on fire and her imagination was working on fast forward. This was excruciating, and now she really was going to have to say something.

'Er . . . I didn't know what you meant *exactly*.' Floundering, she saw Jake's mouth twitch.

His oh-so-beautiful mouth, so perfect it looked as if it had been chiselled from marble.

'You mean was I talking about kissing you? Or the whole bed thing?'

Trust Jake to come straight out and say it. Her toes practically bent double with embarrassment, Kate nodded.

'Well, that's completely up to you. Whatever you decide. Or,' Jake offered, 'we could start off with a kiss and see how you feel.'

Kate's heart was hammering against her ribs; she already knew how she felt. Then an awful thought struck her.

'And you'd want money?'

Jake smiled and shook his head. 'Damsel, I'm not a gigolo. I don't charge.'

'So, um, why are you doing this?'

His smile broadened. 'I'm not volunteering to empty cesspits here. It's hardly an arduous task we're talking about. I love sex. You're a beautiful girl with a hang-up about your face, who hasn't had sex for over a year. I mean, I didn't have a university education, but isn't there a simple solution here?'

Oh God, oh God. Kate was lost for words. Staring blindly at the black and white tiled floor, she felt Jake's hand stroke the back of her neck.

'I like you,' he said softly. 'Believe me, it wouldn't be an ordeal. It would be a pleasure.'

After that, everything seemed to happen in slow motion. Since Norris was outside in the back garden and the sight of him pressing his slobbering jowls against the conservatory windows just might kill the moment, Kate led Jake upstairs to her room. Trembling, she allowed him to undress her. And kiss her. And run his hands over her naked body. And make love to her.

He was right, too, about it not being an ordeal. The next two hours were nothing but glorious technicoloured pleasure.

Chapter 31

'Right. Fun's over.' Fastening his shirt, Jake bent over the bed and planted a warm, lingering kiss on Kate's mouth. 'Back to the real world. Orders to take, caskets to deliver.'

Feeling bereft already, Kate said, 'Malcolm's looking after the business. You don't have to go.'

Was that needy? She didn't care.

'I do.' Jake kissed her again. 'Have to pick Sophie up. You were amazing. What a way to spend an afternoon.'

Needy was one thing, but begging quite another. Resisting the almost uncontrollable urge to ask when she'd see him again, Kate smiled and stretched like a cat.

'You were pretty amazing yourself.' She couldn't *stop* smiling, actually; great waves of happiness kept swooshing over her, she hadn't known it was possible to feel this fantastic.

'Good.' Jake straightened up and headed for the door. 'I'll let myself out. And don't forget, Maddy'll be round later.'

'Maddy.' Kate pulled a face.

'Hey, she's sorry. And she's having a tough time. Go easy on her,' Jake said gently.

He blew her a kiss and left.

Hmm. Settling back against the mass of pillows, Kate pictured herself going easy on Maddy Harvey.

Oh yes, and pigs might perform aerial acrobatics.

Then again, then again . . .

By five thirty, Kate had had a major re-think. It *was* completely ridiculous, carrying on a childhood feud for no other reason than that each of them was too stubborn to apologise. It made matters awkward whenever their paths crossed. Neither of them stood to gain anything from it. The only mature, sensible thing to do, surely, was to forgive Maddy and heal the rift.

Plus, she was Jake's sister.

Saying sorry to Kate Taylor-Trent should have been an excruciating prospect, but nothing was as bad as having to phone Kerr to tell him it was over, that from now on they wouldn't see each other any more, ever again.

'Ever?' Kerr queried. 'How about next year, after the baby's born? Couldn't we try again then?'

Maddy heaved a sigh; she'd thought of that too. But what were the chances of Kerr still being interested and available then? By next year, any girl with an ounce of sense would have snapped him up.

More importantly, he'd still be a McKinnon. Nothing in the world could change that. Some families, Maddy knew, fought like cat and dog. She'd seen enough episodes of *Jerry Springer* to know that plenty of mothers and daughters hurled abuse at each other and didn't care how much pain they caused because they genuinely couldn't stand the sight of each other. They were happy to be estranged, living their own separate lives, carrying on without exchanging so much as a word for years.

But she could never do that to Marcella. They may not be related by blood, but Marcella had devoted her life to her stepchildren and they'd loved and adored her in return. Becoming estranged simply wasn't an option.

'I can't,' said Maddy, her chest aching with suppressed grief. 'We can't. I'm sorry, I just . . .'

'Can't.' Kerr finished the sentence she was incapable of finishing herself. 'OK, I understand. Take care. Bye.'

'Bye,' Maddy whispered, but the line had already gone dead.

That was it, all over.

Done.

'Gosh, this is a surprise!' Estelle, answering the front door of Dauncey House, was clearly bemused by the sight of Maddy on her doorstep. Then her hand flew to her mouth. 'Oh no, not bad news, something hasn't happened to—'

'Mum's fine,' Maddy said quickly. 'Nothing's happened to the baby. I'm here to see, um, Kate. Is she around?'

Still mystified, Estelle said, 'Well, yes, but she's in the bath. Why don't you wait in the sitting room and I'll tell her you're here.'

'It's all right,' came a voice from the top of the staircase, causing both Estelle and Maddy to turn and look up. 'I already know.'

Straight from the bath, wearing an ivory silk dressing gown and with her dark hair slicked back from her face, Kate led the way into the sitting room. It was the first time Maddy had seen her without make-up. Minus the concealing foundation her scars were more noticeable – that went without saying – but the effect wasn't as shocking as she'd imagined. With her renewed air of confidence, Kate was somehow managing to carry it off.

'Sit down,' said Kate. 'Drink?'

Maddy shook her head. As soon as she'd said what she'd come to say, she was out of here.

'No thanks, I'm fine. Look, we both know what this is about,' Maddy blurted out. 'I'm sorry, OK? Really and truly sorry. First I accused Nuala of telling Jake about me and Kerr, and I was wrong. Then I accused you of telling Marcella and that was wrong too. You'd think I'd have learned my lesson by now, wouldn't you? Anyway, I apologise. From the bottom of my heart. I should never have said it, and I'm sorry you were upset.' Trailing off with a helpless shrug, Maddy forced herself to meet Kate's stony gaze. 'That's it really. I'm just sorry.'

Silence.

Finally Kate said, 'OK. Apology accepted. But you were lying about one thing.'

Oh God. A wave of exhaustion swept through Maddy. She simply wasn't up to a heated debate.

'What was I lying about?'

'You said, "No thanks, I'm fine," and it isn't true. You look terrible,' Kate went on with characteristic bluntness. 'You're as white as a ghost – and look at your eyes, you're in a complete state.'

'Well, thanks.' Delighted to have this pointed out to her, Maddy retorted, 'And who says ghosts are white anyway? They don't all go around with sheets over their heads, you know.'

Unbelievable. In less than a minute flat they were sniping at each other again like a pair of twelve-year-olds. Once upon a time, of course, they *had* used white sheets in order to dress up as ghosts on Halloween night and wreak havoc around the village.

Astonishingly, instead of launching into a counter-attack, Kate's tone softened.

'Don't take offence. I'm just saying it's pretty obvious you aren't fine. And I'm sorry too, OK? For the hard time I gave you years ago. Ridgelow Hall may have taught me how to speak like an It-girl and flirt in Italian, but it turned me into a right stuck-up little bitch. I'm not proud of the way I treated you.' As she spoke, Kate's fingers were clenching and unclenching in her lap. 'I said some really horrible things about the way you looked . . . well, I'm sure you remember.'

Remember? The horrible things were etched in sulphuric acid into her heart. 'Rings a bell,' said Maddy, still finding it hard to believe that Kate was actually apologising for all the hurt she'd inflicted over the years.

'Well, I got my come-uppance there, didn't I?' Kate raised her hand to the left side of her face. 'You must have laughed your head off when you heard what had happened to me.'

'I didn't laugh,' Maddy protested. 'I'd never *laugh*.'

'But?' prompted Kate.

Oh well, it wasn't as if she was saying something Kate hadn't already figured out for herself. She'd never been stupid.

'But I did think that now you'd know how it felt.' There, confession over, she'd admitted it.

'I don't blame you. I was such a cow.' Wryly Kate gestured towards Maddy. 'And see how the ugly duckling turned out. Look at you now,' she said bluntly. 'Who'd have thought it?'

Gazing down at her yellow sandals, rather too bright against the tasteful bottle-green carpet of the sitting room, Maddy said, 'For all the good it's done me,' and felt her eyes prickle with tears. Oh no, she mustn't start crying again, not *here*.

'You've finished with Kerr then,' said Kate.

Maddy nodded. 'No choice.'

'I would never have told Marcella, you know.'

'I know. I'm sorry.'

'Don't be sorry. It's my own fault. When you asked me not to say anything, I shouldn't have let you think I might.' Kate paused. 'Are you feeling as bad as you look?'

Maddy's bottom lip began to tremble. 'Worse. Damn, I don't make a habit of blubbing all over the place . . . oh, thanks.' She reached blindly for a tissue from the box Kate was holding in front of her. 'I just can't believe my bad luck. Years and years of being ugly and boys taking the mickey out of me, then getting less scary and going out but never finding the right chap, then finally finding someone and really falling in love for the f-first time . . . and I can't have him. It's not allowed. I don't know, it j-just doesn't seem fair somehow . . . oh bugger, can I have another tissue?'

'Here,' said Kate, 'better keep the box.'

Chapter 32

An hour later they headed together down Gypsy Lane. It was seven o'clock, time for Kate to begin her evening shift at the Angel. Dressed in a geranium-red sleeveless shift dress and high heels, with her face now carefully made up for the benefit of the punters, Kate was looking tall, glamorous and – from this angle – flawless. Next to her, moping along in her frayed denim jacket, old jeans and flat yellow sandals, Maddy felt inferior all over again.

'Well, this is weird.'

'Us, you mean?' Kate turned her head and smiled, revealing her scarred side. 'Actually speaking to each other again?'

'And all thanks to Kerr.' Maddy pulled out her dark glasses as they approached Main Street, acutely aware that her eyes were bulging like a bullfrog's. 'So he came in useful after all, that's good news. I'm sure he'd be pleased.'

'I'm pleased,' said Kate. 'It's not been much fun being back here in the village, knowing nobody liked me.'

'Not *nobody*.' Maddy shook her head. 'Jake didn't care how I felt. He liked you straight away.'

'Really?' Flushing with pleasure, Kate said, 'But I was so prickly with him.'

'Oh well, that's Jake for you. Always up for a challenge.'

And thank goodness he had been. Smiling to herself, Kate felt her heart begin to quicken at the memory of their time in bed together this afternoon – and the thought of the next time, tomorrow with any luck. She couldn't wait for a repeat performance.

'Coming in for a drink?'

Maddy glanced across the road at the pub, then shook her head. 'Not tonight. Hey, did you ever see this?'

Kate turned; Maddy was making her way over to the old bench next to the bus stop. Following her, she watched as Maddy searched the wooden slats for a moment before finding what she was looking for.

'Here we are.'

Peering down to where Maddy was pointing, Kate saw the words gouged into the wood amongst the mass of graffiti carved over the years.

'Kate T-T is a cow,' Kate read aloud.

'I can remember exactly when I did it,' said Maddy. 'September. We'd just started back at school after the summer holidays and I was here one morning waiting for the bus. Then you sauntered past with one of your posh friends, on your way to the shop. Bear in mind that you were both wearing stretchy halter-neck tops and tiny skirts, while I was in my six-sizes-too-big maroon school uniform. And you turned to your friend and said, "God, back to school already, who'd be a pleb?"'

'I remember that!' Kate nodded energetically. 'We still had another ten days of holiday; we fl—'

'It's OK,' said Maddy when Kate stopped abruptly, 'you can say it. You flew down to the south of France and spent a week on your friend's dad's yacht.' Drily she added, 'You boasted about it when you got back.'

'You're right, I was a cow.' Kate marvelled that the wonkily carved accusation had been on show all these years, clearly visible to anyone who'd ever sat on this bench waiting for the bus. Never having caught a bus in her life, she would not have known it was here. 'What are you *doing*?' she exclaimed as Maddy took her Swiss Army knife keyring out of her bag and began energetically digging away at the bench.

'Changing it. Bringing it up to date.' Working at speed with the sharp blade, Maddy brushed away the loosened paint flakes and sat back to show Kate the finished job. Instead of Kate T-T is a cow, it now said Kate T-T *was* a cow.

They gazed at each other in silence for several seconds, then simultaneously burst out laughing.

'Absolutely disgraceful,' a male voice barked behind them. Turning, Maddy and Kate saw a couple of middle-aged rambler types in matching baggy khaki shorts and Save the Countryside T-shirts.

'I know,' said Kate, 'it's outrageous.'

Infuriated, the male rambler boomed, 'Defacing public property, wanton vandalism. You should be ashamed of yourselves.'

'I am,' Kate told the man who was by this time puce in the face, 'but I'm feeling better now. Anyway, it isn't vandalism,' she added with a sweet smile. 'It's local history.'

Fantasy time.

After the best night's sleep she could remember, Kate was lying in the bath with bubbles up to her ears and a blissful grin on her face that wouldn't go away. What a magical day yesterday had turned out to be. What a day today would hopefully turn out to be – heavens, from now on anything could happen.

Closing her eyes to make visualising it easier, Kate conjured up a Christmassy picture not dissimilar to the final moments of *It's A Wonderful Life*. There was Jake with one arm round her and the other round Sophie – actually, no, because then she and Sophie would be separated; far better to have Sophie in the middle, hugging them both and being hugged in return to show how happy they were. Anyway, so there they were, all together, just like a proper family – and if she and Jake ended up getting married there'd be no problem with warring in-laws because Estelle and Marcella got on brilliantly together, and she and Maddy had put their silly differences behind them. God, this was the best fantasy ever, and it could actually come true—

Yeek, phone, that was probably Jake now!

Racing downstairs with bath bubbles cascading down her body and a towel hastily slung round her middle section, Kate skidded breathlessly into the kitchen.

'Was that for me?'

Estelle, eating toast and compiling a shopping list, looked surprised.

'No, darling. Will Gifford just rang, he's coming down this afternoon.'

Wrong answer. *Completely* wrong answer. Who gave a toss about bumbling Will Gifford?

'Expecting a call?' said Estelle.

No wonder she sounds amazed, Kate thought. What with me and my action-packed social life.

'Not really.' Realising she was dripping water and foam onto the kitchen floor, Kate said, 'I'll go and get dressed.'

'Darling, I'm so glad you and Maddy are friends again.'

Kate nodded; Estelle had in fact got quite tearful last night at the thought of happy endings all round. Not that her mother knew yet about the particular happy ending she had in mind for herself and Jake.

Struggling to contain a giveaway smirk, Kate said, 'Me too.'

By eleven o'clock she was setting off down Gypsy Lane with a bounce in her step and a fully-fledged plan in her brain. Because basically, why hang about waiting for Jake to ring when she was perfectly capable of making things happen herself? Even Norris seemed more cheerful this morning, jauntily ambling along, exploring the hedgerows and almost – but not quite – breaking into a run when he spotted Bean cavorting outside Jake's workshop.

Even our dogs get on, Kate thought joyfully, what could be more perfect than that?

It was cooler than yesterday, with an overcast sky and the threat of rain in the air. Instead of sitting outside his workshop with his shirt off, Jake was inside wearing a pale grey lambswool sweater and jeans. He was working on a casket, painstakingly brushing varnish over a transferred painting of a snowy mountain range.

Looking up as Kate entered the workshop, he flicked his sunstreaked blond hair out of his eyes and flashed his trademark dazzling smile.

'Hi.'

He loves me.

'Hi.' Kate felt herself go fizzy all over; when a man smiled at you like that, you knew that yesterday had meant something extra-special. 'Listen, what are you doing tonight?'

This was Jake's cue to do his sparkly-eyed thing and murmur flirtatiously, 'I don't know, what *am* I doing tonight? You tell me.'

Instead he said, 'I've been bullied into taking Sophie to the cinema to see the new Spiderman movie. I must be mad, the last one scared me witless.' He pulled a face. 'But that's Soph for you. What can you do with a girl who has three pairs of Spiderman pyjamas?'

'Well, it's my night off,' said Kate, 'so why don't we all go? Then I can hold your hand during the scary bits.'

'It's good of you to offer, but it's Spiderman.' Jake shrugged good-naturedly. 'Hardly your kind of thing. You wouldn't enjoy it.'

Actually, this was a fair point. Not that she wouldn't enjoy sitting in the darkened cinema holding Jake's hand, but as a breed, movies starring comic-book heroes left her cold.

'OK, better idea. I'll meet up with you after the cinema and we'll go for a pizza.' Kate beamed, pleased with herself, then realised that Jake was hesitating and added hurriedly, 'I meant all of us go for a pizza, you, me and Sophie.'

'Kate, look, I'm sorry, but I have to say no.'

Time stood still. She wondered if she'd somehow misunderstood this last sentence; if, in fact, he was actually saying yes. But that was taking fantasy too far.

Slowly Kate said, 'No to what? Pizza?'

'No to all of it. Meeting up, visiting cinemas together, doing the kind of things couples do, the whole works.' Jake shook his head. 'Yesterday was great, OK? We both enjoyed ourselves. But that's as far as it goes. I keep my private life and my family life separate. It wouldn't be fair on Sophie, introducing her to an endless stream of girls, letting her think I might be getting serious about this one or that.' He paused, then said gently, 'Does that make sense to you?'

It made about as much sense as being hit across the face with a wet towel. This wasn't what Kate had been expecting to hear at all.

Stunned, she said, 'Is it because of the way I look?'

'Oh, please. I thought we'd cured you of that. I just don't want to confuse Sophie, that's all. If I know I'm not going to be settling down with someone, why get her hopes up?'

What about *my* hopes? Kate wanted to scream, and the awful realisation that he meant what he said struck her like a stake through the heart. This was rejection of the most brutal kind, brutal because she genuinely hadn't been expecting it.

Despising herself for being pathetic, already knowing the answer deep down but still needing to hear it from Jake's mouth, she heard herself ask, 'So do you want to carry on seeing me when Sophie isn't around? Or was yesterday just a one-off?'

Jake sighed. 'I wouldn't have put it quite like that. But OK, it was a one-off.'

'So you lied to me.' There was a telltale tremor in Kate's voice. 'I thought you really liked me. You *told* me you liked me. But it was just a big lie.'

'That's not fair. I do like you,' Jake said evenly. 'But we're never going to be a couple.'

Kate felt her fingernails digging into her palms as a glimmer of hope shone through. 'We could be!' Her heart raced as she realised what this was all about. 'Is this because your family's poor and mine are rich? Jake, it doesn't matter a bit, I don't *care* that you don't have any money—'

'Well, nice of you to say so,' Jake interrupted, 'and I'm very flattered, but it's nothing to do with that.'

Helplessly Kate blurted out, 'It is my face.'

'Stop jumping to conclusions and just listen to me. And you do have to stop blaming everything on your face, by the way,' said Jake. 'Because, trust me, it matters to you a damn sight more than it matters to anyone else.'

'Go on then, fire away.' Outside the workshop, Kate could hear Norris and Bean playing, happily rolling around together – not unlike Jake and herself yesterday afternoon. Now, fiddling with the button of her thin navy jacket, she said, 'What, then?'

'It's quite simple,' said Jake. 'When you fall in love with someone, it doesn't happen because you want it to. Sometimes it's the *last* thing you want – crikey, look at the mess Maddy's got herself into – but you don't have any kind of control over it. It just happens.' He paused, and there was compassion – or sadness – in his green eyes. 'Or not, as the case may be.'

And that was that. Stung by the rejection, Kate stalked

back up the hill to Dauncey House at such a rate that poor Norris's paws barely touched the ground.

So much for having thought she might actually be about to discover how it felt to be happy. Now she was back to square one, all over again.

Chapter 33

'Oh God, not you again.'

'Enchanting to see you too,' Will Gifford said amiably, stepping to one side as Kate swept past him. Catching the front door before it had a chance to slam shut in his face, he added, 'Is your mum in?'

'Does it make any difference?' Kate shot him a look of irritation. 'You usually enjoy a good nose around whether anyone's here or not.'

'Ouch,' said Will with a grin.

Contemptuously Kate hissed, 'Oh, grow up.'

Estelle had her mouth full of mint Aero when Will came into the kitchen. Jumping guiltily away from the fridge where she kept her stash of chocolate, she covered her mouth with one hand and gave him an embarrassed wave with the other.

'Just passed the ray of sunshine on her way out,' said Will.

Estelle winced, managed to swallow a giant chunk of Aero in one go and said shamefacedly, 'Hence the comfort eating.'

'Still giving you the runaround?'

'I don't know what's happened. Yesterday she was fantastic, so cheerful you wouldn't believe it.' Seeing from Will's face that he didn't, Estelle went on earnestly, 'Really, it's the truth. She was happy, laughing, she even made up with an old friend she'd fallen out with *years* ago. I thought this is it, we've turned the corner at last, but this afternoon we're back to square one. It's as if yesterday never happened, like Brigadoon, and I don't know what's wrong. I mean, am I being really dense here?' As she said it, a sob burst from Estelle's throat, as unstoppable as a sneeze. 'Other people seem to manage to have children who don't treat them like a pile of poo, but it just doesn't seem to be h-happening for m-me.'

'Hey, hey,' Will crooned, crossing the kitchen at the speed of light. Next moment Estelle found herself being held by him, and realising that this was what she'd been subconsciously longing for ever since Will had last left for London. 'It's all right,' he murmured soothingly, 'it's not you, you didn't do anything wrong.'

Dizzily, Estelle breathed in the fresh Persil-scent of his diabolical plaid shirt. She was struggling to take in this startling turn of events. If she was honest, she'd daydreamed about something like this happening, but never believed for a moment it would ever actually happen.

'I really shouldn't be saying this,' Will's mouth brushed her ear, 'but you have no idea how much I've missed you.'

Estelle's stomach did a pancake flip. She couldn't be attracted to a more wildly unsuitable man if she tried. For a start, Will Gifford was thirty-eight while she was forty-five, and when you weren't exactly drop-dead glamorous, seven years was a lot. Secondly, Will was here because he was making a documentary about her husband, which was scarcely ideal. What's more, she hadn't been involved with any man other than Oliver since her eighteenth birthday. For heaven's sake, if anyone in this house was suited to Will, it should be Kate.

But Estelle's tangled train of thought was distracted by Will's mouth finding hers, and she gave herself up to the sheer mindless pleasure of his kiss. Because sometimes chemistry happened and you made the discovery that you just didn't care. Anyway, when was the last time Oliver had pressed her up against the fridge and ravished her? Determined not to feel guilty, Estelle reminded herself that the only thing that got Oliver excited these days was profit margins and business plans.

If she painted herself pink, like the *Financial Times*, she might have more luck.

'We shouldn't be doing this.' Belatedly, her conscience kicked in. 'What about Oliver?'

'No problem, he's still in London. I spoke to him before he went into his meeting. He won't be home before six.'

'I didn't mean that,' Estelle panted, because Will was still stroking her face. 'I meant he's my *husband*.'

'Really? The one who neglects you?' Will raised his eyebrows. 'The one who doesn't deserve you? *That* husband?'

'He's just busy, he doesn't mean to neglect me.'

'So you want me to stop? You'd rather I didn't come near you?'

Trembling, Estelle whispered, 'No. I just . . . wasn't expecting this. It's all been a bit, um, sudden.'

'Nice sudden or nasty sudden?' said Will.

Estelle smiled. 'Nice sudden. But scary too. Kate could be back at any minute.' This was true, but it had also occurred to her that she hadn't shaved her legs for five days; worse still, she was wearing knickers made from a kind of weird stretchy honeycomb-patterned material that, when you took them off, left an unfortunate honeycomb imprint all over your bottom.

'I've thought of you more often than you'd believe,' Will murmured. 'Seriously. Nothing like this has ever happened to me before.'

The chances were that he wouldn't even notice her honeycomb-patterned bottom. And if he did, he probably wouldn't care. But Estelle couldn't take that risk. The prospect of getting naked in front of another man was terrifying enough. If Will burst out laughing she'd be mentally scarred for life.

Then again, she wouldn't say no to another kiss.

'Don't you have work you should be doing?' Estelle glanced at the kitchen table upon which were piled the bags containing his video camera and filming equipment.

'Just a few background shots. No hurry.' He paused. 'I know what you're thinking, by the way.'

'Wh-what?'

'You're worried about your body. Don't be.' Smiling, Will said, 'If I'd wanted a twenty-year-old stick insect, I wouldn't have spent the last week thinking shamefully erotic thoughts about you.'

Erotic thoughts.

'Actually, forget I said that.' Will pulled a face. 'Erotic thoughts just sounds sleazy, and I promise you I'm not sleazy. It's just . . .' he paused, gently stroking her hair back from her temples and letting it fall through his fingers, 'you've been on my mind.'

'Oh,' breathed Estelle as his warm mouth closed over her mouth and the length of his body pressed thrillingly against hers. It was the most wonderful sensation, glorious in its own right and made doubly so because who would have thought she had the power to instil such desire? She'd honestly thought that once you hit forty all the passion and excitement of youth became a thing of the pa—

'*Oh!*' squeaked Estelle, less breathily this time as the kitchen door creaked open. Leaping away from Will so fast she almost cracked her skull open on the oak wall cabinet, she felt abject terror rise up in her throat like bile.

'It's OK.' Will smiled as Norris, having executed his leaning-against-the-door trick in order to force it open, ambled into the kitchen.

'I thought it was Kate. Or Oliver. God, what if it *had* been?' Tingling all over with a mixture of fear and desire, Estelle rubbed the back of her head.

'Poor you, let me have a look at it. Government health warning,' said Will, tenderly feeling the bump. 'Adultery can seriously damage your health.'

Adultery. Estelle's mouth went dry at the sound of the word. How could she take that risk?

'Will, I'm flattered, but I can't.' As the words spilled out, she didn't know whether to congratulate herself on her moral strength or despise herself for being such a wimp.

'You don't want to?'

Oh, how could he even ask that?

'It's Oliver. We've been married for twenty-seven years.'

Will sounded amused. 'We don't have to tell him, you know.'

'But I'm such a hopeless liar,' wailed Estelle. 'I mean, I've never needed to lie before, so I haven't had the practice. I just know I'd stammer and go red and get it all horribly wrong, and we'd be found out in no time.'

'Sshh, OK, that's fine.' Will's tone was soothing. 'We won't do anything you don't want to do.'

This instantly made Estelle want to do it.

'No sex,' said Will.

Now she *really* wanted to have sex.

'Maybe just a spot of minor flirting,' Will went on. 'How would you feel about that?'

Is that all? thought Estelle, already feeling deprived. Then she gave herself a mental slap, because he was absolutely right. She *couldn't* betray Oliver, she *mustn't* sleep with Will, and flirting was fine, really it was. All the fun and none of the guilt. What could be more harmless than that?

A spot of minor flirtation and the occasional bit of kissing.

'Sounds . . . great.' Faintly flustered by her own thoughts,

Estelle smoothed down her pink and white shirt. In the corner of the kitchen Norris was slurping noisily from his water bowl, which put a bit of a dampener on the seductive atmosphere.

'Well,' Will said good-naturedly. 'Could have been better, but at least you didn't run away screaming in horror. I'm happy with that.'

He didn't know it, but he'd made her year. Talk about an ego boost. Unable to contain the joy bubbling up inside her, Estelle said, 'Me too.'

Nuala's collarbone wasn't the only thing on the mend. Like a wonderful unexpected Christmas present, breaking up with Dexter was turning out to be far less traumatic than she'd imagined. So much so, in fact, that it was almost embarrassing. In the past when boys had dumped her, she had always been distraught, weepily imagining that her life was over and that she'd never know happiness again. Having actually been quite famous for the extent of her declines, Nuala had naturally expected something similar to be happening now, but it simply hadn't materialised. No depression, no sense of utter hopelessness, no weight loss even, which was a bit of a blow.

'I can't understand it,' Nuala told Maddy as she jauntily swung the door of Snow Cottage shut behind them, 'I feel absolutely *fine*. I don't even get that choked-up thing in my throat when I see Dexter. You know what? If I'm honest, it's almost a relief to have it over and done with.'

'Good.' Maddy was pleased for Nuala, but her speedy recovery from breaking up with Dexter was a double-edged sword. On the one hand, it was good that Nuala was cheerful and in such a positive state of mind. On the other hand, there was such a thing as being annoyingly cheerful and positively irritating.

'Two years we were together,' Nuala marvelled, swinging her turquoise shoulder bag by its plaited leather straps as they headed across Main Street to the pub. 'Two whole years and I'm completely over him! It's like a miracle, I can't tell you how *great* it feels!'

Which was all very well, but not what you particularly wanted to hear when you'd never felt more empty and miserable in your life. The thing with Nuala was that she'd spent the last two years being treated like rubbish by a man she should never have got involved with in the first place. Never had two people been less compatible. No wonder she was glad to be out of a relationship like that. But – Maddy closed her eyes briefly – that wasn't how it had been with her and Kerr. Breaking up with someone you *knew* was the love of your life wasn't nearly so easy. Already, in the space of a few days, she had lost half a stone and knew it didn't suit her.

But Nuala had insisted on dragging her out for the evening because moping around the cottage was just – quote – dull, dull, *dull*, and in the end Maddy had run out of arguments. Which was why they were here now, at the Angel.

'We should go into Bath, check out some clubs,' Nuala bossily announced as they queued up at the bar. 'You too,' she ordered Kate, who had come over to serve them. 'I mean, look at us, three single girls without a man between us, how sad is that? And it's not as if we're ever going to find anyone decent in this dump.'

'Charming,' said Jake, who'd arrived just before them. 'And to think I was about to buy you a drink.'

'I am strong,' Nuala told him smugly, 'I am woman. Moping over men is no longer my thing. Anyway, I'm quite capable of buying my own drinks.'

'But sadly not capable of paying your own rent.' Jake grinned at Dexter then winced as Nuala landed a punch on his shoulder with her good arm.

'Just for that, I'll have a Bacardi and Coke.' Turning to Kate, Nuala said, 'And make it a large one. In fact, make it a bucket.'

Dexter, who didn't miss a trick, had already sensed that something was up. The moment Jake Harvey had entered the pub, Kate's body language had given her away. Jake, as relaxed and laid-back as ever, had greeted her with a cheerful grin but Kate's jaw had tightened beneath the polite veneer and she had made a point of avoiding his gaze. Knowing Jake as he did, it didn't take a genius to work out what had happened when Jake had taken Kate home the other afternoon. It was like a Pavlovian reaction, Dexter imagined: the moment you found yourself alone with a girl, you automatically seduced her. What's more, when you were Jake Harvey, it evidently never crossed the girl's mind to say no. Who knows, maybe he'd slept with Nuala too, although Dexter doubted this. If he had, he suspected Nuala wouldn't have been able to resist the urge to boast.

The range of emotions he was experiencing weren't the kind Dexter was used to – he didn't actually know where they'd sprung from but they were no less powerful for that. Whereas the thought of Nuala in bed with Jake didn't bother him at all, imagining Kate and Jake together filled him with a boiling rage. How *dare* Jake take advantage of her like that, when he clearly had no interest in a proper relationship? That was Jake Harvey all over, he was a shameless, morals-free zone.

'And one for yourself,' Jake told Kate, when she'd finished serving the rest of the round of drinks.

'No thanks.' Kate busied herself wiping up the spilled drops of lager on the bar.

'Go on.' Jake's voice softened. 'Hey, no hard feelings. We can still be friends, can't we?'

Dexter, straining to hear the murmured words from six feet away, longed to land a punch on Jake.

Deeply intrigued, Nuala raised her eyebrows enquiringly at Maddy.

Maddy, who'd been lost in thought about Kerr, hadn't a clue what was going on and wondered why Nuala was doing that weird thing with her eyebrows.

Kate shook her head. 'Really, I'm fine.'

Resting his fingers fleetingly on her arm, Jake mouthed, 'Sure?'

Unable to keep quiet a moment longer, Dexter barked, 'She doesn't *want* a drink, OK?' Barging up to Kate, he steered her towards the restaurant end of the bar. 'Table six want another bottle of wine. Sort them out, will you? I'll take over here.'

An hour later, Jake left to pick up Sophie from Marcella's. Fascinated, Nuala watched Kate doggedly pretending not to watch him go. During a lull at the bar she beckoned Kate over to the table she was now sharing with Maddy.

'More peanuts?' said Kate.

Her shoulders were noticeably more relaxed.

'It's not peanuts we're after.' Nuala gave her a complicit smile. 'It's information. Otherwise known as gossip. So,' she went on brightly, 'you and Jake, am I right? What's been going on that we don't know about?'

Kate reddened. Startled, Maddy said, 'Actually, there are some things I'm quite happy not to know about.'

'Oh, don't be so boring.' Eagerly Nuala turned her attention back to Kate. 'You slept with him, didn't you? I can tell.'

'Look,' Kate shuffled awkwardly from foot to foot, 'this isn't—'

'Oh my God, I'm right, aren't I? You really did!'

'Please,' Maddy protested, but Nuala was unstoppable now.

'You lucky, *lucky* thing,' she gasped excitedly, slopping

drink all over her sleeve. 'I wanted to sleep with Jake but he turned me down – damn, I'm so jealous! What was he like?'

'Hello? Excuse me,' Maddy's voice rose, 'but I really don't want to hear this.'

'Just whisper it then.' Nuala gave Kate a nudge. 'I mean, I'm assuming he's fabulous.'

'La-la-la,' Maddy sang loudly, her fingers jammed in her ears.

Hurriedly, Kate said, 'Dexter's going to hit the roof if I don't get back to work.'

Clearly Kate wasn't about to spill the beans. Some people were just plain selfish.

'OK, some other time. We could try that new club down by the train station on your next evening off, have a real girly night out.' Giving Kate a nudge as she turned to leave, Nuala added, 'But he is fabulous, isn't he?'

'Kate, get over here,' Dexter bellowed. 'I don't pay you to stand around doing bugger all.'

Back behind the bar, Kate snapped, 'And there's no need to yell at me.'

'I thought I was rescuing you.' Dexter's voice softened.

This only served to remind her of Jake calling her a damsel in distress. Pushing past Dexter on her way to refill the ice bucket, Kate said coldly, 'Well, *don't*.'

Chapter 34

Was this sad? Was this the kind of thing only truly pathetic people did? Was it really so wrong when it brought her so much comfort?

Well, OK, maybe not *so much* comfort, but beggars couldn't afford to be choosers. Any tiny crumb of comfort going was better than none at all.

Squinting in the darkness, Maddy held her wrist up to her face and peered at her watch. Ten past two in the morning and here she was, sitting in her car at the end of Kerr's road, gazing up at the unlit windows of his flat.

She would have been here earlier but Nuala had stayed up until midnight and Jake hadn't gone to bed until almost one o'clock. Maddy had been forced to wait until they were asleep before sneaking out of the cottage, climbing into her car and driving – hopefully not in a deranged, stalker-like fashion – into Bath.

Oh, but now that she was here she really *did* feel better, just knowing that Kerr was less than fifty feet away from her. These were *his* windows, that was *his* car parked outside, there was his very own dark blue front door . . .

She wasn't doing anything wrong, Maddy reminded herself; this was a harmless coping mechanism, nothing more. OK, so she'd promised Marcella she'd never see Kerr again, but nobody had said anything about not seeing his front door.

247

Behind her a set of headlights swung round the corner into the road. Guiltily, Maddy sank further down in the driver's seat and waited for the car to pass.

When it did, she caught her breath. Now why on earth would a police car be patrolling a deserted backstreet at this time of night? Honestly, when you were desperate for a passing policeman you wouldn't find one for love nor money, yet here were a pair now, tootling around in the small hours, avoiding the city centre where they might actually be needed.

As the patrol car reached the end of the cul-de-sac and swung round, Maddy tugged her purple baseball cap further down over her face. A horrid thought was unfurling like a tapeworm in her brain – surely not . . . oh bugger, don't slow down, no, *noooo* . . .

The car pulled up directly in front of Maddy's Saab, so that their bumpers were almost kissing. Lucky bumpers. Mortified, Maddy watched the door open and a skinny beanpole of an officer unfold himself from the passenger seat.

Bugger bugger bugger.

In response to his hand gesture, Maddy unwound her window.

'Would you step out of the car, sir?'

Bugger.

Slowly Maddy did as he asked. Standing there in her jeans, sweatshirt and trainers, a good foot shorter than the gangly policeman, she mumbled, 'I'm not a sir,' and took off her baseball cap. Her blonde hair slithered down past her shoulders.

'My apologies, miss.' Was the gangly policeman's mouth twitching? 'Um . . . may I ask what you're doing?'

Marvelling at the way your Adam's apple bobs up and down, mainly. Aloud, Maddy said, 'Just sitting in my car, officer. Is that against the law?'

'Do you live in this road?'

'Well, no.'

'So why exactly are you here?'

'Oh, for heaven's sake.' Maddy sighed. 'It's for personal reasons, OK?'

'Perhaps you could tell—'

'Look, I promise you I'm not doing any harm,' Maddy blurted out, 'but personal means *personal* and I don't want to sound stroppy, but shouldn't you be out catching real criminals, like burglars or car thieves, instead of harassing innocent motorists?'

'That is, in fact, our aim, miss. We were called here tonight by one of the residents, concerned that you might be planning to break into their home.'

For a sickening moment Maddy wondered if it had been Kerr, alarmed at the prospect of being stalked by an ex-girlfriend-turned-deranged-madwoman. Then a flicker of movement in her peripheral vision caused her to swivel round, just in time to catch the ruffled bedroom curtain of the house opposite dropping down as a permed head hastily ducked out of sight.

'I'm not a burglar,' said Maddy. 'I promise.'

This time the gangly policeman was definitely doing his best not to laugh.

'OK, I think I know what this could be about. Boyfriend trouble, am I right?'

Miserably Maddy nodded.

'Ex?'

She nodded again.

'Dumped you for another woman?'

'No, nothing like that! We just aren't seeing each other any more, that's all.'

'And sitting in your car in the middle of the night looking at his house makes you feel better, does it?'

'Well, yes,' Maddy admitted wretchedly. 'Yes, it does.'

'It's all right. I know.' Now it was the gangly policeman's turn to nod. 'I've done it too.'

'Have you?' Heartened, Maddy gazed up at him.

'God, yes, loads of times. Practically every girl who's ever chucked me.'

Yikes.

'In fact, every girl.' He nodded vigorously. 'The last one was only a few weeks ago. She swore she wasn't seeing anyone else, but I caught her out.' Smugly he said, 'I'd drive round to her place at four o'clock in the morning and feel the bonnet of her car. If it was still warm, that meant she'd been out with some bloke, see?'

'Um . . . yes . . .'

'Ever tried that?'

Maddy swallowed. 'Well, not really, no.'

'Should do. Handy tip, that. And if you've still got a front door key,' he went on eagerly, 'well, you can do all sorts. Tap their phone, fit listening devices, anything you like. I can give you the address of a shop that sells all that stuff, if you want. Best in the business and very discreet.'

'Gosh, um, thanks. Actually,' Maddy checked her watch again, 'it's getting a bit late, I really should be making a move—'

'Hidden cameras, they're good.'

'I don't think I need to—'

'Hey, this could be fate!' The gangly policeman's pale-lashed eyes gleamed in the moonlight. 'I've just split up with someone, you've just split up with someone – how about we get together some time?'

Urk!

'Well—'

'D'you like pizza? We could go out for a pizza.' His Adam's apple bobbed eagerly. 'Tomorrow night? I'm off duty tomorrow night. I can tell you how to send anonymous letters without getting caught.'

'Look, I'm sorry,' Maddy blurted out in desperation. 'I've got to go!'

As he watched the girl speed off, the gangly policeman smiled to himself before heading back to the patrol car.

His fellow officer, who had been listening to every word, chuckled. 'Poor kid, you frightened the living daylights out of her.'

Helping himself to a Snickers bar the policeman said, 'I did the girl a favour, brought her to her senses. Besides,' he broke into a grin, 'anything to brighten up a dull shift.'

Esme Calloway owned and ran Dartington House Nursing Home. When Kerr had first met her, he'd prompted himself to remember her name by recalling Cab Calloway's song 'Minnie The Moocher', from *The Blues Brothers*. Sadly, all this had succeeded in doing was making him think of the name Minnie every time he saw her. It was only a matter of time before he accidentally called her that.

But this wasn't likely to happen today. Esme Calloway had asked him to visit her in her office and the news she had for him wasn't cheerful.

'I'm afraid your mother's condition is deteriorating, Mr McKinnon. The doctor came out to visit her again this morning. The results of last week's blood tests aren't too good. Her liver function is, as you know, already poor.'

'I know.' Kerr nodded. It had been poor for years, but somehow his mother had survived; liver-wise, she was Ollie Reed in a dress.

'But this time it's serious,' Esme Calloway went on, 'and Pauline is aware of this. All we can do now is to keep her as comfortable as possible.'

'That's fine.'

'One more thing,' said Mrs Calloway. 'She's concerned about her other son. He's in Australia, I believe.'

Kerr shrugged. 'Your guess is as good as mine. He could be anywhere. We haven't seen him in years.'

'So I gathered.' Mrs Calloway rose from behind her mahogany desk, to indicate that the interview was at an end. 'Well, I'm just letting you know.'

'Not long to go now,' said Pauline McKinnon, putting it rather more bluntly than Mrs Calloway. 'Few more weeks and that'll be it. Did you bring me anything?'

Kerr shook his head. She asked the same question every time she saw him and each time he shook his head, because what she wanted him to bring was a bottle of Jack Daniel's whisky. Not that she went without; his mother was known for lavishly bribing the poorly paid domestic staff to smuggle regular supplies of alcohol into the nursing home for her; it was an open secret among everyone who worked at Dartington House.

'Oh well. Down to business.' Pauline McKinnon ran a trembling wrinkled hand over her mouth. Dwarfed by the armchair in which she was sitting, she looked frailer than ever and there was an unmistakable yellow tinge to her skin. 'I need to see Den.'

Kerr shook his head. 'I don't know where he is.'

'Then you have to find him. He's my son and I need to see him again before I die.' Vehemently Pauline said, 'It's *important*.'

Of course it was. Den had always been her favourite son, and he in turn had been devoted to his mother. Kerr hadn't been jealous; their closeness had simply been a fact of life.

'I'll try,' he said now. 'No guarantees, but I'll do my best.'

Pauline dug down the side of the armchair and with difficulty pulled out a silver flask. Her bony fingers shook as she unscrewed the top, raised the flask to her pursed lips and took a gulp.

'And don't look at me like that,' she told Kerr coldly. 'Why shouldn't I have a drink if I want to?'

'It's your life.' He rose to leave, keen to be out of this stuffy overheated room, thick with lavender air-freshener and alcohol fumes.

'Just find him,' his mother said brusquely. Fumbling for a tissue up her sleeve, her eyes unexpectedly swam with tears. 'Please. Find my boy before it's too late.'

Chapter 35

Back at the office, Kerr dealt with a stream of phone calls before turning, without much hope, to his computer. This wasn't the first time he'd tried to track down Den; his last unsuccessful attempt had been just before Christmas.

Dennis McKinnon. He typed the name into a worldwide search engine and scrolled through the list of matches, most of them familiar to him from previous searches, none of them his brother. Kerr knew; he'd checked out each and every one.

There were two new entries, the first a seventy-six-year-old man from Louisiana. The second sounded fractionally more feasible, a member of a brass band in Wellington, New Zealand. Mentally crossing his fingers, Kerr clicked on to the brass band's home page. Could this be Den? Had he moved to New Zealand and taken up trumpetry in his spare time? Anything was possible.

Scanning the page, Kerr clicked 'photos' and waited for them to pop up on the screen.

The third one down on the left was a photograph of Dennis McKinnon playing his trumpet. Black, bald and in his fifties, he looked like Louis Armstrong. Oh well.

Kerr exhaled wearily and leaned back in his chair, closing his eyes and rubbing his hands over his face. Everything that had happened was starting to catch up with him. Sleeping had never been a problem before, but these days it was beyond him. Tormented by wakefulness, he was unable to stop himself thinking of Maddy. When he did finally manage to doze off, he dreamed about her but the dreams never ended happily and when he woke he felt worse than ever. More exhausted too, which made it a struggle to come into work.

Forcing himself to get a grip, Kerr sat up again and opened his eyes. Life went on because it had to go on, but it wasn't easy pretending everything was fine. His mother was dying, his brother was unreachable and he missed Maddy terribly, more than words could—

'Kerr? Catch.' The door swung open and Sara, the receptionist, lobbed a cellophane-wrapped sandwich through the air at him.

Kerr caught it and looked at the label.

'It's egg and lettuce. I didn't ask for egg and lettuce.' More to the point, how could anyone in their right mind possibly *want* egg and lettuce?

'Yeah, well, too bad, none of us got what we asked for.' Sara's tone was as pointed as her pink Faith stilettos. 'But we just have to make the best of it, don't we?'

The Happy Hamper was supplying their sandwiches now, and happiness was in short supply. Aware that his staff all blamed him and were becoming increasingly mutinous, Kerr said, 'OK, but they're better than Blunkett's.'

'And that's supposed to cheer us up? They're not a millionth as good as the Peach Tree.' Sara was looking as if she might be on the verge of stamping her pointy-toed foot. 'The thing is, Kerr, *we've* done nothing wrong. I don't know what happened between you and Maddy, but the rest of us liked her a lot, we liked her sandwiches even more, and we really don't see why *we* should have to miss out just because you two have had some stupid little falling out.'

A stupid little falling out. If only that was all it was.

'And I'll tell you something else,' Sara said accusingly,

'the accountants from the first floor aren't happy about it either.'

Kerr sighed. 'The thing is, there's nothing—'

'You can do about it. Yeah, yeah, you *say* that, but we're the ones who are suffering here and it's all your fault.' Sara fixed him with a look of disdain. 'Which is why we're strongly suggesting *you* sort it out.'

The door slammed shut, Sara flounced back to reception and Kerr returned his attention to the computer screen. Ordering himself to concentrate, he tapped his fingers against the mouse and gazed at the trumpet-toting Dennis McKinnon on the screen in front of him. With his shiny black face and dazzling white grin he looked happier than Den would ever look; throughout the grim years of visiting him in prison, Kerr had never once seen his brother smile.

Forget Dennis. Returning to the search engine, he typed in the words Den McKinnon instead.

Last time he'd tried this, the reply, 'no match found', had flashed up.

This time the search engine came up with a lone match. Kerr clicked onto the site, belonging to a rugby club in Sydney, Australia.

There was the name again, Den McKinnon listed as fly half for an amateur rugby club. No photographs. No further clues. Had his brother even enjoyed playing rugby at school? Kerr couldn't remember.

It was a long and flimsy shot, but he may as well give it a go.

E-mailing the club secretary, Kerr wrote:

Dear Sir,

You have a Den McKinnon on your rugby team who may or may not be my long-lost brother. Could you please pass this message on to him, and ask him to reply letting me know either way? I urgently need to contact my brother as soon as possible. My address and phone number are . . .

Many thanks.

Kerr McKinnon.

When it was done, Kerr pressed send and envisaged the message popping up in the inbox of a computer in an air-conditioned office somewhere in sunny Sydney, Australia. After years of e-mailing, it still never failed to impress him that it was possible to make instantaneous contact in this manner, across the world.

Whether the reply would be instantaneous was another matter. Would he even get one? What if the club secretary mentioned it in passing to Den McKinnon, a grizzled sheep-shearer from the outback, who said, 'Yeah, yeah, I'll give the guy a call and tell him it ain't me,' then promptly forgot all about it?

'Right,' Sara abruptly announced from the doorway. 'Got it.'

Kerr heaved a sigh. 'Got what?'

'That little newsagents on the corner of Tapper Street and Marlborough Hill, where I buy my paper every morning. The bloke who runs it is really friendly and nice.'

'So?' Kerr pictured Den McKinnon scratching his big griz-zled head, going, 'Strewth, mate, what's an e-mail when it's at home?'

'So,' Sara repeated with exaggerated patience, 'I'm going to ask him if the Peach Tree can deliver our order to his shop every morning, and if he can look after it for us until one of us pops down there before lunch to pick it up.'

Kerr forced himself to pay attention.

'Won't that sound a bit weird?'

'Of course it'll *sound* weird. We'll just have to tell him

the truth,' said Sara with a shrug. 'That you broke the deli delivery girl's heart and that's why she refuses to bring us our sandwiches any more.'

'I didn't break her heart.' Kerr imagined his brother shaking his head, snarling, 'Why would I want to speak to that asshole when I haven't even seen him for years?'

Sara gave him an old-fashioned look. 'Of course you didn't. Anyway, I think the newsagent bloke will do it. We'll have to pay him, of course, but you can do that. So shall I pop down now and ask him or—'

Kerr's mobile phone began to ring. Snatching it up, he glanced at the caller number on the screen and felt his heart beat faster.

'Hello?'

'Kerr?'

It was Den. It was weird. Hearing his voice again after so long.

'Yes. Hi. How are you doing?' Kerr's throat tightened. This was his brother. He was also the reason why he and Maddy couldn't be together.

Kerr waved Sara out of the office.

'I'm OK.' Den sounded wary. 'Jed from the rugby club just gave me a ring and passed on your message. What's this about?'

'It's our mother.' God, it sounded so cold, so formal, but Pauline had never wanted to be called Mum. 'She's dying.'

Pause. Then, from ten thousand miles away, Den said, 'And?'

'She wants to see you.'

'Really. And what would be the point of that?'

It was a chilling response from a son who, prior to his spell in prison, had been utterly devoted to his mother.

'She's desperate to see you before she dies,' Kerr persisted, 'and she doesn't have long. She begged me to find you.'

'I don't know. It's a long way to come.'

'She's in a bad way, Den. I had to move her into a nursing home. Look, I can wire you the money for the plane ticket—'

'No need for that. I'll think about it. I may come or I may not,' Den said defiantly.

'OK.' This was a step up from an outright refusal. 'It would be good to see you again.' As he said it, Kerr wondered if he meant it; in truth, his feelings towards Den were very mixed.

'Would it?' His brother's laughter was hollow, tinged with bitterness and doubt.

'Are you married?' It was odd to think that Den could have a wife and children, a whole family they knew nothing about.

'Married? No.' Den paused. 'You?'

'Me neither.' *Thanks to you.*

'Not even seeing anyone?'

Kerr wondered how Den would react if he were to tell him who he'd been seeing up until last week. It wasn't the kind of discussion you could get into, under the circumstances. Aloud he said, 'No.'

'Haven't met the right girl yet?'

Oh, I've met her, all right.

'Something like that.' Kerr's tone was brusque.

'Right, well. Have to go now. If I decide to come over, I'll be in touch.'

'Shall I send you the money for the plane ticket?'

Pause.

'If you want,' Den said awkwardly.

'Give me your bank details then.' If he wired the money, maybe Den would feel morally obliged to fly over.

'I haven't decided yet. I'll be in touch when I do. Is the house still there?' Den asked abruptly. 'I mean, still in the family?'

So that was what was interesting him, thought Kerr. Hillview was worth in the region of three quarters of a million pounds.

'It's still in the family.' Drily he told Den, 'Don't worry, as soon as she dies you'll get your fifty per cent.'

There was a stunned silence, then Den said, 'Fuck off, Kerr,' and hung up.

'All sorted,' Sara announced.

Miles away – over ten thousand miles away – Kerr looked up and said, 'What?'

'Jameson's Newsagents. The bloke who runs it is Mike Jameson,' Sara patiently explained. 'He's agreed to do it, take in our sandwich delivery and keep it in his back room until one of us arrives to pick it up. He's charging twenty quid a week, which you'll be paying because this whole thing's your fault.'

'Fine,' said Kerr.

As she closed the door behind her, Sara thought, Damn, should have said forty.

Chapter 36

Marcella had cut down on her hours at Dauncey House, which suited Estelle down to the ground. With Will staying, acting normally around her family wasn't a problem, probably because in their eyes she was the least likely person in the world to be indulging in illicit naughtiness. But Marcella was a different matter, altogether more observant. Not much got past her. Estelle, terrified of letting her guard slip, was finding it increasingly difficult – but at the same time oddly exhilarating – to maintain an air of normality.

Luckily Marcella had other things on her mind to distract her.

'She's not eating. I took one of my casseroles over to the cottage last night and Jake says she didn't even touch it. And the weight she's lost – you don't think she'll make herself ill, do you?'

'Of course she won't.' Estelle's tone was comforting. 'Girls break up with boys all the time and get over it.'

'I know Maddy's unhappy,' said Marcella, 'and I hate to see her like this, but what's done is done. It isn't as if she can blackmail me into changing my mind, because how can I? She can't carry on seeing him and that's that. Now, give me that cup.' She reached across the table for Will's empty coffee cup. 'And as soon as I've loaded the dishwasher I'll be off.'

'Can I film you doing it?' Will picked up his hand-held video camera.

'What, bending over to stack the plates? Me and my big bottom filling an entire TV screen? What a treat that'd be for the nation,' said Marcella. 'No thanks.'

Estelle said, 'Leave the dishwasher, I can do that. You go home and get some rest. And ginger biscuits are good for stopping you feeling yuk,' she added, because Marcella's morning sickness had kicked in with a vengeance.

'You know, I'm just so glad to be pregnant, I don't even mind the feeling sick.' Her eyes shining, Marcella gave her stomach a protective pat. 'I've spent so many years longing to know what it feels like. It's proof that it's actually happening at last.'

When Marcella had left, Estelle carried on with the ironing. Acutely aware of Will's eyes upon her, she tried her best to concentrate on the sleeves of Oliver's favourite speedwell blue Turnbull and Asser shirt.

'I love the way your bottom wiggles when you do that.'

'Sshh.' Estelle bit her lip and smiled to herself, because it had to be twenty years since anyone had said anything nice about her bottom.

'Slow, slow, quick-quick slow.' Will, coming up and standing behind her, placed his hands on her hips as they swayed from side to side. Into her ear he murmured, 'I thought Marcella would never leave. I've been counting the seconds.'

'And Oliver's upstairs,' said Estelle, as if he needed reminding. Oliver was currently conducting a four-way transatlantic conference-call, before heading off to Zurich on yet another business trip. In order to allay any suspicions of hanky-panky, Will had to return to London. She wouldn't see him for at least a week and already the prospect seemed unendurable.

She must endure it, Estelle knew that. Oliver was basically

a good man, hard-working – if not a bit *too* hard-working – and honest. He didn't deserve to be cheated on.

'You smell gorgeous,' Will whispered, nuzzling the nape of her neck.

Oh, he definitely knew how to nuzzle . . .

'*Bugger*,' squeaked Estelle as the smell of something far less gorgeous filled the air. Snatching up the iron, she gazed in horror at the brown v-shaped scorch mark on the cuff of Oliver's shirt.

'Oops,' said Will with a grin.

'It's worse than oops. This is Oliver's favourite shirt,' wailed Estelle. With his own shambolic Worzel Gummidge style of dressing, Will couldn't begin to understand.

The telltale *ting* of the phone extension told them that Oliver's call was at an end and he was on his way downstairs. Flapping her arms in desperation to get Will away from her and simultaneously dispel the smell of expensive burned shirt, Estelle squealed, 'Oh God, here he comes now, he's going to go *mental* . . .'

By the time the kitchen door flew open, Will's video camera was whirring away. Oliver, instantly aware of it but naturally pretending not to be, said, 'Darling, have you finished my shirts?'

Darling, *ha*.

'Had a bit of an accident, I'm afraid.' Estelle confessed at once, because there was no point trying to pretend it hadn't happened, Oliver would spot the scorch mark in no time flat. 'Burned one of the cuffs.'

His face reddened with annoyance. 'Not the blue one.'

'Sorry,' said Estelle.

Instead of exploding in fury – 'I wanted my shirts ironed, four shirts, is that too much to ask?' – Oliver was obliged to shake his head with good-humoured resignation, because this could end up in the final edit being broadcast to millions.

Helpfully, Estelle said, 'You could always roll your sleeves up.'

His eyebrows raised in derision, Oliver said, 'I'm not Tony Blair.'

No, thought Estelle, Tony Blair has sex with his wife.

'I'll be leaving in ten minutes.' Gathering up the other ironed and folded shirts, Oliver headed out of the kitchen to finish packing. 'A coffee before I go would be nice, if you think you can manage it without burning the beans.'

'Just ignore him,' Will murmured when the video camera had been safely turned off.

'I got off lightly. Thanks to you.' Estelle's smile was rueful.

Will gave her a wicked look. 'You have no idea how much I want to kiss you.'

It wasn't the first time he'd said this, but it still had the most extraordinary effect on Estelle's knees. Like Ker-Plunk, she half expected them to give way at any moment, causing her to collapse in a heap on the ground.

'Sshh.' Scooting over to the coffee machine, she began trowelling in beans.

'D'you know what I love about you? The fact that you have absolutely no idea how sexy you are.' Will followed her, a playful smile lighting up his face.

'Right, all done. What are you two whispering about?' Oliver, barging back into the kitchen with his Louis Vuitton case, glanced at his watch.

'How mean you are to me,' said Estelle and he laughed, humouring her.

'I'll bring you back some of that scent you like from duty free, will that do?' Oliver dropped a fleeting kiss on her forehead. 'Don't bother with the coffee, we need to get going. OK?' he said to Will, who was dropping him at Heathrow on his way back to London.

'No problem.' Ambling around the kitchen, Will collected

up his belongings, the video camera, his tatty, haphazardly packed rucksack and a Waitrose carrier bulging with the battery pack and tapes he'd used so far.

'Ready?' Always loath to waste a moment, Oliver was by this time hovering impatiently in the doorway.

'Absolutely. Just one thing left to do before I go.' Making his way back over to Estelle, Will gave her a clumsy one-armed hug and kissed her noisily on both cheeks. 'Thanks for putting up with me.'

'My pleasure.' Estelle couldn't believe how deliciously naughty this felt. 'See you again soon.'

A whole week without Will. She was missing him already. However would she cope?

Chapter 37

Maddy pulled up on double yellows outside Jameson's, the tiny newsagents on the corner of Tapper Street and Marlborough Hill. She should have said no; the staff at Callaghan and Fox could find themselves another delivery service easily enough if they bothered to scour the Yellow Pages. It felt strange, preparing sandwiches that you knew were going to be eaten by Kerr; for a moment while she'd been making them this morning, she'd been horribly tempted to slip a love note into his chicken and chilli-prawn wrap.

But Sara had been unstoppable on the phone when she'd rung to place the order, informing Maddy in no uncertain terms that the arrangements had already been made. Basically, Maddy hadn't had the nerve to turn her down.

'You're delivering all that stuff to this one little shop?' Next to her in the passenger seat, Kate was incredulous. 'What, you mean the guy sells your food from here?'

It had been during last night's darts match at the Angel that Kate had overheard Maddy telling someone that she drove into Bath before ten o'clock each morning. Kate had said eagerly, 'So you could give me a lift, save me having to get a taxi? I've got some shopping I need to do tomorrow.'

And since they were now officially friends again, Maddy had felt compelled to say, 'No problem, but I don't know

266

what time I'll finish so you'll have to find your own way back.'

Now, lugging the packed cool-box out of the car, she said, 'This is for Kerr's company, Callaghan and Fox.' She nodded in the direction of Marlborough Hill. 'They're in Claremont House, up there on the left. I drop the order here, someone comes down later to pick it up, and I don't run the risk of bumping into Kerr.'

It was pathetic, but even saying his name was painful.

'Actually, here's fine for me.' Peering round, Kate unbuckled her seat belt. 'I can cut through to Milsom Street from the end of that road down there. Thanks for the lift.'

'No problem,' said Maddy. 'Have a good day.'

As she click-clacked her way down the narrow side street, Kate smiled to herself. With a bit of luck she might have a better day than she'd planned.

Five minutes later, when Maddy was safely out of sight, she returned to the little newsagents.

'Hi, I've come to pick up the delivery for Callaghan and Fox.'

'Blimey, you don't waste much time, it's only just arrived. Hang on, love, I'll go and get it.'

Moments later the wiry, middle-aged newsagent handed the cool-box over to Kate. 'Bit heavy, love. Sure you can manage?'

He was doing his best not to stare at the damaged side of her face. Flashing him a broad smile, Kate said reassuringly, 'I'm fine.'

As he watched her leave – pretty girl, shame about the scars – Mike Jameson reflected happily that this was set to be the easiest twenty quid a week he'd earned in his life.

Marlborough Hill wasn't for the faint-hearted. By the time she reached Claremont House, Kate was pink-cheeked and panting like a porn star. Pausing at the entrance to get her breath back, she prayed that after all this effort Kerr wouldn't be out.

Careful not to disturb her foundation, she blotted her face with a tissue. Coming home to Ashcombe had undoubtedly been a good move; against all expectations, the familiar village environment had done wonders for her self-esteem. Just a couple of months ago, she could never have envisaged herself working in a pub, serving customers, sometimes completely forgetting her scars for – well, maybe not hours, but certainly minutes at a time. The fact that people treated her normally and no longer cringed at the sight of her had boosted her confidence no end, proving that a life following physical disfigurement *was* possible. Crikey, just look at what she was preparing to do now! Six weeks ago this would have been out of the question. And yet here she was, acting completely on impulse, ready to reintroduce herself to Kerr McKinnon, upon whom she'd once had *the* most enormous crush.

Who knew what might happen, Kate thought giddily, fantasising already as she made her way up the broad staircase. She and Maddy had mended their differences. They were friends again now and she was truly glad about that. But there was absolutely no need to feel guilty also coming here today, because Kerr and Maddy were no longer together. And just because Maddy wasn't allowed to be with him . . .

Well, it seemed a shame to let a good man go to waste.

'Hi, can I help you?' The plump receptionist's gaze zoomed in on the cool-box as she spoke, her eyes lighting up, her glossy lips parting in delight. 'Oh wow, is that . . . ?'

'I'm a friend of Maddy's,' Kate explained. 'We dropped this off at the newsagents this morning but I thought I'd save someone the bother of coming to pick it up.'

'You're an angel. Aren't they just the best sandwiches in the world? I tell you, I could have *kicked* Kerr when he broke up with Maddy – I mean, how could he? Typical bloody man – ooh, look!' Rooting busily through the contents of the cool-box, the girl let out a yelp of recognition. 'Here's mine, rare beef and horseradish on rye. I'm never going to last until lunchtime. I just want to eat them *now*.'

The girl was either a first-rate receptionist, trained not to react with so much as a flicker of revulsion to the sight of a scarred face, or she was so utterly entranced by her sandwich that everything else faded into insignificance. Mentally bracing herself – she was here, this was *it* – Kate said, 'Actually, is Kerr around?'

'Oh, you know Kerr too! No problem, he's in his office, I'll just give him a buzz.' As she reached for the intercom, the girl said excitedly, 'Is that why you're here? To give Kerr a damn good talking to for being silly enough to dump Maddy?'

'Um, something like that. Don't buzz him,' said Kate, suddenly excited too. 'Why don't I give him a surprise?'

He called out 'Come in' when she knocked but didn't immediately look up from the report on his desk. Kate, rather glad of the moment's reprieve, took in the sight of him in his cranberry-red shirt, black trousers and polished black shoes. His dark hair flopped over his forehead, his bone struc-ture was as stunning as she remembered, and—

'Kate.' Having glanced up and seen her in the doorway, Kerr put down the report he'd been studying. He rose to his feet. His gaze flickered for a split second as he took in the scars.

'Hello, Kerr. Surprise.' Her heart was pounding audibly, Kate was sure. She'd had such a crush on him when she was fifteen; did those feelings ever really go away? More to the point, was Kerr currently experiencing them too?

'What's this about?'

Honestly, typical man-question. You and me, Kate wanted to shout at him. Why else would I be here, you berk?

'Brought the lunch delivery,' she said aloud. 'Maddy gave me a lift into Bath. Thought I'd drop by and say hello.'

'Maddy's here?' Kerr's expression changed at once; you'd think she'd just announced that Madonna was waiting to see him in reception. Naked.

'She isn't here. But she's absolutely fine,' lied Kate.

There was no escaping the disappointment on his face. 'Fine. Well, that's good.'

'We're fine too,' Kate went on. 'I mean, we're getting on really well again. It wasn't me who told Marcella about you and Maddy – she did tell you that, didn't she?'

Kerr nodded. 'It was the TV cameras. I know.'

'Anyway, it's great to see you again.' Keen to move the line of conversation away from Maddy, Kate said, 'You haven't changed a bit.'

Ha, what was he going to say to that? Neither have you? To his credit, Kerr didn't even attempt it.

'Maddy told me about your accident. Nasty business. You're lucky you weren't killed.'

'I wished I had been. When I saw my face, I wanted to die.'

'That's mad.' Kerr shook his head. 'It doesn't matter what you look like.'

Kate, her smile rueful, said, 'Only someone who looks like you could say something as stupid as that.'

Kerr couldn't imagine what Kate Taylor-Trent was doing here in his office. She showed no sign of leaving. In her ruffled white shirt and sleek beige skirt, she looked tanned and fit. Interestingly, the scars on the left side of her face in no way detracted from her air of glamour.

'Remember your last year at school?' Kate was saying now, smiling fondly at the memory. 'Those school discos we all used to go to?'

Kerr could just about recall them but he failed to see their relevance. He had a dim memory of himself as an eighteen-year-old chatting up a group of leggy beauties from Ridgelow Hall, then discovering later that they were only fifteen years old. Then, the age gap had been vast, three whole years. Now, of course, it was nothing at all, but he still failed to see why Kate Taylor-Trent should have come to his office in order to blather on about their schooldays. The only person he was interested in talking about was Maddy, and every time he mentioned her name Kate swiftly changed the subject to something else.

When Kate at last left Kerr's office, she knew it hadn't worked. Back out on the street in the baking sun, she heaved a sigh and headed back down Marlborough Hill. That was it, she'd done her best and failed absolutely. Pulling out all the stops, she had flirted with Kerr with all her might and got nowhere. It had been like trying to flirt with a park bench.

Yet somehow, Kate realised, she wasn't downhearted. OK, it was disappointing in one way, because she'd lusted after Kerr McKinnon for so long, but this hadn't been the kind of rejection you could take personally or blame on your facial scars. Because Jennifer Lopez or Halle Berry or, well, pretty much anyone in the world could have given it their best shot back there in that office and found themselves faced with similar lack of interest.

Basically, unless you were Maddy Harvey, Kerr couldn't care less.

Chapter 38

'My poor baby.' Juliet's heart went out to Tiff, normally so full of life and bouncing Tiggerish energy. Kneeling by his bed stroking his hot forehead, she reflected that these days he had to be feeling really ill before he'd allow her to call him her poor baby.

'Don't go to work.' Tiff's eyes were half closed, his fingers laced through hers. 'Stay with me.'

'Sweetie pie, of course I'll stay with you. I'm not going anywhere.' Checking her watch, Juliet saw that it was seven in the morning. 'Let me just give Maddy a ring. Maybe Nuala can help out in the shop. Would you like some Ribena?'

'I don't know.' Tiff plucked miserably at his Spiderman pyjama top. 'I'm hot.'

It absolutely wasn't a problem, Maddy assured Juliet on the phone, Nuala and her one functioning arm would be only too delighted to step into the breach, she'd go and wake her up now. And give Tiff a big kiss from her and Jake.

Making her way back into Tiff's heavily curtained bedroom, Juliet said, 'All sorted out. Here you are, sweetheart, I've brought you a drink.'

Tiff's spiky head emerged from the duvet, his little face paler than ever. In a high voice he said, 'Mummy, I feel—'

Oh dear. Maybe she wouldn't give him that kiss on Maddy's behalf just yet. Predictably, the fountain of sick managed to end up all over Tiff's pyjamas, pillow, duvet and undersheet.

Tiff whispered, 'Sorry, Mummy,' and the words squeezed at Juliet's heart.

'You don't have to say sorry. It's not your fault you're poorly.' Kissing the top of his head – currently the only part of him safe to kiss – Juliet said, 'Come on, let's get you into the shower. I'll give the doctor a ring when surgery opens, see if he'll come and take a look at you.'

'There's sick on the carpet, Mummy.'

'I know, sweetheart. I'll clear it up in a minute.' Stripping off his pyjamas, Juliet gave him a hug. 'It doesn't matter a bit.'

Jake popped his head round the bedroom door an hour later.

'Maddy just told me about Tiff. How is he?'

Juliet, on her knees in the darkened bedroom stroking Tiff's forehead, said, 'Feeling lousy. He's been sick a few times, you know the routine.'

Jake nodded; Sophie had succumbed to a similar bug at Easter. 'Anything I can do?'

'Thanks, but I'm OK. I'll have Maddy and Nuala downstairs, they can bring me cups of tea.'

Drowsily Tiff said, 'Is that Jake?'

'Hey, look at you.' Crossing the bedroom, Jake gazed down at him. 'Not feeling so good, eh?'

'I won't be able to play with Sophie today,' Tiff whispered feebly. 'Mum, will I be better tomorrow?'

'Of course you will. Full of beans.' Juliet's tone was consoling.

Tiff summoned a ghost of a smile. 'Might have been the beans I ate yesterday that made me ill.'

At nine o'clock Juliet rang the surgery. As soon as the doctor had finished his morning clinic, the receptionist assured her, he'd be over to take a look at Tiff.

At ten o'clock Nuala delivered a handmade Get Well card from Sophie, featuring a large and ferocious bug with pointed fangs and many legs. Inside it she'd written: 'This is what you cort. Love, Sophie XXX.'

At ten thirty Tiff woke up and was sick again, this time retching into the bowl Juliet held under his chin. Trembling violently with the effort, he clung to her and moaned, 'My head hurts, my head hurts.' Then, when Juliet moved to switch on the bedside light he flinched and wailed, 'Turn it off, it hurts my eyes, I want it *dark* . . .'

It was at ten past eleven that what up until then had been an unlovely but ordinary enough day abruptly turned into a nightmare. All morning, at regular intervals, Juliet had been checking Tiff's body for a rash. Each time, encountering nothing, she had felt vaguely foolish for even allowing the thought that Tiff might have meningitis to cross her mind.

Now her heart turned over and her hands began to shake as she took in the dark red spots on his stomach. Where had they come from? What did they mean? Did they *have* to mean what she thought they meant, or could there be other causes? The glass test . . .

Slowly, Juliet reached for the tumbler of water she'd been sipping from, tipped the contents clumsily into Tiff's sick bowl and pressed the side of the glass against Tiff's skin, his precious baby-boy skin . . . Oh God, oh no, please don't let this be happening.

''S cold,' mumbled Tiff, flinching away from the cool-ness of the glass.

Still kneeling next to his bed, Juliet ran feverishly through the options. Maddy was out on her delivery round in Bath. Nuala was downstairs running the shop. The doctor was still seeing patients in his surgery. Stumbling to her feet, she headed across the darkened bedroom and flung open the window.

'Jake, *Jake*.'

Within seconds she saw Jake heading up the road, shielding his eyes from the late-morning sun as he gazed up at her. One look at Juliet's face told him all he needed to know.

'OK,' he called out. 'Don't worry, I'll get the car.'

Too terrified to cry, Juliet watched Jake carry her son downstairs in his arms. When she was settled on the back seat of the car he carefully laid Tiff, by now floppy and pale, across her lap. Juliet cradled him, reassured him and sang to him while Jake drove like a demon into Bath. Finally reaching the Royal United Hospital, they screeched to a halt outside casualty.

'Will he be all right?' Juliet whispered fearfully as Jake lifted Tiff off her.

'Come on, let's get him inside.' Glancing down at the ominous red rash spreading over Tiff's thin legs, Jake added automatically, 'He'll be fine.'

It was nothing like turning up with a cut finger, thank God. No hanging around for hours on end playing spot-the-doctor. Within seconds of their arrival Tiff had been whisked away into a cubicle to be thoroughly examined by a young house officer. The paediatric consultant was bleeped and arrived minutes later. By the time Jake returned from moving the car to the car park, the consultant was on the phone arranging for Tiff to be admitted to ITU.

'As soon as he's settled down there, we'll perform a lumbar puncture,' the consultant told them as Jake gave Juliet's shoulder a reassuring squeeze. 'That'll tell us what's going on. But I have to say, it's looking like meningo-coccal meningitis. We're starting Tiff on IV antibiotics now. You'll be asked to sign a consent form for the lumbar puncture.' He glanced at Jake as he said this, and Jake shook his head.

'I'm not Tiff's dad. Just a friend.'

'I see.' The consultant, nodding briefly in acknowledgement, turned to Juliet. 'You may want to let his father know.'

Gripped with terror, Juliet gasped, 'How serious is this?'

'If it's bacterial meningitis,' the consultant replied, his tone matter-of-fact, 'it's a serious illness. We're going to do our very best for Tiff.'

By the time Jake arrived back in Ashcombe, everyone in the village had heard the news.

'Poor little boy, what a *dreadful* thing to happen.' Estelle, who was in the Peach Tree buying croissants and greengage jam, had tears in her eyes as Jake emerged from the flat upstairs with an overnight bag for Juliet.

'Right, I'll head back to the hospital. You stay here with Maddy and Nuala,' Jake told Sophie, who was sitting behind the counter looking utterly miserable. 'I'll ring you later, I promise.'

'She'll be fine with us.' Maddy gave Sophie a hug.

Sophie nodded; she didn't know what meningitis was, but she definitely didn't like the sound of it. 'Tell Tiff to get better and come home. Does he want some Smarties?'

Tiff was currently semi-comatose and connected up to a forest of machines and drips. Reaching over to kiss Sophie, Jake shook his head.

'Not just now, darling. But he loved your card.'

'Give them both our love,' said Maddy, stroking Sophie's unbraided candyfloss hair.

'Can't I go with Dad? I want to go,' Sophie whispered.

'I know sweetheart, but we can't.' As Jake left, Maddy realised she'd never seen him look so sombre.

'Tiff's my best friend.' Sophie's bottom lip began to wobble. 'I don't want him to die.'

In the ITU, Tiff occupied the bed in the far left-hand corner of the ward. Jake, holding his fragile hand and stroking his fingers, watched Juliet asleep in the chair next to him. Exhaustion had caught up with her; it was midnight and she'd fallen into a fitful doze twenty minutes earlier. As a plump nurse silently approached them, he slid his hand away from Tiff's and rose to his feet.

'Tiff's father just phoned,' whispered the nurse, causing Jake's eyebrows to shoot up.

'And?'

'He wanted to know how Tiff was doing. I told him.'

Curious, Jake asked, 'Did he say where he was calling from?'

The plump nurse shook her head. 'No, just that he was on his way.'

Interesting, thought Jake. So he was about to meet Tiff's mysterious father at last.

Still dozing in her hard chair two hours later, Juliet felt a hand on her arm.

'Juliet? Tiff's father's arrived.'

'What?' Bewildered, Juliet stared up at the nurse. 'But he can't have. I didn't call him.'

'He's here now, in the waiting room.' The plump nurse glanced at Jake, who shrugged.

'He's not in this country,' said Juliet.

'Well, do you want to come and see who's in the waiting room?' Diplomatically the nurse added, 'If it is Tiff's dad, we do prefer only two visitors for each patient at any one time.' This was addressed to Jake, who guessed that it was ward policy to avoid potentially awkward encounters between parents and step-parents, which was presumably what they thought he was.

'Don't worry.' Standing up, Jake said, 'I'll go and find a coffee machine.' Looking down at Juliet, hollow-eyed with concern for Tiff, he murmured, 'Will you be OK?'

Wordlessly, Juliet nodded.

As he left the unit, it occurred to Jake that the field had just narrowed dramatically. Juliet hadn't told Tiff's father. But somehow he'd heard about Tiff's illness. While he was *out of the country* . . .

The waiting room was ahead of him, to the left.

Without pausing, he pushed open the door and came face to face with Oliver Taylor-Trent.

'Thought so,' said Jake.

Chapter 39

Juliet watched Oliver make his way down the darkened ward towards her. He looked terrible; business suit crumpled, greying hair uncombed, the lines around his mouth grown deeper than usual like cracks in parched ground. Then again, she probably wasn't looking that spectacular herself.

Too shattered to move, Juliet sat and listened to the night nurse patiently explaining to him the functions of the various bits of machinery surrounding the bed. Being Oliver, he demanded to speak to the consultant in charge of the unit and threatened to become difficult when it was explained to him that the consultant was at home, asleep.

Finally, Juliet intervened.

'Tiff's getting the best care. Losing your temper isn't going to help him. Oliver, sit down.'

'I can't bear it.' Oliver's gaze was fixed on his son's fragile, immobile body. 'I just want to make him better.' Turning abruptly to the nurse he said, 'Would a private hospital be able to do more? If it's a question of money, I don't care how much it costs—'

'They're doing everything possible,' said Juliet. 'It's OK,' she told the hovering nurse, 'I'll speak to him.'

'He was fine the other day, I saw him playing outside the shop with Sophie . . . absolutely fine . . .'

'He was fine twenty-four hours ago. That's the thing about meningitis.'

Oliver was shaking his head in disbelief. 'Why didn't you phone me? You should have phoned me as soon as it happened.'

Juliet shrugged. 'I knew you were in Switzerland. It would have made it more serious. I just kept hoping they'd say he was getting better. How did you find out?' she said, although it was fairly obvious.

'I rang Estelle. She told me what had happened. I was about to go into a meeting.' Oliver gazed blankly down at Tiff. 'I walked out of the building, flagged down a taxi and caught the first flight out of Zurich. When I was growing up in Bradford,' he went on in a low voice, 'there was a boy who lived opposite me. Billy Kennedy, his name was. We used to play in the same football team. He got meningitis.'

'What happened to him?' The moment the words were out of her mouth, Juliet regretted them. Oliver didn't reply.

Juliet rubbed her dry, aching eyes. 'I need to change my clothes.' Both her blue shirt and long white cotton skirt were spotted with sick and there were bloodstains on her sleeve where she had helped to hold Tiff while the doctor had been setting up an intravenous drip. The bag of things Jake had brought from home was in the waiting room outside.

'You go. I'll stay here,' said Oliver, and for a second she hesitated, because if Tiff were to open his eyes and she wasn't there for him, what would he think?

Except she knew Tiff wasn't about to open his eyes. He was in a coma now, unaware of anything at all, mercifully, and clinging to life by a thread. Wondering how she could bear to be going through this, yet aware that come what may she simply had to, Juliet rose slowly to her feet.

'I'll be two minutes.' She felt older than she'd imagined possible.

'Take as long as you want,' said Oliver.

'I don't *want* to take any longer than two minutes.' Aware of the smell of sick rising from her skirt, Juliet said, 'Did Jake see you?'

Oliver nodded.

'OK.'

The waiting room was cool and deserted. Taking her carrier bag into the bathroom, Juliet changed into the clean silvery grey v-neck top and darker grey crinkle skirt Jake had found in her wardrobe. She'd never been a jeans and T-shirt kind of girl, preferring stretchy, ultra-comfortable clothes that didn't constrict.

Her reflection in the bathroom mirror wasn't comforting but Juliet didn't care. Without the customary crimson lipstick, her mouth was far too pale. Since dragging a comb through her hair was too much to contemplate, she forced herself to brush her teeth instead, then sluiced her face with cold water. Even that felt as arduous as wading waist-high through treacle.

'Hi.'

Emerging from the bathroom, Juliet was unsurprised to find Jake waiting for her.

'I've brought you a coffee.' He held one of the steaming Styrofoam cups towards her. 'Pretty vile, I'm afraid. But better than nothing.'

'Thanks.' Juliet took the cup, knowing she wouldn't drink it.

'So.' Jake paused. 'Oliver Taylor-Trent.'

'Don't lecture me,' she said wearily. 'This isn't a good time.'

'I'm not going to lecture you.' Jake shook his head. 'Who else knows?'

'No one. No one else.'

'Not Estelle?'

'No.'

'Tiff?'

'Of course Tiff doesn't know.' Juliet gave him a how-can-you-even-ask look. 'He's seven years old. Do you seriously imagine he'd be able to keep quiet about something like that?'

'OK, that's all.' Jake held up his hands. 'No more questions. I just needed to know for practical reasons.'

'Sorry.' Of course he did; he would be heading back to Ashcombe now. 'Anyway, thanks for everything.' Juliet moved towards the door, beginning to panic at the thought that she'd been away from Tiff for longer than five minutes.

'No problem.' Jake waited, looking as if he wanted to say something else. Then he shook his head and smiled briefly at Juliet, so clearly desperate to get back to the ward. 'Off you go.'

'You look shattered,' said Juliet. 'Shouldn't you get some sleep?'

It was eight thirty in the morning, grey and overcast outside. Oliver, looking more crumpled than ever, rubbed his eyes.

'Not before I've spoken to the consultant. He's on his way in now.' Straightening up on his chair he said, 'Who's that over there?'

Juliet twisted round. At the nurses' station behind them a lanky youth in a porter's uniform was leaning against the desk glancing over at them and whispering to one of the nurses.

'His name's Phil, he lives in Ashcombe.' Aware that her heart should be plummeting but quite unable to summon up the energy to care, Juliet said, 'He works part-time in the kitchen at the Fallen Angel. Looks like he's recognised you.'

'Here's someone now,' said Oliver as the swing doors crashed open and a middle-aged man with an unmistakable air of authority burst into the unit, trailing assorted minions in his wake. 'Is that him?'

'That's him,' Juliet nodded, her throat tightening with trepidation.

Oliver was already out of his chair. 'About time too. Right, now we'll find out what's going on. How d'you do, I'm Oliver Taylor-Trent.' Oliver stuck out his hand as the consultant, followed by his entourage, reached them. 'I'm the boy's father. I want to know exactly where we stand here,' he announced brusquely. 'No holding back.'

Juliet, her fingers closing helplessly round Tiff's immobile hand, prayed that Oliver wouldn't start going on again about money. She also prayed that the consultant wouldn't be as brusque as Oliver; she wasn't at all sure she had the strength to hear what he might be about to say.

'Pickled walnuts, would you credit it?' Marcella shook her head in disbelief, mystified by her own weirdness. 'I always thought those food cravings were made up, just to get pregnant women a bit of attention, but I swear to God I'm *dreaming* of pickled walnuts. The moment I wake up I have to have them. Nothing else will do. And when I'm not eating them I like to look at them, bobbing about in their jar like dear little shrivelled brains—'

'Whoa,' Estelle spluttered, waving her hands and struggling to swallow her mouthful of Marmite on toast. 'Too much information.'

'Oh, sorry.' Marcella carried on polishing the silver, spread out over the far end of the oak kitchen table like an upmarket boot sale. Peering over at Norris, noisily chomping away at his bowl of Pedigree Chum and Winalot, she said, 'Hasn't put this one off.'

'Nothing could put Norris off his food.' Kate, finishing her coffee, rose to her feet. 'Anyway, I'd better be getting ready for work.' Tilting her head to one side, she said, 'Sounds like a car coming up the drive.'

'That'll be the delivery man,' Marcella joked, 'bringing me my next crate of pickled walnuts.'

Estelle felt her heart begin to race; it couldn't be Will, could it? Had he been overcome by a sudden wild urge to see her again? Oh Lord, if it was him, would she be able to act normally in front of Marcella?

At the sound of the front door being opened, Marcella stopped polishing. All eyes were fixed on the kitchen door now. Estelle did her level best to look as utterly confounded as Kate and Marcella. Only Norris, blithely ignoring the intruder, continued to crunch away at his Winalot.

Estelle couldn't have been more astounded if it had been David Attenborough himself complete with beige safari jacket who had pushed open the kitchen door.

Not Will, but Oliver.

Oliver, mystifyingly looking every bit as dishevelled and ungroomed as Will habitually did.

'*Oliver?* What's wrong?' Guiltily, Estelle prayed he hadn't somehow found out. 'I don't understand, you're meant to be in Zurich.'

Oliver barely seemed to notice them. He shook his head.

'I was in Zurich. I came back.'

'B-but why?' Truly terrified now, Estelle gripped the edge of the table. 'What's happened? You didn't even phone!'

Marcella sniffed the air. 'What's that smell?'

'Oh Norris, not again,' sighed Kate.

'No, not that kind of smell.' Pregnancy had heightened

Marcella's olfactory senses; lifting her head like a meerkat, she sniffed again. 'It's like that disinfectanty smell you get in hospitals.'

Wearily Oliver rubbed his eyes. Still bemused by the unexpectedness of his arrival, Estelle said, 'Hospitals? Is that why you're back? Oliver, are you *ill*?'

The next moment, somehow, she just knew. Maybe it was the expression on Marcella's face, maybe the look of resignation on Oliver's. Whichever, Estelle found herself feeling suddenly weightless with shock, as if someone had just switched off the gravity in the room.

Kate, still worried, said, 'Dad? What's wrong?'

'It's Tiff Price, isn't it?' Estelle heard the words coming from her mouth as if from a great distance. 'That's why you came back . . . that's where you've been. I don't believe this,' she blurted out. 'Are you actually going to tell me he's *yours*?'

Oliver didn't reply.

White-faced with shock, Kate said, 'Dad? Is it true?'

More silence.

'Oh, for heaven's sake!' Estelle was by this time breathing so fast her fingertips had begun to tingle. 'Of course it's true! If it wasn't true, he'd say so, wouldn't he? He's Tiff Price's father.' Swinging round to Marcella she demanded, 'Did you know about this? Does everyone in the village know except me?'

'I've never heard a thing.' Concerned, Marcella said, 'Look, this is private. I should go.'

'I've got a better idea.' Galvanised into action, Estelle stalked over to the door. 'Why don't *I* go? Come on,' she told Marcella, 'you can help me pack.'

Kate looked aghast. 'Mum! What are you *talking* about?'

'I'm *talking* perfect sense. Why should I stay here and be publicly humiliated?' Estelle ran her hands frenziedly

285

through her fair hair. 'Your father has a mistress and a child, living *right here* in Ashcombe. All these years he's been having his cake and eating it, making a complete fool of me—'

'I haven't.' Oliver spoke at last. 'I haven't been making a fool of you, because nobody else knew. And I haven't been having my cake and eating it either. Juliet isn't my mistress.'

'Really? How extraordinary!' bellowed Estelle. 'What was it, artificial insemination?'

'We had an affair once,' Oliver said shortly. 'Not any more.'

'Oh, fantastic, that makes me feel so much better. How *dare* you? How could you do it?' Estelle was still struggling to take in the news; the shock was on a par with hearing Oliver announce he wanted a sex change.

'These things happen. We met when Juliet was living in London. And just to set the record straight,' said Oliver, 'she wasn't the one at fault. I told her I was divorced.'

'You bastard!' Estelle's voice trembled with rage; how could she have spent the last twenty-seven years married to a man who would do something like this?

'You're absolutely right. Call me all the names you want, I deserve them. But right now,' Oliver said heavily, 'my main concern is Tiff.'

He'd come straight from the hospital. Stubble-chinned and ashen-faced, he looked as though he hadn't slept in days. Remembering how she'd felt when the call had come through from America telling her about Kate's car accident, Estelle experienced a pang of guilt.

Next to her, Marcella said quietly, 'How is he?'

Oliver looked as if he was struggling to breathe normally.

'Still alive. And that's about as encouraging as it gets. If septicaemia sets in, they could be forced to amputate his arms and legs.'

Oh God, that poor little boy. A lump sprang into Estelle's throat at the very thought.

'I just came back to shower and change,' Oliver went on.

'Tell Juliet we're all praying for him,' said Marcella, her dark eyes luminous with compassion.

Rubbing his face, Oliver nodded across at her. 'I will.'

Chapter 40

'It's not fair,' Estelle raged. 'It's not fair, he's acting as if I don't have any right to be upset because Tiff's ill. He's making out that I'm being *selfish*, and I don't want to be selfish, but I *am* upset, I'm *bloody* upset! All these years I've stayed married to him. I could have had an affair, you know, but I didn't because I was loyal to my husband, and all the time I was being so loyal he was busy having sex with Juliet Price, telling her he was single, getting her *pregnant*—'

'Is this wise?' Marcella said patiently, sitting on the end of the bed watching Estelle hurl nighties, skirts, shoes and assorted items of underwear into two cases.

'I doubt it, but I'm bloody doing it anyway. How can I stay here?' Viciously, Estelle flung in her hairdryer and a bottle of Chanel No. 19, not even caring if it smashed. 'I'll be the laughing stock of Ashcombe. Why should I let myself be humiliated?'

'You wouldn't be.'

'Anyway, I'm going.' Estelle said it quickly before Marcella could come up with some plausible reason why she should stay.

'Where?'

'God knows. Pass me my pink top, would you? I mean, can you believe he didn't even say *sorry*?'

'It's been a shock,' said Marcella. 'For both of you.'

'Bloody right it's been a shock. Oh, darling . . .' Estelle's head jerked up as the bedroom door swung open and Kate appeared.

'Mum, I don't want you to go.' Fiercely, Kate hugged her. 'I can't bear it that Dad's done this to you.'

Aware that the news of Tiff's existence must have come as a shock to Kate too, Estelle was nevertheless overwhelmed by the emotion in her daughter's voice. Kate was on her side and that meant so much to her.

'It's the only thing to do. I can't stay here. Darling, I love you.' Her own voice wavering, she stroked Kate's face.

'Where will you go?'

'Not sure. Some hotel, I suppose. I'll ring and let you know,' said Estelle.

'You shouldn't have to leave. He should.' Kate was vehement. 'You haven't done anything wrong.'

Yet, thought Estelle.

'Oh God, what a mess,' Estelle sighed when Kate had finally been persuaded to leave for work. In the space of an hour her whole life had been picked up and shaken like a snow globe. From now on, nothing was ever going to be the same again.

Marcella emerged from the en suite bathroom. 'Here, don't forget your razor.'

'To cut my wrists?'

'To shave your legs. Hey, don't cry,' Marcella said encouragingly. 'You'll get through this.'

'God knows how.' Estelle wiped her eyes with her sleeve, determined not to start. 'Why do you keep looking at your watch?'

'Do I? Oh, sorry. Jake's taking Sophie along to the surgery

289

this morning; the doctor at the hospital told him she might need a course of antibiotics. He said he'd let me know what was happening.'

Another great wave of shame swept through Estelle. She truly didn't mean to be a selfish, horrible person, but it was so hard not to think about what had happened to *her*. Right now, her own problems were what were uppermost in her mind, whereas as far as everyone else was concerned, the fact that Tiff was lying gravely ill in hospital was far more important.

It was just as well she was leaving Ashcombe. Under the circumstances, how could she stay?

Poor Tiff, thought Estelle, picturing the little boy and feeling her bottom lip begin to wobble again. Poor Sophie. *Poor me.*

'No danger of a smile, I suppose.'

'What?' snapped Kate.

'You know, that thing people do with their mouths to cheer up the customers, make them feel welcome.'

'Since when have you been bothered about customers feeling welcome? Anyway,' Kate turned her back on Dexter, 'they're all out in the garden. There's no one in here to smile at.'

Drily Dexter said, 'Thanks.'

'Don't mention it.' Really wishing he'd go away – although since this was his pub it was unlikely – Kate did the next best thing and wrenched open the dishwasher, which had just finished its cycle. Instantly she was enveloped in an impenetrable cloud of steam.

The next moment she jumped as Dexter loomed through the steam like Swamp Thing, whisking the hot glasses from her hands.

'You could try telling me what's wrong.'

'Nothing's wrong. I'm fine.' Leave me *alone*.

'And I'm Pierce Brosnan.' Through the haze of condensation she saw Dexter's eyebrows furrowed in anger. 'It's bloody Jake, isn't it?'

Startled, Kate said, 'Sorry?'

'Messing you about again. I told you before, he's nothing but trouble. You don't need someone like that, always messing you around and—'

'Fine, I'll tell you,' Kate blurted out.

Dexter shook his head. 'Not if you don't want to.'

'By tonight everyone in Ashcombe will know, so it really doesn't matter. My father had an affair with Juliet Price. Tiff Price is his son. So you see,' Kate's voice began to waver, 'it isn't only men like Jake Harvey that women should avoid, it's ones like my father too. They're all as bad as each other. And now my mother's left him. She's gone off, goodness knows where, my father's at the hospital and I'm left here like a lemon wondering what the bloody hell's going to happen next.'

'Here.' Grabbing a clean bar towel adorned with the Guinness logo, Dexter handed it to her to wipe her eyes with. Awkwardly, he patted her on the arm. 'And congratulations, that's definitely the best excuse for not smiling I've heard all day. Little Tiff Price, eh? And he's your half-brother. Poor kid.'

Bristling, Kate said, 'Because he's my half-brother?'

'Because he's got meningitis. The bad kind. You're not that much of a nightmare.'

Kate wasn't so sure; her feelings were hideously mixed. When she'd been much younger, her father had made no secret of the fact that he'd wanted a son as well. Well, now he had one, which was absolutely typical of Oliver Taylor-Trent, because he'd spent his life making sure he got everything he wanted.

A more recent memory struck Kate: the morning when Tiff Price had spilled chocolate ice cream down her best cream trousers and she had blown her top. And the way Oliver had laughed the incident off, siding not with her, but with his precious, longed-for son.

'Hey, you'll be fine.' Sounding most unlike himself, Dexter pushed a brimming glass of wine into her hand and steered her on to a stool. Mortified, Kate realised she was feeling jealous of a critically ill seven-year-old.

Was it possible to sink any lower than this?

The Intercity from Bath to Paddington was full of business types endlessly announcing into their mobiles that they were on the train, before launching into tedious discussions of sales figures, past and future meetings and projected targets. It would probably have made their week to overhear Estelle's phone call but she was far too embarrassed to make it from the carriage. Instead, she locked herself in the tiny lavatory cubicle in order to press out the number.

Hanging on to the sink as the train clattered and swayed through the countryside, Estelle held her breath and envisaged the conversation going horribly wrong. What would she do if Will picked up the phone and said, 'Well, for God's sake don't come here, my wife'll be back from school any minute with the kids.'

'Hello?'

Will's voice sent a shudder of joy mingled with fear through her. Was she presuming too much?

'Hi, it's me. I'm on the train.' Taking a deep breath, Estelle said, 'I've left Oliver.'

Silence. Out of the window, fields and trees and Friesian cows hectically zipped past. Why wasn't he saying anything?

'Which train?' said Will at last.

'Gets into Paddington at three thirty.'

'I'll meet you there then.' Will sounded as if he was smiling. 'At the gate.'

Chapter 41

Paddington station had never looked more romantic. Magically, all the filth and grime seemed to have melted away. Estelle no longer saw the heaving mass of grim-faced commuters milling like worker ants across the concourse. All that mattered was Will's arms around her, the wonderfully comforting smell of him and his unstoppable smile.

At the sight of him, she had actually broken into a run. Well, more of a clumsy canter. With her two cases banging against her legs and the music from *Brief Encounter* swelling in her brain, Estelle had cannoned into Will and known at once that this was truly meant to be; *this* was where she belonged.

'I can tell you're an innocent country girl,' Will whispered into her ear.

'Really? How?' Did she have bits of straw in her hair and smell of pig muck?

'Look at your cases.' He shook his head at the sight of them, flung carelessly down onto the platform. 'Do that around here and they'll be gone in two seconds flat. You're in London now.'

'I'm not safe to be let out on my own,' said Estelle.

'I know.' Having gathered up the cases, Will kissed the tip of her nose. 'Just as well you've got me.'

Will's flat was in Islington, on the second floor of a

three-storey terraced Victorian property opposite a tatty rank of shops. Gazing out of the living-room window at the video store, the launderette, the newsagents and the betting shop, Estelle reflected that she was a long way from Dauncey House. Will's flat was exactly like Will himself, scruffy and uncoordinated but welcoming and, against the odds, attractive in its own way. The decor was basic, tidiness clearly wasn't a priority and the wallpaper out in the hall was, frankly, very George and Mildred, but Estelle didn't care. She was here with Will and that was all that mattered.

'Here we go. Should be champagne really.' Will appeared, carrying two mugs of tea, leaving a trail of drips in his wake.

'Tea's fine.' Taking a sip, Estelle suppressed a shudder; he'd put sugar in.

'Sorry, sorry. God, I'm a hopeless case.' Snatching it away from her, Will swapped it with his own. 'I still can't believe you're here, that you've actually left Oliver. It's like a genie has just burst out of a lamp and granted my wish.'

This time the tea was better but the mug was a bit grim, chipped and stained and looking as though it had been hastily rinsed out rather than introduced to the joys of washing-up liquid. Bravely forcing the tea down, Estelle said, 'All these years, I never had any idea. What kind of a man brings his mistress and son to live in the same village as his family?'

'The kind of man who thinks he can do anything he likes and get away with it.' Will's voice was gentle.

'Exactly! That's Oliver all over. Bastard!' raged Estelle. 'Well, I'm not going back. It's over.'

'Bed,' said Will.

'*Really* over. Juliet's welcome to him.'

'Bed.'

'God knows how many other women he's had . . .' Estelle paused. 'What did you say?'

Will removed the chipped mug from her grasp and drew her towards him. 'Let's go to bed.'

She shivered with anticipation. 'Are you sure?'

He grinned. 'Are you kidding? This is my second wish.'

'OK, but there's something I have to say first.' Estelle hesitated, because she might not be wearing her hideous honeycomb pants this time but there was still the problem of her less than perfect body. 'Don't expect . . . you know, too much, OK? I'm forty-five.'

'Fantastic,' Will said happily. 'That's my third wish come true.'

By early evening, everyone in Ashcombe had heard the news. Phil Jessop, who worked as a porter at the hospital by day and in the kitchen of the Fallen Angel at night, had told everyone he knew, and the ripples had spread out from there. Tiff remained in a critical condition at the hospital. Juliet was still with him, as was Oliver Taylor-Trent. Estelle, along with a pair of suitcases, had left Dauncey House in a taxi. Kate was currently serving behind the bar of the Angel, biting the heads off customers faster than Ozzy Osbourne could bite the head off any bat.

Since Ashcombe was currently a hotbed of gossip, it wasn't too surprising that Sophie Harvey had got to overhear most of it before bedtime.

'I might be seven, but I'm not stupid,' she announced to Jake, Maddy and Nuala, who were outside in the back garden of Snow Cottage. Wearing a blue vest and yellow pyjama bottoms and with toothpaste splashes around her mouth, Sophie settled herself on Jake's knee. 'I heard Cyrus Sharp talking to Theresa Birch in the shop. They were saying Oliver Taylor-Trent is Tiff's dad, but he can't be. He's never even bought Tiff a Christmas present.'

Jake wondered how you were supposed to do this. He'd been putting off the birds and the bees lecture for as long as possible, but there wasn't just the technical aspect of procreation to consider. Sophie was only seven, for heaven's sake. How were you supposed to answer the Christmas present question?

'Oliver is Tiff's biological father,' Nuala came unexpectedly to the rescue, 'but it was a big secret. So nobody knew, not even Tiff.'

'Biological.' Sophie was frowning. 'That's the seed thing, right?'

'Right. Anyway, it doesn't matter a bit,' said Nuala. 'All we care about is Tiff getting better.'

'But what if he doesn't?' Sophie's gaze swung back to Jake. 'Theresa Birch said people die of meningitis.'

'Tiff isn't going to die,' said Jake.

'But if he does, will you make a casket for him?'

'He's not going to die,' Jake repeated, because what else could he say?

'You hope he isn't going to,' said Sophie, 'but if he does, he wants one like a batmobile. And if I die, I want a red one with a giant spider on the lid.'

'Poor Kate,' said Maddy when Jake had carried Sophie off up to bed. 'Must be a bit weird for her. I still can't get over it – Juliet and Oliver, of all people. I can't believe they never once gave themselves away.'

'It's good, really, that Estelle's left. Otherwise you wouldn't know whose side to be on, hers or Juliet's.' Finishing her can of Coke, Nuala gazed at Maddy with longing. 'Is it my turn now?'

'No.'

'Oh, go on, don't be so mean. Let me have a go.'

'Look, I'm an expert, I know how to handle these things. You'd just fall out and fracture your other collarbone.' As she said it, Maddy shielded her eyes from the setting sun and watched Jake re-emerge from the house without Sophie.

'Maddy won't let me have a turn on the hammock,' Nuala called out. 'Tell her she's being selfish.'

'What's wrong?' Maddy knew something was up the moment Jake failed to turf her out of the hammock and leap into it himself.

'I just rang the ITU. They let me speak to Juliet.' Jake's throat was working as he struggled to keep his voice under control.

Fearfully, Maddy said, 'And?'

'Tiff's taken a turn for the worse. The doctors have warned her that he may not last the night.'

'I have to go to Ashcombe,' said Will. 'You understand that, don't you?'

It was nine o'clock in the morning. Since waking twenty minutes earlier, Estelle had been torn between revelling in the fact that she had spent last night making love with a man who wasn't her husband, and coming to terms with the realisation that she was a cheated-on wife. The other unfamiliar situation was her nakedness beneath the bedclothes – it actually felt quite weird, when you weren't used to it, not to be wearing a nightie.

'Today?' Hauling the duvet up around her breasts, she struggled into a half-sitting position.

'It's my job. I'm a documentary maker.' Will, already showered and dressed, came to sit on the bed. 'Not including all this stuff in the programme would be like making a film about Hitler and not mentioning the war.'

Estelle nodded; of course he had to go.

'You're amazing.' Will reached out to stroke her cheek.

'You won't tell him I'm here, will you?'

'Absolutely not.' He pulled a face. 'Do I look stupid?'

'Nor Kate,' Estelle insisted. 'I don't want anyone to know.'

'Hey, don't panic. We're on the same side, remember. I'll

be back tonight.' Will held up a front door key. 'Now, this is my spare. Will you be OK here without me?'

Blissful memories of last night came flooding back, of Will whispering how beautiful she was, and how she didn't have to hold her stomach in for him. In a rush of love and gratitude, Estelle decided she'd spend the day cleaning his flat, restoring order from chaos and discreetly bleaching his coffee mugs.

'I'll be fine.' Taking the key, she leaned up for a kiss.

'Typical,' said Will good-naturedly. 'All these weeks I couldn't wait to race down to Ashcombe, and now all I want to do is get back here to be with you.' Then he paused. 'How will you feel if Oliver's distraught about your leaving? Will it make you want to go back to him?'

'I've made my decision.' Counting off on her fingers, Estelle said, 'For a start, nothing's going to make me want to go back to him. Secondly, he wouldn't be distraught, that's just not Oliver's style. And number three,' she concluded, 'I doubt he'll even notice I've gone.'

By midday the flat was looking fifty times better and Estelle was feeling like Wonderwoman. Ironic, really, that back in Ashcombe she paid Marcella to do most of the house-work for her, yet here she was having the time of her life doing it herself.

Smugly, Estelle surveyed the vacuumed carpets, the dusted surfaces and the neat piles of magazines in the living room. In the kitchen, the mugs were now gratifyingly stain-free and the worktops sparkled. Ruthless de-cluttering, that was the key. Now that she'd cleared away all the extraneous rubbish, she could set about improving the flat in other ways, jazz it up a bit with some nice cushions, vases of flowers, bright rugs and a few decent prints on the walls – come to think of it, the walls could do with a fresh coat of paint, maybe she'd go out on a shopping trip this afternoon—

Bbbrrrrpppp went the doorbell. Startled, Estelle froze. Will hadn't said anything about the doorbell ringing. What was she supposed to do now?

While she was wondering, it rang again. Cautiously she made her way over to the window and peered out.

Although there really was no need to be cautious, Estelle reminded herself. She was allowed to be here. And it was hardly likely to be Oliver, begging her to forgive him and come home.

The lanky lad on the pavement was wearing a cycle helmet and carrying a package. Oh well, even she could manage to take a package in. Raking her hands through her hair, Estelle ran downstairs to open the front door.

The delivery boy looked distinctly taken aback when he saw Estelle. In her hurry to get on with cleaning up the flat, she hadn't actually got around to dressing this morning. Double-checking that her peacock blue cotton robe wasn't gaping open, Estelle said nicely, 'Is that for Will Gifford? I can take it.'

The boy didn't hand it over; he was too busy boggling at her. For heaven's sake, was opening the front door in your dressing gown not the done thing in London? Was it against the law?

'Really,' Estelle persisted, 'I can. It'll be safe with me.'

Cautiously the boy said, 'Do you . . . um, live at this address?'

He'd clearly delivered packages to Will before and was making sure she wasn't some madwoman who liked to break into strange houses and steal other people's parcels.

'Yes, yes, I live with Will.' God, it felt lovely saying that. 'He's at work just now, but he'll be back this evening. I'll make sure he gets it then. Where do you want me to sign?' Belatedly, Estelle realised he wasn't carrying a clipboard.

'No need.' Handing over the package, the boy said, 'It's

just the latest tape from the edit suite; Will wanted to check it out himself. You're Estelle, right?'

Startled, Estelle wondered how he could possibly know her name.

The boy broke into a geeky grin. 'Yeah, that's it, got it now. Recognised you from the tape.'

Chapter 42

When he'd wandered into the Fallen Angel in order to innocently enquire why there was no one at Dauncey House, it
had occurred to Will that if Kate refused to tell him what
had been happening, he was going to be stuck.

Thankfully, this didn't happen; Kate sang like a canary.
On tape. Only too keen to bring Will up to date, she didn't
even object to being filmed while the whole sorry story came
tumbling out.

'And now Mum's gone. God knows where,' Kate
concluded heatedly. 'She just took off, yesterday afternoon.
I mean, what must she be going through? She could be suicidal
for all he cares ... that's so typical of my father, the only
person he's bothered about is himself.'

Will kept the camera rolling. This was perfect. In his diffi-
dent, apologetic way he said, 'So you're concerned about
your mum.'

'Of course I'm concerned about her!' Kate looked at him
as if he were mad.

'Not so long ago, the two of you seemed, well, not so close.'

'She's my mum. Until she gets in touch, I won't even
know if she's still alive.' Kate paused, then said abruptly,
'OK, switch that thing off now. Don't try and make out I'm
just some cold bitch who was always horrible towards my
mother.'

Will, having switched off the video, was now replacing the lens cap and fitting the camera back into its carrying case. He said mildly, 'I wasn't trying to do that, but I'm glad you spotted it.'

'Oh, don't practise your amateur psychology on me.' Kate looked defensive. 'I know I wasn't that great when I came back to live here, OK? I was under a lot of pressure.'

'That great? You had an attitude problem the size of Texas.' To soften the blow, Will said, 'Anyway, you've come on in leaps and bounds since then. And I'm glad you appreciate your mother more now.' *I know I do.*

'You sound like a trendy vicar,' snapped Kate.

Will patted her arm. 'Right, I'm heading over to the hospital. See if Oliver'll speak to me.'

When he'd ambled out of the pub, Dexter stopped sweeping up spilled peanuts and said, 'Does he have his eye on you?'

'Fancies me rotten, if that's what you mean.' With a brief smile, Kate said, 'It's pretty obvious. He hangs around our house like a puppy, half the time when Dad isn't even there.'

'I have exactly the same problem with Nicole Kidman.' Dexter nodded gravely, then waited. 'And?'

'Oh please, I know I'm ugly but I'm not *that* desperate.' Kate's lip curled with derision. 'Will Gifford just has a high opinion of himself. He can't quite believe I don't fancy him back.'

Will persuaded Oliver to come outside the hospital and talk to him, just for five minutes.

'I'm so sorry, it's a terrible thing to happen.' Will was genuinely sympathetic. 'How's Tiff?'

'Not so good.' Rubbing his face, which was grey with fatigue, Oliver said, 'The doctors are doing everything they

303

can, but it's . . . you know. Hard.' He paused, indicating the whirring camera. 'Do we have to do this now?'

'Your wife has left you,' said Will. 'We need to see your side of the story. You do have a reputation as a ruthless businessman,' he pointed out. 'This way, the viewers will be touched by your anguish.'

Angrily Oliver said, 'I don't give a fuck about the viewers. It's not their sympathy I'm after. Tiff's my son and I *love* him.'

'Of course you do, of course you do.' Will's voice was consoling. 'It's a tragic situation. What a way for your wife to find out that you had a love child actually living right there in Ashcombe. How did she feel about that?'

'Not too happy, obviously.' Oliver's tone was curt. 'She's gone, hasn't she?'

'Do you think she felt humiliated? Made a fool of? Do you have any idea,' Will persisted, 'where she is now?'

A look of pain crossed Oliver's face. He shook his head. 'Look, I can't concentrate on this. I need to get back to the ward.'

'Would it be possible to have a word with Juliet? Do you think she'd come out and speak to me?'

'I'm sorry.' Oliver had already turned to leave. 'Absolutely not.'

'Hang on, did somebody switch front doors? Am I in the wrong flat?'

'Surprise,' Estelle sang out, flinging her arms round Will, covering him with kisses and simultaneously dragging him through to the living room.

'Oh wow,' said Will, staring. 'Cushion city.'

'I just thought I'd tidy up.'

'And buy some cushions.'

'I might have got a bit carried away,' Estelle admitted.

'Hey, you heard the rumours about the national cushion shortage and grabbed them while you could. That's completely understandable.' Will nodded. 'When you can only buy them on the black market, we'll be millionaires.'

'Sorry,' said Estelle.

'Shh . . . eleven, twelve, *thirteen*.' He grinned. 'Thirteen cushions. In one room.'

'I found this great cushion shop in Barnsbury.'

'And candles.' He did an exaggerated double-take. 'And a rug. God, and everything's so *clean*.'

'I just wanted to help.' Estelle hung her head; the cushions had cost an absolute fortune. Then again, it was Oliver's money, so who cared?

'Hey, listen, you don't have to do all this.' Lifting her chin, Will said, 'I'm just glad you're here. I'd be happy to live with you in a tent.'

You might be happy, Estelle thought, but I jolly well wouldn't be. Unless it was a luxury tent. But it was so sweet of Will to reassure her like this.

'I've been too busy to cook anything. We'll have to eat out.'

He pulled a face, gesturing towards his pockets. 'I'm a bit . . .'

'My treat,' Estelle said hurriedly.

Well, Oliver's treat. Better still.

'Let me just grab a shower first.' Will gave her a quick kiss.

'Hey,' he yelled minutes later from the bathroom. 'Posh soap!'

Estelle smiled to herself, because it was only Camay. Then again, compared with Will's beloved Wright's Coal Tar, presumably any soap was posh.

'Kate's missing you,' said Will. 'She's on your side.'

His words brought a lump to Estelle's throat. It was eight

o'clock and they'd come to an Italian restaurant a couple of streets away from Will's flat. Over fettuccine alla marinara and a bottle of Barolo, he had brought her up to date with the goings-on in Ashcombe.

'I should ring her, let her know I'm OK.' Estelle was overcome with guilt.

'No hurry. Call her in the morning,' said Will. 'It won't do them any harm to worry about you for a change.'

He was right. And he was so lovely. Wondering if she'd ever felt happier, or naughtier, Estelle sat back, heaved a sigh of satisfaction and finished her glass of red wine. Beneath the table, under cover of the cobalt-blue tablecloth, she slipped off one of her shoes and wiggled her bare toes along the inside of Will's jean-clad thigh.

'You're a wicked, shameless woman.' Will shook his head. 'I'm being corrupted. Are we having pudding?'

For once, tiramisu wasn't exerting its irresistible pull. Her toes still wiggling, Estelle murmured, 'You know, I think I'd rather get back to the flat.'

'And count cushions?' Wasting no time, Will signalled the waiter to bring their bill.

Estelle reached happily for her purse. 'Well, something like that.'

Estelle revelled in the feel of Will's arm slung around her shoulders as they made their way out of the restaurant. In her whole life, Oliver had never slung an arm around her shoulders in public; it was an altogether too casual gesture for him. Impulsively, she turned and planted a warm, loving kiss on Will's mouth.

Flash, went a camera somewhere nearby. Well, that was London for you, heaving with tourists snapping away nonstop—

'What the hell . . . ?' Will, his head jerking back, gazed in disbelief at the man who'd appeared from nowhere on the pavement in front of them. Flash flash *flash* went the long-lensed camera. Bewildered, Estelle clung to Will's arm. Her first thought was that Oliver had hired a private investigator to track her down and spy on her, but how could he possibly have known where to find her? How could *anyone* have known?

'What's this about?' Will was every bit as flummoxed as Estelle.

'You're Will Gifford, right? And that's Estelle Taylor-Trent,' said the photographer with a grin. 'Neat twist, making a documentary about some big-shot businessman then running off with his wife.'

The next moment he was gone, vanished into the crowds thronging the pavement.

'Shit. *Shit*,' Will seethed.

Estelle, shaken up but thinking fast, said, 'Hey, it's OK, it's not as if you stole me away from Oliver. He's the one with the mistress and the baby.'

For some reason Will wasn't reassured. 'But how could this *happen*?'

Estelle exhaled, fairly sure she knew the answer. 'I forgot to tell you. A tape arrived for you this morning. It was delivered by someone who works at the editing place. Tall and skinny, in his twenties, funny teeth . . .'

'Garth,' Will said grimly.

'Anyway, he recognised me from the tape. I was still in my dressing gown.' Estelle searched Will's face. 'Could that be it?'

'Oh yes.' He nodded, unamused. 'That could definitely be it.'

'But it doesn't *matter*,' Estelle insisted. 'I mean, so what if Oliver does find out? It's not the end of the world!'

'Of course it isn't,' said Will after a long pause. 'It's hardly going to do my career the world of good, but never mind about that. Come on.' With a rueful nod he took her hand in his. 'Let's go home. Ever been on the front pages of the national press before?'

A jolt like electricity zapped through Estelle's body.

'Oh God, will I be?'

'Duh,' Will teased. 'My name's Will Gifford, not Jude Law.'

Estelle squeezed his hand. Feeling ridiculously happy, she said, 'I'm glad you're not Jude Law.'

She wasn't on the front pages of the national press. Will eventually found the photograph the next morning on page seventeen of the *Islington and Barnsbury Observer*.

'Well, that's OK,' said Estelle, peering over his shoulder to read the accompanying article. 'Nobody I know is going to see this.'

'So long as it doesn't get picked up. Bloody Garth,' Will shook his head, 'blabbing to everyone at work. He thought it was funny, I suppose. I'm sure they had a good laugh about it down at the pub. Then word spreads and some keen young journalist gets to hear about it . . . it just doesn't *occur* to them that something like this could have consequences.'

'Hey.' Wrenching the newspaper from his grasp, Estelle pushed him back onto the bed. 'Consequences don't scare me.'

'God, I love you,' Will sighed as she straddled him, her peacock-blue robe falling open almost to the waist.

Estelle's heart began to race. He *loves* me!

'Bet you say that to all the girls.'

Will ran his fingers lightly down from her throat to her cleavage.

'I've never said it before in my life. And you're trying to make me late for work.'

308

'Sorry, I'll stop.'

'Don't stop.'

'No, no.' Moving her hips, Estelle said seriously, 'You can't possibly be late for work, I'll just let you get dressed—'

'Don't stop.'

Estelle shook her head. 'I don't want to be responsible for getting you into trouble, I'd never forgive myself if—'

'Sshh,' murmured Will, a broad smile on his face as he settled back against the pillows. '*Don't stop . . .*'

Afterwards, when Will had headed off to the edit suite he rented from Carousel Productions, Estelle picked up the phone and called Kate.

Was she only a hundred miles away from Ashcombe? It felt more like a million. Cleverly she remembered to block her own number first.

'Mum?' Kate sounded relieved to hear her voice. 'Mum, where are you? Are you OK?'

'I'm fine, darling.' Estelle was careful not to sound *too* fine; she was aiming for coping bravely in the face of adversity rather than having the time of her life with an adoring younger man.

'Are you coming home?'

'No.' Sitting cross-legged on the unmade bed, Estelle gazed out of the window at the rows of higgledy-piggledy Mary Poppins-style rooftops.

'Where *are* you?'

'In a hotel. How's Tiff?'

She had to ask.

She couldn't not ask.

'Still really bad.'

'And Marcella?'

Kate brightened up. 'Oh, Marcella's OK. She's got a thing for Twiglets now.'

'Well, that's not so terrible.'

'She dips them in custard.'

Estelle still thought this was an improvement on the pickled walnuts. 'How's Norris?'

'Fat, greedy, slobbers a lot. Pretty much the same as Dexter.' Kate paused. 'Are you going to ask about Dad?'

'Go on then.' Estelle was wary.

'I haven't seen him. He's still at the hospital. But if he *was* here, I wouldn't speak to him. He's been a complete idiot. Speaking of idiots,' Kate said abruptly, 'Will Gifford was down here yesterday. Honestly, what a pillock, I swear he thinks he's Hugh Grant. He was wearing that awful green jumper with the moth holes down the front.'

Estelle's gaze slid guiltily to the offending jumper, now flung across the chair in the corner of the bedroom. She'd personally removed it, moth holes and all, from Will's more than willing body last night.

OK, concentrate.

'What did he have to say?'

'Oh, he pretended to be shocked,' Kate sounded scornful, 'but he was over the moon, you could tell. Interviewed me in the pub then raced off to the hospital to see Dad. You can't blame him, I suppose, he's a journalist. All this business has brightened up his boring documentary no end.'

Estelle bit her lip. This was probably true. You couldn't blame Will if he were secretly delighted with the way things had turned out, for the sake of the documentary if nothing else.

'Mum? Norris really misses you.'

'Does he?' Estelle managed a wobbly smile. How completely ridiculous, Norris wasn't even their dog.

'I miss you too,' said Kate.

'Oh, darling . . .' Overwhelmed, Estelle's hand flew to her throat.

Sounding embarrassed, Kate said, 'Bet you never thought you'd hear me say that.'

Chapter 43

Estelle put the phone down and had a little cry. Her life was changing so fast she couldn't begin to get to grips with it. For now, like an alcoholic, all she could do was take things one day at a time. Like today. It was lunchtime, the weather was beautiful and she was going to go out for a couple of hours. *No more cushions* had been Will's parting shot as he'd left for work. OK, but she could buy food for dinner tonight. Roast lamb, Estelle decided as she headed for the shower. Will had always loved her roast dinners. A gorgeous leg of lamb, lots of fresh vegetables, crunchy roast potatoes with garlic . . .

Then glorious sex, probably.

Followed by Belgian chocolate truffle ice cream, Estelle thought happily.

Then more sex.

'Hi! Can I give you a hand with those?'

It was two o'clock. Juggling her house-key, handbag and four bulging carrier bags, Estelle started at the sound of the friendly voice behind her. She knew London was where you went if you wanted to get mugged in broad daylight, but this voice really didn't sound as if it belonged to a mugger. For a start, it was female and quite posh. Secondly, Estelle discovered as she turned around, its owner was less than five feet tall.

She was wearing smart clothes, Estelle couldn't help noticing. Surely someone in a neat white shirt and well-cut black pencil skirt wouldn't kick you to the ground and make off with your groceries.

'It's OK, I don't bite!' The girl, who was probably in her early thirties, said gaily, 'Here, you do the door and I'll make sure your bags don't topple over. That happened to me last week and I smashed a bottle of Pinot Grigio – I was so cross!'

Eventually Estelle managed to get the key fitted into the unfamiliar lock. As a red bus came trundling up the road, she nodded at it and said, 'Is that the one you're waiting for?'

The girl beamed. 'I wasn't waiting for a bus. Actually, I was waiting for you. You're Estelle, aren't you? Let me say hello properly.' Grabbing Estelle's temporarily free hand, she shook it with enthusiasm. 'I'm Lucy Banks.'

Blankly, Estelle said, 'And?'

'Well, the thing is, I'd love to have a chat with you. You see, I work for the *Daily Mail*.'

'Oh. Right.' So the story about Oliver and Tiff had come out. Feeling suddenly sorry for Juliet – this was the last thing *she* needed right now – Estelle said politely, 'I'm sorry, but I don't really want to talk about what my husband did. I'd rather just keep out of it, if you don't mind.' As she said this, it belatedly occurred to her to wonder how this girl had known she'd be here.

'That's completely understandable,' said Lucy, nodding sympathetically. 'But this isn't actually anything to do with your husband. Not directly, at least. You see, this is about what Will Gifford's been up to.'

'Up to? *Will?*' Estelle was by this time thoroughly confused.

Gently, Lucy said, 'Why don't we sit down and have a chat?'

Unwilling to invite the journalist into Will's flat, Estelle took her to a garden square a couple of streets away. There on a wooden bench beneath a sycamore tree, with a tiny tape recorder whirring away on the seat between them, she learned from Lucy that a woman had contacted the *Daily Mail*'s offices this morning after seeing the photograph of Will and Estelle in the local paper and reading the accompanying piece.

'Ever heard of Magnus Jonsson?' said Lucy.

'The record producer.' Estelle nodded rapidly, her fevered imagination conjuring up any number of bizarre images – Will was Magnus Jonsson's son, or his lover . . .

'Did you ever see the documentary Will made about Magnus?'

'No.'

'Well, that's not surprising,' said Lucy, 'considering it never aired.'

'Why not?' said Estelle, because this was clearly what she was supposed to ask.

'Because it never got finished. Because Magnus and Will had a bit of a falling out.' Lucy paused. 'Because Magnus found out that Will was sleeping with his wife.'

There was a high-pitched humming noise in Estelle's ears; she really hoped she wasn't the one making it. A short distance away, on the grass, two small children were battling over a bag of bread crusts, sending pigeons up into the trees.

'So you see, you're not the first,' Lucy said sympathetically. 'Magnus was a workaholic, away a lot of the time. Moira was lonely, she felt neglected. Then Will came along and she found his attentions so flattering it didn't take long for her to succumb. Will told her he loved her. From the sound of things, he has quite a way with him. I can imagine it would be hard to resist.'

Miserably, Estelle said, 'What happened?'

'Magnus came home unexpectedly one day and caught them. Have you noticed a bump on Will's nose?'

Estelle nodded. How many times in the last couple of days had she kissed that bump?

'That's where Magnus broke it,' said Lucy. 'He went berserk – well, who can blame him? He loved his wife.'

'Go on.' Estelle gazed down at her fingers, twisted together in her lap.

'Moira left Magnus and went to live with Will. They spent a couple of weeks together at his flat, then a month in the Caribbean. Moira paid for that. She thought they'd be together for ever, she was absolutely besotted with him, but soon after they arrived back in London, Will ended it. Moira was devastated. Magnus took her back, but the marriage didn't survive. They divorced a year later. When Moira read in the local paper that Will was up to his old tricks again, she felt she had to do something. She's a nice lady,' Lucy concluded earnestly. 'She isn't motivated by spite. She doesn't want you to make the same mistake she did, and give up on a perfectly good marriage for the sake of someone like Will.'

Estelle said stubbornly, 'Maybe she had a perfectly good marriage. I don't. Look, so what are you saying, that Will's nothing but a con man?'

'Not a con man.' Lucy proceeded with care. 'Not *exactly*. I'm sure he does care for you very much, in his own way. But we've done a bit of digging around and he does seem to make a habit of persuading lonely women to fall for him, then fairly rapidly losing interest in them. Usually after they've spent a bit of money on him, I have to say.' She paused. 'According to the receptionist at Carousel Productions, one of last year's conquests bought him a brand new BMW.'

'He doesn't have a BMW.' Estelle was numb.

'I know. But it's how he funded his trip to Australia. Finished with the woman,' said Lucy with a grimace, 'and promptly sold the car.'

Estelle swallowed; she felt as if she were trapped on a fairground ride, being spun round and round and not allowed to get off.

'So I was an easy target, is that it? I'm sorry, I can't believe this. Will told me he loved me.'

Next to her on the bench, Lucy took a slim notepad from her bag then flipped through it until she found the page she was looking for.

'Did he tell you he'd never felt like this about anyone before?' she said, and Estelle felt the palms of her clasped hands break out in a sweat.

She couldn't speak.

'Does he tell you that you're the one he's been waiting for, his whole life?'

There was a lump the size of a conker in Estelle's throat.

'Does he call you the other half of his soul?' Lucy persisted, her French-manicured finger moving slowly on down the list. 'Does he talk about the poem you'll have engraved on your joint headstone when you're both gone? Does he have nicknames for each of your elbows? Is he—'

'Stop!' Unable to bear it a moment longer, Estelle buried her face in her trembling hands. 'Oh God,' she wailed, 'please, just *stop*.'

'You're back!' exclaimed Will. 'Are you OK? When I saw the food on the floor I thought maybe you'd been kidnapped by aliens.'

He hadn't been home long himself. The carrier bags of food Estelle had unceremoniously dumped before going with Lucy to the garden square were still there on the kitchen floor. The Belgian chocolate truffle ice cream had melted, seeping like treacle across the tiles. Estelle stood and gazed down at the mess, as well and truly ruined as her own life.

'Something is wrong.' Will looked wary, like a guilty man opening his front door to find a policeman on the doorstep.

'Smile,' Estelle told him, 'you're going to be in the *Daily Mail* tomorrow.'

'The *Mail*. Oh God, Oliver'll go ape. He might pull out of the documentary.'

'Well, it'll be a real shame if that happens,' said Estelle. '*Again*.'

Now Will looked like the guilty man discovering that the policeman had proof of his crime.

'Moira Jonsson saw the piece in the local paper this morning.' Had it really only been this morning? It felt like months ago.

'Moira Jonsson.' Will shook his head. 'She's just jealous. We were together for a while, then we broke up. She never got over it.'

'You were making a film about her husband!' Her voice rising, Estelle shouted, 'All the things you told me, you'd already told her. And it's not just the two of us, either.'

'Who told you this?' Will's eyes narrowed.

'A journalist.'

'Oh, come on, now you're being naive. They'll make up *anything*—'

'Not this time,' yelled Estelle. 'Apparently there are quite a few older married women around whose elbows have nick-names!'

Trapped, Will said, 'So? It's not against the law.'

'Yesterday,' Estelle said shakily, 'you brought a bag of

travel brochures back here. We spent half the evening talking about going away on holiday. You kept saying you'd love to go to the Caribbean, remember? Because you'd never been there before.'

From the look on Will's face, he knew what was coming next. 'OK, so maybe I have. *Once.*' Sulkily he said, 'But it wasn't much of a holiday, let me tell you, with Moira clinging to me like a leech the whole time.'

'She probably felt she was entitled to be clingy, seeing as she paid for the entire trip. Tell me,' said Estelle, 'is it all a deliberate ploy? Do you do it to spice up your documentaries, make them more interesting for the viewers?'

'*No.*'

Estelle had already guessed as much. After all, Magnus Jonsson had pulled out of filming; his documentary had ended up not getting made.

'So it's just that we're available, is it? Lonely, neglected wives, grateful for the attention. Oops, I almost forgot – lonely, neglected, *wealthy* women.'

Giving it one last go, Will said desperately, 'It isn't like that. I'd never sleep with someone unless I cared about them. The money isn't important.'

'Nice try,' said Estelle. 'Very convincing.' Cuttingly she added, 'But I'm still not going to buy you a brand new BMW.'

His eyes flickered with guilt and she knew it was all over.

'Where are you going?' said Will, as she stalked past him.

Reaching the hallway, Estelle glimpsed her reflection in the mirror on the wall – the mirror that she had bought and hung there yesterday to brighten up the narrow space. She looked exactly what she was: a foolish 45-year-old woman who should have known better and was now living to regret it.

'To pack my things,' she told Will, discovering that she didn't even have the energy to cry. 'After that, I don't know.'

Chapter 44

'I don't know what to do any more,' said Kate. 'I don't even know what to think. I just . . . oh God, I don't know . . . give up.'

'It's like the world's gone mad,' Nuala suggested helpfully. Using the tongs to transfer a cherry Danish from the glass cabinet to a paper bag, she added, 'Like waking up and looking out of your window and seeing that the grass is purple.'

Maddy, who was about to set off with the morning's deliveries, said, 'Have you spoken to Estelle this morning?'

'Like wildebeest stampeding down Main Street,' said Nuala.

'She hasn't been in touch.' Kate shook her head helplessly. 'It's just unbelievable. My mother's run off with a toy-boy who's only out for what he can get. My father's at the hospital with his ex-mistress. They have a son together, I've got a half-brother I never knew I had, and he doesn't even *know* who his father is because he's lying there in a coma.'

'Orang-utans swinging from the trees, the Taj Mahal where the war memorial used to be,' said Nuala. 'Flying saucers whizzing through the sky.'

'Just ignore her,' said Maddy.

'Sorry. That'll be eighty pence.' Nuala handed the bag to Kate. 'But wouldn't it be weird if that *did* happen?'

Maddy rolled her eyes in despair. 'And I have to live with her,' she told Kate.

'What about Sophie?' Along with the rest of the town, Kate knew that Sophie had been prescribed a course of anti-biotics as a precautionary measure. 'Is she OK?'

Maddy smiled, touched by her concern. 'She's absolutely fine.'

Marcella turned up as Kate was leaving. Marcella had a ten o'clock appointment at the hospital's antenatal unit and she was hitching a lift into Bath with Maddy.

'Got everything?' said Marcella as Maddy loaded the cool-boxes into the car along with a bag containing clean clothes for Juliet.

'I've got everything. Have you got everything?'

Smugly, Marcella held up her pink raffia basket. 'Antenatal notes. Spare knickers. Wee sample. What more could a woman need?'

The basket was heavier than that. Pulling it open and surveying the contents, Maddy said, 'Pickled gherkins, a pomegranate, two orange Kit Kats and a tube of tomato puree, by the look of it.'

'Don't curl your lip at me like that,' Marcella protested. 'I have a blood sugar level to think of. It doesn't do to get peckish.'

Having dropped Marcella off first, Maddy parked the car and made her way over to the intensive therapy unit. There was a family, distraught and sobbing, in the waiting room. When Juliet emerged from the unit, Maddy hugged her hard, then said, 'Shall we go outside?'

They found a bench in a patch of sunlight between two buildings. Shaking her head, Juliet said wonderingly, 'I'd almost forgotten how it feels to be in the sun.'

She looked exhausted.

Maddy said, 'How's Tiff?'

'Still alive. Still in a coma. They did another brain scan yesterday.' From somewhere, Juliet dredged up a smile. 'Thank Sophie for the cards, will you? They're beautiful. How is she?'

'Good. Missing Tiff.' Maddy hated having to ask, but it was only fair they should know. 'Has Oliver seen the paper this morning?'

'The *Mail*? Yes. Poor Oliver.' Juliet shook her head. 'Poor Estelle too. What a hideous mess.'

Fiddling with her car keys, Maddy said, 'I'm actually feeling sorry for Kate. And I never thought I'd hear myself saying that.'

'I feel like it's all my fault.' There was anguish in Juliet's eyes. 'Maybe Tiff being ill is my punishment for getting involved with Oliver in the first place.'

'That's not true,' said Maddy. 'You know it isn't.'

'Oh God, I'm so tired I don't know *what* to think any more.' Checking her watch, Juliet gathered up the bag of clean clothes. 'Thanks for these, anyway. Say hello to Jake, and give Sophie a big kiss from me.'

They headed back to the ITU. As they approached the corridor they both heard the sound of hysterical sobbing behind the closed door to the waiting room.

'What's happening in there?' As soon as the words were out of her mouth, Maddy regretted them.

'It's Donna's family. Donna was a hit and run yesterday.' Juliet kept her voice under control. 'She's eighteen. The doctors have just told them she's brain-dead.'

Maddy closed her eyes.

'Anyway,' Juliet went on, 'how are things with you? Are you still missing Kerr?'

Maddy instantly felt smaller than she'd ever felt before. *Yes* she was missing Kerr, of course she was, but compared with everyone else's problems hers was laughably insignificant.

'Don't worry about me.' Giving Juliet another hug, choking back tears at the thought of Tiff lying helplessly in his hospital bed, she said, 'Ring me if there's anything else you need. And give my love to Tiff. We're all praying for him.'

She actually was, too. Despite never having prayed before.

'Thanks.' Juliet wiped her own brimming eyes. 'Me too.'

Maddy returned to the hospital at twelve thirty after finishing her deliveries. Marcella, waiting for her outside the main entrance, thought how pale and drawn she looked. Supermodels might aim for stick-thin limbs and hollowed cheeks but Maddy looked better with a bit more weight on her. There was an air of defeat about her too. She hadn't said anything, but Marcella knew why this was.

Well, there was nothing she could do about that. But she could certainly do her best, as a mother, to cheer Maddy up.

'Lunch,' Marcella declared as she climbed into the passenger seat of the Saab. 'My treat.'

'I'm fine.' Maddy shook her head. 'You don't have to do that.'

'Rubbish. Look at you, skinny as a broomstick! You need feeding up, and Nuala can manage without you for another hour. We'll go to Quincey's,' Marcella announced, because this was one of Maddy's favourite places to eat. 'And sit outside like proper sophisticated ladies wot lunch.'

When Marcella was in this kind of mood, Maddy knew there was no point trying to argue with her. Within ten minutes the car had been parked and she and Marcella were sitting at a table for two on the broad pavement outside Quincey's wine bar with two orange juices, two giant menus and – for ever-ravenous Marcella – a vast bowl of olives. The moment they'd finished ordering, Marcella reached down and began delving into the pink raffia basket at her feet.

This was when Maddy, her attention wandering, gazed across the road and saw who was seated in the window of the restaurant opposite.

The sensation was akin to a giant syringe shooting a gallon of adrenaline into her bottom. Sitting bolt upright as if she'd been electrocuted, Maddy stared first at Kerr, in profile to her, then at the glossy brunette sharing his table.

Oh Lord, this was too much.

'Here we are,' Marcella gaily announced, waving a small, curling piece of paper.

For a moment Maddy wondered if she'd hired a private detective and was now presenting her with evidence that Kerr had found himself another woman.

'Take it,' Marcella urged, 'it won't bite you. Can't bite you,' she added with a grin. 'It hasn't got any teeth yet.'

Kerr was sitting less than twenty feet away and Maddy was having to behave as if everything was normal. She wasn't even sure she could remember how to breathe.

'Are you OK?' said Marcella.

'Sorry, sorry.' Guiltily Maddy grabbed the photograph and gazed at the funny little broad-bean-with-legs that was destined to become her stepsister or -brother.

'That's his heart,' Marcella proudly pointed out, 'and look, that's his bladder!'

'Wow, his bladder.' Willing herself to concentrate, Maddy did her best to keep her hands steady.

Without much success.

'You're trembling.' Marcella looked concerned. 'Darling, are you sure you're all right?'

'I'm fine.' Glancing over the road, Maddy saw that Kerr

and the brunette had finished their meal and were preparing to leave the restaurant. 'Um, you said he. Is it a boy?'

'They always call them he,' Marcella explained. 'I don't want to know whether it's going to be a boy or a girl. It's because you haven't been eating properly,' she scolded, taking hold of Maddy's hand and giving it an admonitory squeeze. 'That's why you've gone all shaky. When our food gets here, you're going to eat everything on your plate.'

The door of the restaurant opened, and Kerr and his female companion stepped out into the street. Terrified that Marcella might turn round and spot him, Maddy hastily pointed in the opposite direction and said, 'Ooh look, there's that actor you like, the one from *Casualty*!'

Peering in vain through the crowd of tourists dawdling along, Marcella leaped to her feet for a better look. The sudden movement, coupled with the brightness of her acid-yellow shift dress, captured Kerr's attention. Turning his head, he focused first on Marcella before his gaze shifted to Maddy.

'Where?' demanded Marcella, desperate to get a glimpse of her favourite actor. 'I can't see him!'

Maddy was unable to speak; she couldn't stop staring at Kerr.

'What's he wearing?' Marcella called out, by now hopping up and down.

What was he wearing? Dark blue suit. Bottle-green shirt. Polished black shoes. Probably his usual aftershave, but from this distance it was impossible to tell. And still he hadn't moved. What must the brunette be thinking?

More to the point, who was she?

'Well, I give up,' Marcella announced, plonking herself back down with a sigh of disappointment. Then she brightened. 'Oh, I know what else I've got to show you!'

In slow motion, Maddy realised what was about to happen. She could read Kerr's intentions in his dark eyes, knew that he'd reached a decision. He was about to come over and confront Marcella, make her understand that enough was enough, that she wasn't being fair. Oh God. Maddy felt herself go hot and cold all over; he really did mean to go through with it.

'How about this?' Marcella, who'd been delving in her straw basket once more, assumed the air of a conjuror triumphantly producing a rabbit from a hat. 'Taa-daa,' she cried, waggling a tiny hand-smocked baby's outfit on a white hanger. 'Isn't it fab? Look at the little cardigan, and the bonnet with the birds on it. They were selling them in the antenatal unit to raise funds for a new scanner. And how about these little leggings, aren't they just adorable?' Her eyes alight with joy, Marcella danced the outfit up and down on its hanger. 'I know I said I wouldn't buy anything yet, but I just couldn't resist it.'

Across the street, Kerr had seen it too. The sight of Marcella proudly waving the baby clothes stopped him in his tracks, reminding him why he and Maddy had stopped seeing each other in the first place. For a fraction of a second their eyes locked again, silently acknowledging that it couldn't happen.

'They had the most gorgeous little striped bootees as well,' Marcella confided. 'I wanted to buy all of them! Will you look at the work that's gone into that embroidery?'

Feeling as if her heart was about to crack in two, Maddy leaned across the table and dutifully admired the workmanship. Out of the very corner of her eye, she saw Kerr and the brunette moving off down the street.

There really wasn't a lot of point in torturing herself further, wondering who the very pretty brunette was and what she was doing having lunch with Kerr.

It's nothing to do with me, Maddy thought resignedly. He's gone and that's that.

'Hooray.' Marcella abruptly whisked away the baby outfit as a waitress approached with their plates. 'Food's here. About time too!'

Chapter 45

The good weather had broken at last and Kate was glad; torrential rain suited her current mood far better than unrelenting sunshine. As she trudged along Main Street, soaked to the skin, Norris veered abruptly off to the left, in the direction of the workshops.

'Come *back*,' Kate groaned, but Norris, with his selective hearing, chose to ignore her.

'Blimey, you look rough.' Kate leaned against the doorway of Jake's workshop, shoulders hunched, hands tucked up inside the sleeves of her grey jersey. Currently drenched with rain, it weighed a ton.

'Pot, kettle.' Jake raised an eyebrow and stopped planing the edges of a casket lid. 'At least I don't look as if I've just crawled out of the River Ash.'

'I don't have stubble on my chin,' countered Kate, because she hadn't been exaggerating, Jake really was looking dreadful. As well as the three-day growth on his face there were shadows under his eyes. Basically, what with one thing or another, nobody in Ashcombe was currently looking that great.

Apart from Bean and Norris of course, who fancied each other rotten and each thought the other one was gorgeous.

'Any news about Tiff?' said Kate, and Jake shook his head.

'No change.'

'Have you been up to the hospital?'

Another shake. 'It's not my place to interfere,' said Jake. 'Juliet's there with Ol— your father.' He rubbed his jaw with a dusty hand. 'How about you? Tiff's your half-brother.'

'If he opened his eyes and saw me, he'd be scared out of his wits.' Kate pulled a face. 'I'm the one who yelled at him, remember, for getting ice cream on my trousers.'

'How about your mother? Any word yet?'

Kate nodded bleakly; it had been Estelle's phone call this morning that had propelled her out into the rain.

'She rang half an hour ago. No idea where from. Not Will's place, obviously. God, can you *believe* it?' Kate blurted out as rain dripped from her fringe and slid down her face. 'My mother and Will Gifford. What *was* she thinking of? It's just . . . gross.'

'It's not,' said Jake.

'Of course it's gross. She's my mother!'

'She's forty-five,' Jake pointed out. 'You're still allowed to have a sex life, you know. Estelle's an attractive woman,' he went on. 'If I was twenty years older, I'd sleep with her.'

'You'd sleep with anyone,' retorted Kate. 'I'm amazed you haven't given Theresa Birch a go.'

For the first time, Jake smiled. 'What makes you think I haven't?'

Two hours later when Kate walked into the Angel to start her shift, she found Dexter bawling into the cordless phone.

'. . . and I never want to see you in this pub again,' he stormed, 'because you're all *barred*.' Then he attempted to ring off with the equivalent of slamming down the receiver, which basically meant pressing the minuscule Off button *really hard*.

'The bloody nerve of these people,' Dexter raged, swinging round and glaring at her.

'Oh, grow up,' Kate retaliated, not in the mood for his rantings. 'Listen to yourself. Why can't you be nice to people just for once in your life?'

'Why the bloody hell should I be? It's midday.' Dexter shook back his hair and jabbed a finger at the clock on the wall. 'We had a table of eight booked for twelve thirty. They've just phoned to cancel. This is how much notice they give me. Let me tell you, I'll shout at whoever I like.'

'Except me,' Kate retorted frostily. 'You're shouting at me now and I won't stand for it.'

'Ha, this isn't shouting. Trust me, you'd *know* if I was shouting at you. What are you so stroppy about anyway?' Dexter's tone was accusing.

'You mean apart from all the other crap that's going on in my life? You really want me to tell you?' For a second Kate was actually tempted to blurt out the truth, that just as she'd been on the verge of getting her confidence back, Jake had gone and spoiled it all by informing her that, in effect, he fancied her mother.

Thankfully, pride kicked in. When Dexter said, 'You can tell me if you want to,' Kate swallowed hard and shook her head. Some secrets were too embarrassing to share.

It was the quietest lunchtime session Dexter had ever known. By one thirty he'd sent the kitchen staff home. Both the restaurant and the bar area were deserted. He could have sent Kate home as well, but sensed she had neither reason nor incentive to go. Dauncey House was empty too.

Outside, the weather had deteriorated dramatically. The sky was charcoal-grey and a full-blown thunderstorm was raging, flinging rain almost horizontally past the windows and bending the trees like springs.

Kate was at the bar perched on a high stool, lost in the pages of a glossy magazine. As Dexter watched her, thunder crashed directly overhead, causing her to jump. He gave up pretending to clean the already clean pumps and moved over to where Kate was sitting. She was wearing a coffee-coloured cotton shirt and a narrow, darker brown skirt. Breathing in the familiar scent of Clinique's Aromatics, Dexter said, 'What are you reading?'

Serve him right if it was an article about thrush. Bit of a conversation-stopper if ever there was one.

But Kate merely flipped her dark hair back from her face and sighed. 'Nothing really. Just being masochistic.'

At least she wasn't shouting at him, informing him he was an ignorant pig. Sliding the open magazine round to face him, Dexter saw that it was something about a trendy New York nightclub. Glossy, superior-looking *Sex and the City* types were sipping drinks, posing and studiously ignoring the camera. None of the women could possibly weigh more than ninety pounds. The designer clothes they were wearing were all lovingly described in the accompanying text. Evidently you were nothing if you weren't teetering on Manolo Blahnik heels.

'None of them are enjoying themselves. Not one person in that photograph is having fun,' Dexter said bluntly, and knew at once that he'd said the wrong thing. Maybe it could have been wronger if he'd been an anti-fur campaigner on a visit to the silver fox factory. Then again, maybe not.

'I used to go there,' said Kate. 'To that very club, in Manhattan. That used to be me. That was my life.'

Biting back the urge to retort, 'God help you, then,' Dexter said instead, 'D'you miss it?'

From the look Kate gave him, he gathered that this was the kind of question only a particularly simple man would ask.

'My old life? Of course I miss it.'

Genuinely bemused, Dexter said, 'Why?' and earned himself another look.

'Because I didn't have these then, did I?' Kate indicated her scars. 'I still had my old face.'

'OK, that's fair enough. What else?' As he spoke, Dexter reached up for two brandy glasses.

'Because I had a great time. I loved my job. I used to be invited to glamorous parties.'

'Thrown by nice people?'

Kate's jaw tightened. 'Of course they were nice people. They were my *friends*.'

'Right.' Nodding, Dexter uncapped a bottle of cognac and poured them both a hefty measure. 'So they'd have been a huge support while you were in the hospital.'

Instead of replying, Kate picked up her balloon glass and took a gulp of cognac.

'And afterwards, of course,' he persisted. 'When you were recuperating at home. I bet it was like a permanent party at your place, wasn't it? Well, that's what friends are for.'

'Look, I just liked New York, OK? I liked looking normal. *Better* than normal,' Kate corrected herself. 'When I walked into a room, people would go, *wow*!' She paused then added bitterly, 'Now they go, *waaah*!'

The next moment, Dracula-style, lightning flashed overhead and the lights flickered spookily in the pub.

'Or that happens,' deadpanned Kate.

'Nobody goes waaah,' said Dexter, 'and you know it. You're just feeling sorry for yourself.'

'And that's not allowed, after the week I've had?' Draining the rest of her drink, Kate held out her glass for more. 'It's all right for you, you've been ugly your whole life.'

Dexter smiled. He'd always been the rudest person he knew, but since Kate's arrival in Ashcombe he'd had serious competition.

'Thanks. Although I'll have you know that my eyes aren't ugly. I've been told several times in the past that I have sexy eyes. And I only gave you a drink in the first place because I thought it might cheer you up. This stuff isn't cheap,' Dexter warned. 'If you're going to carry on being grumpy you can pay for your own.'

Kate flashed him a sunnily insincere smile and kept it in place until he'd refilled her glass. Then she began flipping through the pages of the magazine once more. Dexter watched her sitting with her legs crossed, agitatedly jiggling her left foot. Any minute now her shoe would fall off.

'Tuh,' snorted Kate. Leaning across, he just had time to catch the headline: 'Older women, younger men', before the page was turned over with a *slap*.

'Now that's more like it.' Dexter nodded approvingly at the double-page spread now facing them. Turquoise sky, glittering emerald-green sea, a great swathe of white-blonde sand. Outside the pub, as if to emphasise the contrast, the rain was hammering down even harder than before.

'Maybe that's what I should do.' Kate ran an index finger longingly over the sweeping curve of beach. 'Just get out of here, go and live somewhere completely out of the way. Why not?' she said accusingly, spotting Dexter's raised eyebrows. 'A tropical beach would suit me fine, on a little island in the middle of nowhere. I could run a beach bar.'

'I've heard Weston-Super-Mare's nice,' said Dexter.

'The Seychelles. I'm serious,' Kate insisted. 'I was thinking about it last night. The only reason I came back here was because this was where my family lived. Well, that's a complete shambles now. They're both off doing their own thing. So basically what's left to keep me here? Who'd miss me?'

Having spent the last weeks biting his tongue, Dexter said, 'Me.'

Chapter 46

There, he'd done it. The sensation of a tightly coiled spring letting go and abruptly bouncing undone ricocheted through Dexter's chest.

Kate, who hadn't been paying attention, said distractedly, 'What?'

'I would. I'd miss you. I wouldn't want you to go.' It was such a relief to be able to say it at last. Now that he'd started, Dexter found he couldn't stop.

Kate shot him a pitying look. 'It's only barmaiding, for heaven's sake. Anyone can do it. If you weren't so stroppy you'd find it a lot easier to keep staff.'

'I'm not talking about a replacement barmaid. That isn't why I don't want you to go,' said Dexter.

Kate frowned. 'I'm not with you.'

Suddenly wishing he was better looking – and a stone slimmer – Dexter said brusquely, 'Do I have to spell it out? I like you. A lot. OK, I really fancy you.'

Kate stared at him in disbelief. Belatedly it occurred to Dexter that he may just have terrified her into handing in her notice, grabbing her passport and jumping onto the nearest plane. This could, in fact, be a fine example of shooting yourself in both feet simultaneously.

'What is this?' Kate demanded at last. 'Some kind of

consolation prize? Jake Harvey wasn't interested in me but never mind, you're prepared to step into the breach?'

Another flash of lightning crackled across the sky, followed almost at once by an ear-splitting crash of thunder. The storm was directly overhead now.

'I thought Jake was interested,' said Dexter.

'Oh, he was. For one night only. As soon as he'd got what he wanted,' Kate was defensive, 'the novelty wore off.'

'Good,' Dexter said bluntly. 'I'm glad. His loss.'

'Look, you really don't have to say all this stuff. I'm not a child.'

'I'm doubly glad to hear that. Can I tell you something?'

'Could I stop you?' Kate retaliated, and although her tone was brisk, Dexter saw that her hands were trembling. Whether that was a good or a bad sign was anybody's guess.

'It was you who made me realise Nuala and I had no future.' Dexter came straight to the point. 'We were a disaster together. We brought out the worst in each other. But you're the complete opposite of Nuala. The first time I saw you, I thought you were fantastic. Unique. I remember wishing Nuala could be more like you, except of course she can't, because she just *isn't*. But I knew I'd never felt like this about anyone before. That's why I let Nuala finish with me.' Dexter paused and raked his fingers through his hair. 'So there you are. Now you know.'

OK. Here came the downright scary bit.

'I don't believe you.' Kate was staring at him as if he'd just grown an extra head. 'You're making it up.'

Dexter rubbed the faint growth of dark stubble on his chin. 'Trust me, I don't have the imagination to make up something like this.'

Her tone accusing, Kate said, 'If it was true, you'd have said something before now. I mean, why wouldn't you?'

335

'You weren't ready to hear it. Plus, I'm a man,' Dexter amended. 'We don't just go around blurting this stuff out, you know. It's not the easiest thing to do. We have to be pretty desperate.'

Rain was rattling the windows; it sounded as though shovel-loads of gravel were being hurled dementedly at the glass.

'But . . . but you're so *rude* to me,' stammered Kate.

'So? You're rude to me too. But I don't say the kind of things I used to say to Nuala.' Dexter shook his head to emphasise his point. 'I wouldn't dream of it. Not with you.'

Kate was gazing anxiously into her empty brandy glass. 'I could do with another refill.'

'Forget it, you'd only fall off your stool. Anyway,' said Dexter, 'if I can get through this sober, so can you.'

Kate's foot was jiggling away again. She didn't speak.

'Look,' Dexter ploughed on, 'I'm never going to be Mr Sweetness and Light, that's just not the way I am. Who's that Irish fellow on breakfast TV, the cheery chubby one all the housewives love?'

'Eamonn,' said Kate.

'That's the one. Makes me want to chuck a brick through the TV.'

'Probably because he has more hair than you.'

'I'm just saying, we're not alike. Joky and jovial is not who I am. If I think someone's an idiot, I'll let them know. But that's life, isn't it? We all have our own characters. We're drawn to different people. I was drawn to you that first night you came into this pub with your mother,' said Dexter. 'There you were, scowling, snarling and glowering like the wicked witch in a pantomime, refusing to so much as look at anyone. The next thing I knew, you'd had a show-down with Maddy in the ladies' loo, hurled a couple of insults at Nuala and stormed out. Everyone else in the pub was stunned,' he reminisced with a crooked smile. 'I just thought *wow*, that's the girl for me.'

This was too much for Kate. Sliding jerkily off her stool, she made her way to the other side of the bar, where Dexter was standing. Reaching past him, she grabbed the cognac bottle by the neck, headed back to her stool and sat down again.

'So you've really been thinking that?' Carefully she double-checked. 'All this time?'

'I have.' Dexter nodded.

Talk about a surreal situation. Kate's hand went up to the damaged side of her face. Defensively she said, 'What about this?'

'I love your scars. They're my favourite part of you. I'm a pretty selfish person,' said Dexter. 'From my point of view, I'm glad you've got them. Let's be brutally honest here,' he went on. 'If you didn't have them, you wouldn't look at me twice. I wouldn't stand a chance.'

Kate felt as if she'd been slapped. Outraged, she retorted, 'What makes you think you stand a chance now?'

'Oh, come on, I'm not completely stupid. I've seen the way you look at me.' Dexter was on the brink of smiling now. 'You can't tell me there isn't a spark of interest.'

Kate's eyes widened. Indignantly she said, 'A *spark*?'

'OK, not a spark. Maybe spark's too strong a word. We'll call it a flicker,' said Dexter. 'There's definitely been a flicker.'

The cheek of it. Well, maybe he did have sexy eyes, but she'd never shared this thought with another living soul.

'You're mad.' Kate hadn't realised her foot was jiggling again, but seeing as her shoe had just flown over the bar, it seemed likely that it had been. 'I don't know what you're talking about.'

'You've wondered what it would be like to kiss me,' said Dexter.

'I have not!'

'Yes you have, you know you have. I've been completely honest with you,' he chided. 'The least you can do is be honest with me.'

'You've been a bit too honest.' Touching the left side of her face again, Kate said, 'You're glad I've got these scars because now that I look like this, nobody else would want me? That's sick.'

'It isn't. I'm not looking at it that way. Before your accident, what kind of men did you go out with? Good-looking ones, am I right? You wouldn't have considered anything less,' Dexter said seriously. 'But less attractive men can have just as good personalities as film-star-handsome ones. Better personalities, in fact, because they have to make more of an effort. That's all I'm saying,' he concluded. 'Thanks to your accident, you have the opportunity to find that out for yourself. And you never know, in the long run you may be glad you did.'

Kate wondered if he was deluded.

'But you *don't* make more of an effort. You make no effort at all! And you *certainly* don't have a great personality!'

There was a hint of a glint in Dexter's eyes. 'No? You still want to know what it'd be like to kiss me though. Actually, that's another part of me that's not too bad. If I say so myself, I have quite a nice mouth.'

Kate looked at him. For several seconds she couldn't move, couldn't speak. Then she climbed down from her stool, made her way to Dexter's side of the bar and retrieved her flung-off shoe. Finally, having gathered together her blue jacket and handbag, she said stiffly, 'I'm going home.'

Dexter hung his head. 'OK.'

Wrenching open the front door, Kate stepped outside the pub and shuddered as the full force of the storm almost knocked her off her feet. The wind was so strong she had to lean into it, cartoon-style, in order not to be sent cartwheeling backwards like tumbleweed.

She crossed Main Street, headed past the workshops and made her way up Gypsy Lane, grimly ignoring the rain pelting every inch of her body, soaking through her clothes all the way to her knickers and *undoubtedly* power-blasting the carefully applied make-up from her face.

Oh well, what did that matter now?

Reaching the entrance to Dauncey House, Kate paused and took the front door key from her waterlogged bag. She looked at it, sighed, then dropped the key back into the bag and turned round.

'Oh bloody hell, not you again,' said Dexter.

But not in a bad way.

'You don't scare me.' Kate moved across the flagstoned floor, trailing a small river in her wake. Blinking rain from her eyelashes, she came to stand directly in front of him.

'Don't I? You scare the bejesus out of me,' said Dexter.

'Just one kiss,' Kate told him, 'to see what it's like.'

Dexter nodded seriously. 'Absolutely. That's it. Just one kiss.'

Chapter 47

Juliet listened to everything the consultant was telling her. When he'd finished, she burst into floods of tears.

'No need to cry, Miss Price. It's good news.' The consultant was smiling broadly.

Oliver, relieved and delighted, enthusiastically shook the consultant's hand. 'Fantastic. Excellent news. We're so grateful.' Glancing at Juliet's tear-stained face, he added in bafflement, 'I'll never understand women. Not as long as I live.'

'Sometimes,' the consultant said happily as Juliet flung her arms round him and kissed him on both cheeks, 'I don't mind not understanding them.'

'I can't believe it,' Juliet sobbed, all the pent-up emotions of the last week exploding out of her like a burst dam. 'I was so scared, I thought he was going to . . . to . . . oh, thank you so much, you don't know what this means to me . . .'

'No need to thank me,' the consultant assured her. 'Tiff's the one who did the hard work. Children have the most astonishing powers of recovery. You never give up hope. It couldn't happen this fast with an adult, trust me. But these youngsters, one minute they're so ill you can't imagine they'll survive, and hours later they can be sitting up in bed demanding pizza and a Gameboy.'

Juliet wiped her eyes on the back of her sleeve. Tiff hadn't reached the pizza and Gameboy stage yet, but he had regained consciousness and was still recognisably Tiff. The consultant, sweeping into the ITU, had informed them that the results of the latest blood test, lumbar puncture and brain scan showed that Tiff was off the danger list. His body had escaped the devastation of rampant septicaemia. He hadn't sustained brain damage. It was the miracle Juliet hadn't dared to hope for.

'Mum?'

Her face still wet with tears, Juliet swung round to find Tiff with his eyes open once more, huge and as dark as pansies against the pallor of his thin face.

'It's OK, darling.' Lovingly she stroked his cheek. 'I'm crying because I'm happy. You've been a bit poorly, but you're getting better now.'

'Why's he here?' Tiff's gaze had settled on Oliver.

Juliet wavered. He had to be told now, that went without saying. But not right at this minute.

'He . . . um, came to see how you are, sweetheart. Everyone's been asking after you.'

Uninterested, Tiff looked away from Oliver.

'Where's Sophie and Jake?'

'They're at home. Look, here are some of the cards Sophie made you.' Eagerly Juliet held them up; making cards had been Sophie's way of willing Tiff to recover. 'How about this one, with a picture of Bean on the front and—'

'Jake was carrying me.' Tiff's forehead creased with the effort of remembering. 'Carrying and carrying me. Will he be here soon with Sophie?'

'As soon as you're well enough for visitors.' Juliet gave his hand an encouraging squeeze.

'But they're the ones I want to see.' Tiff's dismissive glance over at Oliver was excruciating; Juliet winced on Oliver's behalf.

'I know, sweetheart. We'll have to ask the doctor. Sophie's missed you too.'

Tiff's eyelashes drooped with exhaustion. Still clutching Juliet's hand, he closed his eyes and drifted off again.

Oliver approached the bed.

'Look at him.' Juliet felt her heart expand with love. 'He's going to be all right.' As a huge yawn overtook her she added, 'I feel as if I could sleep for a month.'

'Right. Well, he's out of danger now. On the mend.' Oliver glanced at his watch. 'Why don't you grab a rest while he's out for the count? If you don't need me any more, I could shoot up to London. See what's been going on while I've been away.'

Juliet nodded. Not allowed to have his mobile switched on in the hospital, Oliver had been reduced to hurrying outside every couple of hours to check out the ever-increasing number of messages and deal with the most urgent to the best of his ability over the phone. After six days, he must be desperate to get back to work. It was completely understandable.

It was also, if she was honest, something of a relief.

'That's fine.' Awkwardly, she offered her cheek up for the kiss Oliver seemed determined to plant there. 'Well, thanks for . . . everything.'

'Ring me if you need to. I'll be in touch tomorrow anyway.'

Feeling horribly guilty, Juliet said, 'Any word yet from Estelle?'

Oliver briefly shook his head. 'No.'

'Will you try and find her?'

'It's not my place to find Estelle, even if I could. I was the one who cheated on her. I let her down,' Oliver said wearily, 'and she left me.'

'For someone else who let her down.' Juliet felt terrible; she'd always really liked Estelle.

'I know.' Checking his watch again, Oliver jangled his car keys. 'Double betrayal. OK, I'm going to make a move. Will you tell Tiff?'

'That you've gone up to London?'

Oliver gave her a measured look. 'That I'm his father.'

'Oh, right.' Inwardly shrinking away from the prospect, Juliet nodded. 'If you want me to.'

'It's not a question of that. Everyone knows now. We don't have any choice.' After a last look at Tiff, Oliver left.

While Tiff was asleep, Juliet phoned Jake from the call box in the corridor outside the ward. Less than twenty minutes later the doors of the ITU swung open and Jake burst in. Still exhausted but too elated to sleep herself, Juliet hastily rubbed her hands over her face and stumbled to her feet. The next moment she was wrapped in a rib-crushing embrace. Jake smelled deliciously of wood shavings and varnish and was wearing paint-smeared jeans.

Fresh paint, she discovered, gazing down at the streak of lilac on the front of her skirt.

As if it mattered.

Jake was grinning too. 'Sorry, I just couldn't wait. I had to come straight away. It's the best news in the world.'

'I know.' Letting him go, her eyes filling with tears of joy all over again, Juliet watched him pull up a chair next to Tiff's bed and gaze at the boy intently. Within seconds, as if by telepathy, Tiff's eyes opened.

'Jake! You're here!' Breaking into a broad smile of delight, he raised his thin arms a few inches from the bed. Careful not to dislodge the IV drips running into his arms, Jake gave him a hug. In return, Tiff's left hand curled round Jake's neck. The look on each of their faces said it all; deeply moved, Juliet almost couldn't bear to watch.

'I'm here,' said Jake, 'and so are you. Now, Sophie's desperate to see you but when your mum asked the doctors, they said it wasn't a good idea. Not for another day or so, at least. But all you need to do is carry on getting better, then they'll move you to the children's ward. Once you're there, Sophie will be able to come and see you as often as she wants.'

'Has she missed me?' Tiff looked pleased.

'Absolutely. We've all missed you.' Jake smoothed a lock of Tiff's hair back from his forehead. 'Nuala and Maddy are looking after your mum's shop. When I went over to tell them you were getting better, they both cried.' Jake shook his head in disgust. 'What a bunch of *girls*.'

'Mum did too.' Grinning, Tiff said, 'Did you cry?'

'Watch your language. We're *men*,' said Jake. 'We never cry.'

'It's because we have willies,' Tiff agreed, indicating Juliet with a knowing nod of his head. 'And they haven't.'

Jake stayed with Tiff while Juliet showered and changed into clean clothes. She put on the long turquoise dress and lilac cardigan Jake had brought along for her – not perfect, but it could have been a lot worse – and applied lipstick and mascara almost as if the nightmare of the last week had never happened.

'Now, are you *sure* this is OK?' Juliet asked Tiff for the hundredth time, ten minutes later.

'It's OK,' Tiff patiently repeated. 'I'm tired. I'm going to sleep in a minute. When I'm asleep, you and Jake are going out for something to eat, so if I wake up you won't be here. But Mel will be here,' he went on, beaming at his favourite nurse, 'so it doesn't matter. She'll be like my babysitter.'

Cheerily, Mel said, 'Better still, I'm free!'

Juliet wondered if all the nurses regarded her as a selfish, hopelessly neglectful mother, waltzing off to a restaurant leaving her fragile seven-year-old son all alone in his hospital bed.

'Oh please,' Mel tut-tutted good-naturedly, catching her look of anguish, 'don't even think it. We're sick of the sight of you! Off you *go*.'

'And Mel's the boss,' said Jake, whose idea it had been. 'Do as she says or she'll zap you with a defibrillator.'

'Jake will have his phone with him,' Juliet told Tiff. 'If you want me, all they have to do is ring us. We can be back here in five minutes.'

'Night, Mum.'

'And we'll be back in two hours, whatever happens.'

''K,' mumbled Tiff.

Oh God, how could she do this to him? How could she heartlessly abandon him? 'Look,' Juliet said in desperation, 'if you'd rather we stayed—'

'Mum?'

'What darling? What is it?'

'Could you not make so much noise?' Tiff murmured. 'I'm *trying* to go to sleep.'

Chapter 48

'I can't believe it. Posh plates,' Juliet marvelled. 'Wine glasses made out of real glass, cutlery that isn't plastic.'

'And candles,' said Jake. 'Major health and safety hazard if ever I saw one. It's playing with fire, having candles at a table.'

Juliet smiled. He'd brought her to Romano's, an Italian restaurant around the corner from Pulteney Bridge with a good reputation for food and an atmosphere lively and buzzy enough to allow them to talk without being overheard. She didn't know if Jake had chosen it for this reason but she was glad to be here.

'Speaking of playing with fire,' Jake went on, 'do you feel like telling me how it all happened?'

Juliet nodded. She owed him that much at least. If she was honest, she'd wanted to tell Jake for years.

'I met Oliver when I was twenty-five. I was working for a catering company, providing directors' lunches in the city. I thought he was wonderful,' Juliet said simply. 'I also thought he was single. But he swept me off my feet, and by the time I found out he was married, I was already pregnant.'

'Carry on,' Jake prompted.

Juliet pulled a face. 'Well, if this was a film, I'd be the plucky pregnant single woman telling Oliver to take a running jump and soldiering on without him. Except I wasn't that

346

plucky. I'm not proud of this, but at the time I was scared witless. I had a threatened miscarriage at five months, which meant the catering company couldn't get rid of me fast enough and made me redundant. After Tiff was born, my landlord refused to renew the lease on my flat. When Oliver came up with his plan, I honestly didn't feel I had any other choice. I was so grateful I just went along with it.'

'So he brought you down to Ashcombe,' said Jake. 'Bought the delicatessen and set you up, so that he'd have his mistress and his child living just down the road from his wife.'

'Ex-mistress,' Juliet said firmly. 'Our relationship ended the day I found out he was married. We haven't been sneakily seeing each other, if that's what you think.'

Jake shrugged and broke open a warm bread roll. 'I don't think anything. I'm just waiting for you to tell me.'

'OK.' Slowly Juliet exhaled. 'Oliver didn't want Estelle to find out, but he really wanted to be able to see Tiff growing up. I was desperate for somewhere to live. It seemed like the perfect answer. I loved Ashcombe from the word go. As long as Oliver's family didn't know about Tiff, where was the harm in it? We were all happy.'

And put that way, it sounded perfectly reasonable. But Juliet sensed that something else was bothering Jake.

'And in seven years there's never been anybody else,' he said evenly. 'Seven years is a long time. So, all part of the agreement, was it?'

There was no point in trying to deny it. Facing him, Juliet said bluntly, 'Yes, it was. Oliver didn't want to see some other bloke moving into the flat he'd bought for me. Maybe it wasn't fair of him, but at the time I was more than happy to go along with it. The last thing I needed, or wanted, was to get involved with anyone else. My number one priority was Tiff.'

Jake was incredulous. 'And in all that time you've never

met another man you'd be interested in getting together with? You've never even been *tempted*?'

'Never seriously.' Shaking her head, Juliet said, 'Of course there have been times when I've been . . . um, tempted. But not getting involved has always worked out for the best.'

'I get it. Now it all makes sense.' Jake paused as the waiter arrived to clear their plates away, and this time Juliet knew exactly what he was remembering. 'That first Christmas after you arrived in Ashcombe. I walked you home on Boxing Night from one of Marcella's parties.'

Juliet nodded; how could she ever forget?

'I tried to kiss you goodnight,' Jake went on. 'You were wearing a blue scarf with silver glittery bits woven into it. And it was really icy outside. Your nose was pink with cold. You wouldn't let me give you a kiss.'

'Wouldn't I?' said Juliet and Jake shot her a don't-try-and-bullshit-me look.

'Then I asked you out and you turned me down flat.'

Oh heck. 'Did I?'

'Now I know why. Because it was in the tenancy agreement. All part of the bargain you'd struck with Oliver. I really liked you,' said Jake.

Juliet realised that it was her own rapid breathing causing the candles to flicker madly on the table between them.

'I really liked you too,' she told Jake, busily pleating the crimson tablecloth between her fingers. 'Which is why I'm extra glad I turned you down.'

Jake's eyes glittered. 'Speak English.'

'Oh, come on, you know what you're like! Goldfish have a longer attention span than you. I've spent the last five years watching you go out with girls and dump them before they've had time to tell you their surnames— *What?*' Juliet demanded heatedly. 'Why are you looking at me like that? You know there's no point in denying it, because it's *true*.'

Jake waved away the waiter, approaching with the sweet menus.

'Of course it's true. I'm not denying it. But has it occurred to you for one second to wonder *why* it's true?'

'That's like wondering why snow is cold. It just *is*. And you're the way you are because you're you.' Juliet prayed she was making sense; the intensity of Jake's gaze was making it hard to think straight.

'OK. Estelle's found out about you and Oliver.' Jake swiftly changed tack. 'She's left him. So, what now?'

'What d'you mean?'

'I mean, is it happy families time? You, Oliver and Tiff?'

Juliet shook her head. 'Absolutely not. I'm completely over Oliver.'

'But you let him rule your whole life!' Jake exploded, causing the group of women at the next table to jump and nudge each other.

'You aren't listening to me,' Juliet shot back. 'I haven't met anyone else I want to *be with*.'

'Haven't you? *Haven't you?*' There was a dangerous glint in his eyes.

Defiantly Juliet said, 'Nobody who'd make me happy.'

'But how do you *know* that?' Jake was becoming more and more exasperated. 'How can you possibly know that when you've never even given anyone a chance?'

'Because I'm not stupid,' Juliet cried, 'because I've got eyes in my head, because I know a heartbreaker when I see one and I don't *want* my heart broken again, plus there's Tiff to consider— Oof, what are you *doing*?'

'Getting you out of here.' Having flung a handful of notes down on the table and grabbed Juliet by the arm, Jake hauled her to her feet.

'Oh, don't go,' protested one of the plump women at the next table. 'It's just getting good.'

'So sorry.' Jake spoke through gritted teeth as he propelled Juliet towards the door.

'She might have wanted a pudding.' The woman, who was squiffy, clutched the back of Jake's shirt and tried to pull him back. 'You can't drag your girlfriend out of a restaurant before she's had her pudding!'

'She isn't my girlfriend.' Jake's tone was brusque as he wrenched his shirt free. 'You're drunk. And if you didn't have so many puddings, maybe you wouldn't be so fat.'

'That was rude,' Juliet gasped when he'd bundled her outside, leaving the rest of the women at the table squawking with indignation.

'Do I look as if I care?' Jake, his green eyes glittering with intent, pushed Juliet up against the Bath-stone wall of the restaurant and kissed her.

Properly. Thrillingly. So completely thrillingly that Juliet quite forgot to put up a fight and push him away. Her body was too busy zinging with desire.

'I've waited five years for that,' Jake murmured, his breath warm on her temple.

Juliet's mouth was tingling. In fact *all* of her was tingling. She wanted to hit him, because it was all so hopeless.

'I love you,' said Jake.

Tears sprang to her eyes. 'And your point is?'

'You didn't answer my question earlier. I said *why* do I go from one girl to the next, never bothering to get to know them properly or settle down?' Jake raised her chin, forcing Juliet to look at him. 'Do you still not see? It's because there's only been one girl I've wanted to settle down with, and she wasn't interested in me. She turned me down.' He paused. 'So I did the next best thing and became her best friend instead. Well, *pretended* to be her best friend.'

'You're just saying that,' Juliet whispered. She was right, wasn't she? This was how Jake operated, how he seduced all the other girls in his life, by sweet-talking them into bed, telling them whatever they longed to hear. Of course she *wanted* to believe him, but what if all he was doing was spinning her a line?

'I love you,' Jake said again, 'and I love Tiff as if he were mine. What would Oliver do if you told him we were a couple? Take the deli away from you and kick you out of the flat?'

Flummoxed, Juliet said, 'Well . . . I, um, maybe . . .'

'Fine.' Jake shrugged. 'No problem. Leave it with me.'

Leaning back against the wall, Juliet felt the smooth stone against her shoulders. For five long years she'd suppressed her feelings for this man and now they were refusing to stay suppressed a moment longer. Her mouth curving into an unstoppable smile, she pulled Jake back towards her until their bodies were pressed hard against each other, then cupped his face in her hands and—

'Whoa, not so fast.' Deftly sidestepping her, Jake tapped his watch. 'It's gone eight.'

'We don't have to be back until half past.' Juliet smiled, feeling deliciously wanton, though what they could get up to in broad daylight in the centre of Bath in twenty minutes flat, she couldn't imagine.

'I want to see Tiff.'

Struck afresh by the fear that she was being a neglectful mother, Juliet said, 'To check he's all right?'

'To tell him everything and get him on my side.' Jake looked pleased with himself. 'And to tell him that his mother has spent the last five years being a complete durr-brain.'

'Oh well,' said Juliet, 'he's seven years old. He already knows that.'

Chapter 49

The next morning Oliver phoned the unit to find out how Tiff was. Juliet took the call and reassured him that everything was fine.

'He's doing brilliantly.' She paused. 'Are you coming in to see him today?'

Oliver cleared his throat. 'Well, er, no. As long as he's doing well, that's the main thing. I've got a lot on, as you can imagine . . . um, give him my best wishes . . .'

Best wishes. Poor Oliver. He did love Tiff, in his own way.

'I'll do that.' Juliet nodded, doing her best to keep the smile out of her voice. 'I'll tell him the other thing as well, shall I?'

'Fine, fine. Far better coming from you. I'll bring him some presents when he's had time to get used to the idea.' Oliver's hearty tone couldn't quite disguise his awkwardness. Now that Tiff was no longer hovering at death's door, he didn't know how to handle the situation.

'They're moving him to the children's ward this afternoon,' said Juliet.

'What would he like? Lego? Scalextric? How about the new Playstation?'

'Oliver, you don't have to do that.' If she left it to him, he'd empty Hamley's. 'Tiff's fine. He's got everything he needs.' He would soon, anyway. Tiff was already counting down the minutes until he could be reunited with Sophie.

Jake left Sophie, who was in a frenzy of anticipation, with Marcella. Considering it was a fairly momentous thing he was about to do, he felt surprisingly calm as he made his way up Gypsy Lane.

Approaching Dauncey House, he removed his sunglasses. It was just gone midday and Kate was at the Angel beginning her lunchtime shift. Oliver Taylor-Trent's car, a silver top-of-the-range BMW, was parked on the gravelled driveway, looking – as it always did – as if it had just been valeted.

Tucking his sunglasses into his shirt pocket, and noticing that the flower-filled stone urns on either side of the front door needed watering, Jake rang the bell.

He heard it jangle inside the house. Finally the door opened. Oliver, back from London and wearing a grey business suit, was on the phone. When he saw Jake on the doorstep he said, 'Right, right. Doug, I'm going to have to get back to you. OK, fine, bye.'

'I wonder if anyone's ever got it wrong,' Jake said easily.

Oliver frowned. 'What?'

'Busy executive businessman barking instructions over the phone to his assistant. They're discussing a takeover bid for another company. The conversation ends and he says bye. But the assistant thinks his boss has just said *buy*, so he rushes off to do as he's been told. Just a thought.'

Oliver said brusquely, 'If he were my assistant he wouldn't have the power to buy a company.'

Jake looked disappointed. 'Not even a little one?'

'Not even a little one.'

'Not even a company as small as mine?'

'What would I want with a company that supplies painted

coffins? And why are we having this conversation?' demanded Oliver. 'Hoping to sell up, are you?'

'No.' Jake shook his head, smiling at the thought of Oliver stripped to the waist in the dusty workshop, painstakingly painting the whiskers of a blue Persian onto the lid of a cat-lover's casket. 'But I'd like a word. Can I come in?'

Oliver shrugged and stepped to one side, ushering him through. In the kitchen, he set about boiling the kettle and locating a pair of coffee mugs with the air of someone unfamiliar with such a domestic task.

Jake, waiting for the coffee to get made, leaned against the dresser with his arms crossed, surveying the kitchen. It was vast, almost as big as the entire ground floor of Snow Cottage, but there was a sense of sadness and neglect about the room. Their own kitchen might be minuscule by comparison and it might not boast a gleaming Neff oven, Smallbone of Devizes handcrafted units and a chrome espresso machine as big as a fridge, but Jake knew where he'd rather live.

It took a while, but finally the coffee was made. Jake stayed standing when Oliver handed him his mug, and guessed that Oliver would too. Sitting down at the table would give away his this-is-my-house advantage.

Jake guessed right.

'So,' Oliver said at last. 'What's this all about?'

As if he didn't already have a pretty good idea.

'Juliet. And Tiff. Juliet and I are a couple now. I love her,' Jake said steadily, 'and she loves me. I love Tiff as well. We've been like a family for years, even you must know that. But everything's changed now. We're going to live together.'

Oliver's jaw tightened with annoyance. 'How can you say you've been like a family for years? I may not always be around, but I hear about what goes on from Marcella and Estelle. You've never settled for one girl when half a dozen

would do. You, stay faithful to Juliet? Don't make me laugh.'
He gestured dismissively. 'The pair of you wouldn't last five
minutes. First you'd break her heart, then you'd break Tiff's.
No, I'm sorry, I can't allow that to happen.'

Jake raised his eyebrows. 'You can't *allow* it?'

'You and Sophie aren't moving into the flat above the
shop,' Oliver said bluntly. 'Now, don't take this personally,
I'm just thinking of Tiff and what's best for my son—'

'Hang on, sorry, we're talking at cross purposes here.'
Jake held up a hand to stop him. 'I wasn't asking your permission just then, I was telling you how things are going to be
from now on. And no,' he went on before Oliver could protest,
'I'm not planning to move into Juliet's flat. She and Tiff will
be coming to live with us. At Snow Cottage.'

'Don't be ridiculous,' Oliver exploded. 'You can't do that!
What about your sister and that dippy barmaid friend of hers?
Are you seriously planning to squeeze six of you, all together,
into that . . . that *rabbit hutch*?'

'Well, maybe we can come to some arrangement about
that.' Jake paused and took a mouthful of coffee; he was
really enjoying himself now. 'You see, Juliet tells me you
bought the deli outright, so obviously what you decide to do
with it is up to you. But she'd like to carry on working there,
and so would Maddy. Which got us wondering,' said Jake.
'Actually it was Juliet's idea. How would you feel about
Maddy and Nuala moving into the flat?' He watched Oliver,
who was clearly wary of being outmanoeuvred, mentally
running through the list of pros and cons.

Finally Oliver said, 'And if I say no?'

'That's absolutely OK. Before my parents moved into
Snow Cottage, Cyrus Sharp's family lived there. And they
had nine children,' said Jake. 'So please don't worry about
us, because I promise you, we'll be fine.'

Oliver was motionless, staring at him. He ran a finger

round the inside of his shirt collar, loosening it. Jake, waiting for his reaction, thought how silent the house was.

Until the tiny mobile phone on the kitchen table began to ring, causing Oliver to jump and glance down at the caller's ID.

'I'll think it over.' Oliver's dismissive manner indicated that it was time for Jake to leave. 'And let you know.'

Smiling, Jake left Oliver to deal with his phone call and let himself out of the house. It was actually really nice, feeling this sorry for a multi-millionaire.

'Hey, this is cool.' Tiff greatly approved of his new surroundings. Gazing around the brightly decorated children's ward, nodding with satisfaction, he said for the hundredth time, 'When will Sophie be here?'

Juliet's eyes danced, picturing the Hollywood-style reunion. Any minute now, Jake and Sophie would appear through the swing doors. Yelling, 'Oh Tiff, oh *Tiff*,' Sophie would break away from Jake and race, in Hollywood slow motion, the length of the ward before throwing herself ecstatically into Tiff's arms.

It didn't happen like that at all. Sophie, who had never lacked confidence in her life, found all the pre-reunion hype too much and experienced her first-ever bout of paralysing shyness. Refusing to let go of Jake's hand, she remained glued to his side, staring fixedly at the artwork up on the wall. For a good five minutes their conversation was as stilted as that of two strangers in the waiting room of an STD clinic.

Finally Sophie said, 'What's the food like?'

'Gross.'

'Oh.' Pause. 'What are the other kids like?'

Tiff shrugged. 'Don't know. I only just got here.'

'Oh. So what are the nurses like?'

'Don't know. I only just *got* here.'

Longer pause.

At last Sophie said grudgingly, 'I told Bean you were better and she wagged her tail.'

Tiff's lip curled. 'That's because she's a dog.'

'Did you like my cards?'

'They were all right.'

'I won't make any more then.' Sophie bristled. 'They took me ages.'

They were glaring mutinously at each other now, like Tom and Jerry.

'You can have them back then,' snarled Tiff.

'Ugh, no thanks, with *your* germs on them.'

'*Right*.' Jake seized Sophie's hand. 'If all you're going to do is argue we'll go home now and—'

'No!' bellowed Sophie and Tiff in unison.

Jake raised his eyebrows. 'So if we stay, you think you can manage to be nice to one another?'

Tiff and Sophie exchanged glances, then both nodded vigorously.

Jake smiled across at Juliet and said, 'OK.'

'I should think so too.' Juliet gave Tiff a behave-yourself look. 'Getting stroppy with your first proper visitor really isn't on. You're supposed to be nice to people who—'

'Sophie isn't my first visitor,' said Tiff. 'Mr Taylor-Trent was here yesterday.'

Juliet stiffened. Of all the subjects to crop up. She'd spent the entire morning attempting to pluck up the courage to explain the necessary facts to Tiff, but the right moment simply hadn't arisen.

Plus, of course, she was a big wimp.

'Did he do you a card?' Sophie's tone was accusing.

Tiff scowled. 'No.'

'Well then, he's not as good as me, because I've done you *six* cards. Anyway, he doesn't count as a proper visitor,' she went on scornfully. 'He only came here because he's your father.'

Juliet felt all the blood drain from her face, although where it went she couldn't imagine. Casting an anguished glance over at Jake, she willed someone, somewhere, to press the rewind button so the words could slither back into Sophie's mouth. Unable to move, she looked across at Tiff.

'What?' Tiff was frowning. 'Mr Taylor-Trent? How can he be my father?'

Sorry, Jake mouthed across at Juliet.

'You remember, the seed thing. Carrie Carter from school told us about it.' Sophie assumed an air of superiority. 'It's called mating.'

Jake was doing his best not to snort with laughter. Juliet was glad he found it so funny.

'Oh, mating.' Tiff nodded equally sagely, like an eminent professor. 'Seeds, yeah.' He paused, his expression thoughtful. 'Mr Taylor-Trent's a bit old, isn't he?'

'He's *very* old,' Sophie grandly announced. 'But quite rich. So that's good, probably.' She beamed at Tiff. 'For when you need a new bike or an Xbox or something. Now that he's your dad, he'll have to buy you presents.'

Tiff blinked up at Juliet. 'So you really mated with Mr Taylor-Trent?'

Never mind hiding under the bed, she wanted to crawl away and die.

'Um . . . yes.'

Behind her, Jake was by this time almost crying with silent laughter.

'Do we have to go and live with him?' said Tiff.

Wordlessly Juliet shook her head.

'That's all right then.' Visibly relaxing, Tiff turned his attention back to Sophie. 'They've got a Playstation 2 on this ward, one of the nurses told me. Do you want to have a look at the tube going into my arm?'

This was the invitation Sophie had been waiting for. Next moment she was perched on the bed next to Tiff, avidly poring over the spot where the plastic tubing actually disappeared through the skin, and bombarding him with questions about how much it had hurt.

Jake drew Juliet to one side, away from the bed.

'Damn, so that's what I've been missing all these years – the ultimate chat-up accessory, an IV drip. Think of the girls I could have pulled if only I'd known.'

Scarcely able to believe that the question of Tiff's paternity had apparently been answered and dismissed as not terribly interesting in half a minute flat, Juliet breathed a shaky sigh of relief and leaned against Jake.

'You didn't do so badly.'

'Ah, but you might not have been able to resist me in the first place if only I'd had an IV tube to enthral you with.'

Juliet smiled, enjoying the feel of his hand on her back. 'You were pretty irresistible as it was. I just told myself that was the problem.'

'You weren't so shabby yourself.' Lowering his voice further still, Jake murmured into her hair, 'Is it time to tell them, d'you think?'

'Tell us what?' said Sophie immediately, her head jerking up like a meerkat's.

Jake and Juliet glanced at each other.

'Something soppy,' Tiff observed with a sly smile. 'Your dad's got his arm round my mum.'

'So?' said Jake.

'Bleeeuurrgh, *gross*,' Sophie and Tiff cried in unison, breaking into fits of giggles and pointing at Juliet and Jake. 'You're in lo-ve, you're in lo-ve.'

It wasn't the first time this had happened. Any fleeting

demonstration of affection between adults was routinely greeted with jeers and the same chanted accusation. As a rule, the best way for the adults concerned to deal with it was to ignore them.

'Yes,' Jake said simply, 'we are.'

That stopped Tiff and Sophie in their tracks.

'What? Are you joking?' Sophie narrowed her eyes, suspecting a trick.

'No,' said Jake. 'Deadly serious.'

'What, you mean you *really* love each other?'

Jake nodded. 'We really do.'

Juliet held her breath.

Tiff and Sophie looked at each other, then started to snigger again.

'What's so funny?' said Jake.

'You've been mating.' Sophie rocked backwards on the bed, whooping gleefully into her cupped hands.

'That's what you do,' confirmed Tiff. Interestedly he added, 'If you've mated, you'll have another baby. What are you going to call it?'

'This could be one of those conversations you wish you'd never started,' Juliet whispered in an undertone to Jake.

'Where's it going to live?' Sophie's eyes were bright with interest. 'I know, if we give it to Mr Taylor-Trent, it can live with him. Then everyone will have a child to look after.'

'Interesting thought,' said Jake. 'But we're not having a baby. Not just yet, anyway.'

'Right. But when you do, can we choose its name?'

Not over-keen on the prospect of any child of his being called Spiderman, Jake said, 'Mind out of the way, the nurse is trying to get through. So are you OK with that, then? Me and Juliet, you and Tiff? All four of us living together?'

'Great!' Sophie beamed as the nurse squeezed round to

her side of the bed. 'Just so long as you don't get married, because I'm not wearing a sissy bridesmaid's dress for anyone. *Oooh.*' She leaned forward ghoulishly as the nurse unwrapped a syringe. 'Are you going to take blood? Can I watch?'

Chapter 50

Kate was working the lunchtime shift at the Angel. Out by the pool at Dauncey House, Norris lay on his side on the sunbaked flagstones, lazily flicking his ears at passing insects and keeping one eye open should anyone feel like volunteering to take him for a walk.

Anyone being Oliver, the only human being currently on the premises. Norris sighed and closed his eyes; he wasn't getting his hopes up.

Inside the house, Oliver was unable to relax. For the past hour he'd found himself pacing restlessly from room to room, visualising the wreckage that was his life. For as long as he could remember, he'd used his position to control people. They did what he said. If the fact that he was a powerful man didn't intimidate them, he resorted to money instead. Whichever, he was used to getting his own way.

Until now.

Oliver paused in the doorway leading through to the drawing room. In a matter of days, his world had spun out of control. Estelle was gone, God knows where. She'd been having an affair with a younger, poorer, *scruffier* man and there was nothing he could do about it. The extent of his reaction had come as quite a shock; it was like assuming that if you had a big toe amputated you wouldn't miss it that much, then discovering afterwards that, actually, you couldn't stay upright.

Too late, he was discovering that Estelle was in effect his big toe and that for some time now he'd been taking her for granted.

In truth, he'd taken his entire life for granted. And where did that leave him now? With a seven-year-old son who didn't know him. A defunct marriage. A daughter who was siding with her mother. And an ex-mistress about to leap into an affair with the local Casanova.

Oliver closed his eyes briefly and rubbed his forehead; if he was honest, he possessed a begrudging admiration for Jake Harvey. Jake had done a good job of raising his daughter. He clearly thought the world of Tiff, and Tiff in turn adored him. The thing between Jake and Juliet wouldn't last, no question about that, but at least they thought it would. And Jake was no tycoon; he might have the looks but he'd never have money. Yet it didn't seem to bother him, he truly didn't care. How people could live like that, Oliver would never understand, but for the first time in his life he found himself almost envious of Jake.

God, what was *happening* to him? As the emotions welled up, Oliver found himself having to swallow hard. The next moment a sudden noise made him jump; having come in search of companionship, Norris had raised himself up on his hind legs and was pressing his wet nose against the closed French windows. Oliver hurried across the room to let him in before he started frantically scrabbling and leaving paw marks on the glass.

Norris licked his hand and Oliver realised that, just now, Norris probably liked him more than anyone else in the world. If that wasn't enough to reduce a grown man to tears, what was?

'Ugly mutt,' he told Norris gruffly, giving the dog's broad silky head a rub.

Norris gave him a not-very-hopeful look.

Oh, what the hell, it wasn't as if he had anything else to do.

'Go on then,' said Oliver, clicking his fingers and pointing out to the hall. 'Fetch your lead.'

Norris couldn't believe his luck. Was he hearing what he thought he'd just heard? This was the one who *never* took him for a walk. Mesmerised, Norris hesitated, awaiting the magic word that would put him out of his misery.

'Walk,' Oliver said at last.

Yay! *That* was the magic word. Joyfully Norris scrambled out to the hall, locating his lead on the cushioned window seat. It was weird, when he'd first come here he hadn't enjoyed going for walks at all. Who'd have believed that these days they'd be his absolute favourite thing?

The phone began to ring as Oliver and Norris were leaving the house. Since it couldn't be anything to do with Tiff – Juliet would have rung his mobile, not the landline – Oliver locked the front door and set off without answering it.

Twenty minutes later, a taxi pulled up the drive. Gulping a bit at the sight of Oliver's car, Estelle dialled the number again and breathed a sigh of relief when it went unanswered. Oliver was probably still at the hospital, at Tiff's bedside. With Juliet.

'I'll be half an hour,' she told the taxi driver. 'There's a nice pub in Main Street if you want to wait there, then come back and pick me up at two.'

The look on the taxi driver's face suggested that if Estelle had an ounce of decency about her, she would invite him into her vast house and make him a nice cup of tea and a sandwich. But for once in her life Estelle didn't care. She didn't have the energy to make polite conversation with a complete stranger. This was her home, where she'd lived for the last twenty-seven years, and she needed to be alone in order to say goodbye to it.

Having watched the disgruntled driver execute a three-point turn and head off down the drive, Estelle fitted her key into the front door.

It felt strange to be back, stranger still to be tiptoeing through her own house. Except there was no need to tiptoe, was there? Everyone else was out. She was here to collect the rest of her clothes, hopefully without interruption.

In the kitchen, which smelled heartbreakingly familiar, Estelle located the roll of black bin liners in the cupboard under the sink and took them upstairs. The suitcases, dauntingly, were piled on top of the wardrobe in the unused spare bedroom. Wasting no time, she rifled through her own wardrobe, pulling out anything she was likely to wear again. When she'd finished doing the same with the chest of drawers and dressing table, she stuffed everything willy-nilly into the bin liners. Oh God, that looked terrible, she couldn't do it. Was there anything more naff than leaving home with your belongings in a bunch of bin bags?

Checking her watch – heavens, five to two already – Estelle told herself not to be such a wimp and braced herself for an assault on the wardrobe in the spare room. This entailed pulling a chair over to the front of the wardrobe, carefully balancing a foot on each of the rolled arms, then reaching up until she was *juuuust* able to grasp the dusty handle of the large blue suitcase stored on top of it.

It was the most ridiculous place to keep them. Estelle couldn't imagine whose bright idea it had been in the first place. Now, maintaining her balance on the padded arms of the chair, she had to *ease* the cobalt-blue case slowly forward then tip it at just the right angle, so that it slid gracefully into her arms rather than crashed unceremoniously down onto her head.

Panting a bit with the effort, Estelle managed this. She was doing fine, absolutely fine, all she had to concentrate on now was— *ohhh* . . .

Falling backwards, falling backwards . . .

'*Fuck*,' gasped Estelle, finding herself flat on her back on the floor with the suitcase over her face. Pushing it off, she clutched the side of her head and felt the sticky warmth of blood where the metal-edged corner of the case had gouged a hole in her scalp. Oh well, at least the damage wouldn't be visible, it was only in her hair.

At least, it wouldn't be visible once the bleeding stopped.

Gingerly levering herself into a sitting position, Estelle brushed dust from her shirt and felt her head begin to throb. Actually, it hurt quite a lot. Having righted the chair and returned it to its original position, she was about to lug the case through to the master bedroom when the sound of the front door opening downstairs reached her ears.

Damn, *damn*. It was too soon for Kate to be back from the Angel, which meant it had to be Oliver. Far too humiliated to face him, Estelle prayed it was only a flying visit home and that in a matter of minutes he'd be off again. Gazing wildly around, she realised that hiding under the bed wasn't an option – the gap between the base and floor was less than six inches, which was completely hopeless with a bottom like hers. Plus she'd drip blood all over the carpet.

Hearing movement downstairs and panicking, Estelle pulled open the door of the wardrobe and plunged in. The door wouldn't close completely, thanks to the absence of a handle on the inside. But that was OK, she didn't want to be trapped in total darkness. Breathing heavily, squashed like a sardine between a musty overcoat and one of her own ancient taffeta ballgowns, Estelle listened to the sound of footsteps on the stairs and prayed she wouldn't sneeze.

Bloody dog, *bloody* animal, Oliver raged as he squelched up the staircase. How was he supposed to have known that Norris could swim? They'd been walking alongside the River Ash when Norris had suddenly spotted a mallard and taken a flying leap into the water. Oliver had experienced no more than a mild jolt of alarm but the next moment, struggling to free himself from a tangle of underwater reeds, Norris had started yelping and scrabbling in a genuinely help-I'm-drowning kind of way. In a complete panic, Oliver had promptly slithered down the steep river bank into the water. Revolting – and disgustingly cold, compared with his own heated pool – but at least he was only in up to his thighs.

That was until he had waded across to heroically rescue Norris, whereupon the bloody animal, wriggling and splashing, had freed his legs from the weeds and launched himself at Oliver, knocking him off his feet.

Spluttering, gasping and spitting out fronds of weed, Oliver had come up for air just in time to see Norris, sleek as a seal, swimming effortlessly past him with something that looked suspiciously like a smirk on his face.

Trudging back up Gypsy Lane, trailing the contents of the River Ash in his wake, hadn't been Oliver's finest hour. Norris, trotting along ahead of him, had begun wagging his stumpy tail as they reached the house and Oliver had lost patience with him. Shooing Norris through the side gate into the back garden, he had let himself in through the front door and made his way upstairs.

With the shower running, Oliver had already stripped off his wet muddy clothes when the doorbell began to ring. Heaving a sigh of annoyance but incapable of not answering the door – what if the bell carried on ringing? – he wrapped himself in a towelling robe and padded downstairs.

'Yes?' Oliver brusquely demanded of the man on the doorstep. On the driveway behind him stood a taxi with the engine still running.

'Uh . . . I'm back.'

'*What?*'

'OK,' said the man, clearly discomfited. 'Could you just tell your wife I'm back?'

Oliver frowned. 'I don't know what you're talking about.'

'I'm here to pick up your wife.'

'My wife isn't here. There's no one else in this house. I'm sorry, but there's been some kind of mistake. You've got the wrong address.'

Oliver waited for the taxi driver to turn and leave, but the man was giving him a decidedly odd look.

'I dropped your wife at this house half an hour ago,' he told Oliver. 'She said she was here to pick up a load of her stuff and that she'd need a hand carrying it out to the cab. This is where I left her.' His eyes narrowing, he said, 'She's definitely expecting me.'

It was Oliver's turn to be taken aback. Why was the man sounding so suspicious?

'*My* wife?' He double-checked. 'Blonde-ish? Plump-ish? About this tall?'

'That's the one. Disappeared into thin air, has she?'

Could Estelle be here and he hadn't even realised? Bemused, Oliver said, 'Hang on, I'll see if she's around,' and closed the front door.

There was no sign of Estelle downstairs. Upstairs, it wasn't until he rounded the corner of the L-shaped master bedroom and spotted the bulging black bin bags that Oliver realised the taxi driver hadn't been hallucinating. Calling out Estelle's name a few times and getting no response, it occurred to him that if she had come back to Ashcombe she may well have popped over to visit Marcella.

Downstairs once more, he yanked open the front door.

'You're right, my wife was here,' said Oliver, 'but she's gone now. Look, she might not be back for a while, so I wouldn't bother waiting if I were you. When she needs one, we'll call another cab.'

The man didn't leave. He backed away a couple of steps, his gaze flickering over Oliver's towelling robe, bare feet and wet hair.

'What's going on here, mate? Your wife asked me to come back for her. Look, is everything all right?'

All right? For crying out loud, his life was in *pieces*; how could everything possibly be all right?

But Oliver knew he wanted the man to go, so he shook his head and said wearily, 'Don't worry, everything's just fine.'

Clearly unconvinced, the taxi driver said, 'Look, mate. Has something . . . happened?'

Upstairs, Estelle could bear it no longer. The taxi driver, it was blindingly obvious, thought that Oliver had murdered her in a fit of rage and was taking a shower in order to wash away the evidence. If she didn't show herself, the man would be on the phone to the police in a flash.

Creeping along the landing, cupping the side of her head so as not to leave a trail of blood, Estelle reached the top of the staircase. Her heart lurched at the sight of Oliver, standing in the front doorway with his back to her. Clearing her throat, she called out, 'It's OK, I'm not dead,' and saw Oliver spin round in disbelief.

Chapter 51

Astounded, Oliver said, '*Estelle?*'

The taxi driver looked pretty taken aback too. Squinting up at Estelle through the gloom, he said, 'Jesus, what happened to you?'

Pulling her shirt collar to one side, Estelle saw that while she'd been squashed away in the wardrobe, a fair amount of blood had trickled down her neck and soaked into the shoulder of her white shirt. No wonder the taxi driver sounded so horrified, she must look like something out of a Hammer horror film.

Unable to bring herself to look at Oliver, Estelle said, 'I fell and hit my head. It's really not that bad. Look, if you could come up and give me a hand with my stuff, that'd be great. As soon as everything's loaded into the taxi, we can be off.'

'Did *he* do that to you?' demanded the taxi driver.

'Of course I didn't bloody do it to her.' Oliver spoke through clenched teeth. 'I didn't even know she was here. You *heard* me calling her name—'

'Sshh,' said Estelle, because Oliver was raising his voice. 'He didn't do it, I promise,' she told the taxi driver. 'Now, can we get my things into the cab?'

'No,' said Oliver.

'Please, I just want to go.' Estelle wondered why she couldn't get anything right, not even leaving her husband.

'We need to talk,' Oliver told her.

'She doesn't want to talk, mate.' The taxi driver wasn't taking his eyes off Oliver for a second, he was on his guard should Oliver suddenly produce a machete from the pocket of his dressing gown.

'Talk about what?' Estelle's eyes filled with tears, something she'd dreaded happening. 'What a complete and utter idiot I've been? Thanks, but I already know that.'

Oliver shook his head. 'Please. We need to do this properly, without an audience. Just tell him to leave, will you?'

Estelle hesitated at the top of the stairs.

'Go on,' said Oliver.

'Look, love, shouldn't you be getting that head of yours seen to? Needs a few stitches, if you ask me.'

Checking her scalp again, Estelle encountered a fair amount of stickiness but scarcely any fresh blood. The last thing she felt like doing was spending the next six hours in casualty waiting for some overworked, sleep-deprived doctor to sew her up.

'It's OK,' she told the taxi driver. 'You can go.'

He looked up at Estelle. 'Sure?'

Estelle nodded. 'Sure.'

'OK.' With a shrug, the taxi driver said, 'That'll be sixty-five quid, then.'

When Oliver had paid him and the cab had disappeared from view, Estelle ventured down the stairs.

'I'll make a cup of tea, if that's all right.' Finding it hard to meet Oliver's gaze, she headed for the kitchen.

'Here. Sit down.' While the kettle was coming to the boil, Oliver pulled out one of the carver chairs. 'Let me take a look at that cut.'

Reluctantly Estelle did as she was told. She felt Oliver gently exploring her scalp with his fingers and wanted to cry.

'How much does it hurt?' said Oliver.

You mean compared with finding out my husband has another child? Hardly at all, thought Estelle. She shrugged and said, 'I'm OK.'

'It's not deep. No need for stitches. So where were you hiding?'

'In the wardrobe, in the spare room.' She'd probably smeared blood all over the taffeta ball gown and Oliver's old overcoat; it had been a tight fit in there. 'You've got mud on your leg.'

'Fell in the river,' said Oliver, 'trying to rescue Norris. I could picture the headlines,' he went on. 'Dog drowns; negligent businessman responsible.'

'He jumped in and started splashing and yelping,' Estelle guessed. 'The reeds tickle his tummy. He loves it.' She paused, watching steam billow from the kettle. 'How's Tiff?'

The kettle clicked off and Oliver dropped teabags into the pot. Carefully he said, 'Doing well. Making a fantastic recovery.'

Estelle nodded, relieved. 'I thought you'd be at the hospital.'

'No. They don't need me there.' He paused. 'How's Will?'

Tit for tat, thought Estelle.

'Sorry!' Oliver blurted out. 'I'm sorry, you don't have to answer that. None of my business. I'm just sorry about . . . everything. The whole lot,' he said tiredly. 'God, what a mess.'

Estelle was speechless; she'd never heard him sound so defeated. Finally she said in a small voice, 'Yes.'

He massaged the back of his neck. 'I never meant to hurt you.'

'Didn't you?' What the hell, thought Estelle, the worst had already happened. Feeling suddenly reckless she said, 'Sure about that?'

'You were never supposed to find out. There's nothing

going on between Juliet and myself.' Oliver shook his head. 'I just wanted to see my son growing up.'

Estelle swallowed as the old ache of longing came back. She and Oliver had tried so hard for another child of their own, but it had never happened. Anyway, that was irrelevant now.

'I'm not talking about Tiff.' Her eyes were bright, her tone accusatory. 'I'm talking about the way you endlessly criticise me, tell me my clothes don't suit me, sneer at the novels I read, complain that my roast potatoes aren't crispy enough. Those are the things that hurt, Oliver. Being treated like a second-class citizen is what *hurts*.'

This outburst was greeted with a stunned silence. She was able to see Oliver mentally checking off each item on the list.

'Do I?' he said at last, clearly shaken. 'Is that what I do? My God, I've never even thought about it before. I suppose I have done all those things.'

'Trust me. You have.'

'And Will was the one who pointed it out to you,' said Oliver.

'I suppose.' Estelle was reluctant to give Will Gifford credit for anything. 'But we were in a rut long before he came along. He just brought it all out into the open.'

'And that's why you ran to him.'

Oh God, she *had* run, practically the length of platform 4 at Paddington station. Wincing at the memory of having thrown herself ecstatically into Will's arms, Estelle swallowed hard and forced herself to nod.

'At least we aren't in a rut now. This is the opposite of a rut,' Oliver said wearily. 'I don't blame you for getting out. Maybe Will's what you need.'

Hadn't he read the papers?

Dry-mouthed, Estelle said, 'I'm not with Will any more.'

Physically, Oliver didn't react.

'No? Where are you staying?'

'Cheltenham.' She may as well tell him; dammit, he was going to be the one settling the Amex bill. 'In a hotel at the moment. But I've been looking at flats to rent.'

'Flats?'

'Well, just the one.' Despite doing her best to sound flippant, Estelle heard her voice crack. Her twenty-eight-year marriage was over, she'd made a complete fool of herself with a younger man and now she was searching for somewhere to live. Waving her arms helplessly, she floundered on, 'It's, you know, a chance to re-think my life, make new friends . . . I thought I might, um, get a job . . .'

'Or you could stay here,' said Oliver.

Had he really said that?

Estelle's eyes filled with tears. 'What?'

'OK, maybe stay isn't the right word, seeing as you've already left. But you could come back,' Oliver said hesitantly, 'and we could try again. I never wanted to lose you. Maybe I didn't always show it, and I *know* I've taken you for granted, but I do love you.' He cleared his throat. 'I've learned my lesson. If you come back, I'll treat you so much better. No more being critical. I'll cut down on my hours, we can go away more often, spend a lot more time together. You wouldn't regret it, I—'

'How many others have there been?' Estelle said abruptly. 'Women, mistresses – other ones like Juliet?'

'None. That's the truth.' Oliver shook his head vigorously, then groaned. 'Oh God, I know what you're thinking, that that's just another lie. But I swear there haven't been any others.'

Estelle paused, then shook her head. 'It's no good. We can't, Oliver. Too much has happened.'

'We can!' There was an edge of desperation in his voice.

'You don't know how much I've missed you. I'll do anything you say!'

'But—'

'Do you want me to retire? Give up work completely? I'll do it.' Oliver nodded, as if work was already nothing but a distant memory.

'Oliver. You love your job.'

'Not as much as I love you.' His eyes began to glisten and instinctively he half turned away, unaccustomed to revealing this much of himself. Rubbing his face with his hands, he said desperately, 'Estelle, you mean everything in the world to me.'

'Oh God.' She was trembling now; this was Oliver as she'd never heard him before. 'But how could I come back here? Everyone in Ashcombe knows what's happened. They'd be laughing at me behind my—'

'They wouldn't.' Vehemently Oliver shook his head. 'Everyone loves you, this is where your friends are, but if you don't want to stay here, fine. We'll sell this place and move.'

'Move?' Heavens, Dauncey House meant the world to Oliver. 'Move where?'

'Wherever you like. Anywhere in the world.'

In a daze, Estelle said, 'You'd do that?'

'Anything.'

Estelle looked at him. Finally she nodded and said in a voice she barely recognised, 'OK.'

'OK what?'

'I'll come back. We don't have to move. We'll start again.'

Oliver was gazing at her, his expression incredulous. 'You really want to?'

'Of course I want to. You're my *husband*.' She managed a watery smile as a great wave of relief swept over her. 'You made a mistake, I made a mistake. Some people never make mistakes, but we did. And we're both sorry. That's allowed, isn't it? If I forgive you and you forgive me, we can try again – oh Oliver, I love you too . . .'

This time Estelle couldn't control the tears, because they weren't only rolling down her own face. Sobbing and laughing at the same time, she jumped up from her chair and fell into Oliver's comfortingly familiar arms. He was still wet and muddy from the river, wearing his dark blue towelling robe, and damp-haired. Thanks to the rapidly drying blood, the hair on one side of her own head was a mass of spiky bits and matted chunks. But when you'd been married for twenty-eight years, Estelle joyfully discovered, it really didn't matter how ridiculous you might look. After twenty-eight years, all that counted was what was going on in your heart.

Chapter 52

'Right, that's sorted then,' Nuala announced. 'The three of us, tonight, nine o'clock, Trash.'

Nuala had been wittering on for ages. Having tuned out long ago, Maddy came to with a start.

'Hmm? What was that?'

'Honestly, you don't deserve a friend like me.' With exaggerated patience, Nuala finished pricing the last few bottles of Tuscan olive oil. 'I'm organising your social life, cheering you up, stopping us all ending up like *this*.'

'What?' Now Maddy was definitely lost.

'Extra-virgin.' Bossily Nuala tapped the label on the rectangular bottle in her hand. 'I mean, let's face it, when was the last time any of us saw any action? It's not natural! We're young and in our prime! Which is why we should be going out to celebrate and have a bloody good night. It's also about time *you* cheered up,' she told Maddy. 'The best way to get over a man is to find a better one, and Trash is *the* place to do it. Just nod and say, Yes, Nuala.'

Oh dear, had she really been that grumpy? Maddy experienced a spasm of guilt. Poor Nuala was doing her best; she was lucky to have her around. At this rate she was in danger of ending up a right Nellie No-Friends.

'Yes, Nuala.' Nodding obediently, Maddy wondered if Trash would be as classy as it sounded. 'We'll have a bloody good night.' They would, she'd manage it if it killed her. 'What is it we're celebrating, again?'

'Tiff's better. My shoulder's better.' Smugly Nuala waggled her sling-free arm like a ventriloquist who's forgotten her dummy. 'Jake and Juliet together at last, and I haven't even been the tiniest bit jealous. I mean, it's *all* fantastic news, isn't it?'

Of course it was. Ashamed of herself, Maddy smiled. 'Definitely worth celebrating.'

'Great. I'll just go and tell Kate.'

Already planning what she'd wear tonight, Nuala scuttled happily over to the Angel. It was almost three o'clock and the pub would be closing for the afternoon. A group of customers was trailing back to the last remaining car in the car park. By the way they were waddling, Nuala guessed they'd had lunch followed by syrup sponge pudding and custard.

They were American tourists, she discovered, overhearing them as they passed her on the pavement.

'What a double act, those two in there,' drawled the taller of the males. 'Like Lucy and Desi all over again.'

'I thought she was going to brain the guy with an ashtray,' said his wife. 'Did you notice if they're married?'

Stifling a smile, Nuala reached the entrance to the Angel. Just wait until she told Kate and Dexter what the Americans were saying about them. Pushing open the door, she entered the pub and exclaimed, 'Hey, you two, you'll never guess—'

That was as far as she got. The rest of the words died before they even reached Nuala's mouth. Behind the bar Dexter and Kate sprang guiltily apart, but there could be no mistaking what had been going on during those brief seconds before her arrival.

Nuala gaped. Kate and Dexter? Dexter and . . . and Kate? It was unthinkable, like discovering that Jake had been carrying on a torrid affair with, crikey, Princess Anne. In fact, given Jake's wicked track record, that was actually *less* unlikely than the scenario she'd just walked in on.

'God, sorry,' gasped Kate. 'Nuala, I meant to—'

'Lock the door?' Nuala tilted her head enquiringly.

'No. Well, yes . . . I mean . . .' Kate stammered, her face the picture of guilt.

'Hopeless.' Dexter rolled his eyes. 'Can you believe it? This is the girl who isn't scared of anyone or anything, and look at her now.'

But incredibly, he was saying it in a good-natured rather than an irritated way.

Unable to resist it, Nuala said, 'You jumped away from Kate pretty smartish.'

He nodded, acknowledging the dig with a wry smile. 'OK, but it's something you needed to know. Kate was the one who didn't want to upset you.'

'Upset me?' Nuala echoed in disbelief. '*Upset* me? Damn right I'm upset!'

Kate was looking even more distraught. Dexter put a protective arm round her. 'Now you're being unfair,' he told Nuala. 'It's nothing to do with—'

'Good grief, I'm not upset about *you*.' Nuala pulled a face. 'I'm upset because I've just arranged a girls' night out for me, Maddy and Kate so we can go out and pull loads of men, but I don't suppose Kate will want to come along now.'

'On a manhunt? Poor sods,' said Dexter. 'Anyhow, Kate doesn't need to any more. She's got me.'

They actually looked like a proper couple. It took a bit of getting used to, but the more Nuala thought it through, the more sense it made.

'I'm really sorry,' Kate apologised again. 'It happened a couple of days ago, took us both completely by surprise, talk about a bolt from the blue . . .'

'It's fine,' said Nuala, 'honestly. You don't have to worry about me.'

Kate looked unconvinced. 'But you seemed a bit put out just now.'

'That's because I thought the three of us could go out tonight and have a great time, then if Maddy got a bit, you know, mopey,' Nuala pulled a Maddy-type face to demonstrate, 'we could gang up on her and *force* her to cheer up. It's OK, I can still manage it on my own,' she said bravely. 'It's just going to take that bit more effort.'

'Like climbing Everest with a motorbike strapped to your back,' Dexter observed.

'Thanks. That's a great help.' As she looked at him, Nuala realised she was well and truly cured. In all honesty, she and Dexter had been the most mismatched couple since that scary egg woman and John Major.

'I'll come with you,' said Kate unexpectedly.

'You will?' Not that Maddy was that much of a liability, not really, but Nuala's heart lifted as if it had been pumped full of helium.

'If it'll help.' Kate was clearly eager to make up for having got together with the ex-boyfriend Nuala was more than happy to be rid of.

'I'd rather you stayed here,' Dexter complained. 'You might get chatted up.'

Kate gave his cheek a consoling pat.

'Don't get stroppy. You don't just drop your friends when you bag a man. Anyway, it's my night off. I can go where I like.'

By the sound of it, Nuala was delighted to discover, Dexter had finally met his match.

'You.' He pointed a warning finger at Nuala. 'Make sure she doesn't get up to anything.'

Grinning, discovering that he no longer had the power to

scare her, Nuala said chirpily, 'You'd have to pay me loads of money to do that.'

Mustn't be a killjoy, thought Maddy as they piled out of the taxi and headed across the road to Trash. Mustn't, *mustn't* be a killjoy, going to have masses of fun, drink loads, chat up heaps of men and not even *think* about Ke— thingy, the one I'm not even going to think about.

Easier said than done, maybe, but she owed it to Nuala and Kate. And to herself. So she couldn't have the man she wanted. So what? Compared with war and famine it was a pretty unimportant reason to go around with a face like, well, the face she'd been going around with for the last fortnight.

Trash was a new club in the centre of Bath, hugely popular and a bit trendier than Maddy was truly comfortable with, but Nuala had been longing to come here for ages, ever since reading in a magazine that it was where the city's movers and shakers went. Nuala, Maddy suspected, was under the impression that this meant everyone would be leaping around, dancing with abandon to Las Ketchup.

Oh well, if she had to join in, she would.

'Cheers,' said Kate, clanking glasses and blissfully unself-conscious of her scars. 'I still can't believe everything that's happened. This morning I was the tragic victim of a hopelessly broken home. Now Mum's back, and she and my father are giving it another go. When I left the house they were being so lovey-dovey together it'd make you sick.'

'Cheers.' Maddy, who could clank with the best of them, said, 'Good for your mum and dad.'

'It may be good for them, canoodling away like teenagers, but what about me? They're my parents.' Kate grimaced. 'It's embarrassing. They're too *old* for all that.'

Too old. Taking a sip of wine, Maddy envisaged herself in fifty years' time. Marcella, aged ninety-something and feisty to the last, had just died in a tragic rollerblading accident. Finally, *finally*, she and Kerr had a chance to be together. Except she was seventy-seven herself and Kerr was eighty. Gazing dreamily into the distance, Maddy pictured the two of them on their Zimmer frames, inching their way across the shabby linoleum floor of the nursing home, dribbling a bit with the effort, peering short-sightedly at each other before she croaked, 'Kerr? It's me, Maddy. I'm free! We can be together at last . . .'

And Kerr, typical man, would pause, bemused, and say, 'Eh? What are you on about, woman? Do I know you?'

Bastard, thought Maddy, outraged.

'Excuse me?'

Oops, maybe she hadn't just thought it, perhaps she'd accidentally said it aloud.

'Sorry.' Turning, Maddy addressed the man behind her. 'Just thinking about someone.'

He gave her a sympathetic look. 'Ex boyfriend?'

'You could say that. Anyway, we're here to have fun.' If she said it often enough, it might come true.

'That's a coincidence, it's why we're here too.' The man beamed down at her; he wasn't what you'd call drop dead gorgeous, but he had a friendly chipmunky face and a decent enough body. 'My name's Dave. Hi.'

Oh well, look where being fussy had got her in the past. 'Maddy,' said Maddy, resolving not to mind about his teeth. He had friends with him as well. Keen to get started on the moving and shaking, Nuala was already eyeing them up.

'Who wants to dance?' she said loudly.

Gosh, they were big, thought Maddy. His teeth, not his friends.

An hour later, on the dance floor with Dave, Maddy spotted a face in the crowd that stopped her dead in her tracks. Dave, boogying on regardless, landed on her right foot and leaped off again yelling, 'Sorry!'

Maddy didn't even notice. She was too busy gazing across at the brunette whose features were indelibly imprinted on her mind.

The last time she'd seen her, the girl had been having lunch with Kerr. If they were seeing each other, did that mean he was here too? Bobbing up and down on her toes, Maddy did her best to see over the heads of the clubbers thronging the dance floor, but it was no good, she couldn't see him. Although actually, surely that was good . . .

'Hey!' Abandoned in mid-bop, Dave shouted out, 'Where are you off to?'

'Um, just to the loo.'

The brunette was wearing a pale green strappy silk dress with gorgeous lilac high heels and a matching lilac clutch bag. It was hard to hate someone, Maddy discovered, whose accessories you coveted. Anyway, she might not need to hate her. There was no sign of Kerr; the girl appeared to be with her plumper, blonder friend – ooh, and now she appeared to be on her way to the ladies'. *Fantastic*.

By the time the brunette emerged from her cubicle, Maddy had installed herself in front of the sinks and was brushing blusher onto her cheeks. She smiled at the brunette in a friendly fashion, via the mirror in front of them both, and the brunette politely smiled back.

See? That was all it took to show other people you were a nice person.

'Busy tonight,' said Maddy, by way of getting the conversational ball rolling.

'Um, yes.' The brunette squirted liquid soap onto her hands and began washing them.

'Quite hot, too. I'm baking!' Maddy beamed and energetically fanned herself. 'Good music, though.'

'Absolutely.' Having finished at the sink, the girl gave her hands a good shake and moved over to the hot-air dryer.

Hmm, not exactly a chatterbox. In desperation, Maddy said, 'I just love your shoes. They're incredible!'

'Uh, thanks.'

'Where did you get them?'

The brunette frowned. 'Gosh, I can't remember. Faith, I think.'

'Well, they're *brilliant*.' This was definitely the way to go about it. Since marching up to complete strangers and asking really quite personal questions was generally regarded as impertinent – unless you were Michael Parkinson – Maddy had decided to go the more subtle route and become the brunette's friend. Then with a bit of luck, once they were chatting away as if they'd known each other for years, the subject would just naturally crop up. OK, maybe with a bit of a nudge in the right direction, but still. 'I bought a great pair of boots in Faith last year,' Maddy said brightly. 'Grey denim, with silver studs up the sides. Remember them?'

The brunette frowned. 'Remember them? I'm sorry, do I know you?'

'Oh no, I just meant do you remember seeing them in the shop?' Seizing the opportunity, Maddy put down the lipstick she was currently applying and held out her hand. 'How rude of me not to introduce myself. My name's Maddy.'

'Right!' After a moment's hesitation, the brunette shook hands. 'Um, Annalise.'

Annalise. Nice name. Maddy pictured Kerr saying it and had to force herself to smile. Was there a way she could ask yet about boyfriend-type stuff without sounding pushy? How about if—

'Well, bye.' Having hastily gathered up her lilac bag, Annalise made a dash for the door and disappeared.

Chapter 53

'Hi,' Dave exclaimed. 'I was beginning to wonder where you'd got to!'

'Oh, right.' It was hard to concentrate on Dave when all she could think about was Annalise currently queuing up for drinks at the bar less than six feet away.

'I bought you a glass of wine,' Dave said eagerly, waving it in front of Maddy's face. 'You don't need to queue up.'

'That's so kind.' Maddy looked suitably grateful. 'And I'll buy you a drink in return, I promise, but could you do me a huge favour and leave me alone for five minutes? It's just, there's someone I really want to talk to.'

Dave's pudgy chipmunk cheeks quivered with disappointment. He held up his paws . . . *hands*, in defeat. 'Fine, I know when I'm not wanted.'

Feeling terrible, but not *that* terrible, Maddy said, 'You *are* wanted—'

'But not until the better-looking bloke's turned you down. Don't worry,' Dave sighed. 'I'm used to it.'

Honestly, life would be so much easier if only she could fall for a nice man who looked like a chipmunk. Ooh, gap in the crowd . . .

'Hello again!' Having wriggled through, Maddy beamed at Annalise, who was with her blonde friend.

'Oh, hello.' This time Annalise's shoulders visibly stiffened and her tone was wary. Since flattery had seemed to work well last time, Maddy exclaimed, 'Gosh, look at your eyelashes!'

Which, in the absence of a mirror, was probably impossible.

Startled, the girl said, 'What?'

'Your eyelashes. They're so long! You lucky thing, how on earth did you get them to grow like that?'

'They've, um, always been long.' Annalise was attempting to back away now. 'Actually, I don't think we'll have that drink. Maybe I'll ring my *boyfriend* and ask him to come and pick us up.'

Maddy tensed; why had she deliberately emphasised the word boyfriend? Did she know? Why were she and her friend exchanging significant glances? For heaven's sake, it wasn't as if she was a mad axe-woman – why couldn't she just ask Annalise a few simple questions and find out what she wanted to know?

Then again, nothing ventured . . .

'What's your boyfriend's name?'

Annalise said, 'Right, we really should be making a move. Come on, Bren. Let's go.'

Avoiding her eyes, the two girls slipped away. As they left, Maddy saw Annalise take a mobile phone out of her bag. Honestly, why did life have to be so complicated?

And where was Paul McKenna when you needed him? He could have quickly hypnotised Annalise, asked the relevant questions, discovered all he needed to know then de-hypnotised her, leaving her none the wiser.

In fact, why wasn't Paul McKenna a member of the SAS? Or was he?

'You're not dancing!' shouted Kate, materialising hot and breathless at her side. 'Come on, you're missing out on all the fun!'

Maddy was touched by her concern. Kate's eyes were shining. After all her exertions her foundation was starting to melt, but she clearly wasn't bothered. Still out on the dance floor, Nuala and Dave and a group of Dave's friends were having a whale of a time lowering the tone of Bath's trendiest club and competing with each other to see who could dance in the least cool manner. Tonight was Kate's first foray into nightclubland since her accident, yet you wouldn't know it. Belatedly, she was discovering that if you smiled instead of scowled, laughed instead of glared, people were far more likely to smile back.

At this rate Dexter was going to have his work cut out keeping her under control.

'Bit hot.' Maddy fanned herself by way of apology.

'*What?*'

'BIT HOT.' Above the noise of the music, Maddy bellowed, 'I'm just going outside for a few minutes, to cool down.'

'Then you have to come and dance,' shouted Kate.

Maddy nodded. 'Definitely. Just give me five minutes. I'll be back.'

Outside, she made a point of proving she was hot, in case any CCTV cameras were pointed in her direction. Well, it *had* been tropical inside the club; what could be more natural than wanting to gulp down a few lungfuls of fresh air, unstick your top from your torso and fan yourself with your hands, Al Jolson-style?

She only had to wait a couple of minutes before Annalise and her friend emerged from the club.

'Oh, hi!' sang Maddy, her Al Jolson hands going into overdrive. 'Hot in there! Just came out for a breather.'

'It's all right,' Annalise murmured out of the corner of her mouth. 'He'll be here any second.' Turning to Maddy, she added, 'My *boyfriend's* coming to pick us up.'

Well, good, because that's why I'm out here, thought Maddy. *Duh.*

Oh dear, was she getting a bit carried away here? If

Annalise's boyfriend did turn out to be Kerr, was she going to be tempted to jump into his car and run away with him? Would she be able to curb the impulse to—

'Look, you've made a mistake,' Annalise began to say as a white Volvo drew up, illuminating them in its headlights. Muttering, 'Thank God for that,' and visibly relaxing, she returned her attention to Maddy. 'I'm very flattered, but the thing is, I'm not . . . that way.'

Puzzled, Maddy said, 'What way?'

'Oh, come on, don't be offended, you know what I'm trying to say. I'm sure you're a very nice, um, person,' Annalise said hurriedly, 'but I'm straight.'

'Hmm?' Not really concentrating, Maddy was far more interested in confirming that the driver of the white Volvo wasn't Kerr.

'You've got the wrong night,' Annalise's friend explained kindly as Annalise wrenched open the Volvo's passenger door. '*Wednesday* is gay night at Trash.'

'Oh, right.' Maddy nodded, relief washing over her as the car's interior light came on. Raising her voice, she called across to Annalise, 'Is that your boyfriend?'

In the passenger seat, Annalise gave the driver a significant, that's-the-barking-one look. Slowly, all three occupants of the car nodded.

Completely unable to help herself, Maddy blurted out, 'How do you know Kerr McKinnon?'

Annalise's plucked eyebrows shot up. 'Kerr McKinnon? The guy from Callaghan and Fox? His company does business with our company.' She paused, bewildered. 'Why?'

'Oh, no special reason.' Feeling as if a ton weight had been winched from her chest, Maddy smiled and waved at them. 'Just wondered. Bye!'

The Volvo pulled away. Feeling fifty times happier, Maddy headed back towards Trash.

From the shadows she heard a male voice say, 'You should have told me before.'

Spinning round, Maddy said, '*Dave?*'

He emerged from his darkened doorway, looking mildly apologetic. 'Sorry, didn't mean to eavesdrop. I came out to see where you were – the girls were worried about you.'

'I'm fine. Much better now.' Maddy smiled reassuringly at him, because Dave was giving her a sympathetic head tilt.

'You know, there's absolutely nothing wrong with being gay,' said Dave.

'I know.' Gosh, it was *such* a relief, knowing that Kerr wasn't seeing Annalise.

'You don't have to be ashamed of who you are.'

Hmm? 'I'm not ashamed of who I am,' said Maddy. Well, slightly embarrassed, maybe, to think that she'd practically *stalked* the girl, just because—

'Nuala and Kate don't know, do they?'

'God, no, they'd be *furious*.' Maddy was completely sick of their lectures on the subject of forgetting Kerr McKinnon ever existed.

As if.

'Well, that's just crazy, this is the twenty-first century,' Dave said crossly. 'Nobody should have to pretend to be something they aren't. Right, shoulders back,' he instructed, linking his arm through Maddy's. 'Chin up, and be proud. We're going to march right in there and tell them *now*.'

Chapter 54

Coming face to face with his brother after a gap of almost ten years was an emotional experience. Kerr had almost given up on the idea of hearing from Den again following that initial strained phone conversation. When the days had stretched into weeks without any further word, he told himself that at least he'd done his best.

And then, on Monday, his mobile had rung and Den had asked without preamble, 'Is she still alive?'

Stunned, Kerr said, 'Er . . . yes.'

'Still want me to come over?'

Stupid question.

'Yes.'

'OK. I'm flying from Sydney tonight. I'll give you another ring on Wednesday, when I reach Bath.' Den paused. 'I can stay at the house, right?'

'Of course.' Kerr's chest tightened as he realised Den's main reason for visiting was to stake his claim on half the property.

'I mean, I'll visit her at the old folks' home, but I don't want to spend hours there.'

'That's up to you,' Kerr said stiffly, because heaven forbid that Den, who had succeeded in ruining his mother's entire life, should have to spend a minute longer than absolutely necessary at her deathbed.

'Fine. OK, I'll see you,' Den concluded laconically, before hanging up.

That had happened forty-eight hours ago. And now he was here. It was Wednesday afternoon and Kerr had taken the message on his phone twenty minutes ago. Leaving the office at once, he had driven out to Hillview. As he rounded the last bend of the driveway, he saw Den sitting on the top step, leaning back against the front door.

He was twenty-eight years old. God, unbelievable. Wearing narrow faded jeans, trainers and a scruffy yellow T-shirt, he looked like a typical backpacker. Kerr wondered if their mother's first comment when she saw Den would be to tell him to get his hair cut.

Exhaling slowly, Kerr switched off the ignition and climbed out of the car. What was he supposed to do now? Before the accident, they had been close, but after it – hardly surprisingly – Den had undergone an abrupt change of personality, cutting himself off from his family and refusing to talk. Kerr had visited him in prison at first, then been sullenly told not to bother any more. By that stage, Kerr had been guiltily relieved to have an excuse not to. Thanks to a single careless moment Den had succeeded in ruining not only the life of the Harvey family, but his own as well. By then, their mother had sunk into alcoholism and was also refusing all offers of help. It hadn't exactly been the greatest incentive to come home. Yet until the fateful day of the accident, he and Den had been close, Kerr reminded himself. A part of him badly wanted to hug his younger brother and tell him how good it was to see him again.

This was easier said than done.

'Hi,' said Kerr, realising that by remaining seated on the step, Den was effectively making sure he couldn't be hugged.

'Hi.' Den waited, his jaw tense. He was very brown, and there were lines around his eyes that anyone else would have called laughter lines. Somehow Kerr couldn't picture him laughing that much.

'It's good to see you,' Kerr said awkwardly.

'Is it?'

Kerr nodded, silently conceding that he had a point. Thanks to Den's actions, he wasn't allowed to be with the only girl he'd ever truly wanted to be with. When you thought of it that way, he wanted to punch him.

But that wasn't why Den was here, and what good would it do anyway? Apart from making me feel better, thought Kerr.

Taking out his keys, he stepped past Den and opened the front door.

'Come on in. There's hot water if you want a shower.'

Lifting his rucksack over one shoulder, Den said, 'Why? Do I smell?'

It was so long since they'd last seen each other that Kerr wasn't sure if he was joking.

'It's OK.' Catching the wary look in his brother's eyes, Den said with a brief smile, 'Yeah, a shower would be great.'

In the kitchen, Kerr put together a couple of king-sized omelettes. It wasn't much, because he didn't keep a great deal of food here at Hillview, but it was easier than taking Den out for a meal. Sitting at a table in a restaurant, forced to make polite conversation for ninety minutes, was a daunting prospect. The awkward silences would be more than he could handle.

So omelettes it was. A couple of cold beers wouldn't go amiss either. Maybe there'd be something sporty on TV and they could watch that.

'Are you tired?' said Kerr when Den came downstairs, having showered and changed into a creased cotton shirt and a different pair of jeans.

'No. Slept on the plane. Which one's mine?'

393

He was combing his fingers through his wet hair, surreptitiously surveying the plates on the kitchen table. It was as if they were teenagers again and Den was trying to decide which of the omelettes was the biggest.

Kerr plonked down the pepper mill. 'Either. They're both the same. If you want to rest tonight, we can visit the nursing home tomorrow.'

Pulling out a chair, Den began to wolf down his omelette.

'Why wait? I've come all this way, like you told me to.'

'Asked you to,' Kerr corrected, because there was an edge to Den's voice.

'Whatever. May as well get over there tonight and see what she has to say.' Den shrugged. 'Be a shame if she popped her clogs just before I got there.'

Maybe he didn't mean to be so callous. Maybe he was secretly dreading seeing his mother again, thought Kerr. For the first time he was about to witness what he'd reduced her to.

'OK,' he told Den. 'We'll go tonight.'

Den held up his empty bottle of Beck's. 'Fine. Got another beer?'

But as he reached out to take the second bottle, Kerr saw that his nails were bitten and his hands were shaking. Den, it seemed, wasn't quite as flippant and careless as he liked to make out.

An hour later they drove over to Dartington House.

'Pretty nice place,' Den remarked as they approached the big old nursing home. 'Must cost a bit, keeping her here.'

She was their mother. Where did Den think she should end her days? In a dog kennel?

'She couldn't carry on any more at home.' Kerr led the way through the wood-panelled painted hall. Spotting Esme

Calloway through the open door of her tasteful eau de Nil office, he paused and said, 'How is she?'

'Oh, Mr McKinnon! Not so well, I'm afraid. And somewhat agitated, I should warn you. We may have to ask the doctor to give her a little something to calm her down. She's still asking to see her other – oh.' Rising from behind her desk and catching sight of Den, Esme Calloway's manicured eyebrows shot up in surprise. 'Is this . . .'

'Her other son,' Kerr confirmed.

'From Australia!' Esme clapped her beringed hands together with delight. 'Well, well, this *is* excellent news! Wait 'til Pauline finds out you're here, she'll be so thrilled!'

Esme Calloway clearly wasn't in possession of the full story, thought Kerr as, still gushing, she swept round the desk in order to shake Den's hand. Needing to see your long-lost son before you died was one thing, but *thrilled* wasn't the emotion he suspected would be uppermost in Pauline's mind.

Esme Calloway, who evidently adored emotional family reunions, led the way upstairs to their mother's room, chattering nonstop about the time she'd visited her cousins in Melbourne and almost run over a kangaroo. Finally she paused outside the door, sapphires flashing on her fingers as she raised her hand to knock.

'Pauline? Coo-ee! Are you awake, dear?'

Behind her, Den glanced in disbelief at Kerr.

'Oh God,' they both heard their mother's irritable voice say through the closed door. 'What now?'

'Visitor, dear!' Turning, Esme gave Den an isn't-this-exciting look and turned the handle. 'Very important visitor, in fact! Here we are, brace yourself for a surprise!'

And that was it. The door swung open, revealing Den to his mother. Pauline was sitting up in bed like a faded, yellow-tinged shadow of herself, wrapped in a cream cashmere cardigan and with her wispy grey hair fastened in a loose bun.

She was only sixty-eight; it wasn't such a great age, Kerr thought. She looked a good twenty years older than that.

He stayed well back, along with Esme, allowing Pauline to gaze in silence at Den. At least his mother didn't appear to have been drinking today; the smell of alcohol was, for once, absent from the room.

Finally Pauline said, 'Oh, Den . . .' and there was a quaver in her voice that made it obvious how much this moment meant to her.

By contrast, Den's face was entirely without expression as he said, 'Hello.'

Esme Calloway looked shocked. This wasn't the deliriously joyful reunion she'd been anticipating. Thinking angrily that Den could at least have the decency to *pretend* to be pleased to see her, Kerr resolved to leave them to it. Maybe Esme's presence was an inhibiting factor. Placing his hand on her elbow he murmured, 'I think they'd prefer to be alone,' and saw Den's shoulders stiffen.

'No,' said Pauline, shaking her head at Kerr. 'She can go, but I want you to stay.'

'I don't—'

'You will,' Pauline said evenly. 'It's important.'

'Ooh, I've had an idea! Why don't I bring you all a nice tray of tea?' Esme beamed at them like a deranged nineteen fifties air hostess.

'Just get rid of her.' Pauline shook her grey head in disgust. 'The last thing I need is an audience.'

Offended, the tilt of her eyebrows signalling despair of the see-what-I-have-to-put-up-with kind, Esme swept out of the room.

Silence reigned. Kerr leaned against the wall with his arms folded across his chest. Den was gazing out of the window like an insolent fourth-former summoned to the headmaster's study. If Pauline had been hoping for a hug from the son who had all but destroyed her life, she was going to be bitterly disappointed.

Finally Pauline spoke again.

'How did Kerr persuade you to come back?'

Den shrugged. 'Told me you were . . . unwell.'

'Unwell, that's one way of putting it.' Snorting at the euphemism, Pauline shakily smoothed the eiderdown over her lap.

'Dying, then,' Den said bluntly.

'That's more like it. On my way out. Not long to go now.' Glancing past Den to Kerr, she said, 'Did you bring anything?'

'I brought Den,' Kerr said pointedly.

His mother reached for a tissue and wiped the palms of her hands. 'A bottle of Jack Daniel's would make this easier.' She looked over at Den. 'So. How have you been?'

'How d'you think I've been?' Den shoved his hands deeper into his pockets and stared back at her. 'I went to prison, didn't I? Served my time. Came out, left the country, went to Australia where no one else knew what I'd done but somehow never quite managed to put it behind me. Still, never mind, eh? I'm young, healthy, life goes on. There are plenty of people worse off than me, I just need to get a grip, sort myself out—'

'Den, don't.' Stricken, Pauline shook her head.

'Why not? You asked me how I'd been. I'm just telling you.'

'I'm sorry.' Her eyes filled with tears; she was squeezing the crumpled tissue between her hands. 'I'm so sorry. That's why I had to see you again, to tell you how sorry I am.' Her fingers shook as she rubbed at her palms. 'Have you told your brother?'

Kerr straightened. Had Den told him what?

'I've never told a living soul,' said Den fiercely. 'You made me promise, remember?'

What? What was this about? Kerr looked from one to the other.

'Right, right. Of course you haven't. I'll do it then.' Pauline nodded wearily, the lines on her face suddenly more pronounced than ever. 'It was me,' she told Kerr. 'Driving the car that day. I was the one who killed the girl, not Den.'

Chapter 55

The only sound in the room was the ticking of the clock on the mantelpiece, a brass carriage clock that Kerr remembered from his childhood. Under any other circumstances his automatic reaction might have been to say to his mother, 'You're joking.' But since she clearly wasn't, he was silent.

'That look on your face, Kerr,' said Pauline McKinnon. 'That's why I've never told you. God, I thought deathbed confessions were meant to make you feel better. I *really* want a drink now.'

Kerr looked at his brother. Den was standing there, by the window, with tears sliding down his thin cheeks.

'Tell me what happened,' Kerr said slowly, but Den was incapable of speech. He shrugged and shook his head.

'We'd been to Evelyn Pargeter's drinks party.' Pauline's voice came out as a monotone. 'I'd had a few drinks, but I felt OK. When we left the party I told Den I'd be fine to drive. We reached Ashcombe and I rounded the bend too fast, hit the girl – well, that was it. There was nothing we could do for her. She was dead. Then I realised what this would do to *me*. I was a Justice of the Peace, remember. Pillar of the community. I knew I'd fail a breath test. I just couldn't bear it, couldn't *bear* it.' She faltered, shaken by the memory. 'But Den hadn't been drinking, and I thought it wouldn't be so bad for him. He was only seventeen, any punishment would be so much easier for him to handle. I was in shock after it happened. And that was it,' Pauline whispered. 'Den loved me. We were always so close, I knew he'd understand. I told him to say he'd been driving. And he did. It was our secret. I wasn't proud of myself, but I couldn't face the prospect of going to prison. Losing my licence for drink-driving. Killing a sixteen-year-old girl. I thought it would be easier for Den. I'm sorry.' She closed her eyes in defeat. 'I was wrong, I know that now. I knew it then, but I couldn't help myself. And I've been punishing myself ever since. I might just as well have taken the blame and killed myself there and then. Anything would have been better than living through the last eleven years, I can promise you that. So you see, I'm glad I'm going to die. In fact, I can't wait.'

Kerr was having trouble digesting this. He couldn't believe what he was hearing.

'Why didn't you tell me?'

'It was our secret, Den's and mine.' Pauline shook her head. 'You would never have allowed Den to go to prison.'

This was true. Jesus, what had Den *been* through, in order to protect his mother? Was it any wonder he'd disappeared to Australia?

'I was wrong,' Pauline blurted out. 'I should never have done it. I'll make a statement to the police.'

'You're about to die,' Den said baldly. 'What good would that do?'

His mother looked at him. 'It'll clear your name.'

'Can they rewind the tape and stop me going to prison? Because otherwise I don't see the point.'

'There's nothing I can do to take that away.' Tears were running down Pauline's face now, dripping into the folds of her cream cardigan. 'I just needed to see you again, to let you know how truly sorry I am. I always loved you so much.

I don't suppose you love me, but thank you for coming back. It means more than you'll ever know.'

It was three o'clock in the morning. In the living room of Hillview, Kerr opened two more bottles of chilled Beck's and handed one to Den.

'I feel like a ton weight has been lifted off me,' said Den, for the fifteenth time that night. Shaking his head in wonderment, he stretched out along the length of the sofa and crossed one foot over the other. 'You have no idea how it feels, somebody else knowing at last. *You* knowing at last. If someone had asked me yesterday if I could forgive my mother for what she did, I'd have laughed and said never in a million years. But now . . . I don't know, I can almost think about it. Because she's dying, and that's what she wants, isn't it? Forgiveness.'

'I suppose.' Kerr couldn't believe the change in his brother, in the space of just a few short hours. He couldn't stop looking at Den, his eyes brighter now, his whole body seemingly more alive. 'You should have told me. I can't believe that you didn't tell me after it happened.'

'Straight after the accident, I was in a state of shock,' said Den. 'None of it seemed real. It didn't occur to me that I'd end up actually going to jail. After a while I began to panic, but by then it was too late. I realised that if I did try and tell them that Mum had been driving that day, they wouldn't believe me. And there'd be no proof if she denied it, just her word against mine – the respected JP versus the seventeen-year-old tearaway.' He pulled a wry face. 'Of course they'd believe her. Anyone would. And I'd just come out of it looking worse, even more despicable, than ever.'

This was true. Kerr felt terrible, recalling how he had regarded Den even while he'd been visiting him in prison.

No wonder his younger brother had been sullen and uncom-municative during their meetings. No wonder Den had told him not to bother any more.

'You never told *anyone*,' Kerr burst out, appalled by the injustice of it all.

'I lied to Mum. I did tell someone once.' Tipping his head back, Den took a swallow of beer. 'A girl I met in Canberra. Moira, her name was. Pretty girl. We started seeing each other. Anyway, one night we got talking about my life in England, where I'd grown up, that kind of thing. I told her about the accident, sticking to the official version. She was horrified. Well, basically, I was a bit drunk and I could see I was losing her. So I panicked and told her the truth. What really happened. Disaster,' he announced with a shudder. 'I saw Moira's face change as I was saying it. Then she called me pathetic, said I was a bullshitter and a sad desperate loser. We were sitting in a restaurant at the time. Moira walked out on me, between the starter and the main course. And that was it, I never saw her again. So much for being honest. I learned my lesson after that.'

'No more telling the truth,' said Kerr.

'No more women.' Den shook back his hair. 'None I cared about, anyway. I'm not saying I was celibate, but I made bloody sure I never got emotionally involved.' He paused. 'How about you?'

Kerr was tempted to tell him everything, but couldn't bring himself to do it. How would it sound? OK, so you've suffered in your own way, but hey, I've suffered too. Don't think you're the only one who's had his life fucked up by what happened. No, that would be just . . . cheap. It wasn't a compe-tition. It may have felt over the last few weeks that his life had been well and truly fucked up, but compared with what Den had been forced to endure—

'Do the Harveys still live in Ashcombe?' said Den.

'Um, yes.' Kerr nodded. 'Apart from the father. Robert Harvey died a few years ago.'

'God, what that family have been through.' Yawning, Den finished the last of his beer and hauled himself upright. 'I'm shattered. It's been a hell of a day.'

'You can say that again.' Kerr rose to his feet too. After a moment's hesitation – because it wasn't something they were accustomed to doing – he gave Den an emotional hug. 'I still can't believe it. I've got my brother back.'

'You think that's weird.' Den's smile was crooked. 'For the first time in eleven years, I'm going to be sleeping in my old room. Any idea what happened to all my old M. C. Hammer records, by the way?'

At seventeen he had been devoted to M. C. Hammer. Bracing himself for outrage, Kerr said, 'I think they went to a charity shop.'

'What was I thinking of?' Den shook his head with heart-felt relief. 'You're sure they've all gone? Thank God for that.'

'I can't,' said Pauline, afraid. 'That's blackmail.'

'So? It's what I want you to do,' Den said evenly. 'You have to, it's only fair. You owe me that much at least.'

Pauline closed her eyes. Her eyelids, flickering with anxiety, were paper thin; she looked defeated and dreadfully ill.

'Don't make me do it. Please.'

'Listen to yourself.' There was an edge of irritation to Den's voice as he paced up and down his mother's room. 'This isn't about *you* any more. I'm asking you to do this for *me*, and I happen to think I deserve it.'

'But—'

'I'll wait outside,' said Den. 'You just get on and do what you have to.' As he turned for the door, he added over his shoulder, 'I'll be back in twenty minutes.'

Den spent the twenty minutes sitting on a bench beneath a vast cedar tree in the grounds of the nursing home, telling himself he wasn't being unreasonable. OK, so Kerr now knew the truth, but it wasn't enough. And their mother was dying, so what difference did it make to her? He hadn't talked this over with Kerr but he knew he'd understand.

A pretty nurse passed by, pushing one of the ancient residents along in a wheelchair. Glancing across at Den, she smiled shyly at him. So preoccupied that he didn't even notice until too late, Den watched the nurse's back view as she headed on up the path. Maybe, once everything was sorted out, he'd feel normal enough to think of forming a proper relationship. Over the past years, not allowing himself to get involved had become second nature to him. Fear of rejection had left its mark.

Right, time was up. Back to his mother's room. If she hadn't done what he'd instructed her to do – well, she just better had, that's all.

'Finished?' Den said brusquely.

His mother's eyes were dull, their whites yellowed, her shoulders slumped back against the pillows in resignation. Prodding at the envelope on her writing tray, she indicated that Den should take it.

'I'll just check what you've written.' He pulled out the sheet of cream writing paper and rapidly scanned the contents before nodding with satisfaction. 'Good. You see? I knew you could do it.'

'It hasn't happened yet,' Pauline croaked. 'It may not happen.'

'Oh yes it will.' Den tucked the all-important letter back into the envelope. 'After coming this far? Don't worry, I'll make sure it does.'

Chapter 56

As the taxi pulled into Ashcombe, Den reached instinctively for his dark glasses. One thing he would never forget was the look on Marcella Harvey's face when she had stared at him across the courtroom during the trial.

And who could blame her?

It was four o'clock on a blisteringly hot Thursday afternoon. Apart from the usual groups of mainly foreign tourists meandering along Main Street, the town was fairly quiet. There was no one around whom Den recognised, but his heart was in his mouth nevertheless as the taxi driver slowed the car.

'This is it then,' said the driver. 'Where d'you want me to stop?'

Where indeed? When you were public enemy number one, discretion was the key.

'Pull into the pub car park.' Den nodded at the entrance on the right, then twisted round to gaze back across the street at Snow Cottage. Did Marcella still live there? Kerr had said the Harveys were still here in Ashcombe, but who was to say they hadn't moved house?

The next moment his question was answered as the front door swung open and a small girl raced out, a brown and white terrier at her heels. The girl, who was around seven or eight, had skin the colour of milky coffee, huge dark eyes and hair braided in cornrows. She was wearing pale green shorts, turquoise sandals and a baggy red T-shirt. As Den watched, the girl slammed the front door behind her, jiggled the terrier's lead and headed off up the street with the dog in tow.

Well, that was good news, at least. He was pleased to see that Marcella had had a daughter of her own.

'OK.' Den handed the envelope, now sealed, over to the taxi driver. 'Just post this through the letterbox of that cottage over there.'

The taxi driver, who had seen it all in his time, said wryly, 'Come at you with a saucepan, would she, if you tried it?'

'At the very least,' Den agreed.

The taxi driver nodded sagely. 'Restraining order?'

'Something like that,' said Den.

'Not going to get me into trouble, is it?' The man was running his podgy fingers over the envelope, surreptitiously checking for wires.

'Don't worry.' Den smiled. 'It's not a bomb.'

As the taxi driver headed across the road, Den realised he was being watched. For a split second he panicked, wondering if he'd been recognised – but it was OK, no one he knew. The girl, in her late twenties, had reddish-brown hair and real curves. Glad of his dark glasses – thanks to them, she didn't know that in return he was studying her – Den admired the way the girl's bottom filled her jeans. Having just emerged from the Angel, she was watching him from the doorway, clearly wondering what he was doing there in the car park when the pub was closed.

Did that mean she worked there?

The next moment the girl had turned left and headed off up the road, out of sight. Something in the pit of Den's stomach went twaaanngg, dimly recalling the memory of how it felt to be attracted to someone. Anyway, too late now.

Across the street, the taxi driver had posted the envelope through the letterbox of Snow Cottage and was making his way back to the car park.

'Right, job done,' he told Den. 'Where to now?'

Where to indeed? Without thinking, Den almost said, 'Home.' Instead, clearing his throat, he said, 'Back to Hillview.'

Sophie, returning from the mini-supermarket with fifty pence worth of sweets in a paper bag, let herself into the cottage. Zig-zagging between her feet, Bean homed in on the envelope on the mat. Post was one of Bean's all-time favourite things. Launching herself joyfully at the letter, she nuzzled it with her nose, scrabbled furiously with her front paws and finally managed to clamp it between her teeth. Now that she'd captured it, she could wrestle it to death, tearing it to messy shreds and—

'*Bad* dog,' Sophie said severely, grabbing the envelope from Bean in the nick of time and whisking it out of reach. 'Mustn't do that to letters. *No*,' she scolded as Bean leaped up once more, 'it's not *yours*.'

Turning it over, Sophie saw that it had Marcella Harvey written on the front. The handwriting was on the wobbly side but that was OK, Sophie could still read it. Her own hand-writing was pretty wobbly too.

'Dad?' Raising her voice, she ran upstairs and hammered on the bathroom door. Her father, with a casket to deliver, had finished work early in order to shower and change before driving over to Cheltenham.

Above the sound of gushing water, Jake shouted, 'Yes?'

'There's a letter for Gran. I'm going to take it to her,' Sophie yelled back. She was allowed to visit Marcella's house on Holly Hill since there was no road-crossing involved.

'What?'

She heard the shower door open inside the bathroom,

enabling Jake to poke his head out and hear what she was saying.

'*Me* and *Bean* are going up to *Gran's*,' Sophie bellowed.

'OK. I'll be back by six,' said Jake. 'I'll pick you up from there, then we'll go and see Tiff at the hospital.'

'OK, see you!' Clapping her hands at Bean, Sophie galloped downstairs clutching the envelope. Delivering letters was easy; maybe she'd be a postman when she grew up.

Marcella had been out in the garden doing a spot of gentle pruning when Sophie arrived. Enveloping her beloved granddaughter in an enthusiastic hug, and feeling her heart expand with love, Marcella wondered if holding a child of her very own could possibly feel better than this.

'Are those really sharp?' Beadily, Sophie eyed the secateurs in Marcella's hand. 'Can I have a go?'

'In your dreams, sweetheart.' Tweaking the end of one of Sophie's braids, Marcella spotted the envelope and said, 'What's that? Love letter from Tiff?'

'It's for you. See, it's got your name on it. What are you going to call the baby if it's a boy?' Sophie was extremely keen to be involved in the decision-making process. 'How about Malfoy?'

'I thought we'd wait until it's born, then see what it looks like.' Taking the envelope, Marcella glanced at her name shakily inscribed on the front and headed over to the garden bench. 'Where did you get this?'

'On the floor at home. The toothmarks are Bean's – I rescued it just in time. Can I have a biscuit?' said Sophie, because nobody kept a better supply of biscuits in their house than Marcella.

'Hmm? OK, just the one.' Having opened the envelope, Marcella's eye slid automatically to the name at the bottom of the letter. It was like bouncing along happily on a cloud, then all of a sudden landing on a tangle of barbed wire.

Marcella's breath caught in her throat and her heart began to race. She wondered if this was someone's idea of a sick joke.

But the wording of the letter seemed honest enough.

Dear Marcella,

Please don't ignore this letter. I have liver failure and very little time left to live. I need to speak to you before I die.

This is very important to me, and will be to you too. Please come to Dartington House on Friday afternoon.

I'm so very sorry.

Once more, Marcella found herself gazing at the signature at the bottom of the page. It looked like the handwriting of someone hopelessly frail. Pauline McKinnon, no less. Close to death. *Saying she was sorry*. Well, that was a first.

Without even realising it, Marcella had risen from her seat and was busy deadheading roses. Needing something to do with her hands she snipped away, doing her level best to block all thoughts of Pauline McKinnon from her—

'*Ouch.*' She snatched her left hand away as a thorn on one of the branches punctured her skin. A bead of blood welled up and Marcella sucked her finger, thinking that if she caught tetanus now, that would be the McKinnons' fault too.

Why the bloody hell should she go over to Dartington House anyway? What had her doctor told her about avoiding stress? And if seeing that woman again wasn't stressful, Marcella thought resentfully, she didn't know what was.

Then again, the woman was dying. Pauline McKinnon had lost her son as a result of the accident, albeit in a less final way than April had been taken from her own family.

And she had just said sorry.

Marcella, barefoot and still sucking her index finger, gazed around the sundrenched garden she loved so much. Her hormones must be getting the better of her; at any other time she would have ripped Pauline McKinnon's letter to shreds by now, and been stomping around the garden calling her the kind of names no granddaughter should ever overhear.

But as Sophie emerged from the kitchen and came racing across the grass towards her, Marcella found herself sliding the letter into the pocket of her white cotton shirt. Not that this meant she'd definitely be going along to the nursing home tomorrow; she simply hadn't yet made up her mind.

'I brought chocolate fingers and Hobnobs, so you can have some too.' There were telltale chocolate marks around Sophie's mouth as she generously offered the opened packets to Marcella. Spotting the letter sticking out of her grandmother's shirt pocket, and keen to avert attention from the number of biscuits missing from the chocolate finger packet, Sophie said brightly, 'Was it a birthday card?'

Marcella smiled; as far as Sophie was concerned, post was either birthday cards or bills. 'No, darling, it's not my birthday until November.'

Breaking a Hobnob in half, Sophie surreptitiously fed it to Bean – who proceeded to chomp away in a very unsurreptitious manner. Rolling her eyes – and looking uncannily like Jake – she said sympathetically, 'Another bill then, I suppose. Electricity?'

'Something like that,' said Marcella.

Maybe it hadn't been electricity, but it had certainly given her a shock.

Chapter 57

'I hope you didn't mind me coming.' Estelle dodged out of the way of a porter wheeling a patient past on a hospital trolley.

'No, no. Jake said you wanted to pop over.' Vigorously Juliet shook her head.

It was a toss up, Estelle realised, which of the two of them was more nervous.

'I wanted to clear the air. Get everything sorted out,' she plunged on. 'It's OK, that's what I'm trying to say. You and Oliver, well, it all happened years ago. Of course it was a shock at first, but I'm used to the idea now, so—'

'I'm sorry, I never meant to hurt you,' Juliet blurted out, her cheeks pink with mortification. 'I'm just so glad you and Oliver are back together.'

'After me making the world's biggest fool of myself.' Estelle's smile was rueful. 'With Will Gifford.'

'Hey, don't be so hard on yourself,' said Juliet. 'If you ask me, it was the best thing you could have done. Made Oliver sit up and take notice, didn't it?'

Estelle moved to one side to allow a group of medical students to pass. Out here in the hospital corridor, it struck her afresh how much she'd always liked Juliet Price. Rather more astonishing was the fact that Juliet had liked Oliver enough to have an affair with him. But now she and Jake had got it together – *at last* – and as a pairing they made so much more sense.

'So anyway, we're OK,' Estelle said hurriedly. 'You and me. No awkwardness, no hard feelings, everything's fine as far as I'm concerned. And we're just so glad Tiff's better.'

'We are too. He's always said how nice you were.'

Touched, Estelle said, 'Hopefully we'll get to know each other even better now. I've never had any nephews or nieces. Maybe I can be a kind of informal auntie.'

'He'd love that. We'd *all* love that.' Juliet smiled automatically as the doors of the paediatric unit swung open, spitting out a doctor she recognised.

'Ah!' Having headed past her up the corridor, the doctor did an abrupt about-turn and said, 'Tiff's blood test results came through. All clear. The consultant wants to see him at the ward round tomorrow, then if everything's OK you can take him home after that. Take Tiff home,' the doctor amended. 'Not the consultant.'

'Tomorrow?' Juliet's dark eyes glinted with tears. 'Are you sure?'

'Unless you want to leave him here,' the doctor said with a grin, before turning and rushing off.

'Here.' Estelle pushed a clean tissue into Juliet's hand.

'Oh, thanks. I can't believe he's actually going home. Wait 'til Jake and Sophie hear this.'

'It's brilliant news,' said Estelle, happier than ever that she'd come along to the hospital. Giving Juliet's arm a reassuring squeeze, she said, 'Now you can really celebrate.'

Kate was in her bedroom getting ready to go to work on Friday morning when she heard the doorbell ringing downstairs. Norris, who was lying on his side recovering from the exertions of their latest walk, lifted his head and cocked an inquisitive ear as the front door was opened and they were just able to make out the sound of a female voice.

Two female voices, in fact, Estelle being the one who had gone to answer the door. Putting the finishing touches to her lipstick and giving her hair a last hasty swoosh of Elnett, Kate said, 'Who's that then, hey? Shall we go and find out?'

Wagging his stumpy tail, Norris trotted downstairs at her heels. Whoever had rung the doorbell was now in the kitchen with Estelle; Kate could hear the mystery voice chattering away in there.

When she saw who it was, she was none the wiser. A tall gangly woman in her mid-fifties was sitting at the kitchen table with a pile of photo envelopes. Her lipstick was a garish shade of orange, her eyeshadow was electric-green and she was waving a photo at Estelle, of herself standing in front of – oh God – the Sydney Harbour bridge.

Looking up, the woman's eyes widened. 'And here he is!' she exclaimed, bending in two like a marionette whose strings have been cut and flinging her arms wide. 'Norris, baby! *Oooh*, look how thin you are, have you missed us terribly?' Peering up at Estelle, she said, 'Hasn't he been eating? Hang on, I've got some chocolate here in my bag.'

'Darling, this is Barbara Kendall, Norris's owner,' said Estelle, just in case Kate thought their visitor was a stray Jehovah's Witness. 'Barbara, this is my daughter Kate.'

'Hello, dear, nice to meet you.' Barbara nodded pleasantly. 'How are you getting on with your face?'

Feeling sick, Kate said, 'Excuse me?'

'You know, settling back here in Ashcombe, letting other people get used to the sight of you. It doesn't do to hide yourself away, you know. After a while they'll hardly even notice, it's like when my daughter had that terrible acne, I told her she was making a fuss over nothing, you just have to get out and get on with it, and it's not as if spots last for ever. Although I suppose it's different for you . . .'

'Have you come for Norris?' Maybe this was a daft question, but Kate was struggling to stay calm. Was this scrawny garrulous woman seriously expecting to just roll up here and take Norris away from them?

'Of course! Why else would I be here?' As if Kate was mentally subnormal, Barbara explained slowly and clearly, 'I said we'd be in Australia for six weeks. It's been six weeks. And now we're back!'

She might be back, but she wasn't making much of a fuss of Norris. Having patted him on the head and looked askance at his reduced bulk, she returned with far more enthusiasm to her holiday photos. Similarly, having lost interest in his owner, Norris had wandered back to sit beside Kate, his head leaning against her leg.

'Oh, and here we are on the steps of the Opera House.' Barbara proudly held the relevant photograph out to Estelle. 'Look at Bernard's socks with kangaroos on the sides! Aren't they a scream?'

Kate definitely wanted to scream. 'We didn't know you were coming today.'

'Well, you know how it is.' Abstractedly, Barbara shuffled through the photos. 'I was going to give you a ring, then I couldn't find your number – anyway, I'm here now! Poor old Norris, he looks so *thin*. Has he behaved himself? Hey, Norris, over here – have you been a good boy?'

'He's been fantastic.' Terrified that she was about to cry, Kate said, 'He was overweight before. We've put him on a diet, taken him for loads of walks – his breathing's so much better now. We-we're going to miss him d-dreadfully.'

'Really?' Barbara looked incredulously across at Norris. 'Well, that's marvellous news! Maybe you'll end up getting one of your own. OK, let's get a move on, Bernard's expecting us back.' Since no one was showing her photos the degree of interest she felt they deserved, Barbara gathered them together and slid them back into their packets. 'Norris, come along, we're going home.'

Kate gazed beseechingly at her mother. Estelle, clearly distraught, could only shake her head. With a quizzical look at Barbara, Norris rose obediently to his feet.

'Say thank you very much for looking after me,' Barbara prompted, causing Norris to wag his tail in a bemused fashion.

'If you wanted him to stay here, we'd love to keep him,' Kate blurted out, causing Barbara to look at her even more oddly.

'But he's ours, dear. Not yours. Right, off we go.'

Crouching down, Kate put her arms round Norris and felt him rest his paws on her knees. Oh God, how could she ever have thought him ugly? Hot tears dripped down her chin as she kissed the top of his broad head. In return, Norris licked her wrist. It was hard trying to say a meaningful goodbye to someone who didn't understand what was going on.

'Bye, Norris,' mumbled Kate as Barbara clapped her hands.

'Right, let's get a wiggle on! Say goodbye to Estelle now,' Barbara ordered bossily.

Unable to watch Norris leaving the house for good, Kate stumbled to her feet and left the kitchen. It was time to go to work, for all the good she'd be. No more Norris, it just didn't bear thinking about.

'Estelle! I forgot to tell you about our visit to the crocodile farm,' she heard Barbara trill behind her.

Bloody Barbara Kendall, thought Kate, how she'd love to feed her to the crocodiles.

Wiping her eyes with the back of her hand, feeling as if her heart had just been squeezed by a giant fist, Kate slammed out of the house.

* * *

Marcella couldn't quite believe she was here at Dartington House nursing home, in the same room as Pauline McKinnon. She especially couldn't grasp what she was hearing.

Feeling light-headed but far too agitated to sit down, Marcella stared at the wizened, yellow-tinged face of Den McKinnon's mother.

'I don't believe you,' she said flatly. 'It's not true. No mother would ask her son to take the blame for something like that.'

'I did.' Pauline McKinnon plucked at the pale blue bedspread.

'I think you're just lying to protect him. You don't have long left to live, so you're trying to persuade me he was innocent all along.'

'Why would I? I didn't want to tell you the truth. I'm only doing it now to prove to Den how sorry I am.'

Marcella took a deep breath. Pauline McKinnon didn't sound as if she were lying. And if Den had spent the last nine years in Australia, why would he need his mother to make up a story like this?

'Is this to do with Kerr?' Marcella was still struggling to take it in. 'Was this his idea? Does he think I'll change my mind about him and Maddy?'

'Maddy who? Your daughter?' Bemused, Pauline McKinnon said, 'What's she got to do with Kerr?'

This time it was blindingly obvious that she had no idea what Marcella was talking about.

'How did Kerr feel about seeing his brother go to prison for something he didn't do?' Marcella was having trouble keeping her voice steady.

'He didn't know. He only found out this week.'

'Does he despise you?' said Marcella.

'He hasn't said so,' Pauline McKinnon shrugged, 'but I'm sure he does. Same as Den. I don't blame them,' she added. 'I despise myself.'

'You were drunk. You killed our daughter.' Marcella's voice began to rise, because she had no doubt now that Pauline McKinnon was telling the truth. 'You forced your own son to take the blame.'

'And I've suffered every single day since then.'

'*Good*,' Marcella hissed, her eyes blazing. 'You don't know how happy that makes me. I hope you rot in hell for what you've done to us *and* to him.'

'I'm sorry.'

'And it's taken you eleven years to say that!'

'I was going to, I swear I was.' Pauline McKinnon swallowed with difficulty. 'Before the trial, we weren't allowed to. Afterwards, Kerr came over to your cottage one day and tried to apologise. You were out. Your husband was there but he didn't want to hear it. He refused to listen and yelled at Kerr to leave. After a reaction like that, how could I risk trying to do the same? I couldn't face either of you. You hated us enough as it was, without even knowing what I'd really done. It was easier to blot it all out,' she concluded wearily, 'and have another drink instead.'

'Look at me,' Marcella ordered, because Pauline McKinnon was avoiding her eyes. 'Can you understand how much we loved April?'

Forcing her head up, Pauline nodded without speaking.

'Actually, I don't suppose you can,' Marcella's voice was cold, 'but let me tell you this anyway. She was every bit as precious to us as our other children. I would give everything I own for the chance to hold her again. The fact that April had cerebral palsy wasn't her fault and didn't make an ounce of difference to how we felt about her. Yet you seemed to think we had no right to be distraught because *it wasn't as if she was normal*.'

'I didn't say that,' croaked Pauline McKinnon. 'I swear.'

'We were told you'd said it.' Marcella was defiant.

417

'Outside the court? I remember. I heard someone else saying those words, but it wasn't me. I've been truthful with you all afternoon,' Pauline went on. 'After everything else, why would I bother to start lying to you now? With a bit of luck by the end of next week I'll be dead. What's the matter with you, anyway?' Her clouded eyes had dropped to Marcella's front. Marcella realised that without even being aware of it, she had been gently rubbing her stomach.

'Nothing.' It was the truth; there was no pain or discomfort. Her family would have a fit if they knew she'd run the risk of coming here today to confront Pauline McKinnon but she had come through it without mishap. Some inner instinct reassured Marcella that her baby was just fine.

'I'm tired,' said Pauline McKinnon tetchily.

'I'm not going to forgive you, if that's why you wanted to see me.'

'I didn't want to see you. This was all Den's idea, not mine.'

Marcella looked at her, experiencing a mixture of hatred, revulsion and disgust. And pity, too. But not for Pauline McKinnon.

As she turned to leave the room, Marcella said, 'My daughter, April, was worth five hundred of you.'

Chapter 58

Outside, Marcella took lungfuls of much-needed fresh air. A warm dry breeze rippled the front of her loose, dark blue shirt. The manicured grounds were deserted apart from a solitary figure sitting on a bench some distance away, beneath a spreading cedar tree. From here it was impossible to tell whether the figure was male or female; all Marcella could make out was longish dark hair, sunglasses, a white shirt and faded jeans.

But she knew at once who it was. Without hesitating, she descended the stone steps and made her way across the freshly mown grass.

He took off his dark glasses as she approached and Marcella saw the eleven years of strain etched on his face. Here was someone who had suffered almost as much as she had. It beggared belief that any son could have a mother like that.

Her heart went out to him. She had spent all these years blaming him for something he hadn't done. He may be a McKinnon, but he was *innocent*.

'Do you believe her?' Den searched her face, his voice taut with uncertainty.

Nodding, Marcella said, 'I do.'

'It's the truth.' Den nodded too and she saw that he was shaking. 'I didn't do it. It wasn't me, I swear.'

Marcella held out her arms and drew him to her, making soothing noises and patting his back as he sobbed on her shoulder like a small boy.

'God, I can't believe it. I haven't cried for years,' Den said finally, using his sleeve to wipe his eyes. 'Not since I came out of prison.'

'You've been bottling it up. Don't worry.' Marcella stroked his face. 'It's all over now.'

'I didn't know she was drunk, that's the stupidest thing.' Den cleared his throat, determined to say it. 'I could have driven that day. If she had only let me drive, it would never have happened. But she didn't want me to know how much she'd had to drink, so she made out she was fine. I should have taken the keys off her—'

'Sshh, stop it.' Her earlier words to Den's mother came back to Marcella now: it hadn't been April's fault she was born handicapped. Well, it wasn't Den's fault either that he had been handicapped by the fact that Pauline McKinnon was his mother.

Marcella briefly closed her eyes, remembering those dark, desperate days after the accident. Her grief had been so overwhelming that directing her hatred at only one person hadn't been enough, she'd needed to encompass the whole family. And that had been wrong, she could see that now.

'Is this what I think it is?' Being hugged by Marcella had brought the curvature of her stomach to Den's attention. Pulling away, he gazed down at the small bump.

'Always one of those embarrassing moments,' said Marcella, 'when you really hope I'm not just fat. And no,' she went on, 'I'm not just fat.'

Den shook his head. 'Congratulations. That's fantastic.'

It was also interesting, Marcella felt, that he clearly hadn't been expecting it, which meant that Kerr McKinnon hadn't warned him.

'Shall I tell you something stupid?' Den was smiling now, crookedly. 'Before the accident, I used to wish you were my mother. I'd seen the way you were with your kids. I really envied them. I thought you were fantastic.'

Overcome, Marcella hugged him tightly. 'Thank you. I hope I'll carry on being fantastic. Now, let's talk about your brother.'

'Kerr?' Den gave her a blank look. 'What d'you want to know?'

He didn't have a clue.

'Kerr and Maddy,' said Marcella.

Den gave her a doubtful look. '*Your* Maddy? Why, does she like him?'

'Just a bit.' Amused, Marcella realised that he was picturing Maddy as she had been eleven years ago with her metal braces, bony knees and those funny NHS specs. All in all, an unlikely contender for his brother's attention.

'Kerr hasn't told you.' As they turned and began to walk across the grass, Marcella tucked her arm companionably through Den's. 'Know where he is?'

'What, right now? At work.' Den looked surprised. 'He's lent me his car.'

'Excellent. Posh one?'

'Very posh,' said Den.

'Even more excellent. So,' Marcella said brightly as another thought struck her, 'does *he* know about *me* coming here today?'

Den shook his head. 'I didn't tell him. This was what *I* wanted to happen. He might have tried to talk me out of it.'

Almost certainly, Marcella thought with secret amusement.

As they headed for the car park – she really hoped Kerr's was the gleaming midnight-blue Mercedes – Marcella said, 'Why don't we go and pay your brother a little visit?'

'Now?'

She gave Den's arm a complicit squeeze. 'Right now. Come on, it'll be a laugh.'

Realising what she was planning, Den said, 'He'll be scared witless when you walk in.'

'But we'll find it hilarious.' Marcella broke into a dazzling, ear-to-ear grin. 'Anyway, if your big brother's serious about my darling daughter, he's just going to have to get used to it.'

Blowing up several dozen balloons had taken it out of Maddy. She was exhausted, but the back garden of Snow Cottage was looking sensational enough for it all to be worthwhile. There were balloons at the front of the cottage too, along with a huge handmade Welcome Home banner and enough curly streamers to tie up an entire herd of wildebeest. Should a herd of wildebeest choose to stampede through Ashcombe.

'Looking good,' said Nuala, carrying out a pile of rugs and cushions.

'Thanks.' Maddy smiled.

'Not you. You look appalling. I was talking about the garden,' said Nuala. 'Poor Tiff's going to take one look at you and have a relapse. Go and put some make-up on or something, before everyone gets here.'

As if moving house and organising the party wasn't enough, Maddy thought, she was expected to get creative with mascara too. And where was everyone else, anyway? Tiff was coming home from the hospital at three o'clock. Jake had driven into Bath to pick up Tiff and Juliet. Marcella had disappeared hours ago, blithely claiming that she needed to buy maternity knickers and promising faithfully to be back before three. Similarly, Kate and Dexter wouldn't be over until after the pub was shut for the afternoon. Sophie had spent hours colouring in the Welcome Home banner. Bean had leaped about like a mini Tigger-on-springs, doing her best to burst the balloons as fast as they were inflated. Quite a few other people from Ashcombe were coming along to the party but none of them had seen fit to offer anything in the way of practical help, evidently more than happy to leave all the boring hard work to her and Nuala.

And what exactly had Nuala done in the last couple of hours, apart from take a long hot shower, paint her toenails turquoise and spend a ridiculous amount of time faffing over what to wear?

'I needed to shower,' Nuala had protested when Maddy had pointed this out. 'We moved house this morning! I had to wash all the dust off, didn't I? For heaven's sake, I was a complete *mess.*'

It hadn't taken long to move house, and Jake had helped. Juliet and Tiff's belongings had been brought over to Snow Cottage, and in return Maddy and Nuala had lugged their things over to the flat above the Peach Tree. It was like a neat chess move. Now that there were going to be three of them working in the deli itself, Maddy had resolved to increase the sandwich delivery side of the business. Last night she had designed a flyer to be printed and sent to businesses throughout the city. Next week she planned to follow this up with visits to the various companies, taking along samples as she'd done with Callaghan and Fox. By this time next year, the Peach Tree delivery service could be a national, international, possibly even a global phenomenon . . .

Oh well, anything to take her mind off the disaster that was the rest of her life.

'Go and have a shower this minute,' Nuala bossily announced. 'And do something with your hair. It's got cobwebs in it.'

Den waited outside in the car while Marcella headed up the stairs to the offices of Callaghan and Fox. Entertaining though it would have been to witness in person Kerr having the living daylights scared out of him, Den's presence would spoil the surprise.

Pushing through the swing doors into reception, Marcella's eye was caught by the clock up on the wall. Ten to three. Back in Ashcombe everyone would be gathering at the cottage, getting ready to welcome Tiff home.

Anyway, never mind about that now.

Behind the desk, a plump girl looked up and smiled welcomingly at Marcella. 'Hello there, can I help you?'

'I hope so.' Since Den had Kerr's car, Marcella was rather counting on him being here. 'I'd like a word with Kerr McKinnon.'

'Do you have an appointment?'

'No, but I'm sure he'll see me.' Primed by Den, Marcella peered down the corridor on the left. 'Is that his office, along there?'

'Er, why don't I give him a buzz?' Apologetically the receptionist said, 'I'm not really supposed to let people in without an—'

'I'm Maddy Harvey's mum,' Marcella confided. 'Maddy from the Peach Tree. Trust me, it'll be worth it.'

This captured the girl's attention. Eagerly she leaned across the desk.

'Is it about Kerr and Maddy? Oh, fantastic! Something's going on between those two, isn't it? I knew there was, I *knew* it, but Kerr just wouldn't admit anything, and for the last few weeks he's been so *grumpy*. Hang on.' The receptionist faltered, belatedly taking in the fact that Marcella was black and Maddy wasn't. 'You can't be Maddy's *mother* . . .'

Marcella said with pride, 'I've been her mother since she was five years old.'

'OK.' Rising to her feet, the girl said, 'You can go and see Kerr. But you have to let me come too.'

The door to his office was closed. The receptionist, having introduced herself as Sara, knocked and said, 'Kerr, it's me.'

From the other side of the door a male voice called out, 'Come in,' and Sara stepped to one side, gesturing to Marcella.

'After you, Maddy's mum.'

'Why thank you so much.' Marcella flashed a mischievous smile at her before opening the door.

Kerr McKinnon was sitting behind his desk talking into the phone. Better looking than his brother, Marcella judged; then again, he hadn't had to go through what Den had been through. Still, she could appreciate what Maddy saw in him. In a purely dispassionate way, of course.

She watched the expression on Kerr's face change as he realised who had just walked into his office. Unsmiling, Marcella stood there and regarded him in silence, exuding menace.

'Er, sorry, I'll have to call you back,' Kerr muttered into the phone. Slowly he replaced the receiver. Marcella couldn't see his hand shaking, but she wouldn't mind betting he was quaking inside.

And now . . . Oh, this was fantastic, the colour was actually draining from his face! If only she'd thought to bring a video camera.

The silence lengthened. It was like *High Noon*. Finally Marcella spoke.

'Scared?'

'Yes.'

'Good. I'd hate to think I was losing my touch.'

A muscle flickered in Kerr's jaw. 'Does Maddy know you're here?'

'No.'

'Right.'

'Your brother does, though. He's downstairs. We've just had a long chat,' said Marcella. 'Everything's been sorted out. I went to see your mother this afternoon, too.'

'You what?' Kerr shook his head in disbelief. 'She actually *told* you . . . ?'

'The whole story, but we don't have time to go into that now. I'm sure you know how I feel about your mother. As for Den, well, I'm just glad the truth's come out. Better late than never. Now, about you.' Marcella paused to check her watch. 'How do you feel about Maddy?'

Lost for words, Kerr said, 'Er . . . er . . .'

'Come on now, we don't have all day.' Marcella widened her eyes enquiringly at him. 'Still interested? Or no longer interested, that was weeks ago, you've met someone else *far* better since then—'

'Stop,' Kerr said hurriedly. 'Still interested.'

'Good.' Marcella's expression softened.

'I *knew* it.' Behind her, Sara was triumphant. Nudging Marcella she said, 'Didn't I tell you? Ha, nothing gets past me!'

'Sara? Could you get back to your desk now? I think I can handle this myself,' said Kerr.

'It's OK, we're going now anyway,' Marcella consoled the disappointed receptionist.

Taken aback, Kerr said, '*We?*'

'You're the boss around here, aren't you? Surely you can give yourself the rest of the afternoon off.' Breaking into a smile, Marcella said, 'It's the least I can do for my daughter.'

'And no gossiping with the others,' Kerr firmly instructed Sara as he left with his jacket over his shoulder and Marcella in tow.

'No gossiping.' Sara obediently zipped her mouth shut. 'You can count on me.'

'And if you believe that, you'll believe anything,' Kerr murmured as they headed down the stairs. 'There's something I don't get here. When you thought my brother had caused the accident, you refused to speak to me. Now you know it was my mother, you're fine. But it was still a member of my family. I don't understand—'

'Hey, don't worry.' Marcella's tone was soothing. 'It makes sense to me. And that's what counts.'

Chapter 59

'Look, you have to cheer up, you knew it was going to happen sooner or later.'

Kate gave the bar a final violent polish. Dexter was doing his best, but he really wasn't helping matters. If she was honest, she'd been quietly fantasising to herself that Barbara Kendall might e-mail them from Sydney, announcing that she'd decided to stay there for good.

'I tell you what, we'll go out this weekend and get you a dog of your own,' said Dexter.

If he didn't shut up, Kate thought she might stuff her polishing cloth down his throat. He might mean well, but another dog wasn't what she wanted. It wouldn't be the same.

'I want Norris.'

'It's ten past three. We've got this party to go to,' said Dexter.

Kate heaved a sigh. Tiff's welcome home party wasn't what she was in the mood for. Was this how foster mothers felt? Just as you began to truly bond with your charge, he was brutally snatched away? God, it was inhuman.

Except Norris wasn't a human, he was a dog.

But it was just so *unfair*. It shouldn't be allowed. Kate wiped her eyes, which had been leaking, on and off, throughout the lunchtime session. She knew she had to pull herself together, but that was easier said than done. The prospect of never hearing Norris's lovely snuffly breathing again, or never stroking his velvety jowls, was just . . . just . . .

'Come on,' said Dexter, 'don't cry. I'll give you five minutes to do your face while I close up, then we're off.'

Locking the front door behind them, they set off up the road. Kate was touched by Dexter's concern; he had his arm round her and was being extra nice. What would happen to the two of them in the long term she hadn't the faintest idea. Would their relationship last? Who knew? She wasn't under any illusions where Dexter was concerned. Nuala may not have been the right girl for him, but he had treated her poorly. It stood to reason that, as time passed, he might start to take her for granted too.

Then again, he might not. At the moment she still got that squiggly excited feeling in her stomach every time she looked at him, but whether they'd last as a couple was anyone's guess. She certainly wouldn't put up with any nonsense. The only thing to do was maintain the upper hand and take the relationship one day at a—

'Watch out,' Dexter said sharply, yanking her back as she was about to cross the road. A grubby red Audi rounded the corner and shot past in a cloud of dust.

Kate wondered if she was seeing things. Her mouth dropped open and her heart began to bang. Was that really who she thought it was, sitting in the passenger seat?

'Norris!' she gasped, and Dexter gave her waist a sympathetic squeeze.

'Sweetheart, it just looks a bit like Norris. You can't—'

'What's going on?' Kate, who knew better, held her breath as the red Audi went into a handbrake turn, circling the war memorial at the end of the street before roaring back up the road towards them.

Another squeal of brakes and it drew to a halt beside Dexter and Kate.

'Oh my God,' Kate said faintly as Barbara Kendall buzzed down her window and Norris, clambering across her with no regard whatsoever for MaxMara trousers, squeezed like toothpaste through the narrow gap onto the pavement. Hurling himself joyfully at Kate, Norris let out a volley of high-pitched yodelling barks.

Rather than follow him through the open window, Barbara Kendall opened the driver's door and stepped out.

'There you are! I just drove up to your house but there's no one at home. Thank goodness I caught you. All he's done since we got him home is howl nonstop.' Her words spilled out in a torrent. 'It's driving us insane. We can't hear ourselves *think*. Can I be frank with you? Bernard and I have actually enjoyed not having the responsibility of caring for a pet for the last six weeks. If we didn't have one, we could take so many more breaks, whenever we wanted, and to be honest, neither of us finds it much fun having to take this one for walks. So we wondered if you were serious about taking Norris off our hands, because if you are, well, we wouldn't mind a bit.'

Kate would have marvelled at Barbara Kendall's couldn't-care-less attitude but she was too busy kneeling on the hot dusty pavement getting her face thoroughly licked by an ecstatic Norris. Dexter, who had heard what had gone on in the kitchen at Dauncey House this morning, frowned.

'So why didn't you say this before? When Kate offered to keep him?' *And save me having to put up with all this grief for the last three hours?*

Barbara Kendall, enthusiastically brushing dog hairs from her smart trousers, looked up and said, 'Hmm? Well, it was one of those silly misunderstandings! Bernard and I have only just admitted the truth to each other. We inherited Norris when his aunt died, you see. Bernard was never wild about dogs, but he tolerated Norris because for some reason he thought *I* wanted a pet. And of course I wasn't that keen at all, but I pretended to be because I didn't want to hurt Bernard's feelings. So that's all sorted out,' she said cheerfully. 'And the thing is, look at Norris now! He seems *so* much happier with you than he does at home with us!'

'I wonder why,' Dexter muttered, just about beneath his breath.

'So?' Barbara was jangling her car keys and looking expectant. 'What d'you think?'

I think you're a cruel heartless witch with a face like a donkey, Dexter was sorely tempted to retort, but heroically he kept this opinion to himself. For Kate's sake rather than Barbara Kendall's.

'We'd love to keep him.' Kate beamed, hugging Norris so hard she almost lost her balance. 'Thank you so much.'

'Well, that's done.' Barbara Kendall looked relieved. 'I must say, from all the things I'd heard about you, I didn't have you down as a dog-lover.'

Norris lovingly licked Kate's neck. As she fondled his gorgeous ears, it crossed her mind to demand furiously what on earth Barbara Kendall meant by that.

Then again, did she really want to know?

Honestly, where *was* Marcella? It wasn't like her to not be here when she'd promised not to be late. Feeling hot and slightly put-upon, Maddy carried two huge bowls of cherries outside, to add to the food laid out on the trellis table. Everyone else, it seemed, was far too busy being one half of a couple and chatting in a couply fashion to other couples, to bother giving her a hand. Kate and Dexter were here, along with Oliver and Estelle. And Jake and Juliet, doing their best not to fuss over Tiff who was – in honour of the fact that he was an invalid and this was his party – holding court from the shaded hammock.

As for Norris and Bean, they were a picture of perfect coupledom, rolling joyfully around together on the freshly mown grass. *Romping* together, *frisking* together, even *frolicking* . . .

Lucky things, Maddy thought, experiencing a pang of envy. What she wouldn't give for a romp and a frolic.

Oh dear, it came to something when you found yourself wishing you could be a dog.

Sophie, tugging at Maddy's elbow, said, 'Dad says we need more ice for the drinks. We're running out.'

'Hang on.' Feeling like Cinderella, Maddy headed inside to the cool of the kitchen, where Nuala was putting together a Waldorf salad. Of course, how could she even think she was the only one on her own? She and Nuala could be batty spinsters together, growing old and becoming increasingly pernickety as the years slid by.

'Bugger,' said Maddy, peering into the freezer. 'That was the last of the ice.'

'Bugger.' Sophie heaved a sigh, rolling her eyes with glee.

'I can get a couple of bags from the Angel,' Nuala offered. 'Dexter's always got loads, he won't mind. If you finish this,' she gestured to Maddy, 'I'll get the key to the pub off him and zip over there.'

Maddy washed her hands and obediently crossed to the table to take over from Nuala. Making salads together, this was only the start. Before long they'd be crocheting tea cosies, writing to the council about the state of the highways, tramping about the countryside in matching patchwork waist-coats and floral wellies—

'*Yowww*,' Maddy yelped. She'd squeezed a lemon with a bit too much vigour and managed to squirt juice into her eye. 'Oosh.' Blinking, she managed to dislodge her contact lens and had to bend double in order to pop it out then neatly catch it in the palm of her hand. This was just one of the drawbacks you learned to deal with when you wore contacts; every so often, like babies, they demanded attention *this instant*.

Luckily her handbag was lying on the window ledge and inside it were the necessary bottles of contact lens cleaning and soaking solution. Grabbing the bag, Maddy headed upstairs to the bathroom, still blinking lemon juice out of her eye.

Chapter 60

'Right,' said Marcella, 'here we go.' Her dark eyes danced as she climbed out of the dark blue Mercedes. 'Kerr, you come with me. Darling,' she turned to Den, 'would you mind awfully waiting here for a few minutes? It's just that Jake's at the party, and I want to be able to explain everything to him first.'

'That's fine.' Den wasn't offended. 'No problem. I'll just sit here on this wall.' At the sound of a door slamming behind him, he turned and saw a girl emerging from the Fallen Angel, the same girl he'd seen here the other day. Her hair was lit by the sun and she was carrying two hefty bags of ice. As she looked up and saw she was being watched, her eyes widened in recognition. Fumbling with the keys to the pub, she clutched both ice bags to her chest, which surely couldn't be comfortable.

'Nuala!' Marcella clapped her hands in delight. 'Just the girl! Will you do me a huge favour, darling? Wait out here for two minutes with this charming young man and keep him company?'

'Um . . .' stammered Nuala, going bright pink and gazing helplessly at Den, then briefly at Kerr, then back again at Den. 'Er, OK.'

'You two just have a nice chat,' Marcella said helpfully, 'and we'll give you a shout when we're ready for you. Now,' she went on, slipping her arm through Kerr's, 'let's have a bit of fun, shall we?'

Nuala watched Marcella and her mystery companion disappear together through the front door of Snow Cottage. Finding her tongue at last, Nuala said, 'Hello.'

'Hi,' said Den.

'Um, did I see you here the other day?'

'You did.' Den nodded, discreetly taking in the gorgeous curvy legs which had previously been hidden by a pair of jeans. 'Watch out for frostbite, by the way.'

'Hmm? Oh!' Belatedly discovering she still had the bags of ice cubes clamped to her chest, Nuala placed them on the ground beside her feet. Attempting to hide the fact that beneath her white top her nipples (yelping, 'Ouch, we're *cold*!') were standing to attention, she said, 'So, um, who was that with Marcella?'

Den wanted to kiss her. OK, not yet, have some decorum.

'Him? That's my brother.'

'And who are you?' Nuala was studying him with just as much undisguised pleasure as he'd been studying her.

It wasn't just his imagination, he realised. She really wanted to kiss him too. Feeling as if he'd truly come home, he took a step towards her.

'I'm his brother,' said Den.

The ice cubes were beginning to melt at Nuala's feet. Moving them into the shade of the garden wall would help, but Nuala was finding it hard to care about the fate of a bunch of ice cubes. She hadn't the faintest idea where Marcella had managed to get hold of these two brothers but she was jolly glad she had. Anyway, that was Maddy's mother for you; you never knew what she might do next.

In a daze, Nuala wondered if Marcella had met the pair by chance in Bath, running into them in the street and persuading them, in that impulsive, irresistible way of hers, to come along with her to a party in Ashcombe. Or maybe she'd been for one of her antenatal appointments at the hospital and had got chatting to them, as you do, in the waiting room . . .

Oh Lord.

Gulping, Nuala blurted out, 'Is your wife having a baby?'

'I don't have a wife.' His thin, tanned face – oh, those cheekbones! – registered amusement at the question. 'Or a girlfriend. And I most definitely don't have a baby.'

Having screwed the tops onto the plastic bottles of cleansing and wetting solution, Maddy checked her face in the bathroom mirror. The contact lens was safely back in place. She could see again – namely, her own unsmiling reflection, in sharp contrast to all the cheerful animated faces out in the garden. This wasn't good enough, it really wasn't, she should be looking jollier, today was a celebration of—

'Maddy, are you up there?'

Maddy looked in the mirror, reminding herself of a tight-lipped, long-suffering mother whose wayward teenage daughter had promised to be home two hours ago.

Except this was no wayward teenager, it was Marcella.

'So you bothered to turn up at last,' she called out, unzipping her make-up bag. 'You were supposed to be back before three.'

'I know. Sorry, darling. I got held up. But I'm here now,' Marcella shouted. 'Are you coming down?'

Why? Did they need her to make more salads? Rustle up a few quiches? Find a mop because someone had just spilled their drink?

Slowly taking out her Maybelline mascara, because all that faffing about with her contact lens had left her with a bald right eye, Maddy called out, 'In a minute. I'm busy.'

There, see? She wasn't a pushover.

'Come down now.' Marcella's tone was cajoling. 'I've brought you a present.'

'What is it?'

'Something nice.'

Maddy finished with the mascara and gravely regarded her reflection. She loved Marcella more than life itself, but when it came to presents her taste could be inescapably dodgy. The last time she'd done this had been after Maddy had happened to mention in passing that she'd enjoyed the latest Harry Potter film. Two days later, following a visit to Aldridge's Auction House in Bath, Marcella had arrived home in a taxi with a moth-eaten stuffed barn owl in a glass case.

'Come on,' Marcella said now. 'You'll like it, I promise.'

Hmm. Maddy squirted on some perfume in an attempt to launch herself into more of a party mood. Her lipstick had worn off. Should she put more on, or not bother? If it wasn't going to cheer her up, was there really any point?

No, sod it, why should she?

'Maddy, will you get out of that bathroom!'

'I'm BUSY,' Maddy bellowed.

'And I'm PREGNANT,' Marcella shouted back up the stairs, 'which means I win, because if I don't get to the loo *this minute*, I'm going to—'

'OK, *OK*.' Conceding defeat, Maddy irritably straightened the straps on her pink dress then unlocked the bathroom door. As she stomped out onto the landing, she froze.

There he was. Kerr. Maddy blinked and clutched the banister rail, wondering if she was in fact awake.

Right, pinch yourself. Go on, pinch your arm really hard – *ow*.

It made no sense, but it appeared to be actually happening. Kerr McKinnon was here in Snow Cottage, at the bottom of this very staircase, with Marcella at his side.

'Hi,' said Kerr, his dark eyes glinting with amusement and what looked like love.

Feeling giddy, Maddy stammered, 'H-hi.'

Marcella said delightedly, 'You see? I *told* you it was a nice surprise!'

Determined not to faint Maddy nodded. 'Um, yes.'

Marcella tucked her arm affectionately through Kerr's and gave it a squeeze. 'My daughter doesn't trust me,' she confided. 'I think she thought you might be another stuffed owl in a glass case.'

'What's going on?' Maddy began to descend the stairs.

'I was kidnapped,' said Kerr. 'From my office.'

'By me,' Marcella added with pride.

Kerr, propelling Marcella gently but firmly in the direction of the kitchen, said, 'Thanks, but I think we can manage the rest of this by ourselves.'

When the kitchen door had closed behind Marcella, Maddy ventured further down the staircase. Scarcely daring to breathe, she whispered, 'Is it really you?'

'Damn, don't tell me you haven't got your lenses in again.' Kerr was smiling now; as she reached the last step, he took her trembling hands in his. 'You're about to be horribly disappointed if you thought I was Brad Pitt.'

If you enjoyed

FALLING FOR YOU

look out for the new *Jill Mansell* novel

THREE AMAZING THINGS ABOUT YOU

Out in January 2015

You can order
THREE AMAZING THINGS ABOUT YOU
now

www.headline.co.uk
www.jillmansell.co.uk

headline
review

🐦 @JillMansell
📘 /OfficialJillMansell

Jill *Mansell*

THE UNPREDICTABLE
CONSEQUENCES OF LOVE

In the idyllic seaside town of St Carys, Sophie is putting the past firmly behind her.

When Josh arrives in St Carys to run the family hotel, he can't understand why Sophie has zero interest in letting *any* man into her life. He also can't understand how he's been duped into employing Sophie's impulsive friend Tula, whose crush on him is decidedly unrequited.

St Carys has more than its fair share of characters, including the charming but utterly feckless surfer Riley Bryant, who is besotted with Tula. Riley's aunt is superstar author Marguerite Marshall. And Marguerite has designs on Josh's grandfather . . . who in turn still adores his glamorous ex-wife, Dot . . .

Just how many secrets can one seaside town keep?

Just *Heavenly*. Just *Jill*.

Acclaim for Jill Mansell's fabulous bestsellers:

'Bursting with humour, brimming with intrigue and full of characters you'll adore' ***** *Heat*

'You'll fall in love with the characters in this lovely tale' *Sun*

'A warm, witty and romantic read' *Daily Mail*

978 0 7553 5593 8

headline
review

Jill Mansell

Books

straight through your letterbox...

The Unpredictable Consequences of Love	£7.99
Don't Want To Miss A Thing	£7.99
A Walk In The Park	£8.99
To The Moon And Back	£8.99
Take A Chance On Me	£8.99
Rumour Has It	£8.99
An Offer You Can't Refuse	£8.99
Thinking Of You	£8.99
Making Your Mind Up	£8.99
The One You Really Want	£8.99
Falling For You	£8.99
Nadia Knows Best	£8.99
Staying At Daisy's	£8.99
Millie's Fling	£8.99
Good At Games	£8.99
Miranda's Big Mistake	£8.99
Head Over Heels	£7.99
Mixed Doubles	£8.99
Perfect Timing	£8.99
Fast Friends	£8.99
Solo	£8.99
Kiss	£8.99
Sheer Mischief	£8.99
Open House	£7.99
Two's Company	£8.99

**Simply call 01235 400 414 or visit our website
www.headline.co.uk to order**

Free delivery in the UK.
For overseas and Ireland £3.50 delivery charge.
Prices and availability subject to change without notice.